The S Curve

Michael Bone

For my people. I have chosen you wisely.

To CAROLE,

THANK YOU SO MUCH FOR YOUR SUPPORT! YOU ARE DEFINITELY ONE OF MY PEOPLE.

SINCERELY,

THE S CURVE

Day One

"Are you ready?" President and CEO Bill Wildeboer asked through a shit-eating grin, "This is a big one." Mark sat in front as Bill took the podium. The bustling crowd dulled to silence. "It is with great pride that I have the honor of introducing our first speaker today, a man of great integrity. For those of you who don't know him already, Mark Deremer has dedicated most of his career to this great company. In fact, this company would not be the spearhead of innovation that it is without him. It is not just seeing the company through its transition that he is responsible for but also for putting EnviroCore on the map of evolution. For undoubtedly, mankind itself will not be what it will be tomorrow without him. Allow me to introduce *your* Vice President of Operations, whiz kid, and personal friend, Mark Deremer." Mark rose from his seat to a standing ovation. He made it to the stage to shake the hand of Bill, who gave him a chuck on the shoulder as he relinquished the podium.

"What an introduction," Mark mumbled sheepishly. Panic started surging through Mark's veins as he stared out at the crowd. He suddenly remembered his introverted nature. Despite all of his success, he was still the skinny little boy that could never seem to fit in. His hand quivered as he reached for his clicker. '*Viridobacter circulofractus* and its Potential in Waste Management' read the screen behind him. *Jesus, I couldn't have come up with a flashier title?*

He felt his confidence slipping away as he was reminded of the numerous awkward social situations throughout his life that laid his path to this point, brick by painful brick. He was frozen. His heartbeat became audible and soon overtook his hearing altogether aside from the voice of doubt, those voices that try to keep the emotions at bay; the rational analysts. They were the

2

'sometimes-neurotic-sometimes-useful-always-logical' team of operators who occupied an abstract space in Mark's prefrontal cortex: the decision center. Their purpose was to make the most well-informed decision with the information given. Though sometimes they asked too many questions and when the philosophical rhetoric got too deep, they trapped Mark in a kind of stalemate. It was a nonsense logic loop that got tighter and tighter as it was dissected, requiring massive energy resources, leaving the body in a near-catatonic state. *These people don't care about any of this. They couldn't care less if I lived or died. Why am I even doing this? My talents would be much more useful back in the lab. Why did I ever agree to this? Why did I ever leave that office? Why did I pick this life? Why didn't I stay working at the store? Why didn't anyone want to be my friend in high school? Why, God, Why?!*

The room suddenly became vacant. All of those faces that were just staring at him disappeared into the black. A screeching whistle of 4 kilohertz accompanied the 120 decibel rhythmic thundering of his heartbeat, which accompanied the figurative lump of sand in his throat and the 74 sweat beads that had amassed across his forehead. The whistle ramped up to 5 kilohertz, then 6, then 7, in lockstep with the increase in Mark's heart rate. Time was perceived as both standing still and as a constant aging and regressing. He stood helpless; frozen in this second.

As the whistle reached the edge of human perception, the logic loop was broken and the auditorium spewed forth its members from the black. Mark's consciousness suddenly returned with no way of knowing how long he had been away in the black out. He could only hope that it was just a few seconds. Only a handful of faces in the crowd seemed concerned which, well, *may* be a good sign. *Oh well. No matter. No choice but to keep rolling along.*

"The world needs our help." Mark snapped, trying to resummon some courage through a loud and authoritative tone. It was a great opening line. "It is not news that mankind is drowning under the weight of its own garbage. For generations, non-biodegradable trash has been pumped into our precious Mother Earth with little regard for consequences; no plan to stop, and no plan to slow down. Environmentalists have vilified the long decomposition time of plastics since their advent. But revenues spoke louder than Mother Nature. In the archeological record, we name epochs after the materials most found in the sediment. When future archaeologists sift through the sediments of today, they will find a thick layer of plastic that has barely decomposed. In fact, for all intents and purposes, it will still be basically brand new. Like The Bronze Age and The Iron Age, ours will be The Plastic Age.

"This is a multigenerational tragedy; a huge black eye on Mother Earth with only us to blame. But lucky for us, on the other side of every problem is an opportunity, to paraphrase Lee Iacocca. We have a tremendous opportunity here to heal that black eye. Just about every company has jumped on the 'green' bandwagon. But going paperless, reducing carbon emissions and offering biodegradable alternatives is not enough. There are still thousands of non-biodegradable polymer factories in operation with only slightly diminishing demand. There are still thousands of landfills filling with more and more plastic as we speak. No one is *reversing* what is already done. That time comes now. We are sitting on the cusp of a new era: a completely untapped market with a large and eternal demand. In other words, mountains of plastic oil sit idle while we have the only drill on earth.

4

"What I'm about to show you here will be nothing short of a revolution. In the painfully dull title of this presentation is the name of a new life form. Most of you probably lost interest immediately, but that bug was created in the very labs of this building.

"A very select few of you may already know of EnviroCore's proprietary genetic translational prediction software. For those of you who don't speak the language, translation in this sense means the creation of a protein through genetic instructions. Understand that bacteria have very short lifespans, making them a quick study when inserting a manmade gene into the genome. However, when trial and error is the only method at your disposal, the wait to see the results is eternal. In order to rectify this dilemma, the fine software engineers in the information technology department partnered with the biologists in the genetic engineering department and, through long hours, long arguments, and perhaps divine intervention, turned out the translational prediction software now known as GLADIS, Gene Ligation and Dislocation Imaging Software.

"This brilliant piece of ingenuity is able to, not only create an image of the protein from base pairs entered into the system, but predict the folding of the amino acid chain and the function of the protein as well. GLADIS is equipped with up-to-date genomes from the worldwide bacterial genome database ensembl.org, GMO patents, and search capabilities for every known scientific journal. Instead of the traditional method of painstakingly regenerating colonies and finding a top down approach to synthetic genesis, GLADIS randomly creates mutations in whatever section is being examined, you can randomly insert, delete, and shift base pairs in any section or sections of the genome then document the growth and compare it to the prediction. Once you stumble on something that looks like it has potential, she'll fine tune the sequence until it appears to do something useful. In this case, that useful thing was an enzyme that broke down Bisphenol A.

"Who cares? Well, Bisphenol A, henceforth referred to as BPA, is a structurally necessary component molecule of many plastics. Still, who cares? When we let GLADIS run with our template genome, she evolved a green-colored sister strain that metabolized the aromatic ring structures, the circles, of Bisphenol A. Hence the name, *Viridobacter circulofractus*, A.K.A. the green circle breaker, A.K.A. *Vir*.

"Every waste management entity on the planet is going to be at our doors, folks, that is, if we don't take over the sector outright. If we were to do this today, by our calculations, the entire world's landfills would be nonexistent in just a few short years.

"That means strike while the iron is hot. Whether you are an investor, a policymaker, or a scientist, make no mistake, *this* is a revolution. We are, quite literally, playing god. If you have your doubts, that's fine. I don't blame you. If you don't want to be a god, well that's fine too. Uneasy lies the head that wears the crown. All I ask is that you consider this chance carefully. The rest of us will be waving to you from the other side of the Styx."

Several decades ago, allegations of unscrupulous lab practices
were encircling the small town of Vandeburgh, one of nine in Ash
County, Michigan. Vandeburgh was the home of Sciencia,
EnviroCore's former name. Rumors abounded; from cloning to
illegal stem-cell acquisition to radioactive pollution of the town's
water supply. All of which were utterly absurd, or at most,
hilariously exaggerated.

Ash County was endless in size but small in population. It
was little more than a farming community before the meager
increase in population that Sciencia's establishment attracted; a
small town with a simple way of life. In the columns of the small
town's monthly newspaper, The County Crier, the speculation
about what went on inside the walls of the biomedical research
company painted a picture of Sciencia that was tantamount to
witchcraft. Even their own employees began to believe the hype, as
no single worker had access to all areas of the facility. Though
they were little more than a tabloid from the imagination of a bored
newspaper columnist, Sciencia was soon overrun with more and
more protesters demanding access to records. Ted Philus,
Sciencia's CEO, was not in any hurry to make public the
company's study folders, which made the unrest of the town that
much more palpable. Even though the allegations of mad scientists
with fetus jar collections were laughable, ethics were not Ted's
strong suit. Philus was prone to getting around regulatory agencies
via any number of loopholes or off-the-record quid pro quos he
could contrive. Aside from that, there was no way he was about to
make any proprietary formulations public knowledge. Ted was a
hardened and slippery businessman. He was the type you may
expect to find selling food-colored grain alcohol under the guise of
some cure-all tonic. He was a fast-talking, mustache-twisting

swindler, but he was good at what he did.

The absurdities that the newspaper poured out through the years eventually prompted sanctions against the company, even in the absence of any real evidence. The town levied draconian ordinances and impossible taxes which crippled Sciencia's operations. It was clear that the county, despite employing a majority of its citizens, wanted Ted gone.

The county could not afford to lose its chief source of revenue, but it had to appeal to the angry mob. Philus met with the mayors of each city in the county behind closed doors. In exchange for turning over a number of hand-picked records to public domain, the facility could change its status from "Biomedical Research Facility" to "Environmental Sustainability Development Company" and could remain in operation free from the shackles the law had placed on it. But Ted offered to, "Do ya one better," by changing the name of the facility and resigning. This way the meeting could be painted as the strong-minded mayors giving the bad old villain what for, and sending him out on his ear while at the same time ushering in a progressive and environmentally friendly economy boost. Hence *EnviroCore* was born.

What an opportunity for long-time family friend Bill Wildeboer to finally make a name for himself. Philus needed a protégé and Bill needed a mentor. A great many failures in his career had left Bill rotting in a pit of despair. Once a bright-eyed and bushy-tailed health care entrepreneur with dreams of making the world a better place, many a failed endeavor had left his wealthy family a little less rich, and his ego a little more bruised. Bill finally submitted to the reality that he was not the fearless and savvy businessman that his father was and took on some meaningless upper-middle management positions with big titles within his father's rolodex. Though running an "Environmental Sustainability Development Company" was not how Bill envisioned making the world a better place, he was not about to let this opportunity slip away. He had the chance to leave a legacy, contribute to society at large, and make a lot of money. Game, set, match. It was a no-brainer.

So Bill was welcomed with open arms as the new CEO of the largest employer in Ash County. In the town's eyes, things had largely gone back to the way they were before the rumors. The newspapers sang praises of Bill and his company and how he would usher Ash County into a new era. But on the inside, things were falling apart. Philus had promised to stay on the board of directors for one year in order to help Bill with the transition. That did not happen. In fact, it was as if Philus never agreed to anything. He didn't show up to the first board meeting. Or the second. His phone number was disconnected. His house was vacant. His relatives did not know where he was. He signed the contract and he was gone. Bill had no idea how to effectively run a single department, let alone an entire company. But he was far too proud to admit that. Everyone was under the impression that he knew what he was doing; Ted wouldn't have brought him in otherwise. But it quickly became obvious that he didn't. Bill became completely reliant on the rest of the executives, who were able to help him keep the business and administrative side afloat for the time being, but with all the changes made in the facility's status transition, the research side was sinking fast. It would not be long before the whole company went under. Bill was in over his head and could not swim. He would have to do some digging and put together a team of advisors for laboratory operations if he ever could expect to make it to shore.

Bill would find a lifeboat in Mark Deremer. Study director for the bacteriology department, Mark, himself, was drowning. He had tens of thousands in college debt and was being held under by the glass ceiling of an obscure degree in a captive job market. Mark had the perfect mix of humility and apathy that made him overlook scholarship applications, which explains the debt. But even though he went off and lived at one of the world's top universities, he couldn't see a world beyond Ash County, leaving him at the mercy of the only game in town, Sciencia.

Mark was born and raised in Middleton, just east of Vandeburgh. Though he graduated high school valedictorian, he promptly went to work in the family's general store in the town of Hayminster. In college, he worked as an intern in a lab that studied hormonal metabolism. Now he was back in the real world where a biochemistry degree isn't worth as much as you might think it would be, especially in the confines of such a rural area. He accepted his first job at Sciencia, developing more effective birth control pills and post-menopausal fertility stimulants. It was a perfect metaphor for Mark's life: one step forward, one step back. It is an eternity in limbo, paying off debt that helped him get a job he never wanted. Always in the distance, he could hear a faint echo of moving up to a more lucrative position within the company, *maybe in a few years when a few more studies have positive results…*

Since he started that first job in the bioanalytical department many years back, he has never made so much as a spelling error on a report. Also curious is that he has never interviewed for a position other than his first. Every step up he has ever made with the company was simply offered to him when someone else quit.

Philus himself had interviewed Mark for the bioanalytical position. Though as smart as Mark was, he did not know his worth. Philus looked at Mark's resume unimpressed and offered him a low-level position as a laboratory technician, paying him little more than he was getting at the family store.

It was solely due to the wishes of his father that he left the general store to live on a faraway college campus. He would have been happy just stocking shelves the rest of his life, eventually taking over the store for his father. Mark enjoyed the routine. He would get up at the same time, eat the same breakfast, stock the same shelves, price the same products, cut the same meats, sweep the same floors and go home to read his articles.

Mark had always loved to read scientific publications from all fields of study. To him, facts were more interesting than fiction. The ideas flowed from the pages into his brain as if he were just pouring a pitcher of knowledge directly into his skull and he flew through them as if that's exactly what he was doing. His father always remarked that there was no way he could read them as fast as he did. But every morning at breakfast, Mark would rattle on in a clear and simple fashion all of the newest and most interesting points of the articles. It was clear enough to his father that Mark was some kind of genius.

However, what Mark possessed in brilliance, he lacked in ambition. He never did one extra thing to make himself stand out or get ahead in school. He was perfectly content just acquiring the information and letting it stack up in his head, never to be used for anything other than being, "something neat," as Mark would say.

Mark's dad was a Vietnam vet and was never all there to Mark's recollection. He would fly off the handle at any moment unprovoked and go out to the deer blind for hours looking through his binoculars into a pass between two clumps of thicket. "I know they're there," he would say under his breath as he slowly scanned the perimeter over and over again. Mark thought that he went up there just to be alone, away from the distractions of reality. He rarely shot a deer. In fact, Mark can scarcely remember a time when he brought one back. He never thought to ask why his father didn't pick a new spot.

When Mark was a boy, he would go up with his father to the blind and just sit in silence for hours. Once in a while, Mark's father would mumble something he saw that was not a deer, "Gopher….. hunter……Al's fence fell down again….that means Slippy's loose somewhere…….'nother hunter," his eyes never leaving the binoculars. For all the endless acreage the Deremer family owned, all the animals that roamed the land, and all the other hunters that consistently brought something back, you'd think that he would have raised his rifle more than a few times. Until he was much older, Mark just assumed that his father liked to look through the binoculars as much as *he* did.

The Deremers owned a staggering amount of land. To young Mark, and to a large part of his adult subconscious, it was the whole world. He could scarcely see the edge of the property, even with the binoculars. The other side of the fence belonged to a man named Alpheus Lichten, who Mark had never met. He only caught glimpses of the wild horse locals called Slippy that ran back and forth through his property from time to time.

Mark still went up to sit in the blind with his father on occasion, but it was mostly for short conversations. Mark still remembered that one fateful autumn day climbing up to the blind to find his father glued to the binoculars, rifle set aside. "What was that you were telling me earlier about the hands?" asked Mark's father as soon as Mark sat down.

"The hands?" Mark puzzled.

"Yeah, you put your hands up together and said they were the same but different."

"Oh," Mark remembered, "I was talking about enantiomers. Enantiomers are molecules that have the same atomic formula but the atoms are arranged in a different manner so that they are mirror images of each other, like hands. There was a terrible tragedy with enantiomers some years back. A drug called Thalidomide was marketed to pregnant women for morning sickness. The only thing was, one enantiomer worked fine but the other one caused horrible birth defects in tens of thousands of babies. Since then, they have changed the drug regulations so that that would not happen anymore."

"Oh yes. Now I remember. And what was it about a pig bladder that was going to change the world?" queried Mark's Dad.

"Oh some folks in a university have extracted extracellular matrix, um, I mean pieces I guess, from a pig's bladder and are re-growing lost body parts for people. It is going to change medicinal healing!"

"That is really something," Mark's dad said patronizingly. "That *will* be a big change. What were you saying about changing the way schools work?"

"I was talking about decoded neurofeedback. It is brand new. It copies brainwaves from an expert and feeds it to naïve brains, that is, students. So learning won't be tough anymore. It is really neat! *That* is going to change the world."

13

"Son," Mark's father said putting down his binoculars and turning to look at Mark with eyes so blue they could be called silver, "you can't work at the store no more." The blunt edge of the comment defined the Deremer personality. The hush and pause that came over Mark was not one of shock, but of computation. Mark was trying to recall even one time when he had made a mistake at his father's store.

"Why?" Mark said without emotion.

"Son, *you're* gonna change this world. Someday people are going to read amazing things about *you*. That's not gonna happen with you playing rain man with the chili cans at the store. You have to get out of the store and into the world so you can have a hand in changin' it. You have to go to college."

Mark was still quiet. He knew nothing about college. The store was what he knew. Ash County was *all* he knew. He knew nothing of the outside world aside from what he'd read about. The Deremers did not even own a television; so quite literally, he had never even seen a person outside the county limits. Not to mention the painful memories of introversion that were summoned upon the mention of high school. He was glad to be done with school. He was in his place where he should be: in the store where he felt safe and knew what needed to be done; a place where he was relevant. Mark felt his ears getting hot. His diaphragm was locked in contraction. He began to feel his heart beating through every vessel in his body. *What the heck is going on?* But before Mark's brain could search its inventory for an explanation, he was out.

Mark awoke some time later to a cold drip of water running into his ear from the damp washcloth on his forehead. "Oh here dear, let me warm that up for you," she said in a soothing gentle voice. "It's probably gotten cold on you."

14

"Thanks ma," Mark uttered. "What happened?"

"Well," she began with a sigh, "your father told me you had a spell after he fired you." It was all coming back to him now. But at least this time the physical symptoms did not return. "I guess anyone might feel a little jolt from that kind of news. But it's nothing to fret over." *Everything was always nothing to fret over.* "Your father's right, son. You are too bright to be frittering away your time in that dusty old store. You ought to be out in the world. Experience a little more of it than Ash County." Mark understood the logic and was able to swallow his wants and continue on down the new path; the *correct* path, the path that he *ought* to take.

Gladys always had a way of making Mark forget his emotions somehow or another. She always made it seem silly that he got so worked up, or that he even cared in the first place. "Now go back out and get your father and tell him dinner's on the table," Gladys said abruptly. Mark arose from the couch and looked at the long and weathered dinner table to find it completely barren of said dinner. He looked back at his mother who was hunched over the sink stirring something in a large bowl. Gladys felt him staring. *What does she mean 'dinner's on the table'?* Mark thought. But Gladys returned the blank stare as if to say, *By the time you two get back it will be.*

"What kind of financial disclosure?!" Bill screamed at one of his advisors.

"You cannot successfully run a company without books. Any first-year business student can tell you that." Don Perry, the CFO shouted back.

"This is not business school, Don, this is a business. It's a shit business. It's a 747 in free-fall with no pilot just a few thousand feet over the Pacific. There were no books when Ted ran the place. We will be fine until we start getting some legitimate revenue."

"Ted was the end of an era. The new regulations, which you agreed to in a binding contract, make it a lot harder to move money around especially if it is off the books. Especially if it isn't actually there. Audits are going to be a lot more frequent too. It's a new ball game now and it is in place to prevent any more Teds ever happening again."

"So what do you suggest we do Don," Bill said at the end of a long silence.

"Well…we'll need to generate some revenue," Don patronized. You could nearly see the smoke coming from Bill's ears.

But he managed to calm himself and rebut, "OK, how do we make that happen?"

"Well, Bill," Don began, his tone dripping with sarcasm, "in order to generate revenue, we have to do some work." You could almost hear the hammer hit the primer before the discharge. Bill capsized his chair as he shot out of it and jumped up on the long, tan marble table. He was halfway across it before any of the others could register what was happening. By the time Don held his hands up, Bill had already gripped either side of his collar and

16

rolled him backwards onto the floor.

"Don't you fuck with me you little cunt! I'll fucking kill you!" With each 'fuck,' an eruption of saliva crashed onto Don's glasses. The rest of the room was on their feet, too stunned to move. The whole incident was seemingly instantaneous. "You don't have to like me you little cocksucker but you do have to respect me and do what the fuck I say!" Bill continued, red in the face, various veins protruding, teeth clenched, breathing heavily.

Don was obviously unprepared for the reaction and his nervous system decided that urine and tear secretions were the best way to handle it. By now, Bill had gotten to his knees and gripped the back of Don's chair with one hand and his necktie with the other. In one quick jerk Bill stood up and lifted a now very disheveled-looking Don back to his place at the marble table, which now bore three long scuff marks down the middle from his shoes dragging across it. All of the papers that had exploded into the air upon impact were scattered about Don's immediate area. Bill calmly, but deliberately, gathered them up and slapped them on the table in front of Don and then lumbered past all of the now standing executives back to his seat. It was a five-second walk that seemed like hours. "Shall we continue?" he asked, clearing his throat and taking his seat, signaling the others to do the same. The room looked around at each other, mouths agape, at a loss as to how to proceed. Since none of them were doing anything, they all decided to do what Bill said and continue. Still shocked at the display but not letting on that they were, they shakily took their seats, hearts pounding, but silent.

Bill then continued as if the last few seconds had not occurred. "So," he directed at Don, who was still trying to regain his composure, "what do you think would be the best way to begin

17

generating revenue?"

In a quivering tone, so quiet it was almost a whisper, he spoke, "Well, pretty much none of the studies running under Ted's employ were up to code," Don's voice cracked as his throat muscles began relaxing again.

"What about the ones that were?" Bill asked.

"Well," Don shuffled through his mess of papers, "it seems that only one group has been consistently producing valid and reproducible data. They weren't bringing in much money, but the studies they ran are the only ones that our new auditor friends have left untouched." Bill remembered the large stack of rejected studies the new auditors had left in a thick, brown accordion folder on his desk. They all had to be discontinued on account of them not following the proper guidelines, improper documentation, or being just plain unethical.

"OK," Bill said with a hopeful inflection, "what's the group and who's in charge?"

"It is a bacteriology group," Don replied, finally fully composed, "the study director's name is Mark Deremer."

Mark was in his 10 by 10 foot cinderblock office adjacent to his team's shared cubical space. The cinderblocks were not so much painted as they were weatherproofed. It was white at one time, now stained a dingy yellow from the humidified test-animal urine that constantly hung about the air in the facility's basement. About 90% of the time, this was where you would find Mark, pouring over medical journals in much the same way he had done since he was a boy. Only now he did so on a computer screen in an office instead of from paperback copies in the deer blind. His reading was a bit more focused now. Most of it was genetics and bacteria but he still made time for the occasional theoretical physics article, just for fun.

Mark could hear the oddly accusatory tone of a voice before which he had never heard ask, "Is Mark here?" from about six feet outside of his office. A few of the techs mumbled lazily back at him some semblance of a sentence which included the word 'office.' Suddenly, Bill Wildeboer was standing in the doorway of Mark's ten by ten workspace, like a ghost who would rather materialize in places instead of walking. He had the face of a movie star which he complemented with impeccable grooming habits and style of dress. He wore a perfectly tailored, black pin-striped suit covering a matching vest over a crisp, bright white dress shirt. The vest was adorned with the long gold chain of a pocket watch, which glimmered even in the drab lighting of Mark's office. A bright red silk tie hung from his collar with some kind of eye-catching geometric pattern woven into it. At the bottom of this figure were brogue shoes brought to such a keen shine that they might as well have been patent-leather. At the top was a $200 haircut, adorning flesh that was just slightly too tan for the season. He definitely looked the part of a man in charge.

Accompanying the sharp dress was an aura of great significance. It was a mixture of power, anger, arrogance, fear, and chemical instability rolled into one indefinable quality. There was definitely an anxiety-provoking presence about him to which was difficult to appropriately react. However the only thing that stood out in Mark's eye was his lack of proper personal protective equipment, i.e. lab coat, safety glasses, and blue polypropylene booties, which was required to enter the laboratory portion of the facility. Though Mark decided to say nothing as this was their first encounter.

"Good afternoon Mr. Deremer," Bill outstretched his hand to a man who he viewed as the opposite of himself. Mark lacked any such pizzazz that would qualify him as anything other than unexceptional. Mark was a little darker than pasty white with a crewcut that he did himself. Under his lab coat, Mark wore a red and black flannel over a rust-stained t-shirt. He wore khaki colored jeans which were faded and riddled with holes. Mark's shoes were what you may imagine a homeless person would find unacceptable. Both men were about the same build but while Bill's physique was acquired through the state-of-the-art health club in the nearby city of Jotunborough, Mark's was molded through summers helping on Grandpa Deremer's farm, the plot of land adjacent to his father's.

Bill took one look at Mark and an avalanche of insults and castigation came tumbling down from his arcuate fasciculus to the back of his teeth, nearly shattering them as he held back. Their hands shook an awkward shake, as neither very much liked what was happening. Each party of the handshake felt as though Beelzebub was behind them having a good laugh. Nonetheless, the two smiled professional smiles and exchanged kind words of

20

introduction.

"Mark," Bill began, "as I'm sure you are well-aware Ted Philus did his best to run this company into the ground." Mark stared blankly, trying to calculate past the following minutes of this introduction. "I'll get right to it Mark," Bill liked to repeat the name of his listener to positively influence their perception of him. "We need your help."

Mark's stare continued. This was at the bottom of the list of statements expected to be heard. The blockade that now stood in front of Mark's calculations was conveyed by two blinks of quick succession. Bill stood puzzled and patiently waited for a response but received none. He continued, "Amongst the jungle of rampant mismanagement that we are now having to deal with upstairs, your lab has a staunch record of regulatory compliance and consistently viable data." Bill's brain was working overtime trying to find the right words to say to establish common ground. Though, it was obvious to Mark and the eavesdropping technicians that these words were not common to Bill's vocabulary. They seemed clunky and lethargic, like his jaw was undergoing tremendous strain to deploy them.

Mark's silence and stare were beginning to fluster Bill. "Mark," Bill said in an almost inquisitive tone, "I'm asking you to come and work upstairs for a while. There are a couple of folks I would like for you to meet who I know would just love to get your opinion on a few things."

To Bill, Mark seemed unaware of what this was going to mean for him. It was most certainly a giant promotion and Bill felt that Mark should jump at the chance to get it. But Mark was too busy connecting the dots and trying to decide if this was a trap of some kind. He was very familiar with the unscrupulous tactics of

Ted Philus and he knew that Bill was brought in by him. *Why weren't they hiring an outside contractor to fix things? Why is he coming to me?* Mark, after all, was a considerably low-level employee to be approached in this manner. He sat back in his twenty-year-old, tattered swivel chair and brought the fingertips on both hands together in front of his lips. "What type of work would you have me doing?" Mark finally spoke. "I have no business experience. I just run a small lab."

"And that's really all we are going to need you to do," Bill assured. "We need you to show us the proper way to run a lab."

Mark piped up just a little before the end of Bill's sentence with, "What will become of my…"

"Nevermind that right now," Bill interrupted abruptly. For a split second, Bill's face transformed almost imperceptibly into a nightmare. The grinding, toothy smile returned so quickly that Mark did not consciously acknowledge what he had just seen. But he did acknowledge it. Not aloud, but internally. *What the hell was that?*

"For now," Bill continued, "we should take a walk; let us go upstairs and discuss terms and meet potential colleagues." As Mark stood from his chair to follow Bill, the blood rushed to his head.

"Whoa," Mark choked as he stumbled to keep his balance, "what the hell am I doing?"

Bill turned around to acknowledge Mark's utterance, "Are you alright?"

"Yeah," Mark replied, "I just lost my composure there for a second."

The two started off walking, the smell of the basement's musty drainpipes returned Mark to his memories of how things used to be while he still worked at his father's grocery store. He had always been allowed to keep his own hours but showed up promptly at 8 and left promptly at 4:15 anyway. He did this every single day from his first day on the job as a boy until he quit to go to college. The other two employees who were actually scheduled to work until 4:30, were told by Mark's father to leave at 4:15 to "stay ahead of the traffic," which Mark never understood. Mark figured that because there were only a few vehicles a day that passed through the town of Hayminster where the store was located, most of them just local farm vehicles or maybe the few amish horse-drawn buggies that passed through from time to time, that it was just something that people say, like an expression. But nonetheless, Mark figured that he would follow suit and leave with everyone else.

Mark knew next to nothing about his father's past. Though they spent countless hours in the deer blind, they spoke nary a word save for the intermittent observations his father would call out from behind his binoculars. For all intents and purposes, they were perfect strangers.

Mark did know that his father was in Vietnam. But the only physical evidence of this was the dusty pair of jungle boots that did nothing but occupy space in the mud room. He also knew that he was rarely in the house. In all of Mark's memories of his father, he was either in the small manager's office at the store or in the deer blind looking through binoculars. As Mark walked with Bill he became determined to find a memory of seeing his father in the house. But search as he did, a memory could not be found. He recalled numerous fights that his father and Gladys had gotten into. But it was not a visual memory of his father that came to mind. It was but the mere fragments of high-volume arguments which came from the bedroom or some other room in the house. As he probed deeper and deeper into his memory, he could find no instance of ever seeing his father and mother together. Though despite the memories of arguments, Mark would not say he grew up in a broken home. Fight as his parents did, Mark never caught any misdirected emotions. It was as if everything was fine between them; in *his* presence anyway.

This lack of memory was troubling though. Surely there were times his father and Gladys were in the same room together. Mark went back to the previous memory that still lingered; the one where Gladys told him to fetch his father from the blind to eat the dinner that was not on the table. Mark remembered walking through the tall grass in the dusk of the early spring. It was warm enough to be without a jacket, but only because the frigid temperatures of a Michigan February had hardened his flesh. The days were getting longer, but the darkness that fell on dinnertime still hung on. Mark walked what seemed to be entirely too long to retrieve his father. Once he finally made it to the blind, he still had the task of climbing up the rickety wooden stakes that were nailed into the tree trunk over a hundred years ago. As he climbed he imagined his grandfather as a young boy who must've climbed these same stakes in this same order to retrieve his father to eat a meal that was not yet on the table. At the summit of this ascent was a hatch that opened up into the private world of the deer blind and there, like a statue, his father sat, eyes pressed into binoculars, rifle propped into the corner.

"Mom says come and eat," Mark said plainly.

"Mm-hmm," his father replied. The night had fallen quickly since Mark first left the house, as if he had walked away from the sun.

"Can you still see?" asked Mark. "It's getting pretty dark."

A deeply weathered and thin layer of skin stretched over sharp, protruding skull bones turned to look at him. It was one of the rare imprints of his father's face lodged into his memory. The wrinkles seemed to be valleys sunken deep into a leathery landscape. The rings from the binoculars encircled two silver spheres that spoke to him in place of a response. Even in absence of words, it was a look that cut through the deafening silence loud and clear. It took no longer than a second for Mark to turn away and retrace his steps from the hatch back to the Deremer residence. The chill of a thousand Michigan Februaries could not compare to that half-second stare.

Mark concluded that his memory must have warped his perception of time, for as he started back to the house, he remembered the sky was completely emptied of light. Adding to the discrepancy was a soft, repetitive thundering; another falsehood perhaps. With each footstep closer to the front door, the booming increased in volume until he went to turn the door knob. As his hand reached it, he was jolted back into the present.

"Mark Deremer," Bill said in a tone obviously concluding a long introduction. Mark had been so deep into his memory that he was living it as his own personal reality, blacking out the common and shared reality of the rest of the world. The walk with Bill from Mark's basement office up two or three flights of stairs to the other side of the building up to and including an introduction of Mark, his history, his work, his credentials and how he was going to turn EnviroCore around was completely absent from Mark's memory. He now stood at the head of the long tan marble table and its adjacent executives.

Mark was a deer in the headlights in front of them. He had no idea what was just said. The confusion engulfed him like a rogue wave that crashes into you harder than the others and knocks you off your feet. But it was not the awkward situation that troubled him, it was the absence of the last... *how many minutes was it? Well, I have to say something.* "Hi," Mark finally punted, "I can't wait to start working with all of you." That seemed like the right thing to say.

Mark's blackouts have been a part of his life since as far back as he could remember. Though he never quite knew when they were coming on, and they seemed to happen at the most inopportune times; moments that needed his full attention. Whenever there was the threat of strong emotion in Mark's life, his mind just dealt with it by dissociating and then returning to consciousness at some undetermined amount of time later. Mark was then left with the task of finding out what happened by a complex guessing game he learned to employ at a very young age. In this case, he used the context of the room, what with its high-grade wood paneling, long marble table, and artistically designed sconces, to discern that this was the showroom and these were important people. Given the recent conversation with the new CEO, it was safe to say that these were the top executives of EnviroCore. After all, some of the faces did look familiar. But that was no measure of confidence as everyone seemed to look familiar to Mark.

"Mark," Bill said after a long awkward silence, "we are going to get you started with Gary over there. Gary was Vice President of Human Resources at Sciencia and now at EnviroCore and you'll be working with him most closely in the early stages." The two shook hands and nodded at each other politely as Bill impatiently ushered Mark away and continued to round the table. Most everyone in the room held their same positions in the transition from 'Biomedical Research Facility' to 'Environmental Sustainability Development Company.' If the title was not the same, the job was. The entire transition deal was basically a dog-and-pony show on the carpeted side of the building. On the lab side, where Mark came in, it was not.

In fact, even though the rumors of what went on beyond the barbed-wire fence of this facility were grossly exaggerated, the truth is that misconduct was rampant. Most of it was unintentional. It was just that the top of the food chain was complacent and unchecked. This trickled down all the way to the lowest rung of the ladder and no one really knew the proper way to do their job. But since the work had to get done, everyone just winged it and the strategy became entrenched. In fact, the unofficial slogan of Sciencia was 'Make it Work.'

In addition to the laissez-faire management style, no one was being called on their mistakes or even on their blatant wrongdoing, so no changes were ever made. The mindset of the company needed a massive overhaul if the transition was even to pretend to work. It was a huge task. In about as nonchalant a way as possible, Bill had just charged Mark with saving the company. This realization was slow to dawn on Mark. But with each passing one-on-one introduction to another executive, the eclipse gradually became total.

"OK," Bill concluded in the most jovial of tones at the end of the last handshake, "that's enough of that horse shit. Let's get you two to work." Gary Planchard, Vice President of Human Resources held the door open and gestured 'after you' and the two left the rest of the executives through the oversized and elaborately decorated glass and metal doors with the giant Sciencia brand still etched into them.

And just like that, Mark was a different person. A few minutes earlier he was in charge of a small and insignificant lab in the basement. Now, as he would soon discover whilst signing his new contract on his new mahogany desk in his new leather chair in his second-floor office looking out over the thick, lush greenery of Valhalla National Park, he was now the Vice President of Operations. Gary didn't say much during the walk until they got through Mark's new office doors, where a manila folder could be seen lying open on Mark's new desk.

"Is this it?" Mark asked as he unstrung the twine holding the envelope closed. Inside was the contract to Mark's new job. It must have been 50 pages of legalese with huge purple arrows everywhere Mark needed to initial or sign. As he stood over it thumbing through a few of the top pages, he heard that soft rhythmic rumbling again that was with him at the end of the last blackout just previous to waking up in front of the executives. This time though, he made the connection that another blackout was coming. The rumbling was getting louder and was now also accompanied by three or four voices chattering incoherently. He picked up a stack of the pages in the contract and let the weight of the big purple paper clips thunder each page back down to the rest of the stack.

"Some view isn't it?" Gary asked.

Mark was sharply jolted from the imminent blackout by the statement. Mark turned to the five foot five inch bucket of charm that stood behind him at the window. He looked like he had just stepped out of a toothpaste commercial, dark-complected with a dazzling white smile. He wore a jet black suit with just as black a tie over a white dress shirt which seemed to match the brightness of his teeth. "Yes," Mark answered in monotone, seemingly disinterested.

"As I'm sure you already know, this region has strong Scandinavian roots," Gary began. He could have been a tour guide. "They named this piece of land Valhalla because it reminded the town's settlers of Odin's kingdom in Norse mythology. Valhalla is the place where Valkyries take the souls of warriors who have died in battle. It means 'Hall of the Fallen.' While there, souls spend the afterlife helping Odin prepare for the apocalypse." Mark watched Gary explain the origin of the park while he looked out into it. "With the snowy owls adorning the pines in the winter, dense canopies of orange birches and maples in the autumn, the Sága Waterfall towering high above them both, spraying her mist for miles, Valhalla is truly the pride of West Michigan," Gary sighed with content. *He could do radio commercials.* The majestic awe that colored Gary's words drained from his next statement as he turned his attention from the scenery back to Mark, "Let me know when you've had a chance to look over the contract. I'll be in my office until about noon. I'll come and get you for lunch and we can go over a few things. Congratulations on the new job." In sharp contrast to the 'pride of West Michigan' speech he just made, he spoke the last four sentences as fast as a legal disclaimer at the end of a loan commercial.

"Yes, I will, thanks," Mark replied as Gary walked away.

30

As he watched him walk out of the office, Mark's hand touched the top of the high-back Italian tufted leather office chair as he remembered the worn upholstery of his old one in the basement office whose back wouldn't even stay upright. He glanced down again at the contract amidst a background of leather binding and wheeled the chair backwards away from the desk so that he may sit and try out his new position. The ball bearings in the chair's wheels were sufficiently oiled as there was no squeak and an impossible ease of motion. As Mark lowered himself into the chair's seat, he did not need to brace himself for fear of falling backward. On the contrary, he found comfort and stability in one.

Mark took one or two minutes to take in the events of the day and soak in the new surroundings. His whole life had changed without much prodding. Though it seemed almost too easy for him to be led the way he was. The analysts began reeling: *Do I really want this position? What will become of my lab and its work? I don't want this kind of responsibility. This is going to add a lot of pressure. Bill is my boss. Do I have to do what he says? Will he fire me if I don't sign the contract? He will probably fire me. Can I even handle this responsibility? On the other hand, this is a huge promotion. There is a lot of money involved. How do I know that? I was underpaid before. I will probably be underpaid again. Is the money worth the stress? There is probably more money in this position than the study director position. Is money all that is important? I do have a chance to do something great here now.*

Mark noticed a stack of purple arrow paperclips had piled up where minutes ago there were none. He also noticed his signature and initials in the spaces of the contract. *What just happened?* While Mark was reasoning, he had read, understood, and signed the entire contract. *Was that another blackout? It must've been.* Though Mark had no memory of the last two minutes, he knew full well what had happened. He was reading the contract while he was reasoning, as if he had two brains. One brain had already decided to go through with signing the contract for the new position while the other brain was still contemplating it. Mark had experienced this many times before. He imagined a Venn diagram with its two overlapping circles drifting apart until one was no longer part of the other; the two were completely separate. When the circles divide, certain thoughts and actions would occur independent of one another, giving him the illusion of multiple states of consciousness, and manifesting in a blackout. There were times like now when only a few minutes would pass and brevity made it seem like a fleeting daydream. Other times, he might lose hours or even pass out.

Mark took a minute to reassure himself that he was one consciousness in the common timeline, staring with finality at his signature on the very last page. He was now officially the Vice President of Operations at EnviroCore. One final breath as the old Mark escaped his lungs as he pushed away from his desk in the ultra smooth and ultra quiet locomotion of his chair, swiveling his direction to the window overlooking Valhalla. Standing up and looking out into its vast majesty, budding plants began to open in Mark's imagination. The reality of the situation came to fruition and began to fertilize Mark's dormant potential. He saw a pink sky filled with surrealistic clouds showering a great flood of dopamine on a dead, gray cortex. Sediments washed away to reveal a vibrant core network of neurons crackling and popping so hard that sparks were jumping off the surface. The cortex began to swell. It began to resemble the pink clouds above it. Popping and sparking became concentrated into lightning bolts that leapt from the surface of the cortex to the sky above it. In turn, the clouds shot them back. The cortex and the clouds were communicating lightning bolts in complex volleys which encoded the grand ideas that bubbled up from deep below the surface and from high above the pink-laced tropospheric marvels. Ideas were flooding his consciousness. He stood firm against a massive tidal wave of inspiration that overwhelmed him, though he did not fall. He breathed the flood into his lungs and exhaled just as naturally as if it were oxygen, feeling every particle of every molecule of the wave tingling past his goose-bumped flesh as he did. He was completely enveloped in a sensation of god-like wonderment, as if every word he had ever read had become reanimated and was now clawing its way out of the soil and arranging itself just as it should be arranged to be useful. He was a lone figure burning brightly against a black background. Enormous thunderclaps echoed in triplet succession, deafening the normal ambience of reality. But suddenly, the strikes sounded familiar. "Are you ready to eat, Mark?" a voice asked from a great distance behind him. With a blink, the thunderclaps turned into Gary's knuckles knocking on the doorframe and Mark snapped back into existence once again. He turned around to greet Gary with wide eyes and a cockeyed smile, "That's three times in one day."

"Umm, what?" Gary asked, betraying his confusion at the odd response.

"Nothing," Mark replied, "Yes, I am ready to eat."

As the two started towards the cafeteria, it dawned on Mark that his tuna fish sandwich was in the refrigerator in the break room down the hall from his former office. "I have to stop and get my lunch," Mark said. "It's in the tech office."

"Don't worry about that today," Gary replied, "lunch is on the house."

Mark had only eaten lunch in the cafeteria one other time during his career at Sciencia and that was for his orientation. Again, nothing of substance was said during the walk. It had occurred to Mark that he would be completely lost if it were not for Gary. Besides the cafeteria, Mark had only rarely frequented the carpeted portion of the building. It was a dark brown commercial grade berber carpet that seemed to go on for miles. This was what separated the business side of operations from the laboratory side: the floor.

In stark contrast to the brown carpet of the business side, the side that handled the money, made the decisions, and made the data look pretty, was the dingy commercial vinyl tile that quite possibly had never been waxed. It was a reminder to all who walked on it that they were the forgotten; the hardened, ragged grunts who plugged away in the lab, hour after hour, with nothing more than a pipette and a calculator to keep them company. The work done on the tiled side was not for the faint of heart. It was thankless and low-paying, with long hours and constant setbacks. It had broken many an up-and-coming scientist with its rude awakening of what the job actually is. It was not glowing jars of slime, violent chemical reactions, or the pioneering of medical breakthroughs which would someday be made into a documentary narrated by Morgan Freeman. It was brutal monotony, constant disappointment, mind-numbing spreadsheets, monitoring, waiting, and analysis; *my god the analysis.* Needless to say, those that had worked their way up to any sort of senior scientist position on the tile side of Sciencia was a different kind of human.

The duo finally reached the cafeteria doors, which like the conference room, still bore the Sciencia brand. Inside was a sea of faces that watched he and Gary enter the room, as if they were two outlaws in some old western; Gary because of his status in the company, and Mark, because he was walking with Gary and was rarely seen outside of his office. Mark was not one to make friends. Even though he recognized a handful of coworkers in the crowd, they were acquaintances at best and did not even acknowledge him. Mark was a stranger in a company where he had worked for ten years.

"Asiago chicken sound good?" Gary asked Mark as they stepped up to the lunch counter.

"Umm…" Mark had no idea if that sounded good or not, but nonetheless decided for the sake of deciding. "Yeah, sounds good."

"Two asiago chicken platters, Tina. Have 'em bring it to the executive lunch room," Gary barked at the cafeteria employee. "You'll like it Mark." Gary moved with an unnecessary sense of urgency. They hurried through the cafeteria to the executive lunch room where two notepads sat. Each took a spot in front of one. The executive lunch room looked like something you might find in the Playboy mansion back in the early 1960s. It was mahogany and Formica and ficus galore.

"Okay Mark," Gary began, "our job from here on out is to organize and assemble something that looks like a functional research facility. As I'm sure you are well aware, the previous CEO did not like to play by the rules and pretty much left this place in shambles. He brought Bill in, but Bill doesn't know what he's doing quite frankly, especially on the actual project and production side. We need to milk the contracts we have and come up with some new ones fast if this thing is going to stay afloat. None of our clients really know what to make of us right now and every day that goes by without an answer to their questions is one more tally on the 'con' side of continuing to do business with us." All of what Gary had just said came out in one breath. Gary did everything fast. He talked fast, walked fast, wrote fast, and twirled his pen fast when it wasn't moving. He continued, "Bill put you in charge because you seemed to be the only one who followed the rules as far as regulatory standards are concerned. Also, you have a good working relationship with your clients and your record is as clean as I've ever seen. In addition, I personally found it curious that we have never met before despite the fact that you've been here ten years and have continued to move up the ranks. I remembered your name but could not place your face and when I finally met you in person that didn't help. That means that you have never interviewed for a position at this company except for when you first started." That was Gary's second breath of the meeting. The speed would have been comical if it weren't so fascinating.

Finally Mark was able to speak, "I interviewed with Ted and since then someone would offer me a new job every once in a while."

"Must be nice to be in such high demand, huh?" Gary chuckled.

"I suppose I never thought of that," Mark replied, taking Gary's statement and rooting it firmly in his hippocampus. "What happened to the previous Vice President of Operations?" Mark asked abruptly and awkwardly out of context.

"You don't mess around do you?" Gary chuckled. "That's good, that's good, get straight to it." Mark had some idea of what happened but wanted to hear it from Gary. "Sean Ascot was the previous VP of Operations at Sciencia," Gary began in a much more relaxed tone. "To put it mildly," he continued, "Sean was complacent. No one kept Sean in check and Sean didn't *keep* anyone in check. I mean, ultimately the downfall of the company rested on the shoulders of Ted Philus, but the current state of EnviroCore, i.e. the mess you and I are cleaning up now, is because of Sean." Just then, Tina from the cafeteria came in with a fine looking plate of food for each of them. Asparagus on a pile of long-grain wild rice next to two honey-glazed biscuits and two steaming chicken breasts with shredded asiago cheese melted over the top of them.

"Thank you so much, Tina," Gary said. "Will you bring us out a carafe of coffee and two cups when you get a chance please?" Mark noticed Gary's tone shifted to reflect his take-charge attitude.

"And some water please Tina," Mark piped up as she walked out the door. She had not heard him. But Gary got up out of his seat and started after her.

"Hey Tina!" Gary shouted out the door after her, "Will you bring us a couple of glasses of water too please?"

"Yeah!" She shouted back, obviously annoyed with the small request.

"Thank you," Gary dropped the door before his words could make it out to her. He continued to tell the story of Sean Ascot but his voice returned to that of a soothing yet deliberate narrator. "So, anyway," Gary continued whilst cutting into his chicken and letting ever more steam escape, "Ted didn't care so Sean didn't care so not many people here did. Those who did care had their hands tied for the most part because whistleblowers would suffer retaliation. But that didn't matter, because anyone with any real power was in Ted's pocket anyway." Mark felt like he was reading one of those tabloids at his father's grocery store. Never before in his life had he ever been privy to such candid yet confidential information.

"Here you go guys," Tina said as she burst through the door with the water and coffee.

"Thanks Tina," Gary said. "Tina this is Mark Deremer, your new Vice President of Operations."

"Pleased to meet you," she said without looking up and with a hint of sarcasm. As she walked out of the room, his mouth became intensely salty, prompting him to take a minute to analyze: *She's pretty, too much makeup.* Analysis complete.

"She's somethin' huh?" was Gary's analysis and with a subtle throat-clearing, got back to his story. "So, Sean kept collecting his paycheck while doing…well, pretty much nothing. He delegated every piece of his job to one of his underlings and never provided them appropriate feedback. Therefore, if a task did get done, it was blatantly half-assed." Mark observed Gary tearing through his chicken as he told the story of Sean Ascot. He ate even faster than he talked. The pieces were cut with once swipe and then thrown down his gullet with steam still billowing out as he swallowed. He never talked with his mouth full but somehow still managed to devour his meal while elaborating on the hairy details of the company's corruption. All the while, he moved with the precision of a Swiss timepiece. "He finally got his comeuppance during the status change," Gary continued. "When the auditors did finally finish, they found thousands of violations and that's just what was *recorded*." Mark noticed that Gary had slowed his speech as a function of his plate contents. "It all fell back on Sean," Gary went on. "Philus was long gone and Sean was left holding the bag."

As Gary continued the story, Mark began to visualize how the scenario played out. Bill sat behind a pile of violations, staring straight through the stack, his rage steadily boiling up to a steam. A blue vein on Bill's temple swelled and shrank to the beat of his pulse, pumping gasoline onto the raging inferno in his chest. Beads of sweat formed on Bill's brow as his temper got hotter and hotter. Then finally the fuse lit. The berserker formerly known as Bill bolted from his chair and threw it behind him with all of his strength. Its impact carved a huge chunk out of the darkly finished wood in the wall. He grabbed as many of the papers as he could hold from the stack, flung his office door open, and burned down the hallway.

A flurry of the red-annotated violation paperwork blew from his arms as he continued to march and to breathe at about thirty miles per hour until finally reaching Ascot's office. Bill's foot was a battering ram that kicked the strike plate out of its nesting behind an explosion of splinters and door pieces. Sean stood up out of his chair with the look of a death row prisoner watching his executioner pull the switch. Before Sean could react, Bill heaved the sizable stack of violations with the force of hurricane winds. What paper did not fly off by means of air resistance clubbed Sean in the chin and upper chest and he fell back onto his hip trying to catch his own collapse.

Bill was not even completely through the doorway of the office before a tirade reminiscent of Benito Mussolini spouted from the top of his lungs. Mark imagined his stomach herniating from the intense flexion of his diaphragm, vocal cords hemorrhaging, ocular capillaries bursting, and body flailing wildly like a conductor in an orchestra struggling through a seizure. He was waving fingers at the end of spasmodic arms, flipping hair

40

follicles in a series of epileptic head jerks, and spitting Vesuvian amounts of foam from a locked jaw full of clenched teeth. Bill's rant was an even distribution of insults, expletives, and threats of violence, peppered every so often with a mention of the misconduct. At times, he seemed to be speaking in tongues, unable to form a coherent communication of his rage. The entire second floor was inching its way to the hall to cautiously indulge their curiosity.

During the whole scene, someone had called security. Everyone thought that Bill was in there beating Sean to death. But in reality, Bill was the one who called security before the whole thing even started. Sean's termination paperwork was already being processed and Bill would not have to see him ever again after the ridiculous and damning report written by the auditor. *So why did he call security?* When the security team arrived they took Bill, not Sean, out of the office.

"They told me off the record that Bill called them to go up to Sean's office and walk him out. But that is usually a job for my team and we were still about a day away from being ready to fire him," Gary explained. "I think the guy has more than a couple of screws loose."

"Maybe he knew he was going to lose his temper and he called security so that he wouldn't kill him," Mark suggested.

"Yeah, maybe," Gary chuckled. "If Bill had one ounce of self-control I might agree with you. Hey you haven't touched your chicken yet. You not hungry?"

Mark *was* hungry. He hadn't started eating because his attention was so intense that it was difficult to pry from its prey. It was both a gift and a curse. His attention and imagination had allowed him to comprehend even the most abstract and

41

complicated subjects from Bragg diffraction to M theory. But he would sometimes lose track of hours as he read his articles, experiencing a dreamlike reality where whatever information was being absorbed would come to life in a surrealistic performance, like an LSD trip but with clarity and purpose.

"I *am* hungry," Mark answered. "So what kind of work am I going to be doing?" Mark finally took his fork and sunk it into the chicken breast. It seemed to have cooled down quite a bit. But as he dragged his knife through the meat a mushroom cloud of steam wafted from the exposed inside.

"Well, it's like this," Gary began, "we need to (a) make sure that we are in compliance with the new standard of operation as an Environmental Sustainability Development Company. (b) We need to make this company profitable and (c) we need to reorganize. That is, we need to weed out everyone slowing us down and hire new people to speed us up. We are at square one right now but we need to make plans yesterday. We need to make plans to make plans to make plans and make them happen. But we don't have much to go on here. Investors are dropping like flies and that is creating a ripple effect."

"OK," Mark said ungracefully chewing his first chunk of the chicken, "so here's what we do…" The fuse of Mark's imagination ignited once again. Though he knew almost nothing about business, he knew plenty about the nature of things. He recalled his knowledge of evolutionary biology and imagined the ultraviolet markings of flowers detectable to the photoreceptors of bees. He recalled the nonvenomous king snake mimicking the venomous coral snake. He imagined the entire process of glucose breakdown from the amylase degrading the asiago cheese in his mouth to the ATP powering his sodium-potassium pumps. Mark's entire body was tense and fidgety and his eyes were wide with anticipation. "Here's what we do," he said again. "We get more money."

Gary looked at Mark like he had just insulted his mother, "Well, yes. Ideally," Gary said, deflated.

"No, no, listen, listen, listen," Mark continued, "OK here goes." With the determination of a gold-medal race runner at the starting line, he launched into his idea. It was now Gary's turn to observe. "We obviously need to overhaul the whole model, right? There is no way to do that without money. But we don't have any. Clients are pulling out and no one trusts us as a Biomedical Research Company so they aren't buying anything that says Sciencia on it. On top of having no money, what money we have is bleeding fast from multiple wounds. So we need to cut off the gangrene and clot those wounds. We need to make believe that this company is, in fact, a new company. Right now we are in a mindset of scrambling to make ends meet when what we really should be doing is promoting EnviroCore. We need to create entirely new departments focused around the environment, not just the biology. We need to seek out new clients and get rid of pharmaceuticals, at least on the surface. We need to make believe that things are better now than they ever have been, and that we are making leaps and bounds over the competition. Our clients will see how we are behaving and follow suit. We need to chew our limbs off and pretend that we are growing two new ones until they actually do grow. We need to have a meeting with a marketing agency or create our own in house to design a new brand. We need to distribute that brand and get on the road to events, conferences, panels, roadshows, whatever platform we can find to say the name 'EnviroCore.' We need to start right now and we need to spend all that we have before we lose it and before anyone can see what we are doing. Every last dime. We are going to lose it all anyway in a similar time period if we do nothing, right?"

Gary gripped the arms of his chair as if he might need to run out of the room suddenly. Mark's intensity and enthusiasm was such that he felt he might be witnessing a psychotic break. Mark had not stopped shoveling food into his mouth during the entire idea. The actions were not as precise as Gary though, and bits of food had flown all over the immediate seating area. Once Mark caught his breath, he held the glass of water to his lips and did not breathe again until the glass was empty.

During this prolonged flash of insight, Mark witnessed the separating Venn diagram of his own consciousness. Though he knew he was talking, he felt that he controlled less and less of what was being said, the more that was said. He only saw bees pollinating the brightest flowers and coyotes avoiding the harmless king snake. He imagined a newt growing back a lost arm. It was a rush Mark had never felt before. He felt godlike. He had the power to adapt and evolve the organism that was EnviroCore. But Mark felt that he was adapting and evolving right along with it and it felt good. "So," he looked to Gary who was still tensed in fight-or-flight stance, "Let's make this happen."

"Well," Gary paused with nervous apprehension, "that was unexpected." Mark silently agreed. He had never been one to take charge or even have a plan to take charge. But it felt good, almost like he was pretending to be someone else.

"It seems a little drastic," Gary concluded. "Plus Bill is not going to go along with anything like that."

Mark continued to wrangle the bull, "We are in charge of this operation, right? Do we even need his approval?"

"If he finds out what we are doing on his own," Gary retorted, "he could get suspicious and throw a stack of papers at us on our way out the door. If we tell him our plan first, he will have the chance to reject it but at least we keep our jobs."

"How long will we keep our jobs anyway if the company goes under?" Mark reasoned, "What is going to happen is that he is going to answer out of fear. He will say no, we will come back down here, drink more coffee, wish we hadn't told him the plan, come up with nothing better, and lose our jobs anyway."

"He will surely ask us what we have come up with," Gary argued. "We will have to tell him something."

"Yes," Mark agreed, "but we don't have to tell him everything. He surely realizes that drastic measures need to be taken to save the company. We can tell him any number of things we are actually doing but leave out some of the scarier details."

"Listen Mark," Gary said in a serious tone, "I have worked closely with Bill for only a small amount of time but a little longer than you have. I appreciate your sense of urgency and you are definitely outside of the box. But Bill will find out somehow and when he does he will lose...his...shit."

Mark was finding it very difficult to empathize with Gary's position. It was crystal clear to Mark what needed to be done. It was the only shot they had. Sure, it seemed extreme, but it was the only way it was going to work. Mark was not used to working together with anybody on a problem. Whenever he could, he worked alone. Anytime anyone else was involved it seemed to hinder his progress. But this was the situation and he would have to try. "What do you suggest then?" Mark asked Gary after a moment of contemplative silence.

"I don't know," Gary finally said with a sigh, "we ought to

go and ask him if there are any guidelines we need to follow."

"If he did not give you any to start, then that works in our favor," Mark said, "if all he said was, 'go and save the company,' then that is what we should do. We should do it independently and as transparently as possible. You said yourself that Bill doesn't know what he's doing. Surely he will listen to reason if we do have to explain the plan in any depth. You also said every day that goes by without an answer to their questions is one more tally on the 'con' side of continuing to do business with us."

One side of Gary's mouth began to climb up the side of his face in a cockeyed smile. "I also told you that you were in high demand," Gary recalled. In that moment, logic had won over fear in favor of urgency. It was a great victory. "We are going to be the most hated people in this company for a long time," Gary realized.

"That is the least of my worries," Mark added matter-of-factly. "We also have to live in the same county."

It was at the very end of that last sentence that a sharp knock on the door to the executive lunch room had broken through the tension in the air. Startled, the two looked over to see Bill standing eerily behind the glass door. *How long had he been standing there?* He was grinning a terrible grin. It was confusing. It was a look that could either be considered happy or angry. Neither Mark nor Gary were quite able to tell what was about to be said. He let himself in and when he spoke it was a most jovial tone indeed. "Howdy boys!" he blared, mocking some southern accent. "How's she goin' eh?" he followed in a Canadian accent.

Gary's blood turned to ice water and he squeaked out the words, "They're goin' Bill." Mark was taken aback. He looked over at Gary whose confidence had been suddenly stolen by Bill's presence. Mark could empathize with Gary in this situation. After all, they had both just made a pact to keep the boss out of the know. What is more, his creepy smile made him look like he knew it. Neither of them knew how long he had been standing outside the door or what he had heard of the meeting. *Was he the kind of person to stand outside of the door and listen to a conversation?* After the story about Sean Ascot, Bill's presence should have made Mark apprehensive as well, but it didn't.

"What about you?" Bill said piercingly. "How do you like old Gary here?" It was obvious that Bill was trying to shake them up.

"Gary is treating me with the utmost respect and professionalism," Mark answered coldly.

"Is that all?" Bill laughed. "Well I guess I'm glad to hear that he's not calling you names and whatnot." Gary laughed nervously, Mark did not. Mark stared back into Bill's eyes, still wrapped in a cloak of friendly jocularity. He was already learning a tremendous amount about him just by being in the same room, as if his intentions were tattooed on his forehead. Bill wanted to have complete control over everything even though it would often hinder the situation. He wanted people to know that he was in charge. He wanted respect, but he did not have the credibility as a manager to command it through any other means but fear. So he used fear and he used it often. But Mark was not dissuaded. He was riding a tidal wave of confidence and he refused to be intimidated in this moment. All of this was unspoken but still understood at some level by everyone in the room.

Much to everyone's surprise, Bill dropped the passive-aggressive attitude. "Well alright," he said with a considerably less offensive tone of voice, "I guess I will let you guys do your work. I just wanted to check in and see if there was anything you needed. By the way, I know this is no easy task. I know it's probably gonna get pretty ugly. I just want you both to know that I will stand behind you no matter how drastic things get."

"We will let you know if we need anything Bill," Mark said dismissively ignoring the sudden change in attitude, and perhaps even pushing the line a little bit.

"OK then great," Bill said as he turned to leave. "Just…let me know."

Mark noticed as Bill turned away from him that in addition to his attitude, his eyes had changed as well. His smile was just as haunting as it ever was, but his eyes were not the same. Mark could see that they were now betraying mournful sorrow at the loss of the verbal standoff. Bill walked out of the executive lunchroom with tears clutching his eyeballs for dear life. He knew he could not be seen showing any weakness in front of his immediate subordinates, let alone in a cafeteria filled with nearly every subordinate in the company. But the feeling overwhelmed him. The frustration inside him was like a frail and bony demon that had hollowed out his thoracic cavity and was pulling at strings that pulled open his glottis. That string was in turn tied to wires that pulled at his tear ducts. Bill clenched his teeth with all of his strength, desperately trying to maintain composure, at least until he could make it to an area of refuge. Try as he did, the tears started falling at great speeds and all he could do was pray that no one would see. But the dissatisfied demon made sure to jump up and let all of its weight hang from the string like he were ringing the bells at The York Minster. Overwhelmed he could not stifle the tears which pleased the demon so much that a second demon spawned out of the first. This second demon crawled up into Bill's skull and started screaming into Bill's ears in celebration which only registered as a binaural squealing whose pitch drifted further and further away from synchronicity. Bill completely lost control and every fiber of his being recoiled. The sinews in his right arm stiffened, his arm drew back, and then swung forward. Slowing slightly as the hand's range of motion was interrupted by a nearby dining table, thousands of muscle fibers popped in Bill's biceps as he flipped it over.

The table was enough of a distraction to buy Bill some time to get out of public and to a nearby elevator. Once inside, he began howling at the top of his lungs. He looked up at the ceiling and cried the angriest cry that has ever been cried. Sobbing and screaming simultaneously, tears streamed endlessly from his bright red eyeballs. Bill kicked a shoe-shaped dent into the metal which held the emergency stop button in the pressed position. He turned around and began punching the metal wall of the elevator repeatedly, still screaming all the while. Before long, the elevator wall was riddled with bloody imprints of Bill's fists. After the tantrum had exhausted him, he fell to his knees and wept uncontrollably. Snot and tears poured from his face and his labored breathing and sob spasms echoed through the elevator shaft, chilling the spinal cords of everyone within earshot. It was a dreadful cry that filled a body with both fear and sympathy for the victim.

The entire cafeteria was now silent and looking in the direction of the table that had just been violently overturned. Mark and Gary had raced outside following the disturbance. A tight coil of paranoia squeezed around both of their necks as they silently pieced together what had just happened. Mark's heartbeat began to throb throughout his entire body. The noise knocked him off the wave and he plummeted towards another blackout. Desperately, he struggled to keep his head up above the waterline of consciousness, but neither of them could ignore what had just happened. Even though Bill had lost a dominance match with one of his subordinates, neither of them drew the conclusion that that was the reason for the table being overturned. They looked at each other, now enmeshed in the surety that Bill had heard them or otherwise knew their intention of hiding details. The reason for the overturned table was all they needed for the seed of paranoia to be planted.

In reality, it *was* the lost dominance match that provoked the meltdown. Even though Bill was no stranger to loss and failure, he had grown hypersensitive to its effects. Coupled with a stark chemical imbalance and general lack of self-control, this made Bill the quintessential time bomb. Worse yet, his horrifying explosion took place without much provocation. *Imagine if somebody were actually trying to offend him.*

Bill's sobs had slowed down long enough now that he decided he could stand up from his kneeling position on the elevator floor. The dented metal in the elevator wall presented a warped reflection, complete with disheveled hair, loose tie flung over his shoulder, bloodshot eyes, and a red face wet with sweat and tears. He inhaled deeply to slow his breathing even further and removed a red handkerchief from his inner pocket. Bill held the handkerchief onto his knuckles and absorbed what blood he could from them. The metal wall dents that dripped his blood were swiped away in a few quick strokes as if he were already tired of the task before he started. The pitiful sniffles turned into snorts of contempt and of disgust, which then turned into single, abrupt guffaws. Soon Bill was chuckling quietly to himself as he ran his fingers through his hair to straighten it out. He pulled at the rest of his disorder until he was presentable enough and then pried the dented emergency stop button out of its newly formed, shoe-print canyon. Then he pressed the button for the second floor, held one hand with the other in a relaxed, patient stance waiting to arrive.

Bill was still chuckling as the elevator doors parted. Striding down the hallway on the way back to his office, he came upon a huddled gaggle of upper middle management. Bill's appearance already made him seem crazy enough. But as he neared the group, he flashed a fortress of polished white teeth still caught in modest laughter. His eyes were little glazed mirrors and his knuckles were dripping blood on the carpet in a trail behind him. One of them swallowed the lump in their throat and dared to speak, "Afternoon, Bill." But Bill did not even acknowledge their presence. As he passed them, the group turned to look at him and his trail of blood but decided it best not to address it. And Bill just kept walking almost cheerfully through the halls and back to his

51

office. Once he arrived, he flung open the door as hard as he could and plopped himself down in his leather, high-back office chair.

The fear by which Bill led EnviroCore transcended multiple dimensions. It was more than just his expensive and masterfully tailored suits that made him intimidating. It was the insanity that constantly lurked in his eyes and smile; a look as if maybe nobody was working the gears upstairs. It was his short fuse. It was because he was a new and mysterious face that suddenly arrived in a company that rarely hired externally. It was the yarns that were constantly being spun about him both before and after his takeover as CEO and president of the company. It was because he never really formally introduced himself to the company and was rarely seen below the second floor. This is why when he flipped the table over nobody really even knew who he was. Bill knew all of this and used it to his advantage. Even if the whole company saw what he had done, nobody would question it. No one would cross him, nobody really knew who he was, and he had just the right combination of style and crazy. He looked important enough not to bother and crazy enough to steer clear of. What he lacked in managerial experience and business sense he made up for with a brute force presence.

Bill sat back and thought about who he was and how people saw him. There was nothing contemplative about his thoughts. He simply sat back and let images of himself race through his head. A few of the faces in the cafeteria caught his eye as the table flipped. They were terrified and jumped out of their seats as the table cracked against the hard vinyl tile floor. Bill's chuckles bounced from the cathedral ceiling of his massive office to the wood-paneled walls off of the white marble floor tiles back to his ears. His voice sounded deep and booming which pleased him even more. He was quite content with the image he projected. He looked around his office and daydreamed of the renovations he would make and the decorations he would buy. He forgot all about how the company was broke and going to go under any day. All that mattered to him was right now. He didn't care about his knuckles bleeding all over the floor or that he'd just caused thousands of dollars of damage to company property. He saw himself as a king. He opened up the left drawer of his desk and retrieved a bottle of twelve-year-old scotch and a glass from it. He tried to slam the drawer shut before he registered the sight of his father's Colt 1911. It was too late. He had already seen the reflection of his smile in the nickel-plated slide. It had a pearl grip which drew up countless memories of its feel. He desperately tried to block the most penetrating of the memories as he poured the scotch almost to the rim of his glass. But they stormed the beaches of his prefrontal cortex before his defenses could be amassed.

Bill recalled the first day of his employment at EnviroCore. He had absolutely no idea what was going on. What he had done in previous positions with previous companies was nowhere near what was going on at EnviroCore. Bill was only typically involved in lower-middle management positions and was notorious for bungling projects. He had a reputation as a loose cannon and was constantly in danger of being fired. Though Bill never knew it, his father drew a lot of water. It wasn't just in western Michigan but at the federal level as well. For that reason, nothing was ever done about Bill. It wasn't as if his father ever intervened or was even mentioned in discussions about firing Bill. It was just accepted that he was there and there was no getting rid of him. Everyone on both sides of the chain of command would avoid him as much as possible because of how much he slowed up progress. Far too much time was spent cleaning up messes that he made, so the lower-level employees went above his head and the upper-level employees didn't chastise them for it.

The way Bill transitioned through his numerous roles before EnviroCore added to the enigma. He never stayed at one place for very long and he would arrive and disappear just as abruptly. He left his previous position as a costing manager at a mid-range pharmaceutical company to be installed as the CEO of EnviroCore the same day. His father, though they never spoke directly, would inform him of his new positions via an email from his assistant and a car would arrive to transport him. There was never an explanation and for some reason, he never questioned it. Bill looked back at his life and summarized it as a long string of confusion of which he was constantly trying to make sense. He remembered how that feeling weighed on him like it never had before his first day at EnviroCore. It was the most responsibility he was ever given and it came all at once. On top of that, the one person who was supposed to help walk him through it had abandoned him. Bill remembered finding that gun in one of his moving boxes which had just been brought up to his office. It was a gift from his father for graduating college. It was gift-wrapped in its case when he received it with an attached card that simply read, 'Aim High.' He decided in that moment he would do exactly that.

Bill took the pistol out of the moving box. He had never fired a gun in his life and wasn't really all that sure how to do it. But Bill decided in that moment that this was how it was going to end. He was sick and tired of being a pawn; a puppet. His life was meaningless and pointless and was going to last forever unless he stopped it now. The constant stress of not knowing how to handle any situation but constantly doing a piss-poor job at trying anyway was no way to live a life. He pressed the magazine release lever and saw that the rounds he loaded the day he got it were still there. Epinephrine flooded his bloodstream as he decided that this was going to be it and that he would not chicken out. He slapped the magazine back in as he had seen it done in the movies and rushed the gun to his temple as fast as his arm would move. He screamed a scream of dramatic intensity and a tear dropped from his eyeball. Bill pulled the trigger.

But Bill's head did not explode all over his moving boxes as he had imagined it would. A loud 'click' echoed a ringing into his eardrums and he dropped the nickel-plated, pearl-gripped 1911 onto the floor. Bill fell to his knees and began to sob into his hands. What Bill did not realize is that a round must be moved from the magazine to the chamber before it will fire. He assumed that when the magazine was in, everything else would take care of itself and all that's left is to pull the trigger. So what Bill saw as some kind of divine intervention was actually naïveté on his part.

So as Bill sat with this unavoidable and intrusive memory, he contemplated his life's meaning. He stared, trancelike into his glass of scotch. Regardless of why Bill's head was still intact, it was, and his life had purpose because of it. 'It *must* have purpose,' he thought to himself, 'otherwise I would be dead already.' And with that thought, he got up, calmer and more clear-minded now than he'd ever been, and walked over to a ficus tree near the door. He started to tip the glass of scotch into the potted soil from which the tree grew but the phone rang and interrupted his entire demeanor. He hesitated a moment and then took the glass back to his desk and answered the phone with a long sigh, "This is Bill."

"Well I'll be damned," a voice said on the other line. It was the voice of Ted Philus. Bill stood from his seat, positively dumbstruck.

"What…the fuck do you want?" Bill asked from behind clenched teeth.

"Well, I was just wondering how you were handling my company. I'll admit I'm a little surprised to hear you. I thought you might have blown your brains out by now." Philus taunted.

"Hey asshole," Bill raised his voice with an added gravelly nuance. "This ain't your fuckin' company anymore, remember? You left us all in the fuckin' lurch you piece o' shit. You don't ever call here again, you got that?"

Bill was nearly able to pull the receiver away from his ear before he heard another word but could not. "Now wait a second there Billy boy," Philus said in a slightly more authoritative tone. "I know you're in over your head here so I'll forgive that vulgar tone you're takin'. But I gave you this spot and it's an opportunity of a lifetime if you don't fuck it up." Bill was silent but for his furiously heavy breathing. "Now listen, if I were to stay there and hold your hand through this whole transition bullshit everyone would have seen right through it and things would be no different from when I was on the payroll. Alright? *You* would have been in the newspapers as Dr. Frankenstein. *You* would be the victim of the witch-hunts. *You* would have been driven out of there by now simply because *I* was by your side." Bill's breathing had slowed to nearly normal levels as he listened to Ted's spiel. "Now I know you want to impress everybody and do this by yourself, and you've done a damn good job already son, I'll give you that. Hell, I thought that you'd have let it crumble by now. But you're keepin' her steady and I commend you for it."

Bill was losing his patience with Ted's backhanded compliments. "Ted whatever point you have to make, I encourage you to go ahead and make it now," he said as his blood pressure began to rise again.

"OK, Billy I'll get to it," Ted continued. "You never were one for patience were you? My offer still stands to help you through this if you want it." Bill sat down and began laughing sarcastically.

"Have you lost your fucking mind?" Bill asked rhetorically. "We're already almost a month into this. The rough part is over. If this shithouse is going to float, the wheels are already in motion to float it."

"Billy do you think that I would just cut all my ties to that place? Huh?" Ted sneered, "I know what's going on over there better than you do. If you think that you've got loyalty over there forget it. Those people know you. They know your track record. Now you may think you've got that hen house figured out over there but I know what you have to do to get them to lay eggs."

Bill was silent again still gritting his teeth. Though his resentment for Ted coursed through his veins like molten lava, he could not help to feel the slightest bit of intrigue. He tried to keep his guard up and not forget the mess that Ted had left behind. "We got our asses handed to us by the fuckin' auditor from your previous escapades," Bill barked. "Stacks and stacks of violations were piled up on my desk; shit you left for me and your lackeys to clean up. If you would have pulled that bullshit after the transition, you would have gone to jail."

"Billy, Billy," Ted rebutted in a calming voice, "you don't go to jail over paperwork." A short silence shored up Bill's intrigue. "Jesus Christ. No wonder you've got such a rotten attitude boy. They've got you thinkin' your balls are in their vice. Count your blessings I called when I did else your voice might actually gain an octave or two." Bill swore that this time he had had enough.

"Again, I say Ted, make your fuckin' point," Bill erupted. Though this time, the impatience was drawn due to anticipation rather than anger and Ted could hear it. Ted knew that the hook was already in and it was all over but the reeling.

"Billy," Ted began, "what do you think that scientist you put in charge is going to do for you? He's got less business savvy than you!" Bill's heart sank. Now he was sure that Philus definitely had someone feeding him information. A rolodex of names now spun frantically in suspicion. "Bill," Philus spoke again, this time in a tone of respect, "you know I make my jabs at you but in all earnestness I handpicked you, and you alone, for a reason. You've got a mountain of potential, kid. It sickens me that all these years that potential has been wasted. That scientist doesn't know his asshole from his nostril. Sure he's done a lot of fine work as an employee for Sciencia but you can't give a man like that so much power without keeping an eye on him. He's either gonna rob you blind or drop the ball big time. One way or the other, he's gonna screw ya." Bill took a minute to process what was being said. Despite his misgivings, Ted was making a lot of good points. Not to mention the fine job he was doing stroking Bill's ego. "Now doing it this way actually works in our favor, Billy," Ted continued. "All you have to do is make sure you're watchin' 'em. Make sure he's playin' by the rules. Make sure he's on the books. Make sure he knows that he reports to you. Make sure he knows you're his friend. Make sure he's makin' all the right moves."

"I won't know if he'll be making the right moves because I

don't know what the right moves are. That's the whole…"

"You just keep your eye on him and we'll be alright," Ted interrupted, "You're gonna learn how it's done, boy. You're gonna right this ship. You're gonna be a fuckin' hero and you're gonna make a shit load of money doin' it." A little bit of blood rushed into Bill's penis. "I'll take your silence as a 'thank you.'"

With those last words, the receiver transmitted the distinct sound of a phone hanging up. Bill swallowed hard and hung his phone up in kind. Bill's mind was racing. He thought about skiing down a mountain of cocaine with strippers perched on both of his arms and shoulders to a podium at the bottom where he would accept his multiple Olympic gold medals and Nobel prizes on an internationally televised award ceremony. He imagined a golden palace lined with rare animal heads and a diverse and exotic harem of large-breasted women. He could see libraries of biographies about him, statues of him, and temples constructed in his honor. He picked up the glass that he had filled dangerously full of scotch and swallowed the entire lot of it in one gulp. Once the liquid had cleared his gullet, he slammed the empty glass down on his desk and sighed a long sigh of content, interlaced his fingers behind his head and reclined to a comfortable position in his office chair.

The Mother of Invention

By now, Mark and Gary had made their way back to Mark's office and were now about an hour and a half through the first stages of the restructuring plan. The paranoia that accompanied Bill's interruption and subsequent table flip was already proving to be a significant roadblock. It was not just that they were making plans behind his back or that they were worried about him watching the whole time through security cameras or microphones, but the fact that the consequences of their plan could destroy the town. Any way they sliced it, people were going to lose their jobs where no other jobs were. But what is worse is that the two were afraid to say anything out loud that may allude to this fact. Finally, Mark broke through the invisible barrier of niceties. "Look this is getting us nowhere," he began. "He said himself that he would stand behind us no matter how drastic things got. So let's get drastic."

"Fine," said Gary, "no more bullshit."

"Agreed," said Mark. "Surely these people knew that something had to happen sooner or later."

The plan was drastic alright. It was less a restructuring and more starting a brand new company. Mark and Gary spent the next several hours together reading government regulations. The clock was ticking and their asses were on the line. But the excitement of the power and their pioneering spirit had largely worn off when they realized how much work it would take and how many layoffs and new hires would be required to make the plan work.

It was Gary's task to get his team together and give them an outline of what needed to happen. Scouts needed to be sent out to hire public relations professionals to downplay the firings and emphasize the hirings for the press. The County Crier, though small, had tremendous influence over the citizens' behavior as was evident during the years of Sciencia. But the company's public relations need to span much further than Ash County if they are going to make any real dents. That means contacting much larger media outlets than The County Crier. These PR professionals also needed to make a big deal out of the change in the facility's status. A change from a small-time Biomedical Research Facility to a large-scale Environmental Sustainability Development Company was grand on several levels. For one, there were not many research companies in the world devoted entirely to environmental endeavors. Secondly, this was about as Podunk as you could put a place like this. Third, it was going to replace the infamous Sciencia. This was a potential goldmine for the press which is what the company needed to get some momentum.

Aside from public relations professionals, the scouts needed to find some big-time scientific talents; people who could run environmentally-centered projects and labs; people who could be put in charge to oversee these huge changes and to make sure everyone is compliant. But above all, a doubling in security was necessary. The layoffs that would occur were going to put a pretty good chunk of the town out of work. This would have a trickle-down effect that would negatively impact the rest of the townspeople *and* the town's surrounding areas; particularly the more densely populated Jotunborough and Feuerstadt. Even though the company was non-union, they had to be prepared to deal with protests and possibly even civil unrest. Needless to say, most of those let go would still have friends on the inside. It was safe to say that sabotage or other internal misdeeds could be expected. Many lower-level employees could possibly be retrained if their departments did not make it through the transition. But many of the specialty positions would not have that option as their services would simply not be needed.

Departmental reevaluation and headcount redistribution would do a lot to save face for the company. It would give the opportunity to have some employees stay on the payroll as long as they were willing to work harder or for less pay. In some situations, both would apply. This would allow some of the weeding out to happen naturally. The affected employees would be allowed to quit on their own while those that chose to stay on would take a pay cut, thus saving the company money. Of course, it would be necessary to address this as a temporary consequence of the transition, however temporary it may actually be.

As the human cost of doing business mounted and congealed into reality, Gary's stomach contracted and churned his asiago chicken slightly back through his esophageal sphincter. He felt like the conductor on the train to Auschwitz. No matter how many times he said to himself 'It's just business,' he could not ignore his conscience. The thought of condemning hundreds of people to either poverty or hard labor and shriveling up a budding town before it could blossom did not sit well with him. Of course it was not his fault. In order to save the company, it had to be done. In fact, if he didn't do it, the company would go under anyway and *all* of the company's employees would be stricken into poverty. However, this fact did nothing to drive his lunch back down.

At the other side of the desk, Mark was completely unfazed by the drastic measures. He saw the same numbers that Gary was looking at but did not see the same toll that EnviroCore's overhaul would take. The restructuring was simply part of the plan which was logically fashioned in order to save the company and the human element simply did not enter his mind. Mark's food was being metabolized right on schedule.

Even though Mark's psychopathic mindset was troubling to

Gary, he had to admit that the rate at which work was getting done was impressive. It was like watching a machine. Mark's eyes would tick across lines three at a time. The reflection of the screen from Mark's laptop in his eyes indicated a near constant screen scrolling until an article was finished. If it were a website that Mark was navigating, the screens would change so rapidly that it was hard to believe that any information could possibly be absorbed. There were times when Gary would sit back to stretch and just watch him go. Mark never stretched. He never even seemed to blink. It was really something to behold.

But Mark was definitely absorbing. His brain was finely tuned from years of reading scientific articles and navigating web pages. In college, he was rarely seen outside of the library. He and his roommates in the dorms never exchanged much more than an introduction in the four years he attended. From a very young age Mark realized that the more he learned the easier learning new things became. It was much easier to draw parallels with the large amount of parallels that had already been drawn. It was like having a very fine soup strainer that added degrees of fineness with each use. After a while, not much is lost.

Mark was pouring over environmental science and technology journals finding the best types of projects for EnviroCore to consider. The 'best' types were those into which current departments could easily transition; ones with minimal resource loss. Ideally, they should have huge impacts with tangible timelines and measurable results. The company had to operate too leanly from here on out to deal with promises and good intentions. Money, of course, was the biggest factor both coming in and going out. It would be possible to secure grants from government agencies for environmental endeavors. But the amount of money they might get from one of those agencies would not sustain much of anything for very long. It was uncertain whether or not anyone would fund them anyway due to the stacks of violations the previous company had accumulated. Plus, whatever transactions Philus made with the mayor probably needed to stay in the dark, for as long as possible. It was becoming ever more probable that no external funding would be coming. Therefore, EnviroCore had to make something out of nothing, quickly.

For this reason, Mark was searching mainly for household products that everyone would be able to use; environmentally friendly and economically viable solutions to common problems. Though, hundreds of papers and hours of Google perusing had yielded next to nothing. With a tinge of frustration, Mark leaned back in his chair, tilted his head backwards and brought both hands up to his forehead whispering, "Needle in a haystack."

But the word 'haystack' resounded deep in the twisted caves of his subconscious and retrieved a very different, but similar sounding word. "HASEP!"

"What?" Gary inquired, only slightly concerned that Mark had lost his mind.

"HASEP HASEP HASEP!" Mark repeated as he tore through the door. Gary was slightly more concerned at this point but had faith that he would return.

Mark continued at an all-out sprint through the hallways of EnviroCore, repeating 'HASEP' the entire way, down the stairs to the basement bursting through labs until he made it to his old office. There were three boxes stacked neatly under his desk that were filled with old papers. He moved the top box aside, tore off the top of the second box and began flipping through about three quarters of the way down through the stack of papers inside. Finally, the coveted packet he beheld. At the header the word 'GLADIS' in all capital letters was printed. Below that, a magnified strand of DNA was illustrated with an artist's rendition of some kind of mythical-looking claw machine replacing one representative base pair letter with another. It was software that fused the prevailing CRISPR-Cas9 gene editing method and a probability algorithm Mark had devised that could theoretically predict outcomes of genetic mutations; an idea that Mark had pitched to the company as a valuable time- and money-saving technique several years back. His bacteriology lab was in the process of developing genetic modification software using HASEP which would repeatedly replace base pairs in a sequence and simulate phenotypes of the organism's mutated gene sequences.

It was an idea born of pain, frustration, and desperate need. Mark's lab was forced to use discount microbial recombineering services due to the insultingly low budget allotted to the bacteriology department. The companies that edited the bacterial genomes had poor quality control and most of the strains exhibited secondary mutations. The impact of these additional mutations was often devastating to the lab's work. It was not uncommon that half of a shipment would be dead on arrival or that two or three iterations of replication would produce nonviable models. The companies that sold the model organisms stood behind disclaimers and liability waivers that basically allowed them to rob their clients without consequence. The amount of money lost on shipments of dead or otherwise unusable bacteria far outnumbered what it would have cost to just use a slightly more reliable supplier. With the amount of money wasted, they could have just bought the equipment to edit their own genomes onsite. This would have allowed them to skip the recombineering service altogether which would have saved the company millions of dollars in the long run.

The procurement department, however, appeared largely disinterested in the long run and told him that bacteriology did not bring in enough money to justify the cost. Mark explained that this was the very reason the department was not making money and a mid-scale purchase of in-house recombineering equipment would alleviate the deficit in one or two quarters. Within the fiscal year, they would even be able to recoup the losses from previous quarters. But, like some antiquated text-to-speech software, they kept repeating that until the department produced some real numbers, the company was not willing to make the investment.

Being turned down by procurement was nothing out of the ordinary though. Undeterred, Mark went to his office and thought...and thought... and reviewed articles...and then thought some more. *How can I change their minds? If only I could get them to understand. If only the equipment were cheaper.* Mark thought about the types of experiments they were conducting. What revenue was not generated by their own work, the company made up by contracting others' pharmaceutical research and development. At the time, the big money grabbers were erection and weight loss pills. Since bacteria are asexually reproducing, his department mostly got stuck with the subject of weight loss. Some of Mark's studies included finding a strain of bacteria suitable for modeling human metabolism. Others were trying to enhance gut bacteria so that people could eat whatever they wanted and not gain weight. Essentially, they were either trying to create lazy, obese bacteria or microscopic tapeworms. Not the most glorious use of Mark's brilliant mind. However, he never cared so much for glory or even making the world a better place as his father had wished. He was simply interested in science.

At any rate, Mark pondered the problem as he did so many differential equations. At the root of all of the experiments, what they were doing was manipulating genomes. A bacterium's life span is a small fraction of most other nonhuman organism models. Therefore, bacteria were the quickest way to manipulate a genome before the advent of genetic engineering. All that has to be done is isolate the good ones and let time do the rest. Once genome sequencing became cheap, the stage was set to begin studying and subsequently altering genes in a cut-and-paste style, radically reducing rates of return. Up sprung startup genetic recombination companies that had not worked all the bugs out but still were charging absurd amounts. Once the kinks were worked out, companies started charging even more for guarantees and warranties and other such customer satisfactions. This inevitably led to the discount guys who offered cut-rate services without the strict quality assurance and cut-rate contract companies were happy to pay the cheaper price. Unfortunately, this is the route Sciencia took and Mark and his team were stuck with the slack.

Mark recalled from some obscure probability theory papers that such random events as single nucleotide polymorphisms, wave forms, or fungal growth could be modeled with Markov processes which were used to predict interacting particle systems. If Mark pooled all the knowledge he had about bacterial reproduction, their mutations, and paired inheritance, he could write a program that would predict an entire genome. But why stop there? If he could do that, it would only be a little bit more work to predict how the genome would translate into the proteins that made up the organism and how those proteins interacted with each other. He could predict whether or not a sequence would yield a viable model. If an exact genomic sequence was given to a higher quality recombineering service, there would be no trial-and-error, no dead bacteria, and Sciencia could get the guarantee. Surely then, the procurement department would see it his way. After the method began paying off, the CRISPR-Cas9 method could be employed, even further reducing costs. *How could they possibly say no?*

But Mark only saw it as a way to make his lab run more smoothly. He did not give a second thought to the fact that if his program worked, it would revolutionize the industry and the course of mankind's evolution soon after. It was a typical demonstration of his phlegmatic temperament, also obscuring his perception to the size of the task. Nonetheless, he put all other projects on hold and got straight to work.

In his 10 by 10 foot brick office he sat with his stack of papers, his notebooks, and his computer and worked for thirty hours straight. Part of Mark's uncanny ability to learn was attributable to his God-like attention span; if you could call it that. It was more accurate to say that his body would go into hibernation when he was performing important tasks for long periods of time. All of his energy would be redirected to brain metabolism and most of the rest of his body would slow down. His body temperature, although he did not realize it, would drop to hypothermic levels. His digestive and excretory systems would shut down so that he did not get hungry or have to go to the bathroom. Even the parts of his brain that were not being utilized would shut down; a way for his brain to sleep in shifts, so to speak, much the same as his multiple states of consciousness would share the burden of attention. If he were so inclined, Mark could have been the subject of countless longitudinal studies, clinical research projects, and investigations into human metabolism and sleep. However, the idea of spending his life lying down in an MRI machine did not appeal to him.

Thirty hours, twenty-three minutes, and eighteen seconds after he first sat down to work, Mark emerged from his office with the final draft of his gene-sequence-altering, single-nucleotide-replacing, RNA translation predicting software; GLADIS, for Genetic Ligation and Dislocation Imaging Software. "Steve," Mark shouted, "Com'ere and take a look at this, will ya?"

Steve was the most senior technician in the bacteriology department. He was completely hairless due to some rare medical condition which only began affecting him in his late twenties. But Steve had just about the same amount of knowledge about bacteria as Mark and was the main collaborator and co-writer of most articles or studies that came out of the department. Steve had about as much of a social life as he did hair, so his work ethic was similar to Mark's. The only other people Steve talked to were fellow clansmen in a video game called Clash of Clans. Steve was completely unfazed by the fact that Mark had spent nearly two full days entirely devoted to this new project. He walked into Mark's office and eagerly asked, "Whaddya got?"

"Look at this," Mark said with a trace of pride lining his tone. The title screen of the new software which artfully displayed the name GLADIS looped through a strand of DNA. The user interface was extraordinarily intuitive for most scientific software. The title screen had two options: 'Predict New' and 'Open.' Mark clicked the 'Open' button to show a single file titled 'showSteve' which he then opened… to show Steve. "*Pseudomonas fluorescens*," Mark said as if he were revealing a priceless museum exhibit for the first time. Steve knew the strain well as it was one of the only ones they used in the lab. He beheld a long list of nucleotides which were divided into codons, which were divided into genes, which were divided into chromosomes. It was reminiscent of software called ChemScript, which enabled the building of molecules using a toolbar on the left side of the screen. Mark hovered over all of the keys to show Steve the labels that popped up. The toolbar was divided into three tabs, DNA, RNA, and protein. Clicking each tab changed the screen to show the corresponding amino acids and mRNA strands of the DNA.

"Hmmm," Steve responded excitedly. Mark's face lit up with satisfaction as Steve stole the mouse from him and began to explore. Steve clicked through single nucleotides, changing the corresponding amino acids. He zoomed out to show the adjacent amino acids and soon far enough to see the structure of one single protein. "Oooh," Steve trilled again as he zoomed out far enough to see the entirety of one of the flagella. He pressed the 'repeat sequence' button over and over to watch the flagellum grow in length slightly with each few taps. "This is fuckin' awesome!" Steve blurted arousing the curiosity of the rest of the lab listening outside.

"That's not all," Mark said as he took back control of the mouse and moved the cursor to the top of the screen to the main toolbar. One of the choices was titled 'traits.' A dropdown menu listed various non-tangible qualities of the bacterium, including motility, diet, replication mechanism, etc. Mark clicked on 'motility.' A second menu dropped down showing which aspects of motility were linked to which regions of the genome. He chose a random region and the view switched to the segment of DNA associated with it. That point of interest popped up with a list of known genes and associated papers which mention the genes.

"Mother of God," declared Steve, "you've incorporated a database?"

"Yes," Mark replied coldly, "this way we can finally go with the higher quality recombinations and get our money back if it's not exactly what we want. The database will help us justify our choices for knock-ins and knock-outs; it'll help us keep track."

"Well, hell," Steve began, "we could skip recombineering altogether with this thing!"

"Eventually, yes" Mark replied. "We need to show that it works first. No, first we need to convince procurement that this will make the better service worthwhile."

"I'm sure it'll work," Steve said, patronizing Mark's conservative attitude. "Even those assholes upstairs will see that once you show 'em this. C'mon let's go show 'em" Mark was gradually coming out of hyperfocus mode and all of the biological necessities that were withheld for the sake of the task at hand were now coming back online all at once. His excretory system kicked on signaling an imminent disposal, grehlin clawed through his cerebrospinal fluid screaming for food, and his pons, the Sinai, choking for sleep's sweet deluge.

"Maybe now is not the best time," Mark said as he calmly stood up and began a purposeful walk out of his office and down the path to the closest restroom or floor drain. Steve stood aside as he dashed past and immediately commandeered the ratty old office chair to play with Mark's creation.

After what seemed like hours, Mark emerged from the bathroom to find Steve waiting for him. "What?" Mark startled.

"You and I are going up to procurement right now to get a signature," Steve commanded.

"It's not ready yet." Mark reasoned.

"It's ready," Steve fired back. "Have some confidence and let's go show it to them."

"I have been in that office for thirty hours, you know? I haven't slept. I haven't eaten. My wits are not about me. Give me a day to recover my senses and we will go up to procurement in the morning," said Mark spiritlessly.

"If you wait, it's not gonna be fresh in your mind and you won't have this momentum. Please, just listen," Steve begged as he moved in closer to Mark's face. "Please man, for the love of god, listen. What you've created in there is a masterpiece. If they don't support you on it, I would suggest quitting. You could easily patent that and sell it for millions. You are cautious man. I understand that. I respect that. Any good scientist should be. But, Mark, trust me, let's go up to procurement now." Mark was too tired to know for sure if Steve was just being overzealous or if the software really could be that valuable.

"OK," Mark finally gave in, "let's go up to procurement."

The reason for his acquiescence was more to get Steve out of his face than for any other reason. But regardless, Mark found himself on the way upstairs to procurement for a second time.

After a short trip back to the office to get the flash drive containing the program, they were off to procurement. Mark was understandably apprehensive as the last trip to this door did not end well. Steve could see this was the case and, not wanting to give Mark a chance to back out, knocked on the door as he pushed his way in, not waiting for a response.

"Good afternoon sir," Steve blurted out. "Steve Williams from bacteriology and this man right here is Mark Deremer, Director of Studies, Bacteriology. We are coming to you this glorious afternoon with an idea that will save the company several million dollars and a good lot of time." He sounded like P.T. Barnum. Mark was mortified. Down in the labs, there was a much different attitude from the office area. It was much more of a relaxed environment than up here on the business side and Steve's lack of professionalism embarrassed Mark to his core.

"Yes," said Greg Sauer of procurement. "I spoke to Mark just a few days ago about..." Greg paused a moment to let Mark finish the forgotten idea.

"Growing bacteria in-house," Mark finished.

"That's right," Greg said with a sigh. "What can I do for you gentlemen?" Steve held up the flash drive with GLADIS on it.

"You can plug this in and let us walk you through the future of Sciencia's genetic modification purchases," Steve said as any carny would say at a ring toss booth. He marched right behind the desk and helped himself to Greg's computer much to Greg's chagrin. It was a nightmare. Though it was awkward, Mark could do nothing to stop what was happening.

"You'll have to forgive him," Mark said to a puzzled and obviously annoyed Greg Sauer. "Sometimes he so excited that he forgets himself."

As he loaded the program, Steve commenced to recounting the situation in bacteriology. He told the story of the discount suppliers standing behind flimsy disclaimers in order to rip the company off and how Sciencia was losing thousands of dollars and months of time with each bad batch of modified organisms.

"The discount suppliers can't offer a guarantee but the quality suppliers can," Steve explained. "This program is essentially a failsafe. It allows us to give the suppliers the exact genome, base pair per base pair, so that if they give us an organism with one base pair out of place, we send it back for a refund."

"You couldn't do that before?" Greg asked.

"No," Steve answered, "the suppliers in our price range usually only have the capability to get it close enough that it might work. We can't send it back if it doesn't."

"So what does the software do?" Greg impatiently questioned.

"Well, I am glad you asked," Steve said excitedly as he opened up the *Pseudomonas* file. He flipped from tab to tab and translated genes for Greg, all the while spitting indiscernible jargon. Greg's eyes glazed over and any flicker of interest he may have had was fading fast.

"Basically it predicts how a strain of organism will behave if you change things around in its genetic makeup," Mark finally chimed in, trying to cut the circus short. "This will cut out trial-and-error and dramatically reduce turnaround time. Right now we are spending three times more using the discount suppliers than we would if we bought the guaranteed strains and wasting, on average, eleven months with restarts. Some types of recombination necessarily must take place in the lab but this program has the added feature of cutting that out as well. One shot, one kill."

"Look Mark," Greg said ominously, Steve still awkwardly invading his space, "I really appreciate what you're trying to do here but it's simply not in the budget. Everyone has to work with what they have for the quarter. I realize that over time an investment might be worth it but this is how Sciencia wants to do it. Until the department makes more money, it won't get a bigger budget. It's a vicious cycle, I get it. But my hands are tied boys."

A silence befell the room like the first few seconds following an execution. Once the dismissal was realized by all parties, Steve ripped the flash drive out of its port and stormed out without saying another word. "Thanks Greg," Mark mumbled in submission as he turned and left the office, quietly closing the door behind him.

Once in the hallway, Steve began ranting, "What kind of fuckin' company do we work for here?! We walk in just handing them millions of dollars and they say, 'no thanks?!' But they don't even give us that respect, they say, 'my hands are tied sorry.'" He was saying it loud enough for Greg to hear and although Mark kept his professionalism by not joining in the rant, he did not remind Steve of his volume either.

Perhaps what drove Steve to be such a good scientist was his ability to get jazzed up. He was an avid hunter and golfer in addition to being a devoted Clash of Clans player/enthusiast. But the qualifier 'avid' does not paint the picture, as he was nationally ranked in all of those hobbies. On the wall in Steve's living room was a mounted fourteen-point buck with a golden plaque in the shape of Michigan underneath it which stated that it was one of the ten largest ever recorded in the state. Mark remembered thinking it was an elk the first time he saw it as it took up most of the living room. To the left of the head was a framed hunting magazine called *Sport Shooting.* It featured a much younger Steve on the cover knelt down over the trophy buck's carcass holding the bow and arrows that felled the mighty beast.

A few feet away from that on the mantle of his fireplace was a line of trophies all related to golf tournaments Steve had participated in. Again, Steve's trophies ranged from local scrambles to several years in a row of placing in *The Michigan Classic,* a statewide tournament in which amateurs compete for a shot at pro status, getting signed with sponsors and going on televised tours. As for Clash of Clans, Steve had managed to build a fictional army that would rival the population of China if it were real. Not only that, he convinced the entire discovery division of the company's research and development side to serve under his leadership as a general. Steve had only downloaded the app less than a year ago but somehow managed to grow his clan in size and strength to be among the top twenty of the fiercest clans in the world. Video game bloggers were constantly sending him requests for interviews and one of the clan's battles was even used in a commercial for the game.

Steve's hobbies were more like obsessions. The tendency was to block out huge chunks of his life and devote them entirely to mastering those obsessions. The only thing that stopped him in any case was the perception of a ceiling. That is, whenever he reached a level in which he felt he could not get any better, he would suddenly experience a sharp drop-off in interest, followed by a lull in all activity until he was struck by something new, followed by another one to two-year long complete hijack of his life. Once he shot that buck, he knew it would be unlikely that he would ever get anything bigger and so it became boring. This was soon followed by leaving early from work on slow days to drive several thousand golf balls on the range.

And so it went. These hobbies made Steve a 35 year-old bachelor with no consistent peer group. The only people with whom he communicated outside of work were the colonels of his clan. This did not bother him in the least. It was what made him happy. Where society might look at his life and say he had some kind of personality disorder for not wanting to be married, have kids, or own nice things, Steve would wonder why anyone would want anything different than *his* life, doing whatever made him happy and not having to put others' needs before his own. This obsessive phenotype also made Steve the ideal research scientist. It was the reason he did not question Mark's thirty-hour work binge. It was the reason the bacteriology was so productive and the reason he was irate at this moment.

"Dirty cocksuckers!" he shouted. Steve was also not known for his charm. "We can't just sit on this," he crowed. "We should just quit and start our own business. It won't be hard to find an investor with this. We're sitting on millions of dollars here!"

"Look Steve," Mark began in a cold, defeated tone, "I can't really tell if this is a dream or not I'm so tired. I appreciate your support and your enthusiasm but I need some sleep before I can rationally plan the next step. You need to calm down too. Collect your thoughts and we'll think of something less drastic than those ideas."

"Fuck him!" Steve shouted, not calming down one iota. "We'll fuckin' sell this shit and buy this fuckin' company and shit on his desk while we fire him. Let's go talk to fuckin' Philus and tell him about this fuckin' douchebag dickin' the company out of millions of dollars!"

"Look!" Mark finally raised his voice, stopping their forward march, "Let's please just calm down and sleep on this before we get fired. I'm upset too but you screaming obscenities won't help our cause."

But the truth was, Mark was not upset. He did not have the same fire that Steve had. Mark was reacting typically: he wasn't. He simply took the failure as a step back and would put the algorithm away. Mark was not a negotiator of obstacles, whereas Steve would employ every contrivance at his disposal to either break the wall down or jump over it.

"Fuck that!" Steve blew back. "If you want to sit in that fuckin' office for the rest of your life while they shit all over you be my guest. But I've had enough of this bullshit. I fuckin' quit. I fuck fuck fuckety fuckin' quit! Kiss my balls bitches!" he screamed as he stormed off down the hall, leaving Mark in his stationary position. He watched him rip his lab coat off and spike it on the floor. People were poking their heads out of their offices, curious to see a lunatic marching triumphantly down the hall, screaming the word 'fuck' with every step.

Steve was prone to rants. It seemed to come with the territory of being a passionate person. But this was a new level. Mark wondered if this time he was serious, or if he was just dreaming the whole scene. But that would indeed be the last time he saw Steve for the next two years. One day he just returned to his desk in the basement with the rest of the old team. He had been rehired and they never spoke of the incident again. Things just went back to the way they were like the two years were just a long weekend.

As Mark stared down the long brown carpeted hallway at Steve's dramatic resignation, a pounding started to overtake him. Knowing exactly what it was, he tried to brace for the impact of returning to a different reality; the present. Once again, Mark had drifted hard into a powerful memory. *Why are some of these memories so much more vivid? Why do they cause me to blackout?* With one final electrifying jolt, he was catapulted back onto the floor of his former basement office, to his own startled shout into Steve's face. The rest of the bacteriology department office was standing just outside, surveying the situation in utter dismay. Their study director, who was walked out of his office yesterday by the CEO and president of the company, was now back, knelt down on the floor clutching some files in a catatonic haze. There was a reasonable cause for concern among the group.

As calmly as he tried to return to present consciousness, this one hit him like a freight train. Sweat beads had formed on his brow and it felt like his heart was trying to escape through his trachea. Steve held a firm grasp on Mark's shoulders and said, "Jesus buddy, are you alright?"

Mark tried to play it off as if he did not look like he just survived a plane crash, "Yes. Yes I'm fine. I just came down to get this." He held up the familiar file so that Steve could see the title.

"Oh, I remember that one," Steve said in a long, drawn out tone. "Be careful with that one, buddy. Yeah boy, that is a sharp one."

Mark looked hard into Steve's eyes trying to focus his gaze but could not. He kept switching between the two eyes frantically, trying to make sense of what was just said. Instead of asking him to repeat or explain it further, Mark decided he didn't have time to clean up the pieces of broken societal behavioral standards and just

81

stood up and walked out of the office. Mark's former team of technicians reacted as if he were escaping his cage at a freak show. Mark, unaffected by the awkward moment, walked out of the office and tried to regain his composure as he headed back upstairs. He was desperately trying to shake this feeling of impending doom. His heart was still pounding, albeit with less thrust, and his skin was still sweating itself back to homeostasis.

The quick footsteps of somebody hustling to catch him bounced into his pinnae. *It has to be Steve.* Just as the thought was internally verbalized, Steve had caught up to him.

"Hey buddy," Steve said, slightly out of breath, "Everything ok? You gonna bring that upstairs?" Mark's pulse quickened again. An intense feeling of déjà vu haunted him now, so much so that he slowed his pace abruptly to look Steve in the eye.

"What did you just say?" Mark said now at a complete stop.

"I just asked if you were bringing that upstairs, you know, to procurement?"

Mark was still experiencing strong waves of the previous memory, forcing him to consider the possibility that he was stuck in a loop, repeating the same memory over again. This fed the anxiety further. His ears warmed and his stomach tightened. He could not reconcile his two conscious states and the fear kept growing; fear with which he could not cope. Mark's knees got weak and the hallway went dark.

In the twilight of the first few seconds of awakening, the blood flowed through Mark's head and into his ears at deafening decibel levels. The rhythmic thunder crescendoed into one giant 20Hz thud brought on by a water droplet which had traveled down his temple from the compress on his forehead.

"Did that get cold on you dear?" a voice entered his awareness. It was a familiar voice that calmed him. It seemed he was reliving the memory of Gladys after his father fired him. Even if he were, he was comforted by the fact that he seemed to be at least aware that he was in a memory. Even if now he knew that he could not trust his own perception of reality, at least he had that. But Mark opened his eyes slightly to reveal the common timeline; the conscious state that seemed to be the most consistent. He was not reliving a memory. The voice was that of a nurse in the company clinic where he now lied. "Here let me take that one and I'll warm it up for you," she said as she left the room.

The nurse just happened to say something that Gladys had said in a memory, just as the action of Steve asking him if he was taking the file to procurement merely coincided with the memory of GLADIS's inception. Mark calculated, reasoned, and concluded that he could, in fact, trust his perception of reality and that the experience was just a fluke. Perhaps it was the endless Michigan winter, or some other environmental factor that was interfering with normal brain function.

"Where's Gladys?" an alternate consciousness whispered aloud as its last remains melded with the first.

"She's right here buddy," Steve said softly tapping on the file under his arm. Mark had just realized that Steve had been sitting beside him the whole time. "Boy," Steve chuckled, "you gotta quit doin' that, eh?"

"If only…" Mark replied.

"What the hell is going on, buddy?" Steve prodded. "We all thought you might be gettin' canned or something when Wildeboer came to get you. Now you come back and you turned into a nutbar."

"Oh, that," Mark said flatly. "I'm the new Vice President of Operations."

"What?!" Steve said in shock. "Get the hell outta here."

"Yeah," Mark continued, maintaining his flat affect. "They say I'm the best they've got." Mark's attempt at deadpan humor fell flat on the floor in front of Steve.

"That's fuckin' unbelievable!" Steve shouted at an uncomfortable volume. "Well let's get you back upstairs buddy! You got some work to do!" He grabbed Mark by the triceps and lifted him out of his chair. Steve was quite a bit larger than Mark and the force nearly lifted his feet off the ground. "We'll let you know if we need anything else!" Steve hollered back at the nurse as he hurried Mark out of the clinic.

The two made their way upstairs to the brown carpeted hallway. Mark still felt a little uncomfortable but was basically recovered. "So what exactly does the Vice President of Operations do, I mean, besides buy a new Bayliner?" Steve asked.

"I'm still learning the ropes honestly but there is a lot of work to do, no question about that," Mark replied.

"Rumor has it that we're in deep shit, the company I mean. Do you have anything to do with that?" Steve joked.

"Well, it's been in deep shit for a while now, I'm not responsible for that," Mark responded, this time it was Steve's humor that was lost. "I can't really say much about it, though. I signed a confidentiality agreement when I took the position. I will show you the new office though." They had arrived at the door of Mark's new office. No name was below the office number; in fact nothing to indicate that it was Mark's office was present.

"Wow, she's a beaut," Steve commented. "You sure this is

you? It curiously looks like this is nobody's office. You just messin' with me?"

"Have you ever known me to tell a joke?" Mark pointed out.

"Well, you really are a big shot now, huh? I guess we can go tell what's-his-name from procurement to fuck off now." Steve remarked. He was quite a bit less hostile than previous mentions of Greg Sauer, even expressing an air of joviality in his tone.

"Wow, you still remember that huh?" Mark asked, as if he had not just passed out remembering the moment himself.

"You don't soon forget a thing like the day you walked off the job in an embarrassing display of delusional rage," Steve chuckled. "Still, are we gonna tell him to fuck off, or what? I've been waiting for that satisfaction for just a little while now."

"The thing is," Mark puffed up, "we don't need Sauer anymore. We are operating under martial law here and I'm the Vice President of Operations." Mark's pride and ego swelled as the shiny metal nine-thousand-pound words escaped his larynx. Testosterone and dopamine utterly crackled beneath his flesh, guiding him to his high-back leather throne and the GLADIS flash drive into his computer's USB port. Steve stood back with a puzzled grin as confidence and character overtook one of the dullest men he had ever known. With robotic precision and wicked speed behind a series of mouse clicks, Mark copied his golden goose to the hard drive and then to a second flash drive for Steve. In less than a minute, the deed was done. Mark popped the copied GLADIS out and flipped it at Steve as if it were a quarter, catching him slightly off guard. "I'm the general. This is a field promotion. You're the study director now. Go move mountains."

"We'll move some fuckin' mountains," Steve said, as if he

had just been handed a detonator.

And with that, without saying one more word, Mark turned back to his computer screen and Steve abruptly left Mark's doorway headed back downstairs. In the milliseconds following the departure the two both looked back fondly on all the other times that neither had ever bothered to follow the structure of a typical socially-governed conversation. Neither of them felt it necessary to waste even a fraction of a second worrying about something even as simple as a departure statement to indicate that the interaction was complete. Both men found societal conventions most cumbersome and so, not ever speaking of the decision, agreed not to follow them in their own interactions. Both men also silently agreed that theirs' were the most meaningful conversations of any colleague. With neither of them having any social interaction outside of the EnviroCore walls, this was an important bond for the both of them.

The sun was now setting over Valhalla. Mark had decided that the number of blackouts he had today was an indicator of just how stressful the day had actually been. The last thing he needed was to slip into one of his prolonged, hibernative states. Gathering his things, he decided that the work could continue tomorrow.

Mark clicked through the turnstiles and pushed through the metal-and-glass front doors that still had the Sciencia name etched into them. This had been, by far, the most unusual day of his life. It didn't even really register how dramatic of a move he made. It was like Mark automatically took on a whole new personality, shedding his old one like a snakeskin.

As Mark drove under the security arm and turned right out of the EnviroCore parking lot onto the long and winding county road like he had for the past ten years, he contemplated the day's events. In a matter of hours, he had gone from study director in a stagnant and unimportant department to one of the company's top executives. Not to mention the monumental consequences GLADIS would have on EnviroCore, Ash County, and before too long, the world. Considering how long it had been since they were bluntly rejected by procurement, it was nothing short of a miracle that somehow all the conditions were met in one day, and everything oddly came together in a single catalytic instant. It was both invigorating and frustrating.

Perhaps the most frustrating of procurement's refusal those years ago, was that the whole setup would have cost them under a thousand dollars. Even a do-it-yourself CRISPR kit was only $169.99 on Amazon and that was mostly materials that the company already had. At one point, Steve offered to use his own money; go behind Sauer's back and put GLADIS into action anyway. It's not like they would ever know. But Mark's ethics precluded them from doing anything even remotely dubious, regardless of the price or the lack of quality assurance. With that said, there was no reason they could not play around with the software.

And that is exactly what they did. For months the two spent their down time using GLADIS to try and solve a problem. As bacteriologists, they were both well-aware of perhaps the only story in which any non-bacteriologist may be interested: the nylon-eating bacterium. By manipulating some parameters of the software, the two simulated the environment of the famous bug to see if they could get the original strain to evolve the enzyme using the program's evolution predictor. For hours, they would watch the built-in, reality-based, mutation statistics apply to the original strain in the hypothetical pond that was their population. Interestingly enough, even with millions of iterations, the gene never materialized. Evolutionary time is so incomprehensible compared to the average human life span that even biologists forget and get frustrated.

"For fuck's sake man," Steve said going into the third hour of the third week of watching GLADIS work. "Good thing I don't have a social life otherwise I might suggest that this thing doesn't work."

"I was starting to think the same thing," Mark admitted.

"You would think that sheer chance would have built the enzyme by now," Steve suggested as he perused the genome similarities highlighted in yellow, and the differences highlighted in red, from the last three weeks. "We've been through several billion years now," he continued. "Maybe we should review the literature again."

"Yes, I concur," Mark conceded. "Something has to be

missing. These population curves are barely getting off the ground."

"Of course," Steve offered, "there is no way to know how much original food source was available in the pond. Plus they probably were only accidentally consuming small amounts of nylon byproduct at first."

"That should be accounted for already," Mark replied.

"What about isolating just the metabolic enzymes instead of the entire genome?" Steve proposed. "I know it's not ideal but we gotta start somewhere."

"I wanted the mutation to be as random as possible," Mark asserted.

"Yes, but we may have to for the sake of making progress," Steve attempted. "We may learn a crucial piece that we'd been overlooking."

"What if there was already a mutation in the original strain?" Mark wallowed. "What if there was a catalyst? What if there was a compensatory mechanism? What if there were epigenetic modifications?"

"Well, before we go back to square one," Steve settled, "let us be the compensatory mechanism. Increase mutation rate in this section by some small amount; say ten percent. Just let that sit for a few days and see if anything interesting happens." A deceptively long moment of silent contemplation fell over Mark to which Steve pleaded, "For God's sake, man."

After some calculation, Mark decided that Steve's suggestion was the best course of action. The proper modifications were made to the algorithm and the hypothetical genetically modified organism was left alone to exist. Much to the chagrin of both engineering pioneers, several billion iterations produced very few mutations in the model bacterium that were worth noting. They decided to handle it in a similar fashion, changing the mutation rate again by an increase of another ten percent. In three weeks, the same results were recorded and another increase was implemented. Even though tedium was a nonfactor for Mark, the long waits before deciding to make small changes was beginning to grind on Steve's nerves.

"Why don't we change it by a hundred this time?" Steve advised. "We've been at this for months now. These are obviously negligible changes we are making. Why don't we ramp it up? We are just playing around anyway. Why not see what happens?"

"Hmmm…" Mark stared deep into the selected metabolic operon comparing the most commonly occurring mutations of one parental strain with another and with the actual nylonase-carrying *Flavobacterium*. "We definitely should have hit it by now," Mark finally said, highlighting the original sequence carrying the famous enzyme as he traced it with the cursor.

For weeks now, Mark and Steve had been waiting for a proper population curve to show itself. But the characteristic 'S' shape was never seen. A typical population growth curve begins with a slowly increasing lag phase, in which there is little cell division, followed by an exponential phase in which the population thrives in the presence of a plentiful food source, ending with a stationary or stabilization phase in which the food source is in equilibrium with the population, and growth approaches zero. Though the 'S' stands for 'Sigmoid,' the curve has an 'S' shape when the food source is sustainable. Instead, what was observed was a slight increase, followed by an immediate tapering off, and then a sharp decline into extinction.

The enzyme of interest was composed of several thousand amino acids, each coded by three base pairs. Even though the odds of stumbling upon that particular sequence were astronomical, with the tweaking of the mutation rate and the billions of iterations, surely at some point, the S curve would have emerged. But it did not. So they pulled out the stops.

On a hunch, Mark manually cut and pasted the gene sequence for nylonase into their virtual *Flavobacterium* and turned it lose on the pond full of nylon byproduct. In horror, the two pioneering bacteriologists looked on as they saw the exact same nosedive shape slap them in the face from behind the screen. "No," Steve muttered breathlessly, "what is wrong?" The two double-checked GLADIS's settings to make sure all parameters were correct. Then, they triple-checked. But the fears were confirmed, "The literature is wrong!"

What Steve meant was that, even though the sequenced genome of the nylon-eating bacteria narrowed down the enzyme's location, there was some confounding variable, something else that was allowing the metabolic adaptation. With the infinite complexities of both known and unknown evolutionary mechanisms, it could be anything. There was essentially no way of knowing.

Mark had done his best to account for as much as he could with probability tricks to model some of the mutations that were less understood. In engineering a software based around genetic modification, most of the power came from the classical theory of evolution; that is, random mutations that are favorable for the environment will propagate as long as they are favorable. Common mutations at the DNA level, such as frameshifts and substitutions, were simply a probabilistic insertion, deletion, or switch of one or more base pairs in the sequence. Similar methods could be employed during straightforward, well-understood transcription and translation. But, as the means by which transcription and translation errors occurred became more and more complex, GLADIS's algorithms became less and less accurate.

Mark did his best to incorporate the less studied mutations into the program. For instance, he could account for environmental influences by inserting random, but known events that affect genetic variation such as radioactivity, climate change, disease, or natural disasters. He even included sporadic introduction of foreign sequences in order to mimic such phenomena as gene transfer and transfection, while randomly enhancing and silencing gene expression to imitate epigenetic modifications. Mark was thorough and meticulous, incorporating everything he could from the literature to capture the impossibly complex nature of all that encompassed what the world knew to be 'evolution.' But mutations are superfluous, inextricable from the environment, and highly dependent on the behavior of the population. Try as he did, there was just not enough information to make GLADIS a flawless model of evolution.

By now, Steve was pacing the lab floor. As far as they had gotten, as close as they thought they were, a blow like this was enough to cause any man to break. But that is the nature of the work. It is comparable to a construction crew spending years building a high rise building only to have it collapse into a mangled pile of rubble, with no clue as to what went wrong. As Steve paced, Mark stared blankly into the screen, drifting away; dissociating from one more harsh reality. He poured over parameters, limitations, restrictions, constants, metrics, rates of change, conditions, algorithms, formulas, code, and settings, as he had poured over hundreds of times before. He examined the amounts of pond pollutants, organic compounds, toxicity levels, oxygen and nitrogen availabilities, temperatures, neighboring organisms, mutagens, and alternate food sources. In the background, Steve kept mumbling, "How? How? How?" over and over, trying to suppress tears of frustration.

"It just doesn't make sense!" Mark exclaimed.

"How?" Steve continued blathering, "How? How could it not have hit on anything?"

"Anything?" Mark asked hopefully.

The two looked at each other as if their brains were somehow connected at the point of epiphany. What the two realized, is that they had only been trying to evolve the nylonase enzyme. They had focused GLADIS on that particular, academically-stated section of the bacterial genome supposed to contain the instructions for producing it, essentially making her blind to all other mutations. A few adjustments and a few boxes unchecked restored them to sanity, and then some.

A history of blank pages and graphs depicting short-lived electronic representations of *Flavobacterium* populations, was suddenly replaced with multiple instances of the S curve. Instead of a failed reproduction of one naturally occurring species, they had created hundreds, if not thousands that nature had failed to produce on its own.

Trying to contain their excitement, they now poured over the fruits of their labor, closely examining the mutations. Some had come up multiple times, making modest switches from, say, digesting one type of plant matter to another or changing from aerobic to anaerobic respiration. But there were a few others that came up only once within the many planetary lifetimes of the pond. These were far more interesting. For instance, one species converted waste hydrogen sulfide of one bacteria to sulfuric acid, which the original would eventually come to need to regulate its own alkalinity. A few others were able to survive off of the inorganic sediments at the bottom of the pond or leave it altogether, burrowing deep into the surrounding earth to find sustenance. One, however, stood alone.

In the original nylonase pond, *Flavobacteria* were only able to digest one or two subunits, not entire polymers. As impressive as it was that bacteria could evolve to eat manmade material, it was only marginally useful as an industrial-scale biotic decomposer, requiring inefficient and costly preparation. What they had here was polymer decomposition of one of the most ubiquitous and stable manmade polymers in existence, bisphenol A. With the ability to metabolize chains of subunits, rather than just one or two, theoretically, the bugs could be set loose on BPA-containing plastics without any type of preparation. The mouths of the two scientists hung open. They had struck oil.

The genome of the strain in question was positively riddled with mutations, far more than the other species that had evolved. Now tinted a green color, the *Flavobacterium* had so many mutations that it could hardly be recognized as a member of that genus. The chance to name a new genus did not happen everyday, and for a bacteriologist, it was a notable accomplishment, even it the genus was hypothetical. But instead of ensuring that their egos would embarrass them through the ages, Mark and Steve went with the modest *Viridobacter,* naming it after the latin for 'green.' The species name, *circulofractus,* was for the rings of the molecule that were broken in the bugs' metabolic process. Hence the binomial, *Viridobacter circulofractus.*

Despite the hell of the turmoil leading up to that proud moment, Mark recalled the memory fondly. He pondered the curious and winding path that *Vir* had taken on its journey to existence. GLADIS evolved *Vir* in a bottom-up fashion, with virtually no guidance and completely by accident. However, if Mark and Steve had not been searching for nylonase in a top-down fashion, she never would have come up with *Vir*.

A branch of mathematics called fractal geometry is able to model seemingly chaotic forms in nature such as snowflakes, coastlines, crystal structures, galaxy formations, trees, rivers, neurons, mountains, clouds, and anything else you'd like. Fractals are everywhere. They are the cosmic storms. They are the tiny worms. But scholars with lifetimes of research in every field will explain that there is no way to predict these patterns with any notable degree of certainty. They will also tell you that no one understands, at a fundamental level, the driving force behind the emergence of these patterns. They are seemingly meaningless and imperfect, and we can only describe them abstractly and within the context of the big picture. How then, can we rightfully call them patterns if they are so irregular? No one would tell you that there is not a pattern. Nor would they say that nothing is driving their formation. We only know that they exist and that is about all we can agree on. Intuitively, innately, intrinsically, we observe a pattern. It is hard wired. Our ability to see patterns is the foundation of our existence. At the same time, the principle of cause and effect is the foundation of humankind's understanding of existence. So, we are blinded by subjectivity; by others' just as much as our own. We can't say that there is anything directing how events unfold, but sometimes a coincidence is too difficult to ignore. Such was the birth of *Vir*, so was GLADIS's interpretation of evolution, so is actual evolution, so are *all* things natural. This includes our ability to analyze in spite of our subjectivity. If we are able to accept the chaos, a pattern will always materialize that we can work with.

Mark slowly climbed backwards out of his rabbit hole as he idled up the pines on either side of the Deremer driveway. Though the sun had gone below the horizon, it cast its memory in a bright red sea of clouds that kept illuminated the vast Deremer landscape.

Mark climbed up the two deck stairs to the front door and flung his hand out to grasp the old weathered doorknob. Suddenly, before he twisted the knob, he remembered the fateful talk that he and his father had many years ago. A figurative bolt of lightning struck him on the top of his skull, sending literal shivers down his spine. That day his father fired him from the store, he remembered his father telling him that he would make a change in this world. Today was the manifestation of that talk so many years ago. Mark felt it only right to climb up to the blind like old times and tell his father of this realization. Not so much to make a connection with a man with whom he'd never formed a real relationship. Nor was it to brag or make him proud or even to thank him. It was merely to state the coincidence and that he was going to change the world just like he told him he would.

Mark climbed back down the two deck stairs and set out walking that old familiar walk to the blind. The snow crunching under Mark's shoes was the only noise that was audible. The air was silent and brutally cold. A Michigan March is unpredictable. The vernal equinox was approaching, but it was still cold enough to freeze Mark's sclerae. Still, he crunched along the long path to the blind, which bore no other footprints. There is no telling how long his father had been up there. *Seems like he's always up there.*

Mark finally made it to the ladder that climbed up to the deer blind. He half-expected to find his father's frozen corpse in the upright sitting position clutching the binoculars to his eye sockets. He did see his father in this position as he began to reach the top of the ladder but he did not seem to be frozen. Mark made his way into the blind and situated himself on a camp stool but his father did not react. He did not move a single muscle. A small and steady burst of breath repeated just below the binoculars to assure Mark that he was still alive.

"I wanted to tell you that I got a big promotion today," Mark began. "The company is going under and they want me to save it. I think I can actually do it." Mark was drastically understating the magnitude of change that had occurred. But he did not want to make the conversation longer than it had to be. "Then," Mark continued, "it dawned on me that the whole reason you sent me away to college in the first place was because you said I should change the world. Well, it turns out I'm going to be able to do that."

"Come and look at this," Mark's father said completely ignoring all that Mark had just told him. But without a spot of offense taken, he climbed off of the stool and knelt down next to his father's chair. His father maintained his position and quietly said to his son, "It's out there on the horizon." He barely engaged his vocal cords as he spoke.

"What am I looking at?" Mark asked, mimicking his father's volume.

"I have no idea," answered his father, finally handing off his binoculars. "But there is something out there, something big." His voice reflected something he had never before heard nor ever expected to hear in his father's voice.

"What am I looking for?" Mark repeated, bringing the binoculars to his eyes.

"It's out there on the horizon," his father's voice quivered slightly.

"All I see is the tall grass sticking out of the snow," Mark reported. To be fair, the slight swaying of the grass could have been construed as animal movement. *That can't be it.* "Was there something else?"

"Just look." His father prodded. Mark desperately scanned the horizon trying to ward off the suspicion that madness had overtaken his father.

After a minute or so of silent scanning, Mark exhaled a long breath of condensed vapor and lowered the binoculars from his eyes. He turned to hand them back to his father. "I can't see any-" Mark's sentence was cut short by his own shock. His father appeared to have aged twenty years since the last time he saw him. His eyes were still the same silver orbs they had always been, but his pupils were so constricted that they were practically nonexistent. The skin around his temples sagged over his outer sclerae so his eyes truly looked like two marbles sunken in to waxy white clay. All of these features were exaggerated by a sincere look of worry; a look which would match what Mark sensed in his voice only much more haunting. "I can't see anything," Mark finished finally.

Mark's father let out a long sigh of disappointment, much like Mark's, and took his binoculars back. He lifted them back up to his eyes and zeroed in on the exact same vision. "It's out there. It's comin'," he said conclusively.

Mark took a long look at his father before turning away. Several weeks ago, Gladys had told Mark that his father had come home in the middle of the day and exclaimed, "I'm retiring." Gladys admitted to Mark that she was being asked a lot of strange questions about Mark's father lately. There is not much more to talk about in a small farming community like Ash County.

Everybody knows everything about everybody. Especially if you own one of the county's only grocery stores. As usual, Mark did not pry. He did not think to ask Gladys about what the questions were or what was strange about the questions. His father was strange. Mark had always known that. But it was clear now that he should inquire.

Mark left his father without saying another word. As he climbed down the rungs of the ladder he noticed that all of the fire of the day's excitement was gone. The grim specter that he beheld in that deer blind had stolen it away from him. How much longer before his father was out walking the streets without pants, ranting about fictional observations. Mark trudged back through the snow following his own tracks back to the deck stairs all the while wondering what his role would be as a caregiver to his stubborn father and how in the world he was going to convince him to see a doctor.

Mark grasped the old weathered doorknob as he'd done thousands of times since he was tall enough to reach it. The door seemed heavier now, like the new burden he had just realized was weighing Mark down. From the deck, the door entered into a mud room and a laundry room combined. Mark kicked off his shoes next to his father's jungle boots and proceeded to the kitchen from the mud room where he found Gladys in her normal place perpetually fixing dinner. "What's wrong with dad?" Mark blurted, skipping his usual evening greeting.

"Oh, what is it now?" Gladys said impatiently.

"Well, he appears to be hallucinating," Mark retorted. "Why? What else has been going on?"

"Well, don't panic," Gladys said with her usual minimizing. "He's just been a little out of sorts lately since he retired."

"Why don't you tell me that story first and we'll go from there?" Mark prodded. "Why did he retire?"

"He didn't say too much about it," Gladys remembered. "He just said that he couldn't do it anymore and that he might as well let Ed do it."

Ed Sorbitt had started working at the store even before Mark, if one could call it work. Being that Eddie was an orphan, Grandpa Deremer had done the noble thing and stepped up to take him in. With few willing or able to look after Ed during the day, he had essentially grown up in the store. Ed's father, Dean, also went to Vietnam, though he never really returned mentally. Ed could be considered a secondary casualty of the war. Dean was a victim of Agent Orange in addition to alcohol dependency. After Ed was born, Dean and his wife fought more and more and eventually the fights became increasingly violent. Mark remembered the horrifying depiction of the end of the marriage written in The County Crier.

The Ash County medical examiner counted one hundred forty-seven stab wounds in Mrs. Sorbitt's body. This did not include the rest of the excessive mutilation wherein method was undetermined. Mrs. Sorbitt's eyeballs were completely collapsed into their sockets, likely caused from Mr. Sorbitt's thumbs. Mrs. Sorbitt's mandible was found in an adjacent room approximately twenty feet in the opposite direction of her body, suggesting it was thrown backwards by Mr. Sorbitt. Blunt force trauma to the back of the head was likely caused by repeated blows against the floor beneath her. Upon regaining composure and realizing what he had done, Dean Sorbitt fled to the bedroom where he retrieved the .357 from under his pillow, put it in his mouth, and launched his brain matter onto the ceiling. Tom Van Beck, the Ash County Sheriff, responded to "complaints of the Sorbitts at it again" as Tom put it. Sheriff Van Beck walked into the Sorbitt home to find Mrs. Sorbitt's body still twitching in the family room, a headless Dean blown backwards on his knees in the bedroom, and little Eddie wailing in his crib from one room over.

Needless to say, the cards were stacked against Ed. Luckily for him, he had Grandpa Deremer who was willing to "raise him up right," as he told The Crier some weeks later. A proper examination from a psychiatric professional would have gone a long way to treat, or at least diagnose the boy. But according to the people of Ash, he was just "slow." Grandpa Deremer allowed Ed to work at the store as soon as he turned twelve. He was only a few years younger than Mark but acted much younger. It was a challenge to work with Ed and some days were better than others. Mark tried to remember that Ed could not help the way he was. But that did little to ease the unnerving frustration that often occurred when the two worked together. Ed often lost count, lost his temper, or simply wanted to make a mess of things. Several female customers had even lodged complaints against Ed as he struggled through puberty. Sheriff Van Beck came to question Ed one time about a break-in at the widowed Mrs. Andersen's house. No charges were ever filed, but the rumors persisted to the present day.

Through the years Mark and Ed learned to tolerate each other and the routine helped to keep the both of them on an even keel. Ed eventually became independent enough to live on his own. Mark's father even trusted him to balance the till on occasion. The store was the only job that Ed ever had and despite his condition, he did quite well and continued to make progress. With that said, Mark's father suggesting that Ed take charge of the entire operation seemed radical. On the other hand, Mark did not know how much responsibility was given to Ed since he had stopped working there to go to college. Considering what he had just witnessed in the deer blind, Ed might actually be the better choice.

"So what should we do about it?" Mark asked Gladys.

"Oh he's fine dear," Gladys returned, not concerned in the least. "He's just getting old and he's probably not able to handle it like he used to. Ed practically runs it by himself nowadays anyhow.. Your father hasn't taken a day off as long as I've known him, dear. You know what that does to a body? If you ask me, you *and* your father should try taking it a little bit easier on yourselves. Take some time to smell the roses. Go out fishing or bowling. You work too hard, the both of you. You take after him in that respect, that's for sure." Gladys did not look away from hand-mashing her potatoes for the entire speech. "Well, don't just stand there. Set the table."

She did make a compelling argument. His father had never taken a vacation ever in his life. He was either at the store or in the blind. That did not mean he was not crazy. But maybe his marbles would return once he relinquished his duties. It is quite possible that a break could be all that is needed and within a few days he would be his old, less screwy self once again. Gladys's ability to sway Mark's logic was uncanny. No matter how blatant the avoidance, he had always taken comfort in her justifications.

All through another silent dinner, Mark stared at the empty plate that would be his father's if he decided to come in to eat. This was not unusual. Only tonight, Mark's brain raced with articles he had read in medical journals regarding schizophrenia and other such illnesses causing hallucinations. He also tried to think of diseases with symptoms that matched his appearance. Mark had never known his father to do drugs. If the symptoms were the result of a head injury or stroke, he would have been dead already. There is the small chance that he was climbing the ladder at the exact moment of the stroke, but then there would have been other obvious indicators. Maybe someone slipped him some LSD when he wasn't looking. But the most likely answer is that he has just been isolating himself too much and the pupils and the rest of his ghastly appearance could be attributed to this never-ending winter. He was snow-blind and his delusions were mild but easily attributable from spending hours alone staring at one spot. *Why the hell was he always up there?* Mark had always figured that he was up there watching out for nuisance animals. In Michigan, a farmer can kill just about any animal they want year round if they are destroying the farmer's livelihood in some way. *Of course, he could just set up traps. Plus, he wasn't really a farmer in the sense that the majority of his income came from the store.* The fact remained that he had always done that and this was not a change in behavior. The only change is that he may be spending too much time up there now that he does not keep his shop. *Why is it suddenly too much for him?* He *was* pushing 70. Working 7 days a week for 50-some-odd years would definitely wear on anyone's nerves. Perhaps he was blowing this out of proportion as Gladys suggested.

A long and steady sound of his own blood flow echoed Mark back from his figuring. Weaving through stacks and stacks of his own condensed internal collection of medical journals and their application in statistical analyses led him to the conclusion that it was probably nothing. It had also led him to another blackout. He was still seated in the same position at the start of dinner; upright and staring at his father's empty place-setting at the table. He blinked a number of times in succession to relieve the dryness that had overcome his eyes and to focus on the hundred-year-old grandfather clock in the living room. He read 2:13. This blackout was much longer than usual although far less jarring. His mother must have just cleared his plate and not bothered to wake him from his catatonia. Either that or his multiple states of consciousness were more incongruent than usual, meaning that he *might* have been carrying on conversations with Gladys the entire time but no short term memories were formed.

Mark wanted to analyze the events surrounding the blackout to get a clearer picture of what was going on with him but he was exhausted. He would get closer to that conclusion tomorrow. Now he had to get some rest for the morning. As he walked by the kitchen window on the way to his room, he glanced out in the direction of his father's blind and wondered if he was still out there or if he had gone to bed while he was entranced. Either way, any reservations about the state of his father's well-being had fled and his mind was clear again.

The sun shone through Mark's window in a steady, condensed beam of light directly into his eyelid. Not a wink of sleep had he forgotten in his slumber. Leaping upright directly from a supine position on his mattress, he rushed to the window and flung the curtains asunder like Ebeneezer Scrooge after the ghost of Christmas future. Not one flake of snow remained from the dreadfully cold and eternal winter and the robins congregated in the yard cheerfully pecking worms from the earth. The smell of coffee and breakfast meat permeated Mark's nostrils and the sound of male and female vocal cords emitting laughter from the kitchen beat in his ears. Upon eagerly entering the kitchen, a very strange sight he beheld. His father sat at his place at the table, looking like a healthy and sane human being. Instead of the white, waxy semblance of a human face that usually occupied the blind, a set of rosy cheeks stood atop the corners of a smile. His father sat there at the table with a cup of coffee in hand wearing his red and black plaid flannel shirt like he had just stepped out of a Norman Rockwell painting. "Well, good morning, son!" his father spoke emphatically. Right behind him spoke Gladys with just as much cheer.

"Good morning, dear," she sang. "How do you want your eggs?" Mark stood in disbelief for another few seconds before replying.

"Sunny side up," he said in monotone. Mark's chest started tingling. His zygomaticus muscles began contracting into a rare and awkward grin.

"So, you got a big promotion, eh?" his father thundered. Gladys kissed him on the cheek as she dropped off a heaping plate of carbohydrates. Potatoes, toast, and pancakes were stacked a foot high and were nearly falling off of the plate as she sat it down. "Have a seat. Let's talk about it a little before you have to go." Mark did not know what to think of this situation. Calculations concerning the likelihood of various explanations ran rampant beneath his skull. *A brain tumor? A parallel universe?* But he was reassured in remembering the conclusion about his father from yesterday. *Mom was right.*

"Well," Mark began as he cautiously sat down and accepted reality. "Basically I'm restructuring the company to make it run more efficiently."

"That is great son!" his father exclaimed. "The wait was worth it, huh? Now you can step in and show 'em how to do it!" He banged on the table with an added note of enthusiasm which made Mark flinch.

"Well, I guess we'll see what I can do," Mark offered as a tear streamed from his eye. The prolonged contraction of such uncommonly used muscles in his face put a tremendous strain on his tear ducts. The obvious question of why his father was acting like a completely different person tried to break through to become speech, but couldn't quite make it past Mark's joy. Instead, he and his two parents conversed through breakfast about unimportant and trivial matters. He could not remember a happier moment in his entire life.

It was typical in Michigan to have grand fluctuations in the weather, especially at this time of year. The birds and the frogs from the pond were deafening, but Mark joined in their exultation when his car only took one crank to start. He drove off in his beat-up white station wagon with the windows down, basking in the strangeness of the morning's events. On the other side of his happiness, Mark's analysts feverishly stirred and scrutinized them.

They could not help but notice patterns, real or imagined, in all that had happened in the past 24 hours. They were, by far, the most extraordinary hours of his entire life and all of the happenings surely could not be unrelated. *I often see patterns where perhaps no patterns are present at all. Of course, there very well could be patterns, but there would be no way of knowing for sure.* He often tangled himself up with these types of thoughts. But the huge promotion, his newfound confidence, the change in weather, the strange behavior of his parents; *these things cannot be unrelated, can they?* If they were related, the common denominator remained to be seen.

Mark shook the paranoia and began to collect all the pieces of his plan to present to Gary. He pulled into a parking space almost to the end of the EnviroCore parking lot, not much further from the one he parked in the day before. But he remembered the VP of Operations space, almost to the front of the parking lot. The feeling of confidence grew back from yesterday's seed into a massive beast, 100 feet high if it was a foot. His consciousness began to enter its mitotic conversion into two separate entities and a calming albeit unsettling darkness washed over him.

In one consciousness, Mark processed the common reality that is shared among all human beings. In another, he saw a metaphor for his thoughts come to life. A giant fault line crackled away on the desert landscape of his brain. From the center emerged an iron cylinder which sprouted numerous long, thin mechanical arms reaching out to beyond the horizon. Claws clasped down on giant crystalline shards from outside the field of view and were retracted to the central black metal cylinder by its multi-jointed extremities. In a short time, the arms had assembled Mark's plan for the future of the company. Glorious and massive, it shone reflections of light which were converted into confidence by Mark's amygdala. As he admired what he had created, his two conscious realities slammed together in a violent fusion, sending a shockwave through Mark's nervous system. Mark's body startled in its seat and he was now ready to deliver the plan to Gary.

Mark sat down at his desk and opened the GLADIS file. It was two-sided page after two-sided page of eight point font computer code with sporadic handwritten notes. Mark did not completely trust a flash drive, or any other drive for that matter, instead preferring several of these ridiculous collections of code, all kept in different undisclosed locations, all made complex enough that only Mark could easily change the program's code. He purposely added lines that negated other lines as well as other such unnecessary code which, though reproducible, would hopefully frustrate a naïve programmer enough to give up. That was Mark's hope anyway. The rest of the world hates tedium. The rest of the world is impatient and hates a struggle. The GLADIS code was just that; a thorny labyrinth of Boolean operators, mind-numbing repetitive sequences, and purposeful misspellings, designed as the final failsafe to prevent the software's misuse.

If Mark had one strength, it was that he was immune to the frustration and boredom that tedium brought most people. In addition to his superhuman imagination, this is what allowed him to read and reread the complex theories of advanced modern science until he understood them. That nagging, whining voice that would plague any other human being within thirty seconds of reading about the isolation and extraction of chemical compounds in undefined bacterial media, was absent from Mark's makeup.

What Mark did not understand was that this was actually a genetic defect. A body craves variety and stimulus. What Mark did to himself as a child with days of endless studying and reading was equivalent to White Torture, an information extraction method utilizing long periods of sensory deprivation. Though this would be a handy tool to have if ever taken prisoner in Iran, behind the scenes Mark's brain adapted to the torture by creating additional states of consciousness to dissociate himself from the world. What could be recognized as a gift was actually a coping mechanism to compensate for his brain's inability to register monotonous torment.

While Mark was contemplating his own resistance to boredom in the tiny scrawl written beside the miniature code, Gary came sauntering into the office in his usual calmness. "Are you OK?" he asked. "You ran out of here like you'd seen a ghost. You don't look much better now either. Who is HASEP?"

"Oh let me tell you about HASEP," Mark said with a rarely seen grin and another sudden, uncharacteristic surge of excitement. "HASEP is going to save EnviroCore and then send it to the moon."

"OK," Gary said with anticipation as he pulled up a chair on the other side of Mark's desk. "I can hardly wait to hear this,"

"Have you ever heard of the enzyme nylonase?" Mark asked.

"Of course I have not," Gary replied dryly.

"Back in the seventies," Mark began, "some scientists discovered a strain of *Flavobacteria* that could digest a byproduct of nylon. Supposedly, many generations of bacteria living in polluted water outside a nylon factory evolved a frameshift mutation producing the enzyme nylonase, which allowed the bacteria to breakdown the nylon byproduct."

"That is really something," Gary said with dry patronization.

"I know," Mark continued, totally indifferent to Gary's tone. "HASEP stands for Harmonic Asymmetric Simple Exclusion Process. It is a continuous-time Markov jump process describing the collective behavior of stochastically interacting components."

"You don't say," Gary continued his playfully sardonic tone.

"I used it to design an algorithm that will predict the phenotype of a bacterial strain based on extrapolations from current literature," Mark said.

"Mark," Gary said desperately, as his attempts to flag his inability to understand were either failing or being ignored, "you'll have to forgive me but I majored in business. The only biology I ever took in college was an introductory class for non-science majors and that was fifteen years ago. So you're going to have to dumb it down."

"My apologies," Mark said. "In a nutshell, the program has the ability to build a virtual bacterium so that we can observe how it works before we build a real one." Mark went on to inform Gary of the current state of cellular engineering both in state-of-the-art labs and EnviroCore. Enough energy and thought was put into the explanation to give Gary a fairly accurate picture of how valuable GLADIS could be. "With *our* technology," Mark went on, "we could design our own strains, in house, which could act to speed up the evolution of a *Flavobacterium* in a pond filled with nylon pollutant. Once we get a firmer grasp of how this process works, we could build them to metabolize *any* kind of pollutant. In fact, we already have one on file that evolved to digest BPA, a popular component of most plastics. We have only to build the real thing."

Gary sat in inscrutable silence. Whether he had understood everything Mark just told him was unclear. "Jesus," he finally said, "we could monopolize waste management." The shock poured over him like warm honey. His eyes were wide, his mouth hung slightly open. "HASEP is going to send us to the moon alright," said Gary in agreement with Mark's insight. "This is going to change the world."

At the same time, both men sat back in their chairs with eyes glazed over. Mark's glaze was the result of another flashback of the deer blind, Gary's was of the stupefaction caused by pondering the magnitude of Mark's invention. Mark felt he had arrived in the place where he was *meant* to be, 'changing the world.' Though he was a man of science, numbers, facts, hard data, etc., he could not ignore the ominously prophetic affirmation Gary had just issued. On the other side of the desk, Gary could not believe this was only the second day.

The two stared blankly at each other, still in awe. Finally, Gary brought them back to reality as he sat forward in his chair, "We need to move on this now. Get this rolling right now before we do anything and we'll get back to the rest as soon as you do. This...this takes precedence." His tone was foreboding, like what you might imagine was commonplace behind closed doors with The Manhattan Project. Gary rubbed his jaw as it hung open. He still could not wrap his head around the potential. Then suddenly, he got up and began walking toward the door, turning around before walking through it, "Make some calls, man," he said, waiting until Mark picked up his phone to exit.

Meanwhile, Mark was still sitting in his office with the phone up to his ear waiting to punch the bacteriology extension into the keys. He was desperately trying to keep his multiple states of consciousness together as one, but it was truly a struggle. In one consciousness, he harkened back to when his father forced him to quit the store and go to college. *'Son, you're gonna make a change in this world. Someday people are going to read amazing things about you. That's not gonna happen with you playing Rain Man with the chili cans in my store. You have to get out of my store and into the world so you can have a hand in changin' it.'* The words played over and over in Mark's head, so loud that he could swear they were almost coming from just outside the office. His father's voice overlaid the voice of Gary saying, *'This is going to change the world.'* Mark felt a sense of fulfillment in this consciousness, as if he had found the reason he was put on this Earth. In contrast, consciousness number two was as barren as the Atacama Desert. Yes, he is about to embark on a fundamental changing of mankind, but there are still about thirty-thousand steps to get there. This consciousness was like a machine, unimpressed with prospects, unimpressed with anything. It only knew to keep going and felt no sense of accomplishment, no reward, no motivation whatsoever except for the glucose it metabolized.

Mark awoke from the small struggle to the sound of dialing in the receiver. He assumed that he suffered another small blackout in which his fingers dialed the bacteriology extension. Steve answered the phone, "Bacteriology. Steve speaking."

The battle with dissociative divide continued which was evident in the monotone voice Mark heard coming from his own vocal cords. "Steve, I need an update on GLADIS."

"Mark," Steve hesitated, "parental generation is a go. The

first filial iteration is in progress. Every single base pair in the genome matches across the board."

"What?!" Mark gasped. "How did you manage that?"

When Mark called the bacteriology department, he expected to hear that all necessary equipment had been ordered, not that they already had a strain. "Oh, I have my sources," Steve said slyly, "I have my ways."

"Is there a significant curve yet?" Mark was champing at the bit now.

"Not yet," Steve replied. "We are still monitoring the population curve. It's a slower start than what was predicted."

"Damn," Mark sighed. "Well we're still way further ahead than I could've imagined. Keep me posted I guess. Thanks Steve."

"Right," Steve said as he hung up the phone, eager to return to watching the stats.

Mark sat back in hesitant excitement, tapping his fingertips on his desk in thought. *He must've worked through the night!* Given Steve's competitive nature, it made sense that he would obsessively immerse himself in this goal now that it was back in the picture. *No matter, at least it's getting done.* But he couldn't shrug it off that easily. What Steve accomplished in one night was unprecedented, considering there was almost none of the necessary equipment in the lab. *Did he drive to lab supply places immediately after I gave him the green light?* But there were much larger tasks at hand than obsessing over minutia. Mark had a future to change.

Mark wiggled the computer mouse to unlock his screen and double-clicked a folder he made titled 'resources.' All that it contained was a long list of documents titled with single numbers. They represented the steps which needed to play out in order to save, or more precisely, rebuild the company from this moment up into a black profit margin and even some tentative pathways beyond that point. The plan now was to put together a team of insiders that would all communicate constantly. Mark had completed enough research to know what professions the team needed, which firms, agencies or individuals he was going to use, where they were going to work and what he wanted Gary to say to each of them to get them to come and work for him. Mark was nothing if not organized. He compiled this information in a spreadsheet and sent it to Gary.

At this point, Mark felt like he had complete control over everything. That warm sensation in his chest that he felt yesterday had come roaring back and, as he began typing the first job description in an email to a lab in Switzerland, swelled up into a firestorm, violently burning his reservations to a crisp.

'Dear Dr. Crisp,

I am writing to you this day to tell you about an exciting job opportunity as a collaborator in a cutting edge environmental research and development lab. As the new Vice President of Operations at EnviroCore, I am looking to put together the best of the best. Having conducted exhaustive research in the field of genetically modified horticulture and subsurface textile irrigation, your name stands alone. We at EnviroCore would be very interested in having you on our team. Please respond as soon as possible to discuss particulars. At EnviroCore, we are changing the world. Sincerely, Mark Deremer'

Mark sent the email with a sharp and solid mouse click. *We are changing the world. Maybe that could be the new slogan.* Mark noticed a reply from Gary about the spreadsheet that simply read, "What's all this?"

"These are the best agencies to use," he replied and began his next recruiting email:

Dear Dr. Brotkletterer,

'I represent an emerging company which is interested in the innovation behind some of your bioprinting projects at The CSIRO. We are EnviroCore and we are committed to developing all things sustainable. Please contact us at your earliest convenience to discuss a possible collaborative effort to make this world a better place.'

Mark slammed the send key again even harder this time. The electronic packet of information blasted from the fingertip of his right-hand index finger and raced over thousands of kilometers of fiber optic cables to the inbox of Dr. Brotkletterer in Canberra. *It's all coming together now.* Mark was going to be the asteroid that killed the dinosaurs. His heart raced and his flesh burned with fiery joy. He opened one more blank canvas on which to compose his next recruitment email when Gary knocked and entered.

"I'm gonna go ahead and handle this part ok, Mark?" Gary said authoritatively. Mark's asteroid fell away in one giant particle dispersal. "All I want you to do is network right now. Get the word out to your pick of potential lab directors and collaborators but don't reveal anything. That is crucial. I will have my people make the arrangements and talk business but we need you to pique their interest. Beat around the bush a bit about what we're doing and start lining them up. We'll be the ones to knock 'em down though."

Mark's face drained of enthusiasm. "I don't believe we have time for a long courtship, do we? We only have a month, right? Isn't that what we figured?"

"Yes but we have to play our cards close to the chest here. If they found out about our financial situation or the pending FDA citations we would quickly be shunned. We might as well turn the lights off now if that happens," Gary explained.

Of course Mark agreed with the logic, but did not want to lose this confidence again. He also did not want to waste a lot of time schmoozing highly acclaimed scientists. The 'straight-to-the-point' attitude which Mark had with Steve was not universal in the field. In fact, it typically took much longer when collaborating on projects. Language barriers, in concert with the field differences, would drag things out to absurd degrees.

"That is not going to work, Gary." Mark said, "Many of these people consider switching from academia to the private sector equivalent to making a deal with the Devil. I am going to need to get them excited. I am going to need to tell them a little of what we have right now if I'm going to pique anything. There may even need to be a bit of fibbing, or perhaps flat out lies, about how far along we are. So I guess what I'm saying is that we need to make that contract pretty sweet if we are expecting them to sell their souls."

Gary stood in silence with his lips pursed in a frown. Three seconds of computation elapsed before he spoke, "I guess this is game time and we've got nothing to lose. Do what you do."

Mark's fire returned with the minor win and he returned to his keyboard. He knew he would need to make it look like they had something really big that they couldn't discuss by any other means than in person. That would buy some time to get GLADIS going;

119

work out the bugs and potential pitfalls. Not to mention lining up the proper regulatory rigamarole. Assembling the departments which he intended to create and have some semblance of work coming out of them would be the next step. There was no doubt that the prospective new hires would do their research on EnviroCore and find nothing, so hopefully Gary could attain the PR guy quickly; today if possible; yesterday would be better. The stress of the situation did nothing but accelerate Mark's fire. Each new step that stacked up in his to-do folder was another liter or so of gasoline pouring onto it. The time was ticking away until the month deadline. Like a death clock hourglass, purging horrible grains of sand into eternity, so was the livelihood of Ash County, Michigan.

Mark wrote a quick email to Gary asking him to focus on getting a PR guy first. If that ball didn't get rolling soon, he would have to throw up an EnviroCore website himself. Though Mark could write HTML, he was not the most creative person. His strengths lied with the facts and soon, the potential facts, as he would have to think up projects that did not yet exist and then get teams together to start working on them. Though they didn't quite know all of the details right now, the whole of the company's workforce was in limbo. And though Mark didn't know it, he was entering his state of hibernation in response to the urgency regarding the new team. He was switching between several different word processor files. Some of the files would appear nonsensical to anyone but Mark. But unlike his GLADIS code, this was not necessarily by design. He was typing in a shorthand which he made up as he went. On one of the documents was written, 'enter after hardware printable time,' which was his way of getting an idea for reducing the amount of time it took for 3D printing fruits and vegetables. On the second document was written, 'The sun has been the most ubiquitous power source known to this planet since earth has been a planet, but it has gone grossly under-utilized by its most intelligent species.' It was a pitch for a different project he would plan for solar panels which would grow from the trees themselves or grow on the backs of high-flying Boomerang Beetles. He was not terribly certain at this point, he was simply jotting down any idea that came into his head. Another document had what was obviously hyper-text markup language. Another, a note to one more scientist. Mark's other states of consciousness had not yet entered sleep phase and he was able to multitask during any lull in creativity in any task performed by any other consciousness.

Hours were going by, people were stopping into his office, conversations were being had, empty documents were being created and filled, phone calls were being made. Then he came to the startling realization that his consciousness seemed to be multiplying geometrically. It was not startling enough to stop his work; just something to remember for when he had a minute to collect them all back into one. Mark likened it to the feeling of running down a steep hill faster than his legs could actually carry him. On the other hand, he felt relaxed, like he was but a mere observer of his own actions; watching his own player-piano-like stamina. Mark drifted away into his work and became vaguely aware that the light of day had gone. But he just kept working.

The clock struck midnight as the sound of metal scraping filled the apartment of Bill Wildeboer. The streetlights shone through the blinds onto the leaves of some exotic plant which sat lilting on a large, intricately decorated metal stand. Playful swearing and laughter came from just outside the door and the jingling of keys accompanied the metal scraping. Nothing was audible of the voices except for the tones. A man and a woman, Bill Wildeboer and Tina Wenthrop, from the EnviroCore food service staff, were trying to unlock the door in a drunken stupor. More than once the keys dropped to the ground outside of the door. Finally, the door flew open, slamming against the wall. They both were stifling laughter and Tina was *shh-shing* Bill as they staggered inside.

"Fuck 'em," Bill said referring to the neighbors or anyone that would dare to complain about the noise at the late hour. Bill slipped his shoes off and kicked them across the room, creating an additional cacophony as they impacted whatever it was they impacted. He searched the wall for his light switch and flipped it on. Tina, dressed in a strappy black dress cut whorishly short *oohed* and *ahhed* at the size of the apartment.

"Vaulted ceilings?" she gasped, which echoed off of the vaulted ceiling. Bill flopped down onto his overstuffed leather couch.

"Yep," he replied as he casually produced a medium-sized baggy of cocaine from his pocket. Tina continued to fawn over things in the apartment as she named them aloud.

"Is this real gold? What type of wood is that? Stainless steel? I love this painting." Bill did not answer any of her questions or even acknowledge she was still in the room. His blood-shot eyes focused intensely on the knot tied in the baggy, which he was trying to negotiate with his shaking fingers. Before five seconds had passed, he gave up and ripped the entire knot off, dumping the contents out on the glass-and-metal modern-design coffee table in front of him. From his other pocket, he fumbled for a twenty dollar bill and upon retrieving it, rolled it into a tightly packed cylinder.

Tina finally ended her tour and found her way to the couch as if she smelled the cocaine spill out from the bag. Bill leaned over the pile and without cutting out a line, snorted a blast of powder through his rolled-up twenty. His body rocked back into the couch as if the cocaine punched him in the face. Tina laughed flirtatiously and took the makeshift straw from Bill's fingers, leaned forward, and repeated his movements exactly. The two laid back together with eyes wide and mouths open, enjoying what the drug had done to their brains. After a time, Tina cooed and wrapped the right half of her body over Bill and closed her eyes.

"Mmm," she whispered, "where have you been?" Her voice was sultry and feminine and though she was probably talking to the cocaine, Bill didn't care.

"Where did *you* come from?" he tried to mimic her playful tone. They both laughed in a drunken, horny haze. "What is someone like you doing out here in the sticks?" he asked. "They don't get very many like you out this way."

"Yeah?" she replied without an ounce of intelligence. "Well, good. I came out here to start over, y'know? I want a life that's more simple." They both laughed again in their stupor.

"Well, I guess you're in the right place," he said. "It don't get much simpler than this honey."

"I just wanted to go somewhere where nobody knows me, y'know?"

"I get it. You've got a past, right?"

"Well everyone's got a past silly."

"Yeah. Maybe your past is your past for a good reason."

"Yeah, you might say that. The wrong people always seem to find me."

"Yeah I know what you mean."

The two laughed together at the irony and decided they were becoming all too coherent and needed to return to the white pile on the table.

As Bill readied his makeshift straw over the pile of cocaine, his pocket started vibrating along with the latest Maroon 5 hit. He drew a huge, harsh breath through his right nostril up through the twenty and shot backward in his leather couch whilst the powder burned all the way up his sinus.

"Whew… Piss! Ass!," he shouted in Tourette-ic euphoria. But as if nothing happened at all, Bill casually reached into his pocket to collect his phone. "It's Ted," he said as he passed Tina the straw. "I'm gonna take this." Though all Tina heard was the muffled voice of Charlie Brown's teacher as she snatched up the straw and dove back into the stack of drugs.

"Yeah," Bill answered, as if he didn't know who was calling.

"Billy Boy," Philus answered back with sarcastic enthusiasm, "I'm not interrupting anything am I?"

"There's nothing that won't wait for *your* call Ted," Bill laughed with sarcastic sincerity.

"That's the attitude I need to hear Bill," Philus chuckled, acknowledging the truth behind the statement.

"What's up?" Bill asked with a combination of impatience and worry.

"I just wanted to keep you apprised of the situation at your company Bill," Philus boomed. "You're doing a hell of a job up there Billy, lettin' those boys play around unsupervised they are really covering a lot of ground."

"Well thank you sir," Bill breathed the weight from his shoulders.

"Oh you betcha Billy," Philus bellowed. "The work those boys are doin' will have us outta the shit in no time. I'm kickin' myself now for not seeing the potential that you saw in that 'Deremer' character. But that's ok because you saw it and we have him now and that's all that matters right?"

"Well what can I say? I'm a genius," Bill joked while simultaneously inflating his ego.

"You are indeed, son," Philus continued with the playful banter. "Now let's get real here for a minute, boy. You don't need to know what's goin' on down there, hell I don't even know what's goin' on down there, but it's gonna be fuckin' huge. It's movin' fast and it has the potential to move out of your control."

Of course what Philus meant was that *his* company was going to get out of *his* control. Deep down Bill realized that Ted was the one pulling the strings. Indeed, he was pulling Bill's strings. However, Bill saw no way out of the predicament except for staying the course. Besides, his life was filled with all the debauchery he could handle, evident in the white powder and blood festooning his nostril. He had gone from holding a pistol to his temple and drowning in panic to the facade of having his shit together; making moves and shaking things up. Who cares if his life was a sham?

"So what should I do?" Bill asked.

"Billy, I swear sometimes I feel like I'm playin' this game all by myself," Philus responded. "You need to talk to the lawyers and draw up some paperwork to protect yourself and the company.

You need them to say that whatever they got goin' is property of EnviroCore. But the papers also have to say that whatever goes wrong is not your fault."

"So I'm taking all of the credit and none of the blame?" Bill asked sardonically.

"Well," Philus laughed, "that is one way to put it Billy. You'll get the hang of it before too long I suspect. Just keep up the good work and stay in touch. Good night, Billy."

With that, Bill looked at the phone to assure he had hung up and then locked his screen. He harkened back to Ted's history and the molten quicksand that he had left him in with the initial changing of the guard that never really occurred. Ted left the company in ruins and jumped ship on the transition, essentially leaving no one in charge. They were scrambling and clawing in vain trying to figure out what to do. He remembered how much he had wanted to kill Ted for getting him in this mess. Then when things started to smooth out, he just waltzed back in and took control of the company again, using Bill as the intermediary no less. He was infuriated with his decision to trust him again and that cold, familiar feeling of regret started to wash over him. It had already submerged his ankles and wet halfway up his shins. A soft sprinkling of paranoia quickly turned into a torrential downpour of panic. Thunder rumbled in his ear the mocking voice of despair in unison with the blinding flash of shame. Before he knew it, he was up to his waist and could hardly see a foot in front of him. He waded to the liquor cabinet, pulled out a glass and a bottle of Chivas and frantically poured himself a life vest. His hand shook violently as he threw it down his throat and immediately splashed another helping into the glass. The second one went down much more smoothly than the first and by the third refill, Bill leaned

126

back on his life vest and bobbed freely with the waves that had now calmed dramatically. The gulps had become sips, the black sky had become orange, and the terrible thunder had now become the calls of sea gulls. He knew all that Philus had done and he knew what he was doing. He didn't have to think about it now. Que será, será. Right now, he was somebody. People thought he was somebody, anyway. Bill knew that he was out here all alone, drowning. It was only a matter of time before he went under. The truth is that in time, Bill could have probably righted the ship without Philus. But fear and impatience had won him over again and he could not stand the thought of failing one more time. Though instead of swallowing his pride and manning the wheel whatever may have come, he chose the fast and easy route of jumping ship and going with the flow. There is something to be said of the statement 'let go and let God.' You can hear the old adage being said in many a church basement. True, you can find some peace in knowing that most of life's setbacks will be resolved one way or another without your intervention. The fallacy is in that God is not going to tie your shoes for you.

Bill walked back out into the living room with his glass half full. "Why are you all wet?" Tina asked, referring to the sweat beads lining and dripping from his brow.

Bill grinned a wide, toothy grin and said slyly, "Sometimes it takes a little heat to run things so smoothly."

"Oh yeah?" Tina asked through a flirtatious smile, "You're in there takin' care of business, huh?"

"Oh yeah," Bill replied gravitating back to Tina's cleavage. "This company would be underwater without me."

"Ooh," Tina keenly feigned her enthusiasm as he sat down next to her, "you're kinda like superman or somethin' huh?"

"You're damn right," Bill said tightening the rolled up twenty for another blast of ill-gotten dopamine.

"Mmm," she mumbled under a stolen sip of his scotch.

"I'm gonna take this company to the fuckin' top," he bragged handing the straw back over to Tina. "Just you wait, babe. I'm gonna be on the cover of fuckin' Forbes. All this shit here is nothing compared to what's about to happen. I got everyone right where I want them and all I have to do is pull the switch!" Tina found Bill's delusional grandeur both sexy and terrifying. She climbed on top of him and laid her hands on his chest.

"Wow," she said startled by his wild, glassy eyes, "you *are* sweaty. You must've really been layin' down the law." Bill's ego was already fully inflated, but he didn't mind the stroking.

"You don't have any fuckin' idea what I'm capable of," Bill growled behind clenched teeth. Tina's arousal was now waxing more towards fear.

"Why don't we get you in the shower and clean you up a little, you dirty boy." Tina said seductively as she pushed Bill's face into her breasts, trying to calm her own terror.

"I am not a fuckin' *boy*," Bill barked as he removed her with firm grasp of her shoulders. "I am a fucking *man*!"

The look of fear was now completely evident on Tina's face as Bill stood up and locked one arm around her waist. But the angry look of psychopathy morphed completely into one of playful animal sexuality which, as is common with most of Bill's conversers, left Tina completely confused and uneasy. She wrapped her legs tightly around him and ground herself into him, using the only way she knew to control someone's actions. Simultaneously, they pulled into each other, locking into a passionate, scotchy kiss and Bill began a long awkward walk, carrying her to the shower.

A tidal wave headed for Mark unbeknownst to him as he found himself floating in the middle of a vast and lonely ocean. In the distance, he saw a fierce and muscular steed galloping on the shore. The horse was running at a full sprint, his eyes wild and his mouth foaming. Through its nostrils, short, panting breaths took the form of steam against the cold air. Hundreds of muscles were working to move the great beast and Mark would swear he could see them all, thinly veiled under shiny velvet skin. His curious awe was broken by his inquisition. *How in the world did I get here?* But before he had time to render an answer, the tidal wave was upon him. The updraft threw him like a fastball pitch right into the path of the horse, whose terror was just as real as Mark's as he barreled helplessly at him. The collision was no less violent than a Louisville Slugger cracking him into the outfield, even though the two never completed the impending impact.

Mark inhaled a gasp of air that one would gasp if held under water until just before drowning. He began violently coughing and gasping and clawing at the flesh on his arms. The shock of reality electrocuted the awareness of his surroundings; the Deremer deer blind in what felt like the middle of winter. Snot was frozen on his upper lip and his pants were filled with frozen urine. A headache like he had never felt squeezed his temples in a vice. The sensation of numbness and tingling in his frostbitten skin was difficult to distinguish from his convulsive shivering. If he could feel his tongue, Mark would realize that he was dying of dehydration and in a few short minutes, hypothermia. He tried to call out, but his vocal cords only let out a raspy grunt of fiery pain. The weakness and cold in his soon-to-be-corpse imprisoned his helpless mind which would only register the experience of the pain of freezing until his heart locked in rigor mortis. *Where is my*

130

father? Conveniently absent. How humiliating. And how did I get
here, *now?* One last look around this horrible and familiar place
would close his eyes forever. One last gasp of arctic air would roll
his eyes back into the endless abyss.

But instead of dropping onto the hard wooden floor of the
blind, his frozen cadaver began a freefall. It fell five good seconds
before crashing hard into another body of water. This was not the
ocean. Its flow was swift and it was adjacent to land on either side.
Helplessly he floated down the river with all the agility of a piece
of driftwood. Standing on one bank was the local runaway Slippy,
carrying a rider this time; an old man, missing one eye and
carrying a spear. The two stared at each other with the intensity of
doctor and gangrenous civil war hero. Realization struck. Mark
was floating down the River Gjöll, which separated the lands of the
living and the dead. The man at whom he was staring was Odin
and the horse was not Slippy, but Odin's horse, Sleipnir, with eight
legs and eyes of solid silver. The soullessness of their appearance
in the animal's deep ocular cavities reminded him of those he
beheld in the deer blind, sunken into his father's head. Though,
Mark could not verbalize the coincidence, his mind drew the
connection unconsciously. As his carcass drifted further and
further from the macabre twosome, he realized he was not alone
floating down the Gjöll. Out of the corners of his lifeless eyes, he
could see other bodies sharing the river. As he drifted further
downstream, the rapids grew thick with them. The cold skin of one
of his fellow travelers brushed up against his, the consistency of
which could be likened to a wet piece of tree bark. But Mark had
no emotion about the matter whatsoever. Yes he was dead. Yes he
was traveling down a river of human remains. And yes, it appeared
that the myths and stories he heard from the old timers over

childhood bonfires were true. But he accepted his fate, with every single brush up against a neighboring corpse.

But then the river's pace began to slow from the logjam. Soon his body was being squeezed next to six or eight others and he found himself face to face with one of them; boatman's coins draped carefully over the eyes of the gray-faced specter. The skin was worn so thin, its nose was all but gone. A collision from further upstream jarred the body suddenly, shaking loose the carefully placed coins. Mark was unable to avert his gaze and, in absolute horror and disbelief, recognized the face staring back at him as his own. His hollow heart suddenly began beating again, reanimating the blood in every vessel under his flesh. In one backbreaking and agonizing jolt, Mark was able to sit up and behold the dam of cadavers stopping up the Gjöll. They were fitted so tight against one another that Mark was able to get to his hands and knees and crawl over them. Once every fourth step or so a piece of the human bridge would break off under Mark's weight and slam him head first into a soft clump of slimy adipose flesh. Reborn, Mark's indifference was gone and was now replaced with nausea. The bodies were all in various states of decomposition but he was beginning to see a rather unsettling pattern. All of the faces he glanced down at bore a resemblance to himself. No longer able to avert his curiosity, he stopped crawling and looked around him. As he bore witness to the expressionless carcasses one by one, Mark was overcome. With welling eyes and a hardened diaphragm, a geyser of green phlegm suddenly spewed forth in a lockjaw dry heave. Recognizing tiny discriminating marks and clothes, he no longer needed an early state of decay to recognize that each and every body in this river was another Mark Deremer. He covered his eyes and began wailing uncontrollably, folding himself into a fetus. Again, the weakness of the brittle flesh and bone gave way and he broke through the wall of death underneath him to plunge into the icy depths of the river. His ears began ringing and his flailing attempt at swimming did not bring him back up. Sinking into black, the ever-increasing pressure flooded his eardrum with the sound of pumping blood. Deafening as it was, he longed for his eardrums to finally explode.

But they did not explode. Suddenly, the overwhelming panic of drowning ceased with one giant, familiar thud. Slowly, his eyelids released their hold on sleep and Mark felt a cold drop of water inching a path from his ear to his cheekbone. The first sight he saw was the Deremer farm cloaked in a sparse layer of white through the living room doorwall. *Where am I now?* Of course he recognized the environment. But he could not trust his own perceptions and was now uncertain of anything. If he was on his mother's couch with a cold compress on the side of his face, was it the common timeline, or was he reliving a memory? He had just experienced the most intense nightmare of his life and the last thing he remembered before it was writing an email to Dr. Brotkettler in his office at EnviroCore.

"Oh dear that's probably gotten cold on you," Gladys called to him upon hearing him sigh. "Let me warm that up for you."

Mark felt worse than he can ever remember feeling. Physically, he felt like he had been hit by a Mack truck and left for dead in the arctic tundra. Mentally, he felt like he had been hit by a Mack truck and left for dead in the arctic tundra.

Raspily, he called out to his mother, "What the hell happened to me?" Talking felt like regurgitating long glass shards and did not sound much different from an electrolarynx.

"Well, your father found you out there in the deer blind half frozen and brought you inside," Gladys stated with impossible indifference. "You must've gone out there last night to look out into the grasses without expecting this darn weather. And how could you expect it? We're almost halfway through April!" A long silence passed as Mark struggled to put pieces together. *Out into the grasses? Is she talking about dad? I don't go out there anymore. Is she starting to lose it too? Am I? What could I have been doing out there? In the dark? Did she say April? What the hell is going on?* But he did not dwell on the strange explanation. He was still barely conscious and not yet sure this was not a dream.

"What time is it?" he struggled to ask.

"It's almost ten." Gladys replied.

"Almost ten?" Mark exclaimed, tasting blood.

"Don't worry about work dear," Gladys assured him. "They called here a little while ago and I told them what happened and they understood you taking a personal day."

Mark shot out of his supine position and flung the blanket off of him. But the blanket was the only thing keeping him above hypothermic body temperatures and he began shivering violently. It felt as if every centimeter of tissue in his body was pulsing with ice water. The sheer ferocity of the shaking caused instant nausea but he was able to grab the metal bucket his mother must have placed on the floor next to him while he slept and heave a few ounces of hot chyme into it. Gladys calmly walked over and sat next to him on the couch. She put the blanket back around him and placed her hand on his back, gently rubbing it up and down until he recovered from the fit.

Fuck! This is it. I fuckin' failed. This was my one shot to prove that I'm worth something and I fuckin' blew it! I'm going back to the store to count inventory now. It won't be so bad. Goddamnit! What the fuck happened? What the fuck is happening to me?

The analysts upstairs in his prefrontal cortex were working overtime trying to come up with logical explanations, but they only returned frantic worry. To Mark, this was a far worse reality than the previous two from which he had awakened. It crossed his mind that he may be passing through different dimensions of hell. But during the terror, an even worse reality manifested: he was not passing out. The defense mechanism he had spent a lifetime crafting in response to troubling emotions was malfunctioning. How ironic that now all he wanted to do was pass out and escape this reality but couldn't. *One thing is for certain, I am awake.*

At the last few vomit-scented exhales, the phone rang. Despite his illness, Mark fled the comfort of the couch and raced toward the corded rotary telephone just on the other side of the half wall in the kitchen.

"Hello," Mark choked on the beginning of the dialogue. The voice on the other end of the line carried all the mannerisms of Steve Williams, but the frequency of the timbre did not match the memory Mark had on record.

135

"Jesus Christ buddy what the hell happened to you? You sound like shit! I knew you didn't look so good the last few days. Musta finally caught up with ya, huh?"

"Yeah must've," Mark complied, fervently trying to assemble a recollection.

"Listen buddy I know you must be sick. You probably have never missed a day in your life have ya? But anyway, ya said to call ya with anything that comes up so here goes. We're really movin' down here with *Vir* but we're still runnin' into some of those critical errors that you and I were getting the other day. It's somethin' in the population algorithm that doesn't make sense. It's those multiple S curves again. I can try and noodle with it until you get back but I know this is one of those things that's gonna require your personal touch; what with your Double Da Vinci Code Slip Shank Knot I'm-not-trusting-anybody-not-even-Steve encryption bullshit an' all." Mark had no idea what Steve was talking about. There was no way he was going to be able to pick up on any clues with this one. His only option was to come clean.

"Listen," Mark whispered, "I think something may be wrong with me."

"I know, I know," Steve said. "You can't talk about it over the phone, Bill may be listening, et cetera. Listen buddy, this ain't the Manhattan Project, alright? It's important work but it's still just the same old little bugs." Mark listened to Steve in disbelief. His conversation suggested that Mark had lost much more time and information than he had previously feared. It also suggested that there had been continuous memory lapses and plenty of paranoia. *What in the fuck…?* What Mark wouldn't give to go back to Gjöll and climb over several thousand copies of his own corpse.

"Steve," Mark labored, "I'm not kidding, I need some

help." Mark's tone betrayed a real fear but Steve's answer suggested he, again, had heard it before.

"I know. OK buddy, we'll see you when you get back, eh? Take 'er easy."

And with those brutally apathetic words, the connection was lost. Mark felt sadness and frustration wash over him. Though it was never really at the forefront of Mark's mind, he considered Steve his only real friend.

Ironically enough, Steve's tone brought to life the conversation that planted this belief, as it revealed a previously unspoken common bond. It was a passionate disinterest in human emotions that seemed to 'get in the way' of humanity's progress. Not in a terribly sociopathic sense, but in that people often held back scientific developments and the evolution of mankind by letting antiquated and unfounded beliefs cloud their judgment. People didn't look at the facts. They let biases and hunches and gods overrule irrefutable evidence. They behaved irrationally and made irrational rules to appease irrational mindsets. The two conversed in depth about how emotions were relics of a time before the cortex when organisms needed to move fast or die and how they have no place in an advanced civilization. Steve and Mark agreed that emotions are an unfortunate poison that necessarily accompanies an evolved human brain. Emotions are unnecessary; they cause pain and suffering and must be avoided at any cost.

However, the dialogue was but a thick mask of intellect covering a declaration of shared vulnerability. How ironic indeed that its memory trace would pervert the essence of the conversation by gushing forth a deluge of long-avoided melancholy. A single tear plowed its way through Mark's tear duct and breathed in fresh oxygen before it was dispersed in a trail down his cheek. It was not just that Steve didn't seem to care about Mark's very real affliction. Nor was it about how he was seriously losing his grip on reality. More than anything, it was *that* he was experiencing the emotion. The sadness was like a thick muck he was wading through to get back to problem-solving. Try as he did to push through and get a foothold on anything, he could only find more sadness. The harder he pushed, the harder it pushed back. It was a positive feedback loop from which he could not break free and before he knew it, he was in an all-out sob, doubled over with his head in his hands.

Gladys descended from the kitchen following Mark to the couch. Again she consoled him by rubbing up and down his vertebrae in an attempt to calm his shaking, heaving body. It was a mournful cry in which Mark lost his sense of identity. The interaction that had just taken place never before would have affected him as it did. The distance he created from these emotions carved his personality into what it was. It might not have been the healthiest manner of maturity but, nonetheless, he matured. Now he was nothing but a lost little boy, uncertain of who he was and what he could trust.

The ancient, mechanical ringer of the rotary phone began again. With a crushing weight of paranoia thrust upon him, Mark lifted his head from his hands to find Gladys suddenly absent from his side. His eyes darted around the room trying to find her, searching too for evidence that he had awoken into yet another hell. Or was it that he was trapped in a memory loop, with subtle changes in each iteration? Gladys was not present and his blood was running hot now, but the setting had not changed and the phone was ringing.

Mark arose and stumbled toward the ringing phone, fully expecting to hear Steve's voice on the other line once again. He held the phone up to his ear but said nothing.

"Hello?" said a voice on the other line that was not Steve's.

"Bill?" Mark asked, forcing his voice through the irritation.

"Mark?" Bill replied cautiously. "What the hell is going on?"

"Bill," Mark despaired, "I need a doctor."

"What's going on?" Bill repeated.

"I've been having these blackouts…these memory lapses…I can't account for the last several hours of my life," Mark confided, feeling his tears well up to the surface once again. To make it worse, he didn't know if he was about to lose his job. As usual, he couldn't tell if Bill was furious or genuinely concerned. It was hard enough to read his demeanor in person. Over the phone, it was impossible.

"Why do you sound like that?" Bill pried.

"That's just it Bill," Mark squeaked, "I have a vague recollection of being outdoors last night very much underdressed. My mother confirms that but…"

"Mark," Bill interrupted, "if you're having substance abuse issues I completely understand. The amount of stress we've been dealing with lately is enough to drive any man to drink but we need to hold it together for now at least until the end of the month. I've got a guy for pretty much anything so just tell me what you need to pull it through to the end of the month and we can get it but this is Hail Mary time bud. We've got the press conference in two days and no one else here knows what the hell is going on except you."

Press conference? "Press conference?" Mark thought aloud.

"Oh Jesus Christ," Bill mumbled in a restrained panic. "You're not kiddin' huh?" A long silence hung over the conversation whilst both parties thought to themselves. Both men were trying to hold on to their composure with every fiber of their being.

"Hello?" Mark finally said, unsure whether or not the silence was indicative of disconnection.

"OK bud," Bill replied, "I'm sending my doctor over to your house right now. He is my personal doctor and you can speak with him in total confidence. Nothing you tell him is going to affect your position with the company. Whatever is going on with you we just need to make it better fast, fast, fast. We'll take on whatever we can over here without you but that isn't going to be very much. Don't get me wrong bud, take the day and relax once Dr. Beecher works you over but get better because we need you. No pressure, but we've got our thumbs up our asses without you over here." Again a silence fell over the conversation. Bill was speaking so fast and Mark was still fruitlessly wandering through his hippocampus. "Hello?" Bill finally said.

"OK Bill," Mark answered. "Thank you."

"Get well bud," Bill said. "Bye Mark."

"Bye Bill."

Paranoia crept up Mark's spine once more. *Why was Bill not psychotically enraged? Who is this doctor? What went on during this unaccounted for time? Press conference?* Despite the haunting suspicions that preyed on his mind like napalm, the promise of seeing a doctor was a welcomed comfort.

Mark handed the phone back up on the base's waiting switch hook. After a moment of quiet introspection, he instinctively called out to Gladys as if she were definitely somewhere in the house. "Can you elaborate on what happened to me?" Mark laboriously squeaked. "Dad found me in the deer blind half frozen? Is that what you told me?" He knew full well that is what she said.

"Yep," she answered, suddenly appearing behind him, "he carried you in and said that he found you out there sleeping in the blind."

"Neither of you thought to get a doctor or drive me to the hospital?" Mark questioned.

"Now what sense would that make, dear?" Gladys asked,

"It's an hour drive to the hospital where we would have just been waiting and waiting. You would have been just as cold if not colder, just as sick if not sicker, and shivering just as hard if not harder. We might still be there waiting for Pete's sake. Even then, they would have just given you a heating pad and sent you on your way. Seems like a big waste of time to me."

As callous as Mark perceived her attitude, she was probably right. They probably would have been waiting long enough that he would have died if it were that severe. Though he knew to never give a hypothermic patient heat pads and the hospital may have been able to perform cardiopulmonary bypass, he didn't bother correcting her, because the logic of keeping him home was still sound.

Plus, he had to keep reminding himself, ever since he returned from college, his folks seemed like they might as well have come over on the Mayflower. They were aware of technology but at the same time, never found much use for it. That was the first time the telephone had rung in months. They didn't even really care to use electricity unless Gladys was toasting some bread for her enormous breakfasts.

Mark remembered his father telling him about a time he was roofing and jumped down off of the last few rungs of the ladder, impaling his foot on a nail in a discarded board as he landed. He said that he pulled the nail out, still attached to the board, wrapped his foot in an oily rag and continued working for twelve more hours until the roof was finished. "That's just the way it was done in those days," he told him. "Folks would rather risk death than go back on their word." With some odd sense of false nostalgia, he missed the old days. Something about, 'the way it was done' was appealing, like somehow it was undoubtedly the right thing to do, with no real logical explanation for *why* it was.

Mark had always felt that he had lost some part of himself when he went off to college. He never had any desire to leave Ash County, but had to honor his father's wishes. In that way, leaving was the right thing to do and satisfied an older way of thinking. But since he returned he has felt out of place in this old way of thinking. Living on campus amongst folks who have never even seen a piece of grass, Mark had little in common with his classmates and kept to himself as much as he could. But in incidental eavesdropping in libraries, in lecture halls before class, in the cafeteria, or any other place students congregated, he learned what the world was like outside of Ash County. People had no respect, were constantly late, talked during lectures, dropped doors on you, didn't say 'please' or 'thank you,' and otherwise didn't care about you unless you could do something for them. In being much more plugged in to the zeitgeist, he realized that this behavior was not confined to campus, but was acceptable in all the world outside of Ash County. To say the least, he didn't like it and couldn't wait to get back home.

But when Mark did return to Ash, he discovered that the people in the town where he grew up were different now. *Their* behavior was abnormal. Risking a gangrenous foot to finish a roofing job in the allotted time now seemed nothing short of insanity. What was worse, it didn't *seem* insane, it *was* insane. A man's word, his pride, his character, his conviction, his honor were things worth *dying* for in this little corner of the world. The fact that Mark now *knew* that this was inappropriate behavior haunted him to his core. He would give anything to return to life before college, before he knew what the world was really like. He would have been perfectly happy with the simpler way of life, candling fresh eggs in the stock room or bailing hay for his neighbors in exchange for a couple of fresh apple pies. But it was too late for that now. There was no going back. As his father always lamented, "You can't turn a pickle back into a cucumber."

A few more moments of quiet introspection in the living room and mysterious stirrings in the kitchen passed before there were four solid knocks on the door. "That couldn't be the doctor already could it?" Gladys asked rhetorically? Knocks on the door happened only slightly more often than phone rings. Gladys wiped her hands on her apron and went to the door. When she opened it, she found two men the likes of whom she'd never seen. Both men were dressed in solid black ensembles almost as if they were in uniform. The one with the gloves must have been the driver as he stood nearest the mirror-windowed Lincoln Town Car. The one standing at the door wore round black glasses that barely covered his pupils and white-blond, slicked back hair. The pair must have come straight from an audition for the parts of Nazis in a World War II movie.

"Mark?" the ghoulish figure asked breathing out a thick cloud of condensation and walking straight past Gladys. The doctor entered the dimly lit Deremer home but did not remove his tiny, shaded spectacles or his drizzle-covered trench coat. A quick survey of the room and the faint scent of vomit led him to the silhouette of a bundled up body stuffed into the corner of the couch.

"Good morning Mark," the doctor said as he seated himself onto the table in front of him. "Do you remember me? My name is Dr. Beecher. You must be pretty integral to the operation down there. Mr. Wildeboer cashed in a pretty big favor to have me come down here like this." With this introduction, Mark already assumed that he disliked Doctor Beecher. He was the perfect embodiment of everything he was just stewing about. His arrogance cast a shadow over the entire Deremer farm. It was a reminder of so many college professors with a false sense of accomplishment that made him feel small for the sole purpose of making themselves feel big; a clear overcompensation for a lack of any real achievement. But even through the added nausea that Dr. Beecher induced, Mark greeted him politely.

"Good morning, Dr. Beecher," Mark squawked. "Have we met?"

"Bill did tell me you were having memory issues," the doctor said, as if that were a proper replacement for the word 'yes.'

"Yes sir," Mark replied, ignoring the doctor's audacity.

"What happened to your voice?"

"I fell asleep outside last night. I imagine it is acute laryngitis."

"Were you drinking or using any illegal substances?"

"No sir."

"Why were you outside?"

"I have no recollection of the last twelve, or so, hours. But Bill made it seem like I may have lost more time based on our conversation."

"What did he say to make you think that?"

"He mentioned details of yesterday that I did not recall. I spoke with another colleague as well who strengthened my suspicions."

"Open up and say, ahh." The whole time the two were speaking, Dr. Beecher was giving Mark a preliminary examination with tools from a large black leather bag, "Did you hit your head recently?"

"I don't think so. But I don't remember."

"Hmm," Dr. Beecher grunted after making his final checks, "have you recently had surgery or any other trauma, any at all?"

"I don't think so," Mark replied hoarsely. "But again, I

can't be sure."

"Mark," Dr. Beecher said gravely, "I'd like to take you up to St. Catherine's to have a few more tests done."

"St. Catherine's?" Mark asked in disbelief. "That's in Feuerstadt! That's a three-hour drive!"

"I know," the doctor said smugly. "There are some more tests I need to conduct in order to make an accurate diagnosis."

"What kinds of tests?"

"Well your voice is not a symptom of acute laryngitis and I want to be sure…"

"What do you think it is?"

"Your left vocal fold seems to be partially paralyzed. If you are experiencing memory loss…"

"You think I might have had a stroke?"

"I don't know if I would call it a full blown stroke but you may have some type of viral infection. I just want to rule that out, get a closer look, and maybe have a colleague observe."

"OK," Mark hesitated a moment. "Let's go to St. Catherine's"

As much as Mark did not want to go, he could not ignore that in the past few days he had blacked out for more than just a few instances, each time worse than the last. Additionally, with every blackout he was losing more and more time; not to mention the newly-accompanying, hellishly-real nightmares. In fact, he realized that his silent prayers for escape were being answered as the now familiar lightheadedness took hold once more. His vision was again becoming cloudy as a function of the intense fear seeping in to his psyche. His diaphragm tightened painfully, his face lost most of its blood, and his teeth began chattering, but he spoke clearly the words, "I need help," before he lost consciousness yet again.

"He's awake," Mark heard a voice say as he regained consciousness. *At least I avoided that car ride.* As many times as it kept happening, Mark was learning to cope with the stress of waking up from a blackout. Even now, waking up face to face with the white plastic surface of the inside of an MRI machine, he was calm. Right away he knew where he was from the telltale clicking and swishing. If not for that, he might have guessed he was in some type of new age casket, inside which they put lights. Though he had some brief show-and-tell type experiences in his college classes, this was the first time he had ever been inside one.

"Try to remain calm if you can Mark," he heard the familiar voice of Dr. Beecher say. "You're nearly done and then we can talk." Mark understood that the doctor was just being cautious, but he was exhausted and too tired to even acknowledge that he heard the command.

Mark transitioned from twilight once more as the mechanical movement of the MRI table crawled out of the coffin and back into a dimly lit room. The jolting stop of the table was enough to wake him completely. Fighting through the torturous aching of his muscles, he turned his head to the left to find a beautiful young nurse holding out her hand to help him off the table. It was a strong yet feminine hand that accompanied the intoxicating scent of its owner. Mark helped her lift him off the bed and found himself flustered and nervous when he sat up and came face to face with her. It was all he could do to hold back his awkward smile, looking away from her in a vain attempt to hide it. But when he glanced back at her, he found her smiling too, and much less embarrassed by the situation. Mark felt a little less uncomfortable and let out a slight laugh as he hopped to his feet. The sudden rise in blood pressure made every bit of his skin flush.

But the romance was cut short in catching a glimpse of Dr. Beecher from his workstation behind the 4 by 8 foot piece of glass in the wall. The unmistakeable look of bad news was written all over his face. But he looked away from that awful reality and back at the almond-eyed beauty before him, who still was showing an impressive mouthful of teeth behind darkly-shaded lips. "Come with me and I'll take you to see the doctor," she said in a friendly voice.

"OK," Mark replied, unable to come up with any other words. Mark had basically no experience in matters of the opposite sex and felt completely embarrassed and uncomfortable, with the strange additional presence of enjoyment. He followed behind her out of the room and into the hallway, breathing in the hypnotic fragrance of her long, black hair as it flowed with the movement of her walk, to the office in which Dr. Beecher waited with his news.

"Dr. Beecher?" she said in an acknowledgement of patient hand-off. She and Mark locked eyes once more before she finally turned and walked away and then suddenly was thrust into this world of potential bad news which seemed to lay thick in the air of the small, fluorescent-lit, white office behind the MRI.

"Mark," Dr. Beecher began in an unmistakable tone of diagnosis revelation, "I'm sure you don't remember much about the car ride over here, but you seem to be aware of your surroundings at this moment, yes?"

"Yes," Mark said with a minute tinge of sarcasm, "I am aware of my surroundings."

"I spoke with some of your colleagues on the ride over here to get an idea of you and your lifestyle," Dr. Beecher continued, ignoring Mark's sarcasm. "From what I discovered in speaking with them, as well as Bill, is that your life has changed a tremendous amount recently. It sounds to me like you've been put in charge of the lives and livelihoods of thousands of people. Those thousands of people are counting on you and they don't even know it. In addition to that, there is a time limit on those lives and livelihoods, a fast-approaching time limit. I imagine that that kind of thing is not easy to live with, especially if you didn't exactly sign up for it. The stress of that burden that you have been carrying around with you for a number of weeks now is surely starting to catch up with you. Do you remember the last time you slept before now?"

"I do not," Mark replied, getting more annoyed with each passing second of communication.

"In the beginning I was absolutely certain that this whole thing was stress related. No one at EnviroCore knows anything about your personal life and no one at EnviroCore knew where you had been going after work for the past week or so. Turns out you haven't been leaving work at all. Security footage revealed that your car never left the lot and at night you did not leave your office. This further suggests that you have a predisposition for stress-related physical reactions; or rather, you've had one for a while and it took this level of stress to finally ignite them."

"How long did you say I have been doing this, sleeping at work?" Mark interrupted after a long and patient period of silence and attention.

"I'll get to that," the doctor quickly replied as if he were on a roll and could not be bothered. "I was quite sure that the reactions and the amnesia were due to an extremely high stress level and a few days off would have done you a world of good. However, in the interest of being thorough, I ordered the MRI and lab work anyway just to be sure that nothing internal was out of the ordinary." The doctor paused to direct Mark's attention to the image of the coronal slice of his brain on his computer screen. "All of the people that I spoke with mentioned your intelligence in some manner; so I am not going to beat around the bush." The doctor used his pen to point to a few small, brightly contrasted outlines in Mark's cortical sulci. It looked like someone had poured glowing white dye into a few of the fissures on the surface of Mark's brain. His heart, however, had managed to find its way into his bowels, as his analysts handed down the diagnosis before the doctor could speak again.

"These bright spots here," Dr. Beecher said tapping on the screen, "are something other than cerebrospinal fluid, meaning something has crossed the blood-brain barrier."

"Meningitis," Mark whispered.

"The good news is that it still looks like it is in the very early stages," the doctor quickly blurted out, as if Mark had sworn in church, "and we can't be certain until we get the results of the cultures. We'll also do a spinal tap before we jump to conclusions but in the meantime I'll give you some antibiotics."

"How long have I been sleeping at work?" Mark asked again, ignoring the bombshell hanging on the X-ray illuminator.

"I don't think you have been sleeping," Beecher answered. "Many bacterial meningitis patients experience insomnia. In addition to the short term memory loss, the vocal cord paralysis, the vomiting, and the fact that you are a bacteriologist, these scans put the finishing touches on a pretty complete picture."

Mark could feel his stomach looking for something to throw up. It was not so much the sickness as it was the doctor's smug attitude. He appeared to be thoroughly pleased with himself; like he was some kind of know-it-all third grader who finished his times tables test before anyone. Suddenly the churning of his stomach had stopped and gave way to a new feeling. His blood suddenly felt electric and his breaths became shorter. His muscles felt charged like he could shoot lightning bolts from his fists. Without warning, Mark's right arm flung forward and shot the computer's keyboard against the wall and out of its port in the computer. Before Dr. Beecher could react, Mark's left hand grabbed him by the collar and shoved him back up against some lockers. "Why don't we get on with the spinal tap?" The doctor was horrified and shaking but still managed to keep his composure.

"Yes Mark," he smiled and raised his hands in submission, "let's do."

Behind those tiny, shaded glasses sat the eyes of cornered prey, waiting to be torn to ribbons by the eager predator. But in the milliseconds it took to process that pitiful sight, Mark was struck breathless by overwhelming empathy. Seeing the doctor's eyes finally revealed behind those ridiculous frames instilled a sense of familiarity; like they were longtime friends. Suddenly, Mark realized the absurdity of the overreaction.

Mark's iron grip on the collar of Dr. Beecher's lab coat abruptly relaxed as his senses returned. "My God," Mark said in a clear voice, "I'm so sorry." His hands slowly retracted from the vicinity of the assault and fell to his hips. "I don't know what came over me," Mark explained frantically. "I'm so sorry." His voice returned to its squawking as if he had suddenly remembered that he had partial vocal cord paralysis.

"It's alright Mark," the short yet intense threat had allowed the doctor to remember his bedside manner. "I completely understand that this is not easy news to take, especially on top of everything else."

"I know that but…" Mark started.

"Now that's enough. Not another word," the doctor interrupted, clearly taking back the dominant position. "I don't blame you for your reaction. I commend you for not tearing my head off." He figured joking would further diffuse the awkward situation. "But this brings me to the puzzle piece that doesn't seem to fit. Have you recently been prescribed steroids or have you been taking them on your own?"

It took a few extra seconds for Mark's analysts to dig before saying with certainty, "No."

"One result stands out to me that is not typical for a blood test suggesting meningitis," the doctor furrowed his brow. "Your testosterone levels are higher than I've ever seen. Normal levels for an adult male are between 300 and 1,100 nanograms per deciliter of blood. You are at just over 5,000. I'm going to take another sample and if it is correct, we need to do some more digging. Some increase is normal under extremely stressful and acute conditions like jumping out of an airplane. Still, it would be nowhere near this unless you were injecting anabolic steroids at a dangerously reckless dose."

Mark took his time. The prefrontal analysts were conducting massive search efforts into the probable cause of this increase. All signs were pointing to coming clean about his hibernative abilities and multiple states of consciousness, to possibly aid the doctor in coming to a more satisfying diagnosis. But despite the threat to his health and the safety of those around him, what came back was an irrational response. *Don't tell him.*

"I have no idea," Mark finally spoke.

"OK," Beecher sighed, "I know you probably won't take my advice to take some time off to calm down. But nonetheless, it is my advice. Let's go ahead and get your lumbar puncture taken care of if you don't mind. Find Shawna at reception. She will take you to get prepped."

She was already walking up to him when he entered the hall. "You ready?" she smiled, forming two deep dimples on each cheek. But Mark could not speak. Again his heart began punching the back of his sternum and he could only manage the shy, awkward smile of an embarrassed child.

Shawna led him to an examination room and had him lie sideways on the bed. The soft feminine fingertips of this goddess brushed against his bare back as she untied his paper gown in preparation for the iodine scrub. This contact immediately engorged his corpora cavernosa, as well as his confidence.

"Shawna," Mark said firmly.

"Yes," the woman replied.

"I'm Mark," as trite as it was, it was all he could come up with to start a dialogue.

"I know," she laughed. Her scent was unnervingly tantalizing. But he felt strong, like a knight entering a dragon's lair, all he had to do was keep going. She continued to work behind him, gathering the tools for the sterile field. The blood raced through Mark's veins and his skin responded by turning a bright red and opening its pores. He was scared to death, but he loved it, like a first-time heroin user.

"He just told me I might die," Mark blurted out, unsure of how to continue.

"Meningitis isn't always fatal and it's still in early stage, if that's what it is. He did just say that the diagnosis was preliminary." Mark was unsure of how to respond. The analysts in his brain were reeling from his uncharacteristic behavior. Their reports were unusable as none pertained to the next right thing to say. *Is she crazy? I'll bet she is really smart. Am I in love with her? What is love? What would our children look like? She didn't*

156

even pretend to be sympathetic. She's still smiling! She is quite sure of herself. She is gorgeous. What would happen if I told her...?

"You are absolutely gorgeous," Mark blurted out without a single instant of hesitation. None of Mark's internal analysts had produced any reliable data that would have previously stopped him from making such a bold remark. Shawna's face lit up and her lips again gave way to a thousand perfect teeth. Each one set in perfect proportion to the rest. The radiant white of each tooth was natural; not a false bluish tint of constant whitening, but the result of a lifetime of good oral hygiene.

In the back of Mark's mind, he found it curious that with all the billions of nodes of information that poured in as usual, what was making it through the filter of consciousness were all the features of her face that made her beautiful; all magnified in stunning detail. The way her eyes closed almost shut from the cheek muscles of her magnificent smile pushing them upward, the unusually perfect shape of her nose, the way her eyebrows lined up exactly to her pinnae. This is to say nothing of her elegant figure, which further seduced him even from under her scrubs.

"I want you to come home with me," Mark blurted as Shawna turned to notice he was no longer lying on his side. This time, a couple of analysts in the back tried to stop the words from leaving but were overruled by this unique and overwhelming desire. More analysts began questioning the decision as Shawna betrayed her feelings with a sharp downward eyebrow flex. For a brief moment, Mark entertained the idea that something was horribly wrong. It seemed that the analysts that represented a reserved and rational mindset were being overthrown by a new lot which set aside societal norms and self-restraint in favor of having sex with this female. But the moment was brief; now gone and forgotten. In its place were varying fantasies of her naked body in various poses and sexual positions. His staunch foundation of decency was being overpowered. The thought that it was unacceptable behavior made it that much more enticing as he sat waiting for her to answer the request.

"I'm seeing someone," she said politely, still smiling, "but I'm really flattered." He should have been grateful that she handled such an odd remark the way she did. But Mark's unbridled confidence would not accept that as a valid answer and he searched his archives for a rebuttal.

"I don't care," was the best he could do. Still she handled it politely. Not speaking, but giving a playful look of disapproval. There were clear indications from the analysts now that Mark should quit and that persisting could result in negative consequences. But this only spurred him on more. The rejection only meant he wasn't trying hard enough and that in the end, she would see it his way. "I'm not kidding," he kept on, "I've never felt this way to be completely honest with you. I know this sounds crazy but I need you to come home with me right now."

"Like I said," her smile now absent as she spoke, "I'm really flattered but I'm seeing someone."

"Shawna," Mark said as he stood from the bed, "I fuckin' need to be inside of you." His arm reached up to grab hers as she backed away from him.

"Listen man," she shouted, "you're barkin' up the wrong tree! Understand?"

Her abrupt shift from goddess to demon was enough to call the rational analysts back to the forefront. His confidence fell like a planned demolition, piling up neatly in a heap of rubble. The blood quickly drained from his face and penis, leaving him in a full-body droop. Shawna stormed out of the room and then, as if the feeling of rejection wasn't enough, panic began to set in. *They are going to call the police. What was I thinking?*

Mark began breathing fast, short breaths. The inevitable fainting spell was sure to follow, but it did not. He paced the room, again praying for the terrible emotions to be interrupted by a loss of consciousness, but this time the prayers were left unanswered. Like a penance for ignoring his own sensibilities, he would be forced to endure all of these dreadful feelings and reactions that accompanied the situation he put himself in. *Why?! God damn it!*

An agonizing five or so minutes went by with Mark alone with his thoughts, pacing the floor in his self-made prison cell of guilt and confusion.

"Mark?" Dr. Beecher snuck into the room in his aseptic garb. Mark whipped his body around to acknowledge the startling presence of the doctor.

"Are you calling the cops?" Mark squeaked.

"No Mark," Beecher said, "I explained what was going on and she's giving you a pass. Why don't you just lie down again like she had you and we'll get this over with?"

Relieved, Mark gladly took the fetal position on his left side once more. The iodine dripped down his back while the doctor encircled the insertion site. The local anesthetic applied, Mark was numb by the time the nine centimeter spinal needle slid into the subarachnoid space between the L3 and L4 vertebrae. Dr. Beecher waited patiently for the expected clear cerebrospinal fluid to drip down from the needle hub and into his waiting collection tube. Instead, it was a cloudy green fluid that bubbled out. "What the…" blurted Beecher in bewilderment, unable to contain his shock. The

159

doctor knew that a condition called hyperbilirubinemia, which indicated physiologic jaundice in newborns, would show itself in this manner. Also, he recalled a case of green CSF being reported following a ventriculoperitoneal shunt infection. Mark fitting neither of those cases, he looked down at the collection as if the martyrs were crying out for vengeance.

Meanwhile, the abrupt change in intracranial pressure caused Mark an instant and severe headache. This was followed closely by lightheadedness and nausea. As the lights went dim once more, the last conscious thought was the sight of transparent, red projectile vomit flowing river-like down the edge of the examination bed.

The Saturnalia

"That was quite the display," Gladys said bitterly.

The transition was nearly instantaneous. No sooner did he lose consciousness than did he wake up in the town car. A vague recollection washed over him of Beecher's voice giving him instructions. However, the memory's voice was too muffled to understand. In his hand he noticed a brown paper bag containing several prescriptions. The pills settled in their bottles as he held up the bag to read the contents.

"What?" Mark asked nonchalantly.

"All this," she said waving her arms at the situation, "was all of this really necessary?"

"The doctor said I have a brain infection," Mark said dryly. "It can be pretty serious. They just want to be cautious. You don't think I have been acting strangely?"

"You always act strangely," Gladys huffed. "You take after your father."

The car ride home was mostly silent. Gladys's disapproval was thick in the air and stifled most of the conversation. It gave Mark a chance to ponder the curious events that had just played out in the hospital. The violent outburst on Dr. Beecher, the unwavering sexual motivation that made forcible advances at his nurse; both could be considered assault. Mark conducted a thorough search through stacks of memories and came up with no comparable situation. He has always been attracted to women as any healthy, red-blooded American male out of Middleton, Michigan should be, but never enough to make him forget that he was a respectable citizen. Same goes with the manhandling of Beecher who had done nothing except for being a smug asshole.

Mark allowed his thoughts to drift. Aside from this trip to the hospital, the most unsettling about the whole situation was the amount of time he had lost. Try as he did, he could not find one shred of a memory which would recount the tale of these missing moments of existence. As far as he was concerned, only a few hours had gotten away from him. But according to the conversations he had with Bill, Steve, and Dr. Beecher, it had been much longer. *Very troubling indeed.*

What has been going on in the lab? Mark didn't even know what questions to ask, or who to ask. If things were moving as fast as Bill suggested, it's possible that the whole restructuring had already taken place. *What was that Bill said about a press conference? And what did Steve say? Multiple S curves?* He would just have to take some time to review what had already been completed and let everyone know the truth. There was no other choice.

The aggregate of self that Mark had pieced together from memories he did have from the time he had been taken from his office in bacteriology to now was a grim showcase of the meningitis that he was now convinced he had. Under this diagnosis, everything makes sense. But this realization was not without consequence and tears began, once again, to well up in Mark's eyes as he considered his own mortality. His files on meningitis reminded him that it was not just *that* he would die, but it was that the last days leading up to his death would be agonizing and humiliating. The physical symptoms had subsided for now and had been replaced with a much worse emotional pain.

Mark reflected on the fact that at some point in his life he had made the decision, conscious or not, that he would distance himself from emotions as much as possible. One way or another, emotions always ended up harming him and taking a piece of him along. In his best effort to leave them behind, he chose to experience life in what he considered the opposite point of view: logic. If he could think logically about each and every situation, he could have distance from harmful emotional experiences and thereby live a more stable, less chaotic life.

Mark disliked change. He disliked anything that was seemingly uncontrollable and unpredictable, which his emotions definitely were. What he did enjoy was logic and a succinct explanation. In time, a minimal sense of enjoyment came with discovering when one thing led to another or when things made sense. He liked order and organization. More than that, he liked finding a way to organize something. This is why he gravitated towards biology in school because it seemed to have the least amount of order. All other subjects had a good amount of order already in place or at least had already made significant progress. But, comparatively speaking, biology seemed to be making the least amount of progress. This was due, in Mark's opinion, to the lack of order. They still didn't have solid taxonomic structure of species or even a widely accepted definition of the word. Mark could see that there is order underlying it all somewhere. It was like a billion piece jigsaw puzzle all piled up for humanity to solve. A corner was started here and a frame had been started there. But it was still mostly just a pile of pieces that needed to be put together which was just the kind of tedium that Mark was into.

But emotions, to Mark, had always just gotten in the way of order and organization, what with the irrationality and all. To Mark, it was like throwing the puzzle pieces up in the air and hoping that they would land correctly. It was clear now why Mark had given up on them long ago. Instead of calmly discussing the problem at hand with Dr. Beecher, he chose to throw the pieces up and punish him for simply showing him his diagnosis. Now he had surely made the impression that he was unstable, and would be treated differently from here on out. As with Shawna, Mark simply thought that if she could see how badly he wanted to make love to her that she would be attracted to him too. Now, since the emotion had passed, it was absurd that the two might magically fall in love during his aseptic preparation for a spinal tap. With patience, he could have made a connection through social media or kept in touch otherwise and, in a more innocuous fashion, persisted with occasional kind greetings and other subtle reminders that he was still interested. But this is not the way of emotion. Emotion wants now. Emotion has no idea what patience is. Emotion thinks that if the goal is not met in this instant, the chance will never come again. It turns people into lunatics in every sense of the word. Once emotion takes hold of people, they can very easily lose their grip on reality.

"Doctors aren't always right you know," Gladys finally spoke.

"I know," Mark said, "but this one seems right."

"He *seems* right," she sneered, "that doesn't mean he is."

"I've been diagnosed with bacterial meningitis," Mark said bluntly. "Given my behavior, my symptoms, and the MRI images I would say the diagnosis is correct."

"You're a smart boy, Mark," Gladys reasoned, "but you are not a doctor."

"No, I am not," he responded, "but neither are you."

"Have you ever actually met anyone with meningitis?" Gladys hounded. "Have you ever seen anything outside of a book that can show you for certain that that's what you've got? That man could be trying to scare you into paying him a wheelbarrow full of money. Have you ever considered that you may just have the flu?"

"I know what meningitis is," he protested. "I know that it could be fatal if I just go on ignoring it."

"All you know is what other people have written down for you," she said coldly. "That's all anybody knows nowadays. Go out and live your life on your terms and don't let the thoughts of others become your own. Have the courage to think for yourself."

"You can't learn all there is to be known on your own," Mark squawked. "There is too much knowledge. You have to trust people and you have to trust the collective knowledge."

"You can't learn *all* there is to be known no matter how much help you've got," Gladys declared. "You can learn all you *need* to know all by yourself."

It was now clear to Mark this was an unwinnable argument, as most arguments with Gladys were. Mark knew that it was not worth trying to make his point to her because her mind was always made up about everything. Also, the troubling fact remains that, she was not wrong. It was a reminder of that all too disturbing paradox that Mark never could reconcile: two people with differing opinions can be right according to their perspective. It was the one variable that could never be controlled. The mere act of observing an experiment adds subjectivity. Objectivity is a concept that can never be too rigorously applied and all scientists, all people for that matter, accept some degree of assumption regardless of subject. We are all locked inside of our own heads and can only know the truth as far as our individual senses and imaginations can take us. As painful as it is, all truth is relative.

When they pulled up in the long driveway on the Deremer property it was already dusk. The two Deremers emerged from the Town Car and waved to the driver as he circled back down the other side of the long driveway. Gladys did not look up as she walked up the rickety old deck stairs and into the house. His mother's attitude added to the bitter cold in the unseasonable April air, making Mark's breath condense upon exhaling. *When is it going to finally warm up for good?*

Mark opened the front door to find his father's dusty jungle boots in their usual spot, where they had been since he got home from Vietnam, unworn and untouched. Even so, Mark was careful not to disturb them, kicking a thin layer of snow off of his shoes before entering the house. He removed his coat, shoes, and socks in the mud room before the kitchen through the second door because in addition to the pervasive cold, a Michigan winter's precipitation is never mild, no matter its form.

"Ceftriaxone, Dexamethasone, and Metoprolol," Mark read off the three pill bottles that spilled out of the brown paper bag and onto the countertop. The antibiotic, Ceftriaxone, was the only one that made sense to him. Dexamethasone, a steroid typically prescribed to meningitis patients, seemed inappropriate considering the absurd testosterone levels. The beta blocker, Metopropolol, may actually contribute to the fainting spells. Perhaps Beecher felt it was more important to control the anxiety in the short term. *Or maybe that wasn't it.* The paranoia that comes with not being able to trust your own judgments surely did not alleviate the anxiety. *What if he knows exactly what he's doing?*

In an attempt to ease his mind in some way, Mark made the decision to give no credence to any thought that things were not exactly as they should be. No matter what comes, no matter how far his mind wandered, he would accept what his brain told him was reality. *No one is out to get me. The doctor's logic is sound.* Instinctually, he knew that this was a dangerous, if not impossible oath to swear. But until he could gather more intelligence, it was his best option.

Mark went into his bedroom to begin his research into meningitis; preparing for the night by changing out of his clothes and into his usual and more comfortable boxer shorts, t-shirt, and flannel. It was a ritual which, despite having always known that it was a ritual, became apparent to him on this night that it was. On the outside, he never put much stock in the arbitrary chants, festivals, or sacrifices made by illogical and primitive people. But in this moment, he realized that on the inside, he had been participating in them all his life.

For years, Mark would end the day by changing garments, firing up the computer, and studying; gaining an ever-greater insight into that which he did not understand. If he added up all the hours he spent in pursuit of understanding the world, he could go bumper-to-bumper with any shaman, cleric, or high priest. Instead of rejecting this ritualistic behavior by making excuses for it, justifying it as different, or otherwise intellectualizing his way out of his hypocrisy, he embraced it.

While the ten-year-old computer continued to whine and crackle its way through booting, Mark went to the kitchen for a tall glass of water with which to complete the ritual's preparation. Tonight, he would enter a new sacrament into the liturgy: taking his pills. One by one, he dumped the night's dosage into his palm. They were to represent the turning over of a new leaf; his acceptance of his situation and his resolve to quit scrutinizing everything so closely. With a deliberate tossing of the pills onto his tongue, the subsequent upturn of the water glass, and the spilling of the water over the pills into his gullet, a rite of passage was complete.

Mark returned to the handmade desk in his room with a fresh glass of water to find the computer still in the final stages of booting. The home screen was loaded but the frenzied clicks of the hard drive were not quite finished. In the meantime, Mark examined the pill bottles again to reread instructions, side effects, anything he may have missed. All three medications were manufactured by Axiom Pharmaceuticals, as was evident by the prominent logo in the lower right corner of each label. All three had similar side effects: drowsiness, nausea, headache, dizziness, confusion, and mood swings.

"Great," Mark scoffed aloud as he aligned the bottles neatly in a row on his desk. The computer's clicking had slowed considerably but was still not complete. Mark folded his arms across his chest impatiently and leaned back in his chair, awaiting the silence of a complete boot.

A loud slamming noise shook Mark from sleep, if you could call it that. In one blink, the sun had completed its journey back to the eastern horizon. The computer's screen was black, but its fan was whistling away; a clear indication that it had been idle for longer than the selected screen saver time. In addition, his water glass was just as full as he remembered. Beneath the radar, his analysts were incoherent, but his instincts were shrieking the paranoid utterances of a universally understood tongue. The accompanying panic reminded Mark of the futility of the oath he swore last night. Axonally speaking, instinctual impulses had far less distance to cover and their reports always made it to the surface before a rational analysis. Though he could not reconcile why he dove headlong into stage 4 non-REM deep sleep, it was perfectly clear why ignoring his instincts would be impossible.

Once he gathered his nerves somewhat, the analysts finally concluded that the meds were responsible for the uncharacteristic crash. It was not a blackout and he had not lost a significant amount of time. Rather, it was merely a departure from what *he* considered normal, beginning his assimilation with the rest of the human flock. Put simply, Mark had fallen asleep.

Though, his suspicions were aroused once more after his morning routine by the rare yet familiar sight of his folks at the kitchen table, laughing and playfully enjoying an immense breakfast platter. *It's only déjà vu.* He joined the other two Deremers at the table amongst the plethora of breakfast meats. Gladys appeared to be more cheerful this morning anyway; much more so than the car ride home yesterday.

"I heard you snoring from your room last night. You fell asleep in your chair," Gladys said softly. "You must've been exhausted. Take it easy in there today, okay? Don't work too hard."

"Yes ma'am," Mark replied, gnawing on a huge strip of bacon.

"Son," his father followed, "don't be afraid to tell them you need some more time off. Your health is more important than saving the company, believe it or not."

"I'm not afraid," was Mark's response, and with it, he uprooted himself from the hundred-year-old wooden farmhouse table, grabbed a piece of toast off the pile, and started out the door without another word.

The air outside was brisk but the sun was warm on his skin. As most Michigan residents have accepted, spring comes when it comes and getting your hopes up won't help. Climbing into the musty old white station wagon, Mark prayed. Lo and behold, the ignition gods smiled down upon him and with an abrupt burst in RPM, Mark started west towards EnviroCore.

Mark could not remember looking at the clock before he fell asleep last night. Time was another sense that seemed to be malfunctioning as a result of this mystery ailment. At any rate, he felt like he got no sleep at all. Usually, if the situation calls for it, he will remain alert as part of his self-described 'hibernations.'

With that thought, he considered one of the meningitis symptoms Beecher had mentioned, 'insomnia.' Suddenly, it clicked. *It has to be!* Desperate to explain his prolonged time loss, he resolved that it *had* to be the longest hibernative state of his life. It was the metabolic decrease, his excretory shut off, and all of those other curious system adaptations that *had* to be to blame for it all.

This 'ability' did not happen overnight. It took many years for Mark to unconsciously hone and perhaps this was a sign that he was getting too good at it and that his control of it was getting away from him. If he was awake the entire duration of these lost weeks, as Dr. Beecher alluded to, then as far as Mark was concerned, the case was closed. No meningitis. After all, Beecher was not aware of this special talent. If he were, surely the good doctor would come to the same conclusion.

These rationalizations that rattled around Mark's skull were blatantly trying to bury a body that wasn't quite dead. The MRI scan of his glowing sulci was the smoking gun which could not be defended by the hibernation. Not yet anyway. Nonetheless, it was one less check in the meningitis box. All he had to do was ask for the security tapes. Even if the cameras did not catch him working around the clock, as long as he was there, that was evidence enough. "Damn you Gladys," he said out loud trying to believe that his mother had won the argument.

And then Mark did something he had never done. Like a child pushing off the wall in the deep end, he believed in something for which he had no evidence; the unthinkable. As much as he did not want to turn away from logic, he wanted meningitis less. A new page turned, feeling his way through the dark, he went with his gut, and let blind faith lead him into the deep end. As Mark found his new parking space, he looked down at the giant 'Axiom' label on his three pill bottles in the passenger seat, and exited the vehicle, leaving them behind.

Upon the security cameras catching Mark enter the premises, a domino effect of phone calls fell across select staff members of EnviroCore starting with the first to Bill from Large Marge, the ex-rugby player security guard usually manning the guard shack. Within minutes, the conference room upstairs was filled with executives awaiting Mark's arrival. Just inside the glass doors at the turnstiles was a large and intimidating member of the security staff wearing a brand new uniform complete with a shiny black pistol belt and Kevlar vest. "Mr. Deremer, will you follow me upstairs please?" the man said in an unexpectedly low-pitched voice.

"Yes I will Gerald," Mark said, reading the gold nameplate on the man's uniform. Mark had some idea of what was about to happen. Even though they surely sent the most intimidating guard to escort him, he was sure it was some type of happy, surprise occasion; a get well soon/glad you're back kind of thing. Or maybe even something better.

After several minutes, a short elevator ride and a five-minute walk brought them to the oversized and elaborately decorated glass and metal doors through which he walked the first day of his promotion to Vice President of Operations, though the Sciencia brand had been removed and replaced with the stylish and futuristic-looking EnviroCore name. The brand looked familiar. And why wouldn't it? Mark had probably seen it dozens of times in the previous weeks but he apparently had never really acknowledged it in his torpor, as he still beheld it as if it were brand new. Sticking to his decision, he accepted everything, all these changes, as they came. The place looked much cleaner since he last remembered and the security uniforms were a nice touch. Mark remained optimistic that he would be able to transition back into his role with relative ease.

"Right through there, sir," Gerald said guiding him to the door.

"Thanks a lot, Gerald," Mark said with a smile. He looked in to see a team of both familiar and unfamiliar faces rising from their seats. As soon as his hand grasped the handle, the room erupted in applause. It was a great feeling. It might have been greater if he could remember what he had done to deserve it, but that didn't stop Mark from enjoying every second of it. Amidst the cheers and claps he made his way around the table, shaking hands with everyone he passed by.

"What in the world is this for?" Mark asked the first person in the line. But, unsatisfyingly, the unfamiliar face simply laughed as if he did not hear the question. He continued his walk around the large marble table, shaking every outstretched hand with a false enthusiasm that hid his confusion. At the end of the line was Bill, smiling his usual maniacally satanic smile. The empty seat next to Bill was presumably his and once the clapping died down Mark turned, waved to everyone, and took his seat.

"What did the doc say?" a voice shouted. It was that moment that Mark decided he would not make his diagnosis common knowledge. He would still tell Gary and Bill, but telling the entire team might throw a wrench into things. Operations seemed to be going well, gauging by the introduction, and a perceived weakness might lead to a negative shift.

"Acute viral rhinopharyngitis," Mark shouted hoarsely. A silence beheld the room following the answer. "It's a cold," he said realizing no one understood, "just a cold."

Following the awkward silence of Mark's stab at humor, Bill snapped out of welcome mode, stood up, and pointed his remote at the projector above the table, not even attempting to recover the fumble. He launched into a fast-paced monologue which drew the intense attention of all in attendance.

"OK everyone," he began, "we lost a day of normal operation yesterday but we are still right on track. Thanks everyone for pulling together to pick up the slack. Everyone is still

ready for the press conference tomorrow right?" Bill looked to
Gary and one of the unfamiliar faces. The two nodded in reply.
"Good. Make sure we're still running mock-ups with the
department heads and keep them talking. Make sure everybody has
their shit straight so we don't look like assholes in front of these
assholes. Mark, if you're able, I want you to take a look at what
you're working with downstairs. Take one more walkthrough to
make sure these fuckers are impressed. Gary, how are the
transitions going? I won't except any answer other than 'smoothly'
so don't even try it." The crowd grumbled a short laugh after Bill's
remark.

"Anything to report from the carpet?" Bill looked to the
direction of CFO Don Perry.

"I'll get with you afterward Bill," Don said.

"Compliance?" Bill called, as if taking attendance.

"Everything's good," a representative from the new
compliance department shouted back.

"Relations?" Bill boomed at the unfamiliar face next to
Gary, who threw a thumbs-up back to Bill.

"OK then," Bill moved along, "I'm not going to keep you
very long today as Mark will have nothing to report and you all
have a lot of work to do to prepare for tomorrow. Just make sure
everybody is ready. Call if you need to. Go to work everyone.
Mark, you hang back a minute." With Bill's dismissal, everyone
filed out of the room with a purpose. There was no small talk or
chatter that usually accompanied a meeting's end. It was beautiful.

Mark kept waiting to see Rod Serling outside the glass
doors smoking a cigarette. This was not the Bill Wildeboer that
Mark remembered. It seemed that in the time he had lost, Bill had
turned into a competent man. This is to say nothing of the

atmosphere and the attitudes of the executives which had shifted from one of subdued acceptance of total annihilation to post-9/11 revenge type fervor. It was organized, deliberate, and cooperative. Wildeboer was Patton, and the rest were his Allied commanders on the Western Front.

What was curious was the rate at which Mark was adapting. The speed, the precision; it is what he always knew the company could be. But so long as he went with the flow, he was sure he could get up to speed by sundown. Surely some memories of the past few weeks would materialize if the memory loss was indeed a hibernation event. They would have to, unless he wanted to accept the alternative explanation.

Bill slapped Mark on the shoulder and ushered him out through the glass doors along with Gary and one of the unfamiliar faces lagging behind. "Nice move not telling everyone," Bill said under his breath and out of earshot of the two stragglers. Once outside the door Bill gestured the three of them through his office doorway.

"OK," Bill began, "Mark I feel like you may want to take this time to fill us in as to what the hell is going on with you."

"Actually Bill I would," Mark started. "I planned on having a meeting with you and Gary about that." He looked at the unfamiliar face that followed them in the room.

"I get it. I'll be in my office if you need anything," the stranger said removing himself from the room.

"OK here it is," Mark crackled, "Dr. Beecher's preliminary diagnosis is meningitis." The room fell silent.

"Jesus Christ Mark," Bill said, tears instantly welling in his eyes. "I'm so sorry." But Bill's reaction was more of a shock than the news itself.

"He hasn't officially confirmed," Mark said, "and it isn't fatal if it's caught in time and treated immediately." The story continued as Mark now second-guessed leaving his pills on the seat, "I can't tell you how grateful I am for setting me up with that appointment, Bill. I wouldn't have gone on my own until it was far too late, I'm sure. So thank you for that. Dr. Beecher said that stress is a huge factor, which is unavoidable at this point. But a far more pressing matter for now is that I have lost my memory of the last few weeks or so. The last thing I can truly remember is my second day on the job, in my office, typing a letter to Dr. Brotkettler. So I'll need to be brought up to speed as much as possible. For instance, who was that man who just left the room?" A hush fell over the room as a mixture of anticipation and disbelief. Bill and Gary looked at each other as if the entire operation was now doomed.

"That was Alec Reill," Gary said. "You were in the room with me when he accepted the position. You seriously don't remember him?"

"No," Mark sighed a deflating sigh, "I don't."

"He is the head of the new Public Relations department," Gary kept on in incredulity, "which was your idea." He looked back over at Bill in shock.

"Fuck." Bill started chuckling, "this shit storm just keeps getting thicker and thicker. Mark, you do whatever you need to do to get better. No one is asking you to sacrifice your health. I'm glad that Dr. Beecher was able to do something. Just be sure you are taking the medicine."

"How did you know he gave me medicine?" Mark was stricken with sudden and intense paranoia and the outburst took the room by surprise.

177

"I assume he did give you medicine if he diagnosed you with something that serious." Bill said in total tranquility. "Easy does it Mark."

"He did," Mark squeaked. "Sorry."

"You can come with me to my office, Mark," Gary invited. "I can show you a progress report that you started, to which you have added each day. As for Alec, of course it's up to you whether or not you want to disclose your health condition to him but, if you don't remember, he has been working very closely with us since the day we hired him and it would save a lot of confusion if you just told him what's going on."

"OK," Mark agreed. "My god this is frustrating."

"I can't imagine," Bill empathized. "You guys go ahead and get it sorted, I know Don's waiting for me outside that door right now."

Gary and Mark started towards the door guided by Bill. As predicted, Don was standing outside making small talk with Alec. "Bill," Gary said looking downward and stroking his chin with his thumb and forefinger, "let me finish with Mark before you and I meet again." Bill took about two or three awkward seconds to process the request before nodding his head.

Try as he might, Mark only felt the paranoia growing stronger. Gary looked very much like he was holding back a large amount of rage. That last statement did not help to extinguish the feeling. *It has to be frustrating for them too, all but losing a key player in the fight.*

After an eternity of hard-soled footsteps on thin commercial-grade berber carpet, the three finally arrived at Gary's office. Once inside, Mark noticed a prominent superficial temporal vein protruding and pulsing hot, angry blood through Gary's head.

It looked like it could explode at any second.

"OK," Gary said quietly, almost under his breath, desperately trying to maintain composure. "That meeting going on right now between Don and Bill is about the solvency of EnviroCore." This time, Gary was the one to make the room go silent. "He and I discussed it last night and came to the conclusion that unless we open up an investment round we are going to be out of money before we even start. So the press conference tomorrow is going to double as a recruiting event and triple as an investment round."

Hearts sank in unison. It was clear that Gary was unravelling. The calm and collected man in Mark's memory did not fit this man's description. A few moments of heavy breathing and pacing previewed the following explosion.

"I fuckin' told him that we should get ahead of it before we tell him. I told him that it was only going to hurt us if we told him anything before we had a solid plan. It makes us look like idiots! Why the fuck is this my problem anyway? I am the Vice President of Human Resources. This should be Don's problem, not mine. What were we supposed to do anyway? This was going to happen no matter what, so what's the difference." A few seconds of silence separated Gary's spewing thoughts. "Fuck 'em," and again, a few more seconds, "fuck 'em," and again. "This is it. If he told him that we're done than we *are* done. If he would have fuckin' waited a few hours we would have been able to come up with something and Bill wouldn't be going into berserker mode right now, which I'm sure he is. He's just trying to cover his ass. He only cares about himself. You'd think after Bill came over the table at him that he would learn to keep his fucking mouth shut, but, whaddya gonna do? Fuckin' asshole." Some more heavy breathing and pacing, "Now you're whole memory of everything is wiped clean? Sorry I know that was supposed to be up to you to tell but I don't give a fuck. How are you gonna be able to talk to the media about our progress when you have no idea what progress we've made?"

"OK listen," Gary said calmly, closing his eyes and resting praying hands underneath is chin, "I'm sorry about that. I was just venting. We've all been under a lot of stress lately and it just needed to come out before I had a heart attack. I can't imagine how you must be feeling Mark."

"It's OK," Mark whispered. "We'll get through it."

"I'll put that fire out in a minute. Now why don't I introduce you to Alec Reill, EnviroCore's Public Relations Director."

"What?" Alec said confusedly. "Introduce?"

"I have amnesia," Mark crackled. "I have a preliminary diagnosis of bacterial meningitis."

"So you don't remember…you don't know me?"

"Nope."

"Not at all?"

"Nothing."

"Wow. Sorry."

"Yeah."

"OK now that that's out of the way," Gary interrupted, "Alec why don't you take Mark to your office to see what is going on on the publicity front and show him how to access the progress reports."

"The progress reports that you write each day?" Alec asked.

"I guess so." Mark answered.

"Wow. OK," Alec accepted, "Sure. Let's go. I'll get you caught up. Good luck with Bill, Gary. Let security know you are going up there."

"Yeah, no shit." Gary chuckled. Even though it was meant to be a joke, Gary didn't think it all that bad an idea.

Alec swung the door open to allow Mark ahead of him.
Alec was a thin, pale, beanpole of a man with thinning red hair
slicked back into a bun on the back of his head. *What the fuck is
that, a bun?* Reill felt Mark's icy stare pierce through him like an
estoc through a bull. The tiny red hairs beneath Alec's bun rose up
in terror. Mark could only feel anger and contempt for this tiny
man and visions of strangling him to death flooded the forefront of
his mind's eye. Ample evidence of fear colored Alec's face,
reminiscent of Dr. Beecher before he gripped him up by the collar.
It gave him a sadistic sense of control. More correctly, it made him
high. The feeling of striking this degree of despair in a fellow
human being was intoxicating to say the least, and through a stare
nonetheless. Mark couldn't help but smile at the quivering jellyfish
before him. His body was pulsating with joy as he juxtaposed the
reality of Alec's horrified expression onto a twitching corpse he
created in his imagination.

"Uh," Alec trembled, "is everything alright Mark?"

But before Mark could respond, he felt vomit rising
precipitously up his esophagus accompanied by a withering
vertigo. Mark's kneecaps clapped against the floor as he erupted
undigested bacon and bread from the Deremer breakfast table onto
Alec's hipster brogues. It was a sea of shiny, warm, pink, white,
and brown followed by a catatonic heave. Still on his knees, he
struggled to his feet by means of grasping and pulling himself up
using Alec's tweed suit coat for help, aggressively huffing the
whole way up. A final empty stare was given through two slits
between Mark's eyelids before he simply walked away from the
mess to find the nearest bathroom. Alec was horrified by the
warmth and the stench of what was now soaking into his corduroys
while at the same time relieved that the psychotic Mark Deremer

was out of sight.

Meanwhile, a few minutes down the hall, Gary was preparing to lose his job or possibly take a beating. His pace slowed to a halt just before he turned the final corner to Bill's office. With one long deep breath, he stiffened his sinews before finally turning the corner to find an open door and Bill calmly talking to Don. Upon notice, Bill motioned for Gary to come in. 'Maybe he didn't fuck me over,' Gary thought as he confidently walked into the office to hear the last few, inaudible words of the conversation.

"Hi Gary," Bill said, in no way reflecting a meltdown. "Don was just telling me about opening up a round of investment following the press conference."

"Sorry Gary," Don said. "I know it was your idea but I had to be the one to tell him, being the Chief Financial Officer and all."

"Uh-huh," Gary offered as a response, knowing Don's attempt to throw him under the bus had backfired, and still not completely certain that Bill was not going to kill them both. "You and your modesty Mr. Don Perry," he said jokingly, but with a straight face. "I just don't know what to make of it."

"Any big names coming?" Bill asked, folding his arms.

"There are a couple of representatives from Axiom coming to see the presentation and a few nobodies from Jotunborough Capital but I think we'll be surprised who shows up," Don answered without blinking an eye. Gary was impressed.

"Axiom?" Bill asked in disbelief. "How the hell did you get them interested?"

"Mr. Reill was responsible for that nab," Don said. "He's unbelievable."

"Damn," Bill declared, raising his eyebrows, "make sure

you keep *him* in the loop on the cold calls."

"I will. We're gonna go ahead and get started now, Bill. We'll let you know what we know when we know it. It's gonna be a full house," Don said before Bill could eek out another question.

"Alright boys keep it up," Bill said, slapping them both on the shoulder. "We may just get out of this thing yet."

The two forced laughs as they exited the office. Once in the hall, Gary sang a sigh of amusement and kept smiling. "That was really some display in there, Mr. Fuck-ass," Gary said. "I'll tell you what Fuck-ass, if you ever do some shit like that again I'll cave your Fuck-ass head in. Do you hear me Fuck-ass?" Don smiled a fearless and daring smile at Gary.

"We'll talk later Gary," Don said in a raspy tone. After a two-second stare, the two parted ways in opposite directions.

Mark, meanwhile, was still in the bathroom, splashing cold water into his face and occasionally looking up into the mirror. His mind was emptier than it had ever been. Not one thought was given to puking on Alec's shoes. Nor did he care about the startling visions produced by his imagination or the pleasure he got from them. It seemed his analysts were away from their desks. A good fifteen minutes or so had passed since he entered the restroom and in that time, no guidance was offered. No guidance was sought either. The stirrings in Mark's brain had ceased. He was like a passenger in his own body; an observer.

Just outside the bathroom, an outline of vomit was being shampooed from the carpet by one of the company's janitors. But to Mark, it was as if the man did not exist and he nearly walked through the stain on his way past. A switched-off Mark Deremer was on his way to the bacteriology lab to fix whatever mess had been made of his GLADIS.

As Mark descended into the bowels of the building, his senses returned to him in short order. What were usually empty hallways were bustling with urgency and chatter. Ghostlike, he made his way through the crowds unnoticed as the intense focus of the employees did not allow him to enter their perception. An aura of combat seemed to hang over the cinderblock and drop-ceiling hallways as if the battle plan mentality from upstairs was being executed down below. It was both appealing and alarming as if to describe too strong a work ethic.

But there was something more than that affecting the crowd. Even though Mark had kept to himself in his years at the company, the bodies in this crowd seemed less familiar. At first, he thought perhaps layoffs and hirings had taken place and the new wave of employees had thrown him off. But this was different.

185

Though he had never made the effort to get to know his colleagues, he could still recognize them as people he passed in the halls.

Their faces looked haggard; unshaven and oily skin stretched tightly over prominent facial bones. Adding to the disheveled presentation was unkempt hair and glassy eyes, with an almost dirty appearance in their flesh tones. *Was Bill working these people too hard?* In contrast to their apparent lack of hygiene, overall, they looked healthy. There was certainly no shortage of energy and as far as their bodies, they all looked…somewhat larger.

Though possibly the most troubling was the ill-tempered demeanor that came along with the urgency. Many of the voices Mark heard in the crowd were boisterous baritones harshly commanding orders at one another. Even a shove here and there was not an uncommon sight. The attitude was one of cooperation combined with irritability. It had all the hallmarks of a time bomb.

Mark uncomfortably slinked through the commotion only to notice the chaos thickening as he inched toward bacteriology. Evidence of past aggression was strewn about a warpath of broken glass and other varying chunks of debris. Lab benches were littered with melted hunks of white plastic, black smudges of burnt ash, and even several easily identifiable puddles of dried up brown and red.

This scene was about as surreal as Mark could fathom and he fought the urge, once more, to doubt his senses. Just outside the once familiar bacteriology lab, the beeping sound of the security badge scanner precluded Steve blowing the door open with a leaning shoulder.

"Hey buddy!" Steve hollered as he wrapped one of his arms around him. "Just the person we've been waiting for! Glad you could make it!"

"What the hell is going on?" Mark asked in bewilderment.

"Whaddya mean?" Steve asked, oblivious to the change that Mark perceived in his environment. Steve turned on his heel and forced Mark back through the door and into the lab. "Okay buddy. Have a look." Mark was sat face to face with a screen shot of the multiple S curves that Steve described over the phone next to the fluctuating statistics, enzyme abbreviations, and changing codons of the GLADIS analysis.

The population curves effectively illustrated that the bacteria would never run out of food. When the organism has a sustainable food source, the stabilization phase continues indefinitely. If not, the population dies off and the curve slopes downward, somewhat like what was seen in the painful weeks leading up to *Vir*'s discovery. In this case, the curves were stacked, meaning that the top of the 'S' begins the bottom of a new one. Each ending stabilization phase begins a new lag phase. It was hard to believe that this had gone unchecked before the organism was produced.

Remembering back to when the two first tinkered with the mutation rates, Mark was unsure of how to force the evolution of an enzyme organically. It seemed that no matter how high they set it, the curve always declined after the stationary phase as the population eventually died off. In nature, mutations occur at rates of about 0.003 per genome per generation. In the lab, Mark and Steve had programmed GLADIS to induce them at nearly a thousand times that, perhaps as an artifact of their impatience. As Mark scrolled through a few lines of the code, he realized they had never changed that back.

It was at that moment that Mark made sense of the 'melted'

plastic piles. Among the chaos into which the lab had descended, he hadn't given them a second thought. Now, looking at these S curves, he knew exactly what happened.

"I need the list of chemical components for these plastics," Mark said, as if that were a common thing to ask for.

"The containers were all BPA-free," Steve said proudly anticipating Mark's inquiry.

"These melted puddles here were incubators?" Mark asked, already knowing the answer.

"They were BPA-free bud," Steve assured, "I promise."

"How did they get like this?" Mark asked, pointing to one of the globs.

"Somebody probably got pissed," Steve brushed off. "There were no bugs in them. The population had already died out."

"Somebody got pissed?" Mark asked in anguish, "Like, they got mad and melted them?"

"Yeah," Steve answered, confused by Mark's disbelief.

"How long have these been sitting here?" Mark asked, growing more and more frustrated with Steve's ignorance, "Why haven't they been cleaned up?"

"I dunno. A week?" Steve guessed. "We've got bigger things to worry about than cleaning."

"You are a bacteriologist, right?" Mark laid on the sarcasm before beginning his diagnosis. "These," he continued, pointing to the connecting points in the stacked S curves, "are most certainly periods of adaptation." He looked over at Steve, whose focus was fixed on the screen. What seemed obvious to him was apparently not to anyone else. "It is not a glitch. *Vir* ate the bisphenol backbone in the Petri dish media and then just kept eating. I'm sure

I don't need to tell you that this is hugely bad. Or maybe I do. Why are you not aware of the abnormal behavior of your colleagues? Why did you just accept that someone destroyed our equipment? Aside from that, why is this lab not under BSL-4 cordon? And perhaps most importantly, why did you not tell me about this sooner?!" The familiar high-pitched whistling accompanied the rise in Mark's blood pressure.

"Uh, Buddy?" Steve retorted angrily, "I told you about the S curves two weeks ago and you told me to 'find my big boy shorts and get it done.' So now you can go fuck yourself!" There was no mention of the new culture of hostility in the basement.

"OK listen," Mark said trying to calm his heightened agitation. But before he could finish his thought, an overhead page for him to call Don Perry's extension interrupted the potential fistfight. "Cordon off this fuckin' area. Start luciferase ATP-testing. Jesus Christ."

The commands quivered with both fear and anger as this was the *last* thing Mark needed right now. It seemed entirely out of character for Mark to just blow off a legitimate concern about his own creation, especially in such a priggish manner as Steve described. But then again, everything about the lab seemed entirely out of character. Nobody seemed to notice the bedlam. Perhaps it had been a gradual descent, each day the madness becoming a little more accepted.

Mark stood staring at the middle row of cinderblocks just outside the bacteriology lab with his hands on his hips; his breaths directing the rise and fall of his shoulders. *This is a nightmare.* If Mark was right about the S curves, then he was dealing with an epidemic of mutant bacteria and EnviroCore was ground zero. "This would make a great science fiction novel," he murmured.

189

As much as Mark did not like jumping to conclusions, he knew he was right and the next step would be to implement emergency quarantine procedures until such time that Steve could confirm a negative ATP test in the lab. But this was uncharted territory and technically there was no protocol on how to handle this situation. This fact brought Mark to a very ugly crossroads. If he did the ethical thing, that is, lockdown the building, call the mayor, the CDC, and initiate HAZMAT procedures, then tomorrow's press conference, followed soon after by the company and then the county, would be sunk. Therefore, was it really the ethical thing? The pathogenic properties of this bug, other than its startling adaptability, are yet unknown and could very well be nonexistent. *Is it worth the gamble?* Mark was not one for probabilities. He liked binary much better. The analysts were always good for coming to *the only* conclusion rather than *the best* one. Unfortunately, they were nowhere to be found.

"Hey Mark," said Don from the other end of the phone, "meet the team in the executive lunch room, would ya? We're going to rehearse a bit for tomorrow and we need your insight."

"On my way," Mark said, trying to hang up the phone abruptly but being called back before the receiver could hit the hook.

"Hey Mark," Don repeated, "you ought to call your doctor back, Doctor Beecher is it? He's called here a couple of times already."

"I will," Mark replied coldly, blasting the phone down so hard that the tiny digital screen cracked from the force.

Mark's autopilot kicked on again during the walk to the lunchroom. Beecher probably didn't have great news. He figured that the diagnosis was confirmed with his cerebrospinal fluid analysis. Now he had to try and get caught up to speed with this press conference tomorrow, which would undoubtedly include Mark a great deal. *No matter*, he heard dim voice of his mother somewhere off in the background trying to calm him down. She always did her best to guide Mark's emotions in a more positive direction.

The usual suspects sat around the table awaiting Mark's arrival. Though Bill was still absent, Mark could see Gary and Don were feigning polite small talk with modest hand gestures and inexpressive eyebrows. Facing the glass door which led to Mark's eye contact, now wearing a different outfit, sat Reill. His facial expression had changed markedly as soon as Mark broke the plane of entry.

"Where's Bill?" Mark blurted before getting all the way in the room.

"We thought we'd surprise him with this one," Don said eagerly.

Mark noticed Gary smiling his toothpaste-commercial smile ear to ear, while Alec still sat expressionless. He had obviously not mentioned the earlier incident to anyone in the room.

"Remember what I said earlier about being broke?" Gary asked. "Well forget that. We just got an offer from Axiom Pharmaceuticals for a buyout. Lock, stock, and barrel."

"When did this happen?" Mark asked.

"Just a few moments ago," Don piped in, "when I called to confirm their attendance tomorrow. They were very interested in your GLADIS project." Just then, Tina, the attractive food service employee, and one of Bill's many vices, walked through the back door holding a tray with a large coffee kettle, four mugs, and a basket of cream and sugar. Her tightly-curled platinum blond locks bounced like springs with each step. She set the tray down and began passing out mugs and filling them with dark black liquid. Tina's eyelashes were so long, so black, that her eyes appeared closed. The scent of the air changed as she made her way around the waiting mugs; it was cheap but seductive, something reminiscent of pineapple.

"What do they know so far?" Mark asked, trying to decide whether he should mention the situation in the basement.

"They know that you created a technology that writes and tests hypothetical genomes before the organism is engineered," Don recalled. "They also know you created a garbage-eating bug with it."

"It eats plastic," Mark corrected. "Bisphenol A to be exact."

"Whatever," Don brushed the correction off and grinned.

"It's gonna be worth a shit load, yeah?"

"Well, that depends," Mark began, interlacing his fingers and leaning forward, "what if we haven't yet worked out all the bugs?"

"What do you mean?" Don asked.

"What if it's gotten loose in the basement and has begun breaking things down that it shouldn't?" Mark paused to allow the question to register. "What if we told them that an epidemic has begun with their bug, that it's rapidly mutating, and that there's no telling how long it's been going on or what type of pathogenic properties it possesses?" Mark's tone had a sharp tinge of sarcasm even though he was not exaggerating very much. Nonetheless, the room fell silent in horror.

"Jesus Christ Mark," Don exhaled. "Don't scare us like that you sonofabitch!" He chuckled nervously, still not sure if it was a joke.

"Yeah that might be a problem," Gary joined along breaking the awkward silence. After all, he knew Mark wasn't one for humor. Reill, on the other hand, did not join in the nervous laughter. He could do nothing but stare into Mark's silver pupils as he slurped the first drops of his coffee.

"I thought it might," Mark sipped calmly.

"Mark Deremer please call the operator," a human yet mechanical-sounding voice called over the EnviroCore intercom, "Mark Deremer please call the operator," it repeated.

"For fuck's sake," Mark grumbled as he rose to comply with the page. In walking over to the lunchroom's phone, he had to walk past Tina, who was bent over slightly in order to pour into Reill's mug more carefully. Just before she had tipped the kettle back to end the pour, a firm, open hand struck her squarely on the backside. Tina yelped in a surprised, yet playful fashion, acknowledging the bold gesture with an unexpected flirtatious smile. Those who remained seated looked at each other in disbelief. To Mark, it seemed as natural as offering 'gesundheit' to someone who had just sneezed. Mark barely looked up as he passed her by, but she bit her bottom lip as if to restrain her libido as she looked him up and down.

"This is Deremer," Mark spoke to the operator at the other end of the line.

"Mr. Deremer, I have a Doctor Beecher on hold for you," the operator announced. "He says it's urgent."

"Fine," Mark's speech colored with annoyance.

"Mark?" Beecher questioned a few seconds later.

"Yeah hi doctor," Mark said with urgency, "what's up?"

"Mark," Beecher hesitated, "are you sitting?"

"Wow," Mark answered, "that bad huh?"

"I knew it was bad when I saw the first drop coming out of your back," Beecher said. "It was green for Christ's sake."

"Green?" Mark nearly swallowed his tongue. Turning back to survey the room for a reaction to the unusual word he had just uttered, he found three disinterested men sipping coffee and one beautiful female gazing in his direction before letting the door close behind her.

"According to the labs," Beecher continued, "you are positively crawling with an unknown strain of bacteria. They are thriving. They have never seen so many in one sample."

"Okay," Mark kept up his calm appearance. "What's next?"

"You need to get to St. Catherine's as soon as possible," Beecher explained. "Once you get here, you will go into isolation. Try to avoid as many people as you can before then."

"Out of the question," Mark barked. "It has to be something else."

"In case you don't understand the gravity of the situation," the doctor condescended, "there is an unknown life form that has taken you over. We can't be sure that it won't kill you and everyone you have come in contact with since you've had it until you come in. We already have a sterilized room and staff members waiting. Don't you understand? You are patient zero! If you don't come in, we'll come and get you!"

"We'll see," Mark said slamming the phone down.

Mark blistered through Bill's door to find him in some sort of hard-nosed negotiation on the phone. "Yes, I do understand how serious it is and I'm sure he does too," Bill beckoned for Mark to come in and sit down with some kind of sloppy circular hand waving motion. A long silence on Bill's end was cut with the chattering of some semi-frantic voice on the other end, "OK thank you again for your call, sir."

"Hey there Mark," Bill greeted in a friendly tone after the phone call was ended. "Did they get you up to speed for tomorrow?" *What an odd way to follow that phone call.*

"Not quite," Mark queried in paranoia. "Are *you* all caught up?" Of course Mark was talking about the conversation that was just ended between Bill and, obviously, Dr. Beecher. Though what was not so obvious was that Bill *was* all caught up. If he were, would there not be a maelstrom of office supplies and expletives emanating from Bill's general direction?

"Well," Bill exhaled hard again, only this time into a thin stream of air forced between his lips, "here are my thoughts. You are entitled to a second opinion from another lab. That gives us about one more day. However I don't fault you one bit if you feel you need to leave now."

"Well," Mark began to talk, not knowing exactly what he was going to say, "here are my thoughts. There is no way of knowing how long I have had this. If I were going to spread it, chances are it has already been well-spread. There is a chance that it's not even contagious. I'll turn myself into the hospital's clean room once we complete the press conference tomorrow. But with doctor-patient confidentiality, no one will ever have to know about this." It was a superb display of winging it, perhaps Mark's finest. He was getting used to playing the odds. Making no mention of

196

what was happening in the basement, he only acknowledged what he had heard Beecher and Wildeboer talking about on the phone a few minutes ago. There was no need to mention that it was definitely *Viridobacter circulofractus* that spilled thick out of his back yesterday into Beecher's test tube.

"Your voice is not getting any better," Wildeboer said after a moment of thought. Mark chuckled a single time to show Bill he acknowledged the joke. Though the rattling and squeaking was getting quite annoying. "You know this win means a lot to me right?" Bill leveled, "You're a good man, Mark," Bill's hand was outstretched in a gesture of gratitude. Taken aback, Mark did not hesitate to reciprocate the handshake.

"We've come this far," Mark said, "let's make it work." Unsure if Bill would get the reference to the unofficial Sciencia motto, it still seemed like a good way to say, 'you're welcome.'

Staring back into the eyes of a man whose reputation for instability preceded him, Mark saw a well put-together individual. Never would he have expected to see such a dramatic transformation. Some people deal with the stress differently. This was Hail Mary time and Bill's chips were all in. Perhaps at some point, he understood that coming apart at the seams would do nothing to help the situation. Or maybe he found his way to a mental hospital and some antipsychotic medication. Whatever was going on with the infamous Bill Wildeboer, it was working. *Amazing what can happen in a few weeks.*

"Wildeboer," Bill answered the ringing phone.

"Just what in the hell is going on there Bill?" the agitated voice of Ted Philus spoke from the other line.

"To what are you referring?" Bill questioned in absolute tranquility, as if he expected the call.

"Goddamn it boy," Philus prodded. "Don't you know what the hell is going on at your own company?" Bill noticed that it had become *his* company.

"There is a lot going on here Teddy," Bill patronized. "You'll have to be more specific."

"Bill," Ted was seething, "for the moment I'll ignore the fact that you have forgotten who you're talking to and ask you about an outbreak in your bacteria lab. Do you know there is an outbreak in your bacteria lab? Do you know about Axiom Pharmaceuticals?"

"I have heard of Axiom Pharmaceuticals," Bill continued to sarcast. "You *are* going to have to fill me in on the outbreak though."

"Have you lost your fuckin' mind boy?" Ted nearly screamed. "Or are you just trying to piss me off?"

"A little of both I guess," Bill mused.

"Don't make me come down there and embarrass you son," Ted threatened.

"I wish the fuck you would come down here!" Bill blasted back, standing up from his laid back position and punching the air with his index finger. "We'll see who gets embarrassed!"

"Now *there's* the Bill Wildeboer *I* know," Ted delighted. "I just wanted to make sure you still had that fire boy! Seems news doesn't travel as fast as I expected from such a well-oiled machine." Bill was still standing and frowning hard. "Billy, Axiom is going to make a substantial offer tomorrow in time for the press conference. We'd be fools not to take it."

"I heard they were coming," Bill said, slowly finding his chair behind him, "but I did not know they planned on making an offer already."

"Well don't feel bad," Philus consoled. "It's hot off the presses. Now these rumors of an outbreak that are spreading in certain circles," Ted continued, "just ignore that. In less than twenty-four hours, that won't be our problem anymore."

Bill noticed that the company was back to being *ours*. "How did *that* get started?"

"You know how these things go," Ted minimized. "Hell, Axiom probably started that themselves to scare off the competition." A brief pause interrupted the dialogue, "God damn Bill. You fuckin' did it! You pulled it off, boy! Can you believe it?!"

"Don't act so surprised," Bill melted into his own ego.

"Champagne and cocaine Billy Boy!" Philus screamed, "Woo hoo!"

A hard 'click' signaled the end of the call. Bill calmly hung the phone up and buried his face partway between his praying hands. Suddenly, the calm, collected Patton reincarnate was overcome with emotions. In the hard-driving confusion that ensued since he had been handed the reigns, he had turned into a bulldozer, unable to pay much attention to anything but what was in front of him. The call from Philus had pulled him out of that state of mind all at once. Ironically, the chaos that was his life made him more stable; not the worst way to handle stress. It was not until this moment that Bill realized all of this, and was now desperately trying to hang on to it.

Tears welled in Bill's eyes. They represented a sort of Stockholm Syndrome. Kept prisoner by the stress of trying to pull the company out of a tailspin, he found serenity in the extreme focus that the task demanded. Now he was free and recognized exactly how much good it had done him. Once he came to grips with the realization that the stability had all but slipped from his fingers, a flood gate opened, taking him with the current. The joy of success, the anger for Ted, the excitement for tomorrow, the fear of what was to come, the pride of his ego, the belated anxiety of the past month, and the shock of it all hitting at once, flowed into his lungs, robbing him of breath. A deep gasp accompanied more tears and a fierce exhale. This blend of mania and anguish produced a laughing, bawling lunatic, the likes of which flipped tables and kicked doors off of hinges. So loud was the fit that even a now faraway Mark Deremer could swear he heard the faint screams of a madman echo through the halls behind him.

After what seemed like an absurd amount of time in the executive lunchroom trying to stay focused on getting caught up and practicing the monologue for the press conference, Mark had conceded that it was to everyone's detriment to continue trying. Though his lack of focus troubled him greatly, Mark accepted that torpor was not coming and the best thing to do was sleep. "Everyone get as much sleep as you can," Mark said as he flicked the light switch to the off position, "tomorrow is just a normal day." The comment was a flaccid attempt to ease minds, but it was so antithetical that tired scoffs burst from each set of lips.

Mark retired to his office to honor the wishes of Bill and Dr. Beecher to stay 'isolated' from the general population. Unaware of how much time he had spent sleeping, or not sleeping, nights in his office, he found it quite uncomfortable to give up what he now perceived to be nightly rituals he had been performing his whole life under the familiar ceilings of the Deremer farmhouse. He got as comfortable as possible, getting out of his shoes and dress shirt, and logging in to the security system to answer the question of how he spent his lost time.

While Mark waited for the program's progress bar to completely fill, two boomerangs came swooping back to him. One, Steve had never gotten back to him with the results of the ATP test and two, he had no memory of ever being granted access to the security system, but managed to navigate it and even type in a complicated password. The memory loss was only affecting declarative memory, not procedural memory, meaning, at this stage anyway, that if it was meningitis after all, it was still confined to the hippocampus, and the more automatic functions remained untouched. *Maybe.*

Mark easily ran through the steps of the program to retrieve the proper cameras and footage from the prior two weeks. Time lapse of the parking lot revealed that indeed his white wagon had not moved from its parking spot. The camera outside of the office agreed that he had been spending nights in this very room, though it could not be known whether or not he had been sleeping. *Why would Gladys not have mentioned this?* Up until two days ago, when the car finally left its space, he had been going into this office and staying until the morning. *Have I not been conducting my own hygiene?* Then he remembered the disheveled lab members. *Have they been staying too?* The parking lot was always filled with cars at any hour of the day. Checking the cameras of the lab area would reveal whether or not everyone was burning the midnight oil. Indeed, the time lapse showed a bustling lab at all hours of the night. Mark's jaw hung open as he watched the footage, but not at the conclusion of EnviroCore's recent work habits.

Inside one of the camera's fields of view was the melted incubator that Mark had beheld earlier. Though during the first several twenty-four hour periods, it was not yet malformed. As time elapsed, he observed the incubator melting all on its own over the course of two weeks. This confirmed Mark's hypothesis about the stacked S curves. *They are adapting.* But what was more startling was that other plastic items in the lab were melting as well. These objects he had not noticed, but for good reason. The rates differed depending, probably, on the different properties of the plastic items; thickness, density, etc. The melted plastic objects he had not seen earlier in the day, were no longer present. Once they began their deformation, they continued until they were gone. Mark backed the footage up several times to be sure. He changed speeds, made notes of the objects and their locations, calculated frames per second from start to finish of decomposition, and watched them over again.

If the rational analysts had been at their desks, they would have made known that this was horrifying on many levels. For one, it was quite probable that everyone near the bacteriology lab had spinal cords and brain ventricles pulsing with thick, green fluid. Two, considering the aggressive speed, the route of transmission was probably airborne and not direct contact. But instead of looking at the situation from the perspective of safety, health, welfare, and regulatory compliance, Mark saw the positive. In fact, this was serendipity. Nobody in the lab has died since the bugs got loose approximately two weeks ago. Everyone down there *has* to be crawling with them. Aside from the agitation that comes with working long, long hours, no serious health impacts have been reported. In addition, quite to the contrary of trying to hide this incident, he was going to show this footage tomorrow at the conference for everyone to see. It would be the icing on the cake. With this footage, they had proof that it worked and was safe. Because it was not deliberate, and virtually no regulations are currently in place regarding a novel genus, which it was, there could be no repercussions. *No harm, no foul.*

"Ha!" Mark shouted through the stale office air, slapping his monitor clear off his desk. Needless to say, Mark was elated. This was the capper. Nothing was even going to be remembered about this press conference except for that footage. Without any regard for the property he had just damaged, Mark kicked his feet up on the desk, folded his hands behind his head, leaned back and closed his eyes. A smirk crossed his cheeks as he imagined the faces of the audience, especially his colleagues, as they watched the evolution of humankind unfold in front of their eyes. As his eyelids sagged shut, the sound of a xylophone plinked off-key notes from the breast pocket of his dress shirt which lay on the floor in a pile.

Mark's hand flailed in the dark through the fabric in search of the cacophony. Once the familiar square shape filled all the familiar spots on his fingers, he brought the black yet blinding screen to the view of a tiny slit carved out of his right eyelid. It was an alarm he had set earlier in the day as a reminder to take the pills Beecher had prescribed. But those pills were at least a quarter mile roundtrip, complete with putting shoes back on and breaths of frost-ridden air. Sleep was far too near. Plus, as he proudly demonstrated, the bug that infected him was not dangerous, so pills were not a matter of life or death. *No matter*, the calmness of Gladys's tone washed warm salt water over his consciousness, until it drowned in relaxation.

A rational Mark Deremer would have definitely continued the medicinal regiment prescribed by the doctor, especially with a diagnosis of bacterial meningitis. This is not a rational Mark Deremer, at least, as far as the can-stacking, egg-candling, bacteriologist Mark Deremer is concerned. *That* Mark Deremer would be meticulously reviewing his notes at the office and practicing his presentation, especially if he didn't remember anything that was in it. But *this* Mark Deremer was taking on the persona of a mover and shaker; the arrogance was an uncharacteristic side effect which he did not fully realize was corrupting his behavior. Why would he? Mark knew on some deeper level that there was something different about him but, because of the conspicuous absence of logical analysis, he did not label it as 'wrong' or 'strange.' It was not just the newfound power that came with the position. Nor was it that there was absolutely nothing they could do now to replace him. It was the perception that he was free. Whether it was the unconscious fear of his looming infection, the lack of sleep, the stress, the confusion, or the fact that he could no longer trust his own awareness, he ironically found liberation in a lack of control.

When a brain operates unconsciously, it is doing work behind your back in a sense. Of course it is more efficient to leave constant, vital, repetitive functions out of immediate thought space. However, sometimes the judge, in charge of what needs to be brought to the prefrontal cortex for analysis and what can remain behind the scenes, gets it wrong. Mark's judge deemed that there was some problem with either the feedback coming in or the analysis. There was a substantial information deficit accompanying the duties of a Chief Operating Officer. Outcomes of situations were not readily predictable. Far-reaching and ordinarily irrelevant factors had to be taken into consideration, and black-and-white decisions were just not possible. For these reasons, Mark's judge seemed to be rerouting most of the relevant information behind the scenes and leaving the rational analysts' inbox empty. For now, all that Mark had was confidence. Hopefully that would be enough to get him through tomorrow.

The antique cuckoo clock in the Deremer living room fired mechanical bird sounds into Mark's eardrums. The time was 10 o'clock, matching the alarm set on his cell phone for his pills. Confused, he fished around the couch cushions for the amber bottles with the Axiom brand, but came up empty. Outside, Mark noticed that despite the time, the moon lit the ground with such luminosity that it might as well have been noon. Quite a spell he remained on the living room couch staring out the doorwall at a thin layer of frozen snow that still clung to the ground. It was so thin that it only appeared to be ice at the scale of centimeters. The vast empty field was an infinite network of branching fissures that followed their pattern up into the branches of the forest of leafless trees that lined the horizon. All Mark wanted to do was stare out into the distance. Hours and hours passed as millions of thoughts raced through and turned over in his mind. He considered the fractal geometry that could be used to model the branching of both the cracked ice and the tree branches against the skyline. He pondered the complexity of the tissues and electrical signals that made up his brain and the trillions and trillions of chemical reactions all taking place that were making up the environment he was viewing. It was virtually an infinite number of events that had taken place, were taking place, and would continue to take place in order for him to have this singular and insignificant experience. It was an odd sensation that Mark had never felt before. Most people might call it beauty.

The smell of frying bacon and eggs finally cut through his intense focus. Mark was famished and voraciously tore through two-thirds of everything on the table. Gladys usually made so much food that no one could possibly finish. But today, thanks to Mark's appetite, nothing remained but empty plates and greasy napkins. The County Crier sat ready for perusing; likely more embellished stories of the strange happenings of the long winter. But before he could begin reading, something inside jabbed at him. Presumably, some inscrutable signal had broken through from one of his rational analysts. Mark had all but forgotten the introvert that used to occupy this corpus with all of its reserve and caution. Still, there was this signal, like he had forgotten to turn off the stove or something. As far as Mark was concerned, he didn't care if he ever heard from the rational analysts again. After all, he could see now that they had held him back in a great many ways. Mark was never one to take a chance. He kept to himself his whole life unless it was absolutely unavoidable. He never would have even tried to get another job under the old regime and now he was the Vice President of Operations. It was a tremendous opportunity to be a different person and Mark fit the role well. It was as if he were awake for the first time in his life; a free man with a lot of time to make up for.

But the signal persisted. Thumbing through the pages of the paper, he realized he was unable to process any of the words. It might as well have been a foreign language. Amidst the cadence of dialogue between his parents, he realized that their words were meaningless as well. Gladys's inflections denoted a question, but the harder Mark tried to concentrate, the louder the antique cuckoo clock distracted him, until he felt his head might explode. *What is it now, a stroke?*

"Mark!" Bill shouted from just inside the entryway, "it's time!" Mark lie curled in the fetal position with his suit coat acting as a blanket. Shivers drew him to near convulsions.

"Is there no goddamned toothbrush?" Mark hollered back, as reality returned and sleep faded.

In the time that had passed between waking up on the floor of his office and now, beholding a much larger auditorium than he remembered fill to standing room only, Mark had reviewed the script for the presentation and added the security footage to the PowerPoint presentation. Perhaps, he had underestimated Reill after all. This crowd was unlike anything he could have imagined. In addition to the unfamiliar faces who had worked at the company for many years, the crowd was filled with congressmen, reporters, and investors from around the country. Aside from the absurd EnviroCore security presence, there were more state police than he thought existed, interspersed throughout the crowd and two standing at every door.

Through the dull roar of the auditorium, Mark picked out bits and pieces of various conversations between long-time colleagues that, 'hadn't seen each other since grad school' or 'saw their talks on such-and-such back in 19-sometime-or-another' or 'went to the Go Green conference in Seattle' or some other such icebreaker. Others included details of trips to Washington, this or that hedge fund analysis, or 'how far out in the boonies' the company was. The situation chilled Mark to the bone with anxiety and nervousness. Whatever confidence he prayed for did not show up, and he was absolutely quaking. *Perhaps I am not prepared.* "This is a nightmare," he said aloud, surveying all the suits in the audience.

Mark found the rest of the executives up front and took his place between Bill and Gary. He was ghost white, and the fact that he had just awoken from sleeping on the floor of his office was apparent. On the inside, he felt just as crazy as he looked, and the rest of the team unconsciously began to mirror his state of mind.

"Are you ready?" Bill asked desperately trying to fight off

his nerves, "This is a big one." The audience lights dimmed slightly as the stage lights brightened and Wildeboer made his way across the stage to the podium. The noise from the crowd's conversation was replaced with polite applause.

"It is with great pride that I have the honor of introducing our first speaker today, a man of great integrity," Bill boomed into the microphone. "For those of you who don't know already, Mark Deremer has dedicated most of his career to this great company. In fact, this company would not be the spearhead of innovation that it is without him. It is not just seeing the company through its transition that he is responsible for but also for putting EnviroCore on the map of evolution. For undoubtedly, mankind itself will not be what it will be tomorrow without him. Allow me to introduce *your* Vice President of Operations, whiz kid, and personal friend, Mark Deremer."

Taken aback, Mark rose from his seat to a standing ovation. Dark black pupils guided his darting eyeballs in a trillion directions. This was not the man of confidence that the team had come to know, and that the crowd had expected. Somehow, it had slipped Mark's mind that he was the introductory speaker. There was no turning back now.

Mark climbed the five stairs of the stage as if they led to the gallows. The weight in his shoes nearly held his legs in place each time he tried to lift them. When the march completed, he reached for the waiting, outstretched hand of Bill Wildeboer, who gave him a chuck on the shoulder as he relinquished the podium.

"What an introduction," Mark mumbled sheepishly over the applause, wondering exactly where Bill drew the line between puffery and flat out lies. Pure panic started its surge through Mark's veins as he stared out at the crowd, hand quivering as he reached for his clicker. '*Viridobacter circulofractus* and its Potential in Waste Management' read the giant screen behind him. *Jesus, I couldn't have come up with a flashier title?*

The room suddenly became vacant. All of those faces and cameras that were just staring at him seconds ago had disappeared into the black. A screeching whistle of 4 kilohertz accompanied the 120 decibel rhythmic thundering of his heartbeat, which accompanied the figurative lump of sand in his throat and the 74 sweat beads that had amassed across his forehead. The whistle ramped up to 5 kilohertz, then 6, then 7, in lockstep with the increase in Mark's heart rate. Time was perceived as both standing still and as a constant aging and regressing. He stood helpless; frozen in this oddly familiar moment.

His mind's eye beheld a giant pile of papers with the word 'STOP' written in a font size that took up the whole page, except for the signature, 'Mark Deremer' at the bottom. From the darkness appeared an African shaman who wore some mask of ritual; his hands clasped in prayer as he moved step by step towards the pile. Once he reached it, he stood above it chanting in monotone tongues whilst a drum beat along to his eerie, rhythmic pattern of speech. The drum gave one final beat which silenced the shaman. In one abrupt movement, his praying hands abducted, like a reverse clap, to drop tiny particles over the papers, which ignited into green flames just before reaching the pile. A blaze of green spread wildly over the pile and shot high up into the sky where the auditorium's ceiling used to be, much to the delight of the shaman who screamed a horrible howl of delight and began dancing vigorously next to the fire. The vision only lasted an instant in Mark's mind, but the imagery was clear enough and the sounds of the crackling flames turned back into clapping hands and the spell was broken.

  Mark's time was now. He stood at the turning point; a cliff off of which he needed to jump. His heart pumped pure adrenaline as he ran towards it, unsure whether he would fly or fall. The violent but muffled uproar of the rational analysts desperately tried in vain to pierce this armor of courage and every fiber in his being told him to retreat. Indeed, everyone was watching and waiting to see him fall into a flailing and helpless descent to the ground below. He looked over the crowd one more time to see that the sea of faces had returned, which was his prompt to take his last few running steps on solid ground and leap off of the cliff and into the abyss of uncertainty.

  "The world needs our help," Mark said enthusiastically. In saying those words, he discovered that if he concentrated tension on his diaphragm, his hoarseness all but disappeared. The shaman's magic had returned his voice, along with his confidence. That giant tidal wave that had bowled him over so many times before, he now rode with command and grace.

  But the return of his confidence was not the only effect the shaman inspired. Assessing the crowd, he began recognizing the faces of the scientists which he had invited to work for EnviroCore, the venture capitalists, the scouts from Axiom, the senators, the reporters, everyone. Their recognition summoned the memory of the invitations that had been sent out to all of them and what they said, word for word. Silently and suddenly, his veil of amnesia was lifted, just as he knew it eventually would be. Packets of energy in his brain exploded in a daisy chain across his synapses. The blackened ash that fell and hardened on the surface now broke to reveal the glowing, flowing orange lava underneath. The agonizing treasure hunt was over. A clear memory of the events that took place in the last weeks suddenly appeared. As if it were the tip of a tyrannosaurus femur sticking out of the sand, he frantically brushed it free. Mark remembered everything.

"It is not news that mankind is drowning under the weight of its own garbage. For generations, non-biodegradable trash has been pumped into our precious mother earth with little regard for consequences; no plan to stop, and no plan to slow down. Environmentalists have vilified the long decomposition time of plastics since their advent. But the revenues spoke louder than Mother Nature.

"In the archeological record, we name epochs after the materials most found in the sediment. When future archaeologists sift through the sediments of today, they will find a thick layer of plastic that has barely decomposed. In fact, for all intents and purposes, it will still be basically brand new. Like The Bronze Age and The Iron Age, ours will be The Plastic Age.

"This is a multigenerational tragedy; a huge black eye on Mother Earth with only us to blame. But lucky for us, on the other side of every problem is an opportunity, to paraphrase Lee Iacocca. We have a tremendous opportunity here to heal that black eye. Just about every company out there has jumped on the 'green' bandwagon. But going paperless, reducing carbon emissions, and offering biodegradable alternatives is not enough. There are still thousands of non-biodegradable polymer factories in operation with only slightly diminishing demand. There are still thousands of landfills filling with more and more plastic as we speak. No one is *reversing* what is already done. That time comes now. We are sitting on the cusp of a new era: a completely untapped market with a large and eternal demand. In other words, mountains of plastic oil sit idle while *we*, EnviroCore, have the only drill on earth.

"People have been tearing down this planet since they discovered ways to tear it down. Even when we discovered that it was a very bad thing to tear it down, we didn't stop. But it wasn't just the bad ones that didn't stop, the good ones did nothing to prevent the bad ones, which in effect, made them just as bad. It was Edmund Burke who said, 'The only thing necessary for the triumph of evil is for good men to do nothing.' Government intervention has done little to stop the treachery. Nor has the threat of global annihilation even remotely hindered the mass production of greenhouse gases in the corporate world. And why would it? To shareholders, the future of our descendants means little in the face of short-term profit.

"Meanwhile our landfills are exploding, war is desolating nations in the name of fossil fuel consumption, and pollution of all types is ravaging ecosystems across the globe. We, as people, need to change strategies. Instead of standing up to the tidal wave, we need to grab our surfboards. We, as EnviroCore, are not fighting the garbage with legislation and tax incentives. We are fighting fire with fire. We are taking advantage of the recklessness of generations past. You've all done your research on EnviroCore. This is not an academic institution. We aim to make a profit, make no mistake about that. Most politicians will have you believe that profit and the environment are church and state, that is, mutually exclusive. We are hereby debunking that myth. We are a self-supporting business with absolutely no government funding whatsoever. The demand for renewable resources is there and the demand for a viable product is there. The shortfall is that no one could ever seem to marry the two and when you have to choose, people will choose the viable option every time. We are telling you, you can have both. A cleaner Earth for the generations is within our grasp with plenty of profit to go around for our efforts and all you have to do is grab a surfboard.

The crowd went from attentive silence to unrestrained applause. Alec looked at Gary who looked at Don who looked at Bill with the obvious understanding that Mark had not gone crazy and may actually pull this off. "What the hell was that?" Bill asked in disbelief through the roaring crowd, referring both to the speech and to Mark's thunderous presence. This opener was not part of Mark's original presentation. The three thumbed through their notes and looked over at each other's notes throughout the speech but came up with nothing even close to what was just said. The truth is that Mark had made it all up on the spot. It was an amalgam of inspirational speeches, TED talks, and his own imagination flowing from his cortex to his partially paralyzed vocal cords in a waterfall of abundance. The audience was hooked, which only gave Mark more momentum to deliver the meat and potatoes.

"EnviroCore is focused on the most pertinent problems of our lifetime, both in the short term and the long run. Already in the making are realistic development strategies for technologies such as increasing storage capacity and efficiency in photovoltaic cells, cell-cultured meat, water desalinization and efficiency solutions, pollution clean-up, and biodegradability technology just to name a few." Mark was counting on his fingers at the mention of each technology. He was sure to mention the fields of those potential hires in the audience with the most influence in the industry. It was all part of an intricate strategy. Mark was catering to the subliminal desires which motivated the audience. Not simply the individual members of the audience, but the audience as a being of its own. The most dubious part was that, all he was really saying was that the company had some big plans. There was only one technology that he could prove they were working on.

"EnviroCore will be on the cutting edge of technological advancement," Mark continued. "Primarily focused around research and development, the EnviroCore mission is to invent, investigate, and implement ideas to save the world and to arise with the new dawn of abundant renewable energy and resources. We are committed to advancing civilization by means of environmental technological advancements."

"What I'm about to show you here will be nothing short of a revolution. In the painfully dull title of this presentation is the name of a new life form. Most of you probably lost interest immediately, but that bug was created in the very labs of this building.

"A very select few of you may already know of EnviroCore's proprietary genetic translational prediction software. For those of you who don't speak the language, translation in this sense means the creation of a protein through genetic instructions. Understand that bacteria have very short lifespans, making them a quick study when inserting a manmade gene into the genome. However, when trial and error is the only method at your disposal, the wait to see

215

results is eternal. In order to rectify this dilemma, the fine software engineers in the information technology department partnered with the biologists in the genetic engineering department and, through long hours, long arguments, and perhaps divine intervention, turned out the translational prediction software now known as GLADIS."

Mark recalled a meeting with the team about spreading out credit to some 'potential' departments, a member of all would be Mark. You couldn't stretch the truth much further. But they decided that a crack team of developers sounded better than one golden goose.

"GLADIS stands for Gene Ligation and Dislocation Imaging Software. This brilliant piece of ingenuity is able to, not only create an image of the protein from base pairs entered into the system, but predict the folding of the amino acid chain and the function of the protein as well. GLADIS is equipped with up-to-date genomes from the worldwide bacterial genome database ensembl.org, GMO patents, and search capabilities for every known scientific journal. Instead of the traditional method of painstakingly regenerating colonies and finding a top down approach to synthetic genesis, GLADIS randomly creates mutations in whatever section is being examined, you can randomly insert, delete, and shift base pairs in any section or sections of the genome then document the growth and compare it to the prediction. Once you stumble on something that looks like it has potential, she'll fine tune the sequence until it appears to do something useful. In this case, that useful thing was an enzyme that broke down Bisphenol A.

"Who cares? Well, Bisphenol A, henceforth referred to as BPA, is a structurally necessary component molecule of many plastics. Still, who cares? When we let GLADIS run with our template genome, she evolved a green-colored sister strain that metabolized the aromatic ring structures, the circles, of Bisphenol A. Hence the name, *Viridobacter circulofractus*, A.K.A. the green circle breaker A.K.A. *Vir*." Again, a bit of dramatic license in the story of the bug's manifestation, for effect.

"Even before you ask, I will answer that, due to her novelty, GLADIS is limited to bacteria and I can't show you any screenshots either. Nor will I be sharing any of the proprietary algorithms that perform these feats of which I speak. All I can say if you don't believe me is, 'watch this.'"

Mark clicked the screen forward one slide to the surveillance video file of the bacteriology lab. Before he clicked the play button, he made sure every eye in the audience was fixed on the screen. Mark's finger slid the dimmer switch down from the control panel set in the podium to further dramatize the moment. With an extra amount of force, 'CLICK' went the left mouse button to begin the video.

It was the same footage that Mark had just seen for the first time yesterday, that no one else in the world had seen, nor anyone in the world would forget. The execs in the front would have been worried if he had not just belted his last improvisation out of the park. The footage showed an energetic bacteriology lab stirring through its work in fast forward. The plastic items melted away, just as he remembered, but nobody reacted, just as he expected.

"Did you see it?" Mark asked, knowing that nobody would

be looking for plastic objects spontaneously melting. "That was *Vir*." He began a different version of the same video saying, "This time pay attention." The surveillance video played again, this time with red circles outlining the plastic objects. As it dawned on the audience what was happening, gasps of amazement radiated upward, and eyes became wide with amazement. This version of the footage played on a loop and a circle appeared over the timer after the first loop completed. Mark's finger rolled the dimmer switch back upward to drink in the sight of shock burned in to the faces of the audience.

"As you can see," Mark trumpeted over the murmurs of disbelief, "this takes place over a period of two weeks. There are still a lot of variables we need to calculate to get a more accurate picture of decomposition rate, but that field of view contains about three total pounds of plastic that disappears."

What nobody knew was that they were looking at time zero of a possible public health emergency. Everyone in attendance assumed that this was a controlled demonstration. No one would think that Mark would deliberately show them an escaped potential pathogen. Furthermore, following Mark's talk, everyone assumed that the plastics being broken down were strictly made of Bisphenol A. No one knew that *Vir* was adapting, eating plastics of all different types. The magic of Mark's presentation was that, even if these thoughts did cross the minds of audience members, the prospect was so exciting that they did not dare rain on the parade.

Mark was unbelievably charismatic, radiating success. Through his yarn, EnviroCore was an established player in an up-and-coming field of play, employing teams of creme de la creme in environmental science, and mass producing the innovations of tomorrow. Every brain in the house was hypnotized by his performance, responding to his claims and gestures as if he were charming a snake.

"Every waste management entity on the planet is going to be at our doors, folks," he continued. "That is, if we don't take over the sector outright. If we were to do this today, by our calculations, the entire world's landfills would be nonexistent in just a few short years."

This was an absurd claim, especially given the fact that he just said they needed to perform many more calculations. But again, no one questioned his prophecy. "That means strike while the iron is hot," he continued. "Whether you are an investor, a policymaker, or a scientist, make no mistake, *this* is a revolution. We are, quite literally, playing God. If you have your doubts, that's fine. I don't blame you. If you don't want to be a god, well that's fine too. Uneasy lies the head that wears the crown. All I ask is that you consider this chance carefully. The rest of us will be waving to you from the other side of the Styx."

With those bold words the audience began hysterical applause, followed by a standing ovation. Bill could not help himself and ran up on stage with Mark and put his arm around him in a forceful hook inward. He then let go and raised up Mark's hand as if he had just won a boxing match. Shutters and flashes strobed wildly as the two stood and basked in the glory of what could be described as a rabid dog-and-pony show. Funny, Mark knew that the audience's applause was not for either of them but for the show, for the promise of money, and the implications for their own self-interests. But in the moment it didn't matter. In the minds of Bill and Mark, they were cheering just for them.

THE S CURVE

Looking to the familiar faces that were seated in the front row, Mark noticed the vacant chair of Don Perry. *Strange.* This was perhaps the most significant moment in his career and not the best time to take a bathroom break.

"Thanks everyone," Bill spoke into the mic. "We're gonna take a short break. Feel free to grab some coffee, stretch your legs. We'll be back in about fifteen."

Mark was escorted backstage by the guiding hand of Bill. "You sonofabitch!" he screamed with a terrifying look of joy coloring his face. Unable to contain his exhilaration, Bill bear-hugged Mark, slapping him continuously on the back and lifting him off his feet, sinking delirious laughter into his chest. "What the fuck was that?!"

"I don't know," Mark said, smiling but much calmer than Bill. "I just got caught up in the moment, I guess."

"Mark," said a voice behind him. It was Don.

"Where did you go?" Bill wasn't done being excited. "Our boy just mopped the floor with 'em!"

"Axiom just made us an offer," Don said quietly, as if he were afraid.

"What," Bill piped in, "for the whole thing?"

"That's right," Don replied. Bill froze in shock, his eyes wide, unable to process the news.

"Wait," Mark said, "based on what? That speech? They don't have any questions?"

"I told ya that boy was on fire!" Bill screamed.

"Listen," Mark said, "GLADIS is not ready. Vir is not ready. All of that out there was a sales pitch…"

"A goddamn fine sales pitch!" Bill added.

"That security video is a fluke," Mark continued. "I didn't

221

see it until *last night*. There is a whole lot of testing…"

"That doesn't matter," Don interrupted. "That was good enough for them and they want to talk particulars. Anyway, I'm pretty sure this was their plan before the speech."

"Listen Don," Mark leveled, "I cannot, in good conscience…"

"Mark," Bill interjected, "you just saved the company. You did. Whatever tweaking you need to do, you can do. But this is it. This is what we wanted; what we needed." Bill's hands landed on Mark's shoulders and squeezed.

Just then, Gerald opened the door he was guarding and thundered above the crowd he was holding back, "Hey Mark, a few people want to talk to you." Gerald grinned at his own sarcastic underestimation. A veritable swarm of reporters all chorused his name, trying to get some kind of statement.

"Why don't you slip out the back Mark," Bill said. "We can take it from here and you promised to go into quarantine today. I don't care if you do. But if someone from Dr. Beecher's office isn't here already, they will be looking for you soon."

Mark nodded reluctantly and Bill beckoned for Gerald to walk Mark out with a quick flick of his index and middle finger. It was now officially out of his hands.

'Out the back,' as Bill put it, meant passing through a door backstage which led to the kitchen. This led out to the food service personnel lot, where Mark would less likely be seen. But before they made it out, Tina came bouncing from out of nowhere.

"Hey," she said as she approached, "I just wanted to tell you 'congratulations.'"

Tina put her arms around Mark and forced his head into her thick blond hair. The aroma captivated him as it had in the executive lunchroom and he felt his erectile tissue engorging. Though the awkwardness of the situation quickly shifted as her fingers locked behind his back and she pulled herself into his tumescence. Then, as if she had been practicing the choreography for months, her fingers separated and began traveling in opposite directions. With her left hand, she pulled Mark in and kissed him softly on the cheek. With her right, she slithered under his waistline and encircled his erection in a firm grip. Mark remained calm and collected, practicing otherworldly restraint as she squeezed. And then, as if her actions were as commonplace as a handshake, she fanned her lashes at him once more and bounced away. Mark looked back at Gerald, to behold his raised eyebrows and misshapen smirk. It was a sudden and confusing cherry on top, but Mark figured it had to be a response to his actions in the executive lunchroom the day before. "Did she look different somehow?" Mark asked, to which Gerald replied with shrugged shoulders both as a response, and to challenge the impertinence of Mark's query. "She sure is strong," he remarked behind a frustrated exhale, finishing the walk to the exit.

When Gerald held the door open, Mark could vaguely hear Gary rattling off facts about West Michigan from the auditorium, trying to get everyone back to their seats to finish the conference. Though Mark had his reservations about letting Axiom take his presentation at face value, he could not help but smile a large, genuine smile. Bill was right. He *had* done it. Why couldn't he just *enjoy* a rare victory, just for today?

The temperature must have gone up at least fifty degrees from the night before. In pulling his suit coat off, he accidentally ripped both shoulder seams away from their stitching. "What the…" Mark said aloud. *No matter*. After a minute or two of walking, his fingertips were pulling his car door handle and he was throwing the ruined garment atop the pill bottles that littered the passenger seat. Key in the ignition, the wagon started right up and when it did, the windows rolled down soon after. Mark even decided he would listen to the radio. 'Country Roads' by John Denver was in progress as he found a clear station. It was as if God himself had put the song on at that moment just for him to hear. Though not a religious man, Mark felt a connection to some higher power. He always did love a good coincidence.

Mark contemplated what had just taken place as he glided down those country roads on a restrained sense of power. All of those academics would be signing their names on dotted lines for employment consideration, Axiom would be signing their names on the deed to EnviroCore Labs, and Bill would be in news publications nationwide. It was only a matter of time before the rest of the dominoes fell. The landfills would empty, carbon emissions would drop to zero, and EnviroCore would be the most profitable company of all time. Above all, Mark would have finally honored his father's wish for him to change the world.

Instead of going straight home as he always had, the winds of fate pulled him into the old familiar gravel parking lot of Hayminster Grocery, a Deremer family heirloom. He had not been back to the store in a great many years. Up to this point, it had represented a sort of hallowed ground. Honoring his father's wishes to go out and change the world had made Hayminster Grocery a place of resentment and mourning. Not only would Mark have been perfectly content minding the menial maintenance of the store, but he took a quiet pride in carrying on the family tradition and holding down one of the only supply hubs in a twenty-mile radius. The painful request that his father made for him to leave attached a source of sorrow to the store, even more so as the years passed and he had yet to change the world in even a small way. The events of today shattered that sorrow. It was as if he had been waiting for this moment since he left; like he drove to the store instinctually. It was more than just confidence. Mark was certain that he had changed the world.

As he walked through the door, his senses were suddenly awash with familiarity. The musty smell of damp wood invaded his nostrils, the floorboards creaked underneath him, the cowbell above the door clanged, and the air that remained thick even in the winter time clung to his flesh. The store had not changed much in 100 years and it had certainly not changed since Mark's last day stacking cans and candling fresh chicken eggs.

Upon entry he saw the familiar face of Ed Sorbitt. Though his hair had thinned considerably since they last saw each other, he was the same stocky, ruddy-faced, happy-go-lucky character he had always been since the two first started working together. No matter the situation, Eddie was always smiling. "Hi Mark," was all he said. It had been well over ten years since they had seen each other but Ed wasn't one for small talk. He always looked like he wanted to add more to a conversation but didn't know what to say.

"Hey there Eddie," Mark said. "How the hell have you been?"

"Good!" Ed replied with an even wider grin. Ed loved when people used foul language around him. It made him feel more grown-up, which was a rare thing for him, even in his thirties.

"Dad said that he made you the manager," Mark continued. "How are you liking that?"

"I like it," Ed said, beginning to drift away. Ed never could hold his attention for very long. He would stare through you, like someone behind you was trying to get his attention. "My girlfriend is over there," he said, pointing to a girl less than half his age. "Her name is Sara. We're in love." They looked over in Sara's direction and waved. "Sara," he called to her more loudly than was necessary, "it's Mark."

"Hi Mark," Sara called back smiling. Mark figured she was a local high school girl who played along with his flirting.

"Nice to meet you," Mark said.

"Do you have a girlfriend?" Ed asked.

"No Ed," contemplating the question deeply for a second, "we can't all be as lucky as you. I was wondering if I could pick up some fresh wine. I am celebrating a victory today. Maybe a nice dry merlot with some of Mabel's canned spaghetti sauce."

Ed's face suddenly turned sour, "The sheriff said I can't talk to Mabel anymore." Mark could only guess, but was sure it had something to do with Ed's 'friendliness.' Ed wanted to flirt with women the same as any other man but didn't quite know the rules, sometimes overstepping his bounds and making the recipient uncomfortable. Ed didn't always pick up on that either and persisted until it became awkward and troubling.

"Well that's ok because you have Sara now," Mark said, easily lifting Eddie's spirits.

"Yeah," Ed said as if he just had an idea, staring off again. Mark figured he would be on his own trying to find the wine.

"I'm gonna take a trip down memory lane through these aisles," Mark said. "I'll tell you goodbye before I leave." Ed didn't say anything but walked a million miles away from the conversation before it was even through.

Mark chuckled to himself and started walking up and down the aisles. Looking back, it seemed he had spent his whole life in this store. There were no speakers to play music like the stores in Jotunborough. There weren't ceiling tiles with fancy fluorescent lights. There were long wooden planks lining the ceiling with light bulbs hanging down from their cords. No matter anyway, the store didn't stay open much past dusk.

Mark spotted the old rickety stairs that led to where Ed now lived, the attic. It was an old room where Grandpa Deremer lived when he was running the store. Mark's father was born in that little room. In those days, people gave birth in their own homes. Back then it was the only option but people still carried on the practice to this day. They figured if their folks had done it that way, there was no point in driving all the way to Jotunborough.

In those days, most people in Hayminster lived in what now would be considered a shack. But back then, folks rarely went indoors in the summertime and in the winter the close quarters helped trap in the heat. These small shacks would be so full of people that it was not uncommon for the whole family to share one bed. As a result, the infant mortality rate was startling, as folks would often roll over on their babies in their sleep. To combat this, Grandpa Deremer would give the parents of newborn children a wooden soup crate filled with cloth diapers, mushed up corn in a jar and a onesie that had probably been second-hand to every baby in Hayminster, just to congratulate them. The empty crate could be used as a crib and thus protect the child from someone accidentally suffocating it in the middle of the night. Grandpa reckoned that Hayminster survived and even grew because of those soup crates. So in much the same way, Mark was carrying on the family tradition by helping the town survive and, when this acquisition was all said and done, helping it grow.

Just about everything in the aisles was merchandise from someone in town. Different folks in town grew different things. They would all bring in what they harvested or slaughtered to the store in return for other types of food and supplies. It used to be that everything in the store was produced by someone in the town. For the most part, Ash County was self-sufficient and nearly off the grid until the old ways of farming were phased out in favor of technology. *How ironic.* Mark's company was now producing technology to phase out *those* ways of farming and make Ash County more self-sufficient and nearly off the grid.

Mark brought Mabel's canned spaghetti sauce, the VerBeek Family's merlot, and Spartan brand spaghetti noodles to the counter where Sara would ring him up on the eighty-year-old cash register. "$19.59," Sara said cheerfully.

"My goodness," Mark said pulling out a twenty from his wallet. "It has been a long time since I've shopped here."

"Thank you sir," She said, handing him four dimes and a penny. "It was great to meet you."

"Yes," Mark said, "you too."

Mark found Eddie chucking huge bags of feed into a semblance of a neat stack at the front of the store. "Well it was great to see you again Eddie," Mark said, interrupting his rhythm. "Say, has dad been in lately? I know he said he was retiring but I didn't think he actually would."

"I do a good job Mark," Eddie said, seeing through the euphemism.

"I know Ed," Mark said, slightly embarrassed that he was caught. "You must. I know he wouldn't have left you alone with the till if you didn't."

Ed was clearly offended and didn't say anything in response. He just kept stacking feed. Mark was remorseful and sorry to leave the store on a sour note. "Let me know how things work out with Sara. She's cute," Mark said. Eddie slowed down his chucking to think very hard. He still didn't speak to him but he couldn't help smiling. "We'll see ya later Ed," Mark said finally, throwing his groceries in the passenger seat and driving out of the gravel parking lot down the old county road.

By now, Mark thought, probably at this very moment, Alec was telling them all about his PR campaign, regaling them with stories of 'billboards with the EnviroCore name from New York City to Jerusalem.' There were professionally designed EnviroCore brands placed on genetically modified fruit, irrigation systems, and petri dishes. He spoke of future press releases and social media, smartphone applications and possible political backers, public forums and tours through the facility, and even hosting their own televised environmental conferences to bolster their image and make the competition come to them. He even dared to show the crowd the analytics he had pulled to display how well he knew the market and how they were going to beat out anything that resembled competition. It was all very exciting. Alec thought it to be the best work he had ever done and, to be fair, it was exceptional. But it was mostly for naught now. Axiom certainly would be able to put up any number they wanted. No one in the world was in a position to compete with them. Nonetheless, Alec, Gary, Don, and Bill would go through the motions to completion. After that, they would probably be getting liquored up and taking tomorrow off.

After that though, the plan got a bit foggy. He was still adjusting to thinking in probabilities rather than rigorous 'yes' and 'no.' Even so, he was adjusting. And though he was swimming with *Vir*, he wondered just how harmful it was. *Nobody has died yet*. Perhaps Beecher had decided it wasn't worth the isolation efforts. After all, he hadn't called. Nor was he waiting for him at the gate or in the conference. *Yes, it is just some kind of mix up*. But that hope was dashed as he looked at his phone to notice that, in its silence, had been called six times from Jotunborough General Hospital.

When Mark pulled up to the driveway, he half expected to see Beecher or one of his minions waiting there for him, but found none. Upon entering the house, he was waiting to hear Gladys start in immediately about Dr. Beecher or some reporter but she said nothing. She took her usual place in the kitchen, mashing up potatoes for dinner. "I got some VerBeek Family merlot," Mark called to the kitchen.

"Beautiful dear," Gladys responded. "What's the occasion?"

"I've changed the world," he said proudly.

"Beautiful," Gladys said, not asking how or even looking up from the potatoes. Though, Mark was not offended in the least.

This was the Gladys he knew and he was glad to have her back. Things were all falling into place.

The halls of EnviroCore seemed oddly still. Beneath a furrowed brow, a fiercely concentrated pair of pitch black pupils scanned the pages of the freshly printed acquisition contract. Buried under piles of complex legalese was the agreement that all assets, past and present, now belonged to Axiom Holdings LLC. The reader, Bill, though not particularly well-versed in business law, could not help but notice a few glaring issues in the liability section of the document. One clause read, 'the company will assume no responsibility for transgressions, violations, disputes, or infractions, civil or criminal, past or future, intended or otherwise, of individual Axiom employees.' This meant that the company itself took no responsibility for the actions of its employees, even if they were acting on the company's behalf. In sum, they could do no wrong. Bill glanced down at the bottom of the signature page to observe the remaining empty line that stood next to his printed name.

Bill opened up a blank email to query the EnviroCore lawyers about the peculiar language that implied Axiom would take all the credit and receive none of the blame. But as he began typing, the now constantly ringing phone was at it again.

"Wildeboer," Bill barked into the mouthpiece.

"Well Billy," Ted Philus sang in surprise, "I didn't expect you'd answer. You've got a lot of celebrating to do."

"I'm not signing this contract," Bill blurted, "not until I talk to the lawyers."

"Hang on a sec there Billy," Ted said. "Don't you think they've already looked it over? After all, yours is the only name missing."

Bill looked up from the contract and took a moment for the statement to sink in. How much, he wondered, did Ted still have his fingers in this operation? He knew it was deep, but this seemed more than deep. It was like he knew what was going to happen before it happened. Was he bluffing? Now steeped in paranoia, Bill set his pupils darting around the office, looking for cameras and tiny microphones. Not wanting to let on, he answered as if nothing were out of the ordinary.

"Ted," Bill started, trying not to show his hand, "this language effectively separates the actions of the company from the actions of its employees regardless of..."

"That is a standard clause Billy," Ted downplayed, "It safeguards the company. It's something Sciencia should have had. It protects the many from the actions of the few. You get that right?"

"Limited liability," Bill quoted, "does not mean..."

"Listen Bill," Philus condescended, "I know you are new at this and that is why I have to talk to you so often. You go ahead and email the lawyers, Bill. They are going to check their inbox and say, 'ol' baby Huey needs some more advice.' Then they will joke about the sum of money they are paid for each question they answer. Then they will get back to you and tell you everything I am telling you right now. Believe me, I am not downplaying your due diligence here Billy. But you are a powerful leader now. Everything you do will be under the microscope. You have to at least appear to know what you are doing."

Though Bill knew exactly what Ted was doing, he could not deny that it was working. So much did it affect him that his bottom lip began to quiver at the thought. His upper central incisors bit down onto it and held it still as if his life depended on it. The thought of one more failure was too much for him to bare, no matter how small. The thoughts of himself as a helpless, clueless failure, pulled his tear ducts open.

"That Deremer kid gave a great speech," Ted continued, "didn't he Billy?"

"Yeah," Bill snorted, unable to restrain his sorrow, "that was really something."

"It sure was," Ted patronized. "Everyone thought that *he* was running the company."

"Who thought that?" Bill asked.

"Well, the paper labeled *him* as the CEO," Ted taunted, "because he stood out. He blew them away. They were eating out of his hand. Don't think he won't try it either."

"Try what?" Bill was slowly changing moods. "How do you know about the paper? They only just left."

"Billy, Billy," Philus laughed, "You oughtta know by now. I run in some pretty small circles. I have been in this game a while. I ran that company the way it needed to be run. People won't hesitate to stab you in the back. People you've known a long time. People you thought you could trust."

Bills eyes were now focus-less, staring straight ahead, considering Mark as a threat to his imaginary empire. Long past memories of failure mixed with the captivated audience of today and it wasn't too far of a leap for Bill to associate the two.

"Now now," Ted consoled, "don't get too down on yourself. I only know these things because I've lived them."

"How do I know *you* aren't going to stab *me* in the back?" Bill demanded.

"Have I ever steered you wrong?"

"As a matter of fact…"

"Billy, everything happens for a reason. You are Ralph Macchio. I am Mr. Miyagi."

Bill sat silently, finally submitting to Ted's philosophy.

"Wax on, young grasshoppah" Ted said in a racist Asian accent before the line disconnected.

Bill hung the phone up, changed. Trancelike, Bill flipped the contract to the signature page, scratched his name onto the remaining line beneath the others, and slammed the contract back down on the desk in a heroic triumph over his feelings of inadequacy. His silver pupils guided the mouse cursor to the 'x' in the corner of his blank email to the lawyers and his index finger slammed the window closed.

"I'm sorry Mr. Deremer," Large Marge said to him from inside the guard shack, "your security badge has been wiped of all clearance access and I got specific instructions not to let you in." Mark stood outside 4,000 feet of razor-wire fencing trying to reason with Marge. Fed up with the 'buzz' and red light flicker that accompanied his security badge scan, he finally exited the car and left it running with the door open. Ash County's weather had regressed to the dead of winter. The night brought thick frost to the grass and angry steam to the exhaust pipes. Cars lined up behind him violently slammed in reverse and cut into the other entry lane.

"Listen Marge," Mark's frustration was becoming evident in his voice, "I know you are in this situation cold but there must be some mistake. Just let me talk to Bill. Hell, let me talk to *anyone*. You understand right? You know me. You know I'm not some crazed lunatic. I just saved this company, this town, your job for Christ's sake. Just give me the benefit of the doubt or at least call Bill."

"I'm sorry Mr. Deremer," Marge stood fast. "Bill called security himself yesterday and told us to keep you out. He didn't seem too happy either from what I heard."

Mark's fuse was burning fast. In the back of his mind, the brutal flowers of paranoia were beginning to bloom. Had Bill used him to make the presentation and now that he had Axiom, his services were no longer needed? *That can't be it. Maybe it has something to do with the quarantine that was supposed to happen.* No matter the reason, the time bomb was ticking.

"Goddamn it Marge," Mark punched the chain links. "This is my fuckin' company now. You wouldn't even be here to keep me out right now if it weren't for me!" Marge picked up the phone to call for backup. "Yeah you bring those cocksuckers out here! I'll fuckin' show ya!"

Mark's fury had reached Adolf Hitler proportions. The dried up voice of the rational analyst knew that he was melting down, but no longer had a say. All that was left was to buckle up and watch the terror unfold. Mark had begun banging on the gate with both hands and shaking the chain links free of each other. His knuckles were bleeding enough to start a puddle. Interlocking his fingers tightly in the links of the fence, his body compacted into a coil and sprang back. Large bunches of links were untangling and it wouldn't be long until there was a big enough hole for him to enter the premises. Marge slapped the little red button on the desk and backed herself up against the far wall, unsure of how to proceed.

Gerald and another security guard of equal size had already begun lumbering to the guard shack in response to the first call. The red button that Marge had slapped sent an intermittent, high-pitched tone through the radios of the security guards accompanied by a voice sounding which button was tripped. 'Main gate,' 'main gate,' 'main gate.'

In the distance, Mark saw the two guards now running as they realized it was no false alarm. "Mark! Mark! Mark!" Gerald said excitedly. "It's gonna be alright man. Believe me this shit ain't worth it." Mark was definitely beyond reason at this point though. No part of his brain was screaming as loud as his amygdala. He could not think, or talk, or hear anyone. The anger overwhelmed him. It *became* him. He just kept screaming and pulling at the chain links. Steam was coming off of his entire body as his temperature rose well above normal. The guards just stood there watching, hoping that he would tire himself out before the rest of the team arrived. But Mark was not getting tired. With each passing second, Mark got evermore violent and his strength seemed otherworldly. The guards beheld every blood vessel trying to escape his red-skinned face while he screamed and pulled and punched.

Then unexpectedly, the twisted pieces of metal unraveled enough for Mark to get through. The look on their faces betrayed fear rarely seen in men of their stature. Despite the very notable size difference between Mark and the two guards, they were nearly bowled over as Mark plowed into them. Knocked back slightly, they regained composure enough to hurl Mark down hard on the frozen blacktop. Much to their surprise, he was giving them a run for their money. It took every bit of both of them to keep him subdued. But Mark was still screaming and fighting to get the two beasts off of him. In the midst of the struggle, he expelled another half-digested Deremer family breakfast through the air and into Gerald's collar. The immediate reaction was to drop his hold on Mark, nearly setting him free. Mark got to his feet and began pulling his leg away from the other security guard in one last violent pull. Marge was frozen in fear and could only watch Mark vomit again as he picked up his pace toward the building. He accelerated to an all-out sprint up to about one hundred meters from the building when one of the doors flung open to reveal what looked like riot police. They all held shotguns and shields and wore all black armor and gas masks. It was a very intimidating sight to behold. But Mark did not slow down.

How ironic. The quiet little voice of a rational analyst observed from behind the wall of fury. EnviroCore's Quick Reaction Force was now being deployed in response to the panic button that Marge had tapped. Both the Quick Reaction Force and the panic buttons were Mark's brain-children, installed in the event of civil unrest due to layoffs. Now they were coming after him.

They were all shouting orders on deaf ears. He got to within 10 meters of them before one of the guards raised his shotgun and fired. Mark felt no impact. He saw the muzzle flash and then suddenly lost control of all motor function. His eyes remained open as he crashed to the blacktop unconscious. A high-pitched ringing was all he could hear, but he was still able to register the sight of the Quick Reaction Force lifting their masks with faces of shock. The vision in Mark's right eye clouded with red and the last thing he was able to process was Marge holding her hands up to cover her face.

Like so many times before, Mark awakened to an uncertain timeline. The drip of the IV bag was the first image that his vision clarified. Combined with the slow materialization of the rest of the scenery, confirmed was his suspicion that he was in the hospital. His head was throbbing, but unlike many of the awakenings under uncertain awareness. The events that brought him to this point were vivid in his memory, even though he was missing what he knew to be a good chunk of time between then and now.

Mark hadn't taken his eyes off of the IV bag since he opened them. While he laid there pondering what was being delivered to his bloodstream, none other than Dr. Beecher walked into the room.

"Hello Mark," he chirped as if it were no surprise at all that they would meet again so soon.

"What is in the IV?" Mark skipped the pleasantries and other glaring issues for the moment.

"It's antibiotics and painkillers," the doctor replied looking at the bag of fluid hanging next to him. "The police searched your car after the paramedics took you away and found your pills. Why weren't you taking them? The beta blockers probably could have done you some real good considering you pulled a prison-grade fence down and then blew over two men twice your size. I am going to say it is for the best that you weren't taking the steroids."

"Did they shoot me?" Mark asked.

"Yes they did," he answered, "it was a rubber bullet that got you in the side of the head. You're lucky you're not dead."

"Where are we?" Mark asked, ignoring the doctor's coldness, "Am I in St. Catherine's?"

"No," he replied, "you're at Jotunborough General. Why didn't you come in yesterday? We could have avoided all this."

The doctor's complete lack of bedside manner did not bother Mark in the least. Though he clearly remembered their last encounter and how much his demeanor had infuriated him, there was no such fury. *Must be the painkillers.*

"Am I in quarantine?" Mark cackled.

"No," Beecher answered, "we'll be moving you up there as soon as we can. We had to make sure you were going to live first. Plus we had to give *your* reservation away. This damned weather is wreaking havoc on people."

"Sorry about that," Mark gargled.

"No matter," the doctor replied. "Bill made a pretty compelling argument for the bug being benign anyway. Just lay back and enjoy the drugs until we get a room upstairs for you."

No sooner had Beecher left the bedside, than a beautiful woman wearing scrubs sauntered in with a purple, plastic-covered dinner tray. "You hungry hun?" her sultry voice asked. But Mark had no response. "Here, let's get you all settled in." She nearly climbed on top of him trying to fluff his pillows. Her giant breasts pressed against his cheek and she even managed to exhale into his ear, as if she were trying to get a reaction. But Mark sat expressionless. "Here's your remote darlin'," the woman said handing it to him. "If you need anything at all you just call." Before she left him alone, she massaged his forearm gently and let the tips of her fingernails drag down his flesh as she walked away. Alas, the nurse's flirtatious behavior escaped Mark's perception entirely.

As he inspected the food that was just presented, he heard a news reporter talking about Vandeburgh. From behind the steam of his cordon bleu emerged a picture of EnviroCore and footage of a repair crew installing two new rows of fencing on the front gate.

241

The report then presented the security footage from the west gate of what had taken place earlier. He calmly watched himself banging on the gate, then ripping it off, then the struggle with Gerald and the other guard, then the shot to the head and subsequent rag-doll drop. Throughout the duration of the news story, Mark's vital sign monitor showed no change in activity whatsoever. Why should it? That is simply what happened earlier; and that's all it was. As the reporter wrapped up her report by calling Mark a 'crazed ex-employee that sought revenge on the company that scorned him,' Mark cut into his cordon bleu and watched the steam rise, waiting to see the next news story.

As the last few green beans of his meal were being stabbed, Mark noticed the gravity pulling sharply on his eyelids. Sounds of cars zooming by on the wet streets of Jotunborough entered Mark's consciousness as he drifted, but the twilight received them as waves crashing against the bow of a ship. Fewer and fewer photons made it to his pupils and he could only vaguely see the outline of a body standing in front of him. Though, in an instant, the realization of the familiar shape forcefully threw his visual cortex into action and he could see that indeed a person had somehow made it this far into his room without warning. It was a figure clad in blue pinstripes and a solid red necktie, arms hung at sides, face locked in a cockeyed smile. Mark's hippocampus finally pieced together the unmistakable personage of Bill Wildeboer.

"They really got you a good one didn't they?" he said in a tone deeper than Mark remembered. "You really got *me* a good one too." The voice was drawn out and deep, like a man who had smoked for many years and had just woken up. "Listen Mark," he said ominously, "things are not going to go your way if you try to run them. C'mon. We are old friends now. I could have pressed charges but I didn't. I know you're going through a hard time with the stress and the illness and all. I only asked that you keep me in the loop. I asked you that, didn't I?"

What the hell is he talking about? Mark saw through Bill's bullshit like he was holding it on a flashing neon sign. If Bill would have pressed charges, then Mark would have countersued for excessive force and maybe worse. It was nonsense. Nonetheless, Bill was up to something. Meanwhile, Mark made only the slightest attempt to acknowledge that he was in the room.

"I'm not going to beat around the bush," Bill continued, vocal cords hitting even lower notes, "There is no way you can come back after that display yesterday. Why didn't you just go into quarantine like you said you would? None of this would have happened. Anyway," Bill paused opening up a thin trifolded stack of recycled paper, "this here is a liability waiver, confidentiality agreement, and notice of termination all in one. It basically says, 'you're done.'" Mark made no reply.

"I'll take your silence as an agreement," Bill said turning his back to Mark to look out the window. "You can sign it when you're up to it." With his hand placed on the wall next to the window, he stared out into Jotunborough for an uncomfortable minute. "You thought you could take advantage of the power I gave you and implement some kind of takeover? You must've been outta your mind. You were brought in to help save the company, not run it. That is my job. It will always be my job." Bill turned away from the window, looked straight through Mark's forehead, and then walked towards Mark with ever increasing speed. Once he reached an arm's distance, Bill outstretched his hand, grabbed a huge chunk of Mark's cheek in his fist, and lifted him out of bed and held him by it. Mark winced and pawed at

Bill's wrist trying to redistribute the weight but Bill kept batting away the attempts with his free hand.

"Give me some indication that you understand me right now," Bill said as calmly as he could during the struggle, "or I'll fucking kill you right here."

Though Mark did not believe that Bill would actually kill him, he didn't particularly enjoy what was happening so he desperately complied with Bill's request, nodding his head the best he could. With one final squeeze, Bill slammed him back down onto the bed revealing a new purple mark with squiggly outcrawlings where capillaries had broken in Bill's grip. Blood and tears rolled down the side of Mark's face, from the popping of two stitches in Mark's rubber bullet wound and from the newest pain in his cheek, respectively.

"Is everything alright?" the nurse asked, hurriedly responding to the commotion. Mark lay clutching his cheek and breathing heavily, obviously not alright. But Bill was more than happy to speak for him.

"Everything's fine dear," Bill said. "Looks like your patient here isn't a very sound sleeper."

"What the hell happened?" she asked as she rushed in.

"I'm fine," Mark whispered loudly as he regained his composure. "Do you have a pen, Bill?"

Bill smiled so hard that his cheeks pushed his glass-textured eyes back into their sockets. They disappeared under the surrounding flesh and all that he could see were two eye-shaped shadows.

"In fact I do," Bill said, retrieving a thick, silver pen from his breast pocket. Mark signed the dotted line without reading one word of the document. As he slithered out of the room with the deed to Mark's dignity, Bill nodded unassumingly and said in thunderous baritone, "Take care now."

From the lobby rose the clatter of chairs crashing into disorder, ending any nearby sleep. Mark's eyelids opened in a panic to the sight of an empty IV Bag. The fracas continued as Mark sat up in bed, peering through his room's door in a vain attempt to relieve his confusion. Finding no satisfaction, he less-than-carefully lunged from bed, wheeling his IV line behind him. Outside the door, he bore witness to a collection of limbs swinging wildly and fists landing into faces. Two or three fighters catapulted through the peace of the lobby, clearing a path as they went.

A dispute over the position of names on the sign-in sheet prompted the first shove, which was quickly rectified with a blow to the jaw, which spewed blood onto a bystander, who then lost his composure and kicked the first offender in the sternum, which then elicited a grappling contest between all three. The struggle was a brutal display; one rivaling anything televised. Two giant men wearing security uniforms rushed in and were able to pull them apart but could only subdue one each. The third man continued to blast one of the restrained until one of his eyeballs burst and his body went limp. That guard then dropped the limp body to pursue the free man. A great chase ensued, followed by a crash to the ground, the smaller civilian trapped under the weight of the giant security guard. Tenaciously, the tackled party continued to throw blows in the form of backwards head butts into the nose of the tackler. With an initial splatter of blood, a shower of red then rained down on the man below. The crowd looked on in horror when the guard decided he had been made a fool of long enough. He placed his knee in the center of the man's back and pulled his chin upward in a headlock. Mark watched as his blood-soaked head turned purple from the pressure. Then, in a flash, Mark had placed the face that was being pulled upwards. It was Vince

Winters, one of Ash County's garbage men. Vince's fingernails scratched hard at the security guard's forearm to no avail. Then, in a sudden and deafening pop, his hands fell away from the struggle and his face went dead. Mark's analysts suddenly reappeared and immediately told him that Vince Winters had just been killed in front of him.

Of course he had never seen a man killed. He had seen animals killed, and in that way, Vince's body fell like an animal's when it is killed. There is no dramatic bounce back or jump up, the body simply stops doing what it was doing at the moment of execution. But an animal's face does not share the same familiar expression as that of a human face. A human face has discernible, relatable features. All the same, the face simply stops whatever it was doing in one anticlimactic motion. The guard had pulled cervical vertebrae four and five apart, ripping every nerve fiber in the cervical spinal cord in two, leaving frayed ends on either side of the break. Upon realizing what he had done, the guard quickly let go of the man's head and all but jumped off of his back. Vince's body hit the large white porcelain tile beneath him with a slap. Bent unnaturally far upwards, Vince's neck was a grotesque perversion of the human form. His eyes rolled up, revealing only the bottoms of retina from under their lids and his mouth hung open revealing the limp red slap of flesh that was his tongue. That one or two seconds that it took the crowd to realize what had occurred before their eyes, cast a shadow that would encompass the rest of their lives.

Immediately following the incident, four more hospital security guards appeared and swarmed the offenders. The first man was still fighting to get away from the steady grip of the other security guard, while the second man lay unconscious in the middle of the lobby. Both of the living men were placed in zip ties. The third man was encircled by healthcare personnel until a gurney could arrive. There was no question to anyone else in the room that the thing they had just lifted onto the gurney was a dead body, but they went through the motions anyway, checking vital signs and covering the face, until they were out of public view.

The whole scene had ignited and extinguished in an atypically short period of time. A janitor was already in to mop up all of the blood puddles. Mark found this man to be the least interested of anyone. He calmly unfolded his wet floor sign and went to work mopping. One would get the impression, by watching him, that he had dealt with this very situation too many times. It was a look of annoyance, as if he had been mopping up blood his whole life.

Whether it was the horrifying scene that just unfolded, the rude awakening, or the empty IV bag, Mark made the decision to flee. The room, the gown, the crowd, all became contributing factors to an overwhelming claustrophobia which he could not bear. Not to mention the fact that he was expected to go into quarantine. There was no way he was about to sit in isolation until they said he was free to go. But as he wheeled the IV bag back into his room to pack up his clothes, he remembered that the last place he saw his vehicle was outside the security arm outside at the EnviroCore gate. Mark could not contain a quiet, "fuck!"

No Matter. Mark unstrapped the tape from his forearm that held the IV catheter in place. Admittedly, the list of people he was friendly enough with to pick him up from Jotunborough General Hospital was slim. Steve, Mark thought, was probably the only one who would. Without another second of hesitation, he used the hospital phone to dial the number to the bacteriology tech office.

"Bacteriology this is Brian," spoke the voice of Brian MacPherson, the associate who took over for Steve when he became study director.

"Brian," Mark grunted, "is Steve there?"

"Is this Mark?" Brian bellowed, "Didn't expect to hear from you!"

"Brian," Mark repeated, "let me talk to Steve. It's an emergency."

"Steve's in jail," Brian said casually. "He got into a fight at Sideway's last night."

"What?" Mark was shocked, "That biker bar?"

"Yeah" Brian assured, "It was in the paper and everything."

"Fuck," Mark swore, not terribly concerned about Steve being in jail, but more about the fact that he would not be delivering his car.

"Listen Brian I have a huge favor to ask," Mark began. "I need my car."

"You want me to bring it to you?" Brian asked, "It's actually still in the lot here with the keys in it. Bill did you a favor by not having the cops tow it."

Mark was a bit shocked, "Would you mind?"

"Nope not at all," Brian replied. "Where are you?"

"Jotunborough General Hospital," Mark said. "I'll be out front."

"OK," Brian said, "I'll see you there."

"Thanks a lot Brian," Mark said.

"Sure man," Brian said as he hung the phone up.

As Mark hung the hospital phone up, he pondered the willingness of Brian to help him. Not that they were enemies, but they definitely weren't close. Mark's paranoia about the whole situation hung thick in the air like a dense fog. Taking a deep breath, he grappled with the odd notion that maybe Brian was just willing to do him a favor, just to be kind. *And what was that about Steve?*

It was the worst kind of weather. A mist hung in the air made up of all three states of matter. The air stung the flesh and turned exactly half of the precipitation solid. Meanwhile, the ground was warm enough to steam, which kept the other half liquid. It was a painful sort of feeling that dominated the spirit; a desperate yearning for the winter to finally give up and allow the long, long awaited chance for new life to bloom. But the stale winter would not let go. It was determined to hang on until all hope was gone. Each year, the souls of Ash County were kept trapped under ice until they accepted that spring would never come. It was a fifth season that only an unlucky fraction of the human population had the displeasure of experiencing. It was unlovingly referred to as 'Limbo.'

      Mark sat sweating and shivering on one of the benches in the sheltered cul-de-sac outside of the hospital. With the commotion in the lobby, Mark figured he would be able to slip past anyone who might care about him leaving. Seeing no familiar faces on his way out, he figured he was in the clear. Though that did nothing for his paranoia. There was a shabbily dressed man in the grips of winter's madness sitting on one of the other benches, ranting to himself about the government. He seemed harmless enough, but difficult to ignore. On the bench directly across from him sat a new mother waiting for her family to carry them home in a warm vehicle. Though, the mother seemed unaffected by the weather; in fact oblivious to anything except her baby. She rocked it back and forth, both of them silent. Across from her, the drifter rocked as well, but in distress, as if he were trying to ward off demons that had escaped the confines of his skull and tormented him in the subzero ambience surrounding Jotunborough General.

      In the distance, finally, Mark spotted the white wagon

pulling down the long drive. But no sooner were his spirits lifted than they were pulled back down by the call of some familiar voice behind him. "Mark," it was Dr. Beecher, "what are you doing?" At first he said nothing, hopeful that either Brian would get there first or that Beecher would be convinced that he was not Mark by the lack of response. But there would be no such luck. "Mark I need you to come back inside right now please."

"I don't think I will," Mark finally acknowledged. "I can't stay here anymore."

"Mark," Beecher said in the tone of a parent, "if you leave now, I have to call the police. You're not thinking clearly. Please come back inside."

By now, Brian had pulled the car up to where Mark stood and, seeing the two in some kind of confrontation, put the car in park and got out. Brian, always one to be a part of the drama, made his way around to the conversation.

"What's the problem?" Brian said in his best tough guy voice.

"Sir," Beecher started, "if Mark leaves the premises he will be in violation of the law. There will be a warrant issued for his arrest and then you will be in violation of the law for harboring a fugitive."

"What's he done?" Brian persisted.

"He's contracted an infection of unknown pathology," Beecher said. "It is unknown whether he is contagious and he needs to remain in quarantine until a diagnostic battery can be performed and we can assemble a pathogenic profile."

Brian looked to Mark with a combination of fear and betrayal. Though Mark did not fully realize the gravity of the situation until now, his mind was not changed about returning to the building. In a split-second decision, his legs snapped into sprint and he dove past MacPherson and Beecher. Though the two gave no pursuit, Beecher for legal liability reasons and MacPherson for the new fear of contagion, Mark jerked the shifter into drive and floored the accelerator, squealing the tires against the wet pavement as he sped away. As Mark's car tore recklessly out of the drive, the doctor and the scientist watched the brake lights remain dim. Throughout the entire scene, neither of the two bystanders looked up once. While the new mother admired her creation, the drifter hummed and clicked and spoke to nobody, both rocking rhythmically in unison.

The Sun Dance

That old white wagon, though not much to look at, had a 3 liter V6 and was plenty familiar with the county roads. Mark made short work of tearing off into the trees and the dirt where the Jotunborough police seldom traveled. Twist after turn after twist, Mark dug deeper and deeper into no man's land. As well as Mark knew these back roads, they were a mess of centuries-old Indian trails, hunting passages, trade routes, and former railways, even he was not immune to the entanglement of the labyrinth.

With each mile travelled, houses got fewer and farther between while the woodland canopy grew denser. It had been a great many years since Mark had been this far into the woods, though he could tell where he was by the sheer mass of the trees. It had gotten the nickname of 'Zululand' for reasons no one could really remember. All that Mark had heard of it was that it was full of wild boars and a few hermits with many miles of land in between. Traveling for enough time in one direction would land him in Valhalla National Park, while in the other direction, he knew there was an opening that would lead directly to Deremer land. There was an unobstructed view of the clearing from his father's deer blind where he often saw Slippy milling around in the tall grass. If he could find his way to that clearing, he would be able to make it home.

These less-traveled roads were far less forgiving than the paved roads in Ash County. Mark found it necessary to slow his car to a mere ten miles per hour in order to keep the least bit of control. In keeping with the obstinate weather, patches of ice still covered what was not made of loose rocks and mud. The slow going allowed him a chance to admire the majestic scenery, as well as some hermits of which childhood rumors spoke.

On his right was a broken, rusted trailer with a huge snow-covered mound in the backyard that seemed to be made of garbage. In the front yard was a dirty mattress where children were landing as they jumped off the rickety porch. Even though it was only about thirty degrees, the kids seemed content in undershirts and short pants. As Mark passed, they stopped what they were doing because here, he was the one out of place.

It was approximately another mile of terrible road conditions before he saw another clearing where a second small dwelling had been built. In the front yard was a clothesline from which hung a line of frozen clothing. Socks, underwear, flannel shirts, and jeans, tattered, faded, and aged with tinges of yellow, all hung stiff on the line, as if someone had been optimistic when the weather began to change. It was obvious from the look of the place that it did not contain a washer and dryer, or running water for that matter.

Mark drove slowly enough by the house to see an old man in a rocking chair on the porch. Overall, he looked shabby and unkempt, clad in jean overalls and a plaid shirt. Judgements began leaping off the desks of his analysts: *I wonder if he has running water at all. I wonder if he has ever changed clothes. He probably has never owned a toothbrush or received a paycheck. He probably stays drunk on homemade moonshine to keep him warm.*

The old man's face was wrinkled to the bone, which was only slightly visible underneath a long, wiry beard. White hair with tinges of yellow crept out just as long and wiry from underneath the flaps of his Stormy Kromer hat. Mark noticed that the man's left eye was completely absent of pigment and could very well have been a ball of cotton. The man's appearance was altogether ghoulish and he could have been mistaken for a corpse that was sat upright in a rocking chair.

But after a few seconds of eye contact at Mark's 10-mile-per-hour pace, the old man raised his right hand up in a wave of acknowledgement. Mark raised his hand up in kind until the old man and his decrepit shack were out of his sight. Another mile of gravel, dirt, and ice passed under his tires. Then another. Mark was losing his bearing. He assumed that the road would eventually empty him on to something familiar, but it just kept on winding through ever-denser thicket.

The road did eventually behave as Mark predicted insofar as it emptied onto something familiar: a yellow metal sign peppered with buckshot holes indicating an S curve lie ahead. As Mark cautiously took the first turn, Slippy, Ash County's unaccountable wild horse, raced directly across his path like it was the last quarter mile at Churchill Downs. Even at a modest speed, the brakes could not stop the car's barreling into the adjacent ditch and the terrible thunder of two and a half tons of Great Lakes Steel echoed through the hollows of the forest. A shower of pills and paperwork filled the air inside the vehicle and left Mark hanging sideways by the seatbelt. The horse, meanwhile, continued galloping through the woods unscathed.

Mark just hung there. It was not a bad wreck. The grade of the turn, the ice on the road, and the depth of the ditch were just enough to make it seem more violent than it was. Though the wreck was minor, he had no idea what to do. Among the pills and papers, his cell phone flew beside them, hurling into some crevice of the vehicle that might as well have been another dimension. *On top of everything else...*

Mark's silent stewing session was interrupted by the abrupt landing of a child on the front driver's side wheel well of the car. It was a ragged looking boy dressed in a shiny black overstuffed winter coat. "Wow! That was so cool!" the boy said admiring the damage to the wagon, "I think you may need a tow truck mister!" Mark did not know what to say. The boy leapt from the wheel well to the door and offered his bony little hand. He was so dirty he looked like a chimney sweep. "Give me your hand sir," the boy said cheerfully, "I think I can help you."

"I'm too heavy for you to lift," Mark struggled to say. "Get off the car, it may tip over any second."

"I don't think so," the boy answered back while surveying the area. "I think you're stuck."

"I'll pull you down with me," Mark said, struggling to unfasten his seatbelt. "Can you get an adult to come and help me? Or at least call a tow truck?"

"I think my sister is right over there," the boy said.

"Great," Mark said, "thank you."

"Moon!" the boy called out and the sound of dead leaves rustling under tiny running feet did not give Mark hope that the situation would improve.

"Holy smokes!" another little voice called back as a girl of the same age and stature jumped down onto the car and perched next to her brother, "I don't remember seeing you before!" The two were obviously twins. She was just as dirty as him and wore the same shiny black coat.

"Where do you guys live?" Mark grunted, blood pooling to his right side, "Do you have parents or someone who can call a tow truck for me?"

"I think Grandpa Ray is home," the boy said. "He can probably pull you out with the winch."

"I remember every stump he ever pulled," the girl said. "C'mon Hugh, let's get Grandpa Ray."

"We'll be back mister," the boy called.

With that, the two jumped off of the car together and dashed away. Both of the kids' coats were slightly too big for them and they were both able to pull their hands inside the sleeves. They both flapped their arms as they ran, flailing the empty cuffs like wings.

Mark was able to find a spot on the floor where he could support all of his weight with both legs. With enough weight taken off of the seatbelt, he was able to release the latch of the seat belt buckle, dropping him to the passenger side window. Little Hugh was right. The car did not move an inch as he hit the lowest point of gravity. Since now he was free, and the car was good and wedged, he took the opportunity to search for his cell phone, just in case Grandpa Ray didn't come. He searched high and low but found nothing but pills and papers. Finally, he decided that the phone must have flown out of the car as he had just noticed that the driver's side window had shattered with the fall.

Mark stood up on the console and placed a hand on either side of the window. In one motion, he thrust himself up and out of the vehicle and leapt off the car onto the bank beside him. Tracing his tire tracks back to the point of control loss, Mark scanned the ground and kicked through the nearby snow but saw no phone. *It must still be down there.*

The woods had a stillness that seemed deeper somehow. Even though most of Ash County could be considered rural, there was never complete silence. Some evidence of man could usually be heard year-round, whether it was a tractor, a chainsaw, a gunshot, or a sneeze. But in this moment, Mark experienced pure quiet. There was the rustling of leaves and clacking of branches in the breeze, there was the occasional bird call or squirrel bark, but the influence of man had left this so-called 'Zululand' alone. It was a strange and satisfying sound and it went unheard by most of mankind. To hear it properly, Mark had to sacrifice a minute of the worry of his phone, his car, his job, his ailment, indeed his whole life. It was not the past, not the common timeline, not a plan for the future. It was not even one second before or one second after this moment. He was truly, and simply, present.

Though he had not blacked out or altered consciousness, it seemed only a second or two had passed in his dwell before the distinct sound of a very old engine shook his peace. A completely rust-covered 1948 Ford F1 was on its way. From this distance, Mark could see the peculiar Hugh and Moon twins riding in the bed of the truck, standing on either side of the cab. As the distance lessened, he could see two coon dogs riding shotgun on the bench seat, but the driver's face was obscured by the glare of a bright sun behind a blanket of overcast. Mark stood in the middle of the one-lane road with his hands on his hips trying to see past the glare to the face of the driver but could not. It remained obscure until the truck came to a complete stop. The door squeaked open and the driver and his crew all dismounted at once. The two dogs ran up to him howling and wagging tails. "Easy boys," the voice of the driver called to the dogs. It was the old man from the porch. He grabbed some gloves from the cab before squeaking the door shut behind him. "Havin' some trouble eh?" the old man said as he donned his gloves. Mark could not ever remember laying eyes on a more ghastly figure. He was even more frightening at two feet away than he was at the twenty or so that separated them when he passed earlier. "Hi stranger," the man outstretched his hand, "I'm Ray." The eye that Mark thought could be a piece of cotton was, in fact, a piece of cotton.

"Mark," Mark replied, trying not to stare. "Thank God your kids came along when they did."

"Yeah," Ray said, "they're always into somethin' 'er 'nother." The old man went straight to work. He grabbed the hook from the winch on the front of his truck and jumped down into the ditch just as spryly as the children.

"Can I do anything to help?" Mark asked.

"When these wheels hit the ground," Grandpa Ray replied, "jump in and put 'er in neutral." After the wagon was hooked, Ray jumped out of the ditch and began reeling the winch cable by means of an elaborately decorated control lever, sharp at the tip. As the vehicle righted, Mark clumsily tripped down to the door, hopped in, and shifted to neutral. The ditch didn't seem steep at all as the winch made easy work of pulling him out.

As the cable had retracted all the way back, the twins began cheering and flying around the scene, clucking and cawing like birds. The racket of the mechanical winch and children wailing in unison made the hounds howl in concert. Ray smiled humbly and chuckled as he stopped the cable's winding, "We don't get many visitors out this way."

"That's probably how you like it," Mark conversed.

"We do like our privacy," Ray said, "but I reckon most folks might fear this kind of livin'. And so they fear those who live this way…us. I can't blame 'em. Hell, just look at me." A chilling yet rib-tickling cackle bellowed out of Grandpa Ray and Mark couldn't help laughing right along with him. "He thinks himself wise, who can ask questions and converse also; but conceal his ignorance no one can, because it circulates among men." Ray widened his eyelids and, with a deliberate and swift motion, tapped one finger against his temple with an almost comical force.

"C'mon in," Ray said as he climbed in the F1, "we'll get you fixed up."

The twins and the dogs jumped in the bed of the truck as the old man pulled the wagon a few miles back to Ray's tiny, dilapidated house. Once there, he offered Mark the run of it until he returned. "There's meat in the freezer. You're welcome to it if you get hungry."

"Where are you going?" Mark asked.

"We're going to town," Ray replied. "Don't often get much reason to."

"Is the car broken?" Mark was thoroughly confused. "How long will you be?"

A moment of deep reflection fell over Ray and his face took on a serious expression of contemplation as he stared thousands of miles down the road. "Reckon however long it takes," he finally said, bearing the remainder of his rotten teeth in a smile under his scraggly white beard. Taking Ray's offer, Mark dismounted, and with a final, one-finger salute, the odd bunch was on their way to town, doing whatever it was they set out to do. Mark assumed it was to have the car fixed but was puzzled as no real inspection was done. *Surely, he knows something I don't.*

The stress of the day seemed to be wildly insignificant in this context. He had these people figured all wrong. The whole town had this area pegged as something it wasn't. Mark was ashamed that he had listened to the crowd and just believed everything that everyone said. But this event had forgiven all of that. '*Conceal his ignorance, no one can.*' The words were a glowing iron that branded his memory for all time. In this moment, he understood that there was more to perception than face value, and vowed never to take anything at face value ever again. From now on, he would question everything.

Mark watched them drive down the icy, jagged road, which Ray navigated with the skill of a stunt driver. A few beams of sunlight had even made their way from behind the overcast through the canopy, seeming to light the road in front of them. And though the truck shook and swayed recklessly over the terrain, Ray demonstrated a lifetime of handling Ash County's neglected rural passages in a manner that put Mark to shame. *None of this ever would have happened if I hadn't slammed on the brakes*. He considered both sides of the connotation carefully as he made his way to the cabin.

Grandpa Ray and his crew were not completely out of sight before one or two rain drops measuring at least one inch in diameter slammed onto the top of Mark's head. He would have thought it bird droppings if it weren't so cold. Still, Mark looked to the sky only to be hit with five more cold drops in rapid succession. A mad dash to the tin roof of the porch only narrowly saved him from becoming completely drenched. The downpour on the tin sounded like combat and nary a thought could be heard over the racket.

Ray's rocking chair seemed like just as good a place as any to rest and wait out the storm. Even though it was offered to him, there remained misgivings about going inside the little red cabin as the two were still basically strangers. But with the wind picking up and the tin no longer providing much shelter, Mark decided to forget their personal status and seek refuge inside.

The interior of the structure was somehow much smaller than the exterior let on. A basic, metal frame bed fit snug against the west wall and a tiny tray table hugged the northeast corner, upon which sat a lantern and a small radio. In the southeast corner was a comically small wood burning stove. It was nothing more than a metal cylinder, laid horizontally on a tripod, which opened up to hold a single log or maybe three pieces of kindling. On the stove's flat top was a cast iron skillet and an antique tea kettle. There was a second door that led out to a back portion which was twice as large as the living area, covered by a corrugated metal roof which also kept a seven-foot-high wall of firewood dry. Within the plywood walls was a chest freezer and ten or twelve gas cans. Too curious, Mark went over to the deep freeze and opened the lid to find it filled to the brim with venison steaks and salmon fillets. *Does this place have power?* He noticed the freezer appeared to be plugged in to an outlet in the plywood but it didn't sound like it was on. Upon venturing to the opposite side of the plywood wall, a generator sat just outside. The weather had been cold enough to store meat outside. Grandpa Ray had probably been conserving gas by not having the generator running. Mark put together the puzzle of this simple life. *I could get used to this.*

The smell of the cabin reminded Mark of the store; a combination of mildew, campfire, and rust. Having such a closed in area was surely a plus when it came to retaining heat. Mark could still feel the warmth of body heat and the little stove despite the room being unoccupied or some time. The violent taps on the single window had more volume than anything, but whatever lined the plywood under the sheet metal roof had gone a long way to keep the space much quieter than the porch, though the weather raged on.

Foreseeing a decent wait time for the storm and for the odd bunch to return from town, Mark decided to try the radio to ward off boredom. One of the largest AM radio towers in the country sat no more than ten miles from Mark's current location. On clear days, its broadcast could be heard in Florida, so there was hope that if nothing else, that station would come through. Just as suspected, the weather reduced all other stations to static except for WAC. It was a 60-story, red and white tower lined with flashing red lights that sat at the base of the infamous 'Mount Trashmore,' a landfill converted to ski hill during the winter months. The lights kept the tower visible to airplanes at night and in dense fog but could be seen two counties over in the light of day. So powerful was its signal that those living close enough received its transmission on their garage doors if tipped at the proper angle.

Before the advent of FM, WAC played the latest hits from Fats Waller to Glenn Miller. Now a dinosaur, the air time belonged to the broadcasting class of Jotunborough Community College, the local classical enthusiasts during public radio hour, and a broadcast of Sheriff Tom Van Beck reading the top stories from the daily edition of The County Crier which repeated four times a day. Mark tuned in just in time to hear the end of a loud and clear 'Ride of the Valkyries.'

The hours kept passing. Though he was unsure of exactly how long he had been waiting, and though unable to see past the curtain of rain draped outside the window, Mark did know that the day was being overcome by the black of the night. Then, over the volume of the radio, which was at its maximum to overcome the tapping on the window, a discordant howl pierced through the night inviting Mark's arm hair to stand. The Deremer Farm was filled with endless species of wildlife from coyotes to barred owls to numerous variants of frogs and toads. There was a vast collection of animal sounds in Mark's memory. However, this one was as unrecognizable as it was chilling.

The darkness, Mark decided, was now too dark and he reached down under the table to retrieve a long matchstick from its box to start the kerosene lantern. As the hours passed, odd sounds reverberated into the night, but he was unable to discern his paranoia from reality. Each one could be explained by different animals, faint radio frequency disruptions, or cabin fever, though none were familiar. Before long, he became accustomed enough to let his consciousness drift.

A very simple dream. The long grasses flowed, swaying side to side. Eyes glued to binocular eyepieces told their tales. All the fractal branches occurring in nature could be seen. Rivers flowing to an ocean, vines crawling up pines, tree branches reaching towards the heavens, cracks in a snow-covered ice sheet, lightning crackling from the sky.

A deafening thunderclap rose Mark from his dreams and nearly out of his skin. If not for his sternum, his heart would have punched a hole in his chest as he looked out over the flooding landscape. The rainstorm had not stopped throughout the night. Still no sign of Grandpa Ray or the twins. *The truck couldn't have made it through this*. The ground was completely underwater and the downpour was still torrential. Mark felt the burning irritation of sweat-soaked clothes on clammy skin and a voracious hunger of an empty stomach.

It was early morning, which was only evident by the switch in exterior from black to gray. The kerosene lamp had burned out overnight, chilling Mark to a shiver. Adding to the ache of the temperature, was hunger. Nearly every morning for most of Mark's life, Gladys had prepared a giant breakfast. To say that he was hungry was an understatement. It felt like he hadn't eaten in a week. Though he felt even less comfortable eating Ray's food than sleeping in his bed, he considered the situation. It was many miles back to town in an unknown direction, all of which were submerged by several inches of water. Moreover, the rain was not warm. Thin condensate clung to the air at the trough of his exhales as he surveyed the sinking woodland outside the door. If Ray had not made it back by now, there was a good chance he would not be back soon. His options were to wander aimlessly in cold rain for hours, live with the hunger pangs until Ray returned, or prepare one or two choices from the offered meat in the freezer. Again, Mark chose to forget their personal status.

He went back to the freezer and pulled out a single venison steak to thaw while he muddled around with the stove. An axe lay next to the immense pile of wood. A single log could be split into four pieces of kindling, which would be enough to cook his steak and hopefully dry his clothes. Mark was no stranger to splitting wood. He had spent many a lonely hour hauling a maul up and over his head and back down onto logs until his trapezius muscles burned. He swung once, 'POP,' twice, 'POP,' and once more, 'POP' to leave four thin logs lying among splinters on the concrete floor. Collecting them and carrying them inside, he retrieved another match from the long thin box with which he would light a fire inside the tiny stove.

A crackle of lightning branched out across the sky in a bright flash, reminding him of the grass fractals in his dream, as the logs went into the oven followed by the fractal flames lit by the match. The wood had probably been drying for years considering the speed with which it caught fire. Within minutes, the room became too warm and Mark stepped back outside to bring the venison steak in to thaw the rest of the way. The cabin sat on a slight hill, so the flood waters were still quite far from being a threat to it. The modest dwelling was a model of efficiency. No form, all function.

Mark picked up the radio from the tray table and adjusted the frequency knob to clear up the static. It was not music and it was not the voice of the sheriff, which meant it must have been the broadcasting students of Jotunborough Community College. It was some type of interview, but it didn't take long for Mark to realize that the two men were talking about EnviroCore. Then he realized one of the men was Alec Reill.

"We are expected to dump the first wave of *Viridobacter circulofractus* by the end of the week at Mount Trashmore. With Axiom behind us now, we have the capacity to speed up the process of growing a much larger number of bacteria by means of industrial vats. I've seen them. They are in a giant airplane hangar and there are twenty to thirty large copper vats that you would see in a brewery, but they are growing *Viridobacter circulofractus* instead of yeast."

"Virico-what? What do you call it?" the host asked.

"*Viridobacter circulofractus*," Reill replied. "We like to just call it *Vir*."

"Veer?" the hosted sounded out.

"Yep, Veer," Alec repeated.

"OK, so you just grow the *Vir* and dump it on some plastic and they eat the plastic?" the show's host asked.

"Yep. That's all it is." Alec answered. "*Vir* breaks it down and the plastic disappears."

"That's unbelievable!" Of course the host was only lobbing him softball questions. In fact the whole show was produced using a large donation from Axiom. *The interview was probably written by Alec himself.*

"So somewhere there is a large airplane hangar growing this particular strain in these huge quantities. How much are we talking here?"

"It's going to be several thousand gallons that will be dumped on the hill on the first run. We are quite sure that one run should be enough to get through a pretty big chunk of the hill. Once we get a realistic timeline of decomposition, we will adjust our level of production and tinker with the rate of metabolism."

"And you can do that how?"

"Proprietary information I'm afraid," the two laughed. "But you will definitely be hearing much more about it before long."

Mark couldn't believe his ears. They were talking about GLADIS. *Thousands of gallons?* The scale was monumental considering he had only just discovered the security footage three days ago. The regulatory agencies alone should have added years to the process. *What the hell is going on?* Mark tried hard to concentrate on the rest of the program, but a combination of hunger and the incessant speculation of his rational analysts prevented him. Throwing the half-thawed venison steak onto the skillet, Mark summoned all of his attention.

"So what happens when *Vir* eats all the plastic in the landfill?" the host asked.

"They die out," Alec said. "We'll have to wait another few decades for the plastic to build back up."

"So how will you make money after that?"

"Bacteria is not all we do. Mount Trashmore is not the only landfill in the world. Plus, there is still plenty more garbage that can be reduced."

"Ah, so you have a few tricks up your sleeve, eh?"

"Again," Reill laughed, "proprietary information."

Something up your sleeve? This is illegal! And nobody knows it! They are completely circumventing the regulatory agencies! Mark thought back to the dubious nature of his own speech at the press conference. *No one would ever question whether or not they were breaking the law if they broadcast what they are doing to half the country.* After all, this was Axiom. *No one was going to question it anyway.*

The sizzle of the steak was starting to slow, meaning it had been ready to eat for some time. Mark rifled through the room in search of a dinner plate and utensils but found none. Hanging from the side of the stove was a hunting knife. *This will do*. He plucked it off the hook, stabbed the meat, and held the knife upright allowing steam to roll off of it. Before it had even begun to cool, the steak was swimming, in its entirety, in Mark's stomach acids.

When the radio interview ended, WAC was transmitting dead air. The Jotunborough broadcasting students had allowed the interview to run short, with no back up plan. With a full stomach, Mark's eyelids began to gain weight with each blink until he noticed a tiny green bug that had landed on his forearm. It jumped up very high and landed in the exact spot from which it had launched. It kept doing it over and over. Then, a second one appeared. Then four. Then eight. *Where did these come from?* More and more kept appearing. *16 now, 32.* He soon lost count and became slightly alarmed. They were doubling every two or three seconds. Mark started brushing them off and trying to find their entry point. The more he brushed off, the stronger in numbers they seemed to return. *What in the fuck?!* It was no use brushing them. He made his way to the door and turned the doorknob but when he pushed, it wouldn't budge. He turned around to the other, but it was the same case. He was trapped in the tiny cabin. The heat in the cabin was now overwhelming. Mark held his arms out straight in front of him to find that both were covered with thick layers of the tiny green bugs. He looked down where he found the cabin floor's planks had disappeared under the layers of green that now grew up past his ankles. "Fuck!" He said out loud, "What the fuck?!" He continued flailing around the cabin to no avail. They were so numerous that they were now audible, filling the air with millions of tiny clicks. Tiny green bugs now flooding up to his knees. Tiny green bugs on the walls, the bed, the stove, the table, everything in the cabin was covered. Tiny green bugs were invading every crevice and orifice of his body. There were dozens in his inner ear and under his eyelids. There were hundreds in his nostrils up into his sinuses. Thousands piling out of his mouth. As much as he spit, they were still thick enough in number to chew. He vomited up huge chunks of moistened millions. The cilia in his lungs could not move fast enough to prepare them all to be expelled and Mark found himself choking. He was in full blown panic mode and operating solely on basic instinctual motor functions. He looked around for some form of answer but only found bugs. Then in the corner of the window where a tiny bit of light was still showing through, he noticed a dream catcher that did not hold a single bug. He looked at it, desperately trying to use his prefrontal cortex and decide why it was different.

Like a shot, Mark leapt from the bed and began flailing and screaming in fear, his body drenched in sweat. He quickly surveyed his surroundings to find not a single bug. The floor, the bed, the window, everything was barren. When he realized it was a dream, Mark gained back his higher-level functioning. He was again able to internally verbalize, *Jesus.* He noticed that his hands were shaking and his breathing was deep and accelerated. He looked around one more time as a final confirmation that he was again in the common timeline and it was, in fact, only a dream.

The door was nearly pulled from its hinges as Mark threw it open. The cool air was as refreshing as the warm steak had been some time earlier. Steam billowed off his damp clothes and followed him out from the cabin like he had just stepped out of a sauna. Though the rain had slowed slightly, the amount of flooding which had taken place was somewhat concerning.

In the distance, a mechanical-sounding buzz cut through the gentle raindrops on leaves and tin. At first, a wave of exhilaration washed over him as he thought it could only be the return of Grandpa Ray's F1. However a few seconds more of closer inspection revealed it to be too unlike an old truck engine. Through the lowest-hanging clouds, Mark made out a low-flying crop duster; not uncommon for rural western Michigan. What was out of the ordinary was the condition of the plane. It was a newer model with a shiny new paint job. Mark focused hard on the side of the plane. As he processed the information his pupils fed him, he could not help but question his senses, his state of mind, his perception of reality. In huge yellow letters was written the new EnviroCore Axiom brand.

I am losing huge amounts of time again. Or I am still asleep. Or I am hallucinating. Mark remembered Alec saying in the radio interview that the planes would fly at the end of the week. *Maybe this is a practice run. Surely I have not lost another week out here.*

Though quite useful with the complexities of everyday life, out here the rational analysts were beginning to wear Mark down. What was usually a welcome augmentation to cognitive processing now seemed like a constant reminder to stay worried. The paranoia and the mistrust of judgment that accompanied the state of multiple consciousness had returned and here, in the wilderness, it was much louder, badgering him at every turn.

The rain was gentle enough that Mark decided to take a walk so that cabin fever did not get on top of him. The drops were freezing, but far enough between that they were more of a relief on his steaming flesh than a nuisance. In the distance, thunder struck softly, as if held underwater or muffled by a pillow. The wind-whispering leaves clapped here and there when struck by one of the stout water droplets that fell from heaven. Mark started north away from the building floodwaters but still encountered impassable puddles and deceptively soft mudbanks. Though he barely made it a quarter mile, he was fearful that he might lose his way and kept turning to make sure the cabin didn't get too far out of sight as the thickening marcescent foliage continued to obscure his view. At some point, he became so obsessed with avoiding obstacles that he forgot to look back. When he remembered and jerked his head around sharply, the red exterior of Grandpa Ray's cabin was no longer visible. In response to the abrupt waves of panic creeping up his spine, he immediately began to retrace his steps until the faded crimson planks reappeared to calm him. "It's starting to pick up anyway," Mark said out loud, referring to the rain and simultaneously making an excuse to go back.

As the raindrops multiplied, the return trip seemed to take much longer than the departure. Before long, Mark was soaked and picked up his pace in favor of watching where he was going. A deep sinkhole swallowed Mark's leg all the way up past his knee. "God damn it!" Mark shouted as he lifted himself out of the hole. As he found solid ground, he noticed something about 50 feet ahead of him that he had not noticed at the outset.

A pile of brightly-colored clothes that stood out under the damp leaves and earth, as if a spotlight shone upon them. Rising to his feet, Mark walked toward it, as it seemed no less than a beckon from God. But as he approached, that voice of silent intuition belted out the observation that the shape had to be a human body.

As Mark made it to the edge of the scene, the pile began to take shape and Mark's intuition was confirmed. It was in the early stages of decomposition wherein the sulfur emitted from bacteria had begun to bind with the hemoglobin molecules in the blood, evident by the characteristic orange and yellow 'marbling' of the flesh. Though the mouth hung open, the tongue had not yet begun to protrude, and no traces of fly larvae could be seen. Also curious was the absence of scavenger marks. Other than the bacteria, it seemed that nothing would touch it. *What does it mean?*

More than the oddity of the decomposition was the familiarity of the body. It was a woman. She had dyed red curly hair that was hiding most of the disfiguration, her features, and hence, her recognizability. But Mark knew he had seen those pearls and the flower dress somewhere before. Deep in his brain, he felt some kind of connection to her as someone he knew in his childhood, like a mother figure. But then, the cortex-dwelling analysts came up with an explanation.

Mrs. Andersen. It was Mrs. Andersen. The woman about whom Sheriff Van Beck had questioned Ed some time ago. Mrs. Andersen was an older woman, but sparked Ed's interest because of her naturally flirtatious personality. She was attractive for her age. Mark remembered how she used to kiss them on the lips when she came in the store. It made Mark blush every time. Now here she was in a pile of disgrace, staring straight up through lifeless, cloudy eyes.

He wanted to be sick, not because the decaying corpse of a childhood acquaintance lay at his feet, but because it had to be Ed. Speculation still surfaced from time to time about the goings-on of Ed and Mabel Andersen. Some people still try to pry it out of him, threaten him even, about what they think might have happened. But Mabel doesn't come in to the store anymore and Ed won't talk about it. Mark knew Ed all his life and knew in his heart that he would never do any of the things people talked about. It was easy for people to make assumptions and spread rumors about him because of his disability. Ed didn't have the mental capacity to explain himself to folks' satisfaction, but still, they felt it odd that he had nothing to say to anyone about the alleged incident, not even to Grandpa Deremer. Of course, all of this coincidence did not amount to Ed killing Mrs. Andersen, but still…here she was.

The rain was nearly back at full throttle, but Mark felt guilty leaving Mrs. Andersen's corpse to rot without some sort of societal ritual. She was swimming with toxins so he couldn't take her anywhere by himself and he had no way of communicating her presence to law enforcement. *So here she must lie.* Though Mark's feelings about religion had not changed, he felt a simple moment of silence to acknowledge his respect for her life and the impact she had on him would suffice for now. Mark bowed his head, closed his eyes, and let the pelting rainfall be her dirge.

Approximately twelve seconds was deemed an appropriate amount of silence and Mark slowly opened his eyes to look upon the putrefying carcass one last time. He scanned the dirty flower dress, assaulted by mud and leaves, from the hem on upward. From curiosity's point of view, Mark admired the waxy, autumn-colored flesh. After all, he may never get another chance to be this close to an un-embalmed cadaver. *I wonder why the smell did not…* Before Mark's analysts could finish the verbalization, Mark noticed that the eyes were no longer gray and they weren't looking up anymore, but straight into his. He looked closer to be sure, then noticed a tear rolling down her cheek. *It's just a raindrop.* But then, the departed Mrs. Andersen turned her head to match the gaze of her eyes, and raised up her stiff, leathery arms as if to reach for an embrace. Mark jumped backwards so fast he nearly came out of his shoes. His left foot landed in the hole out of which he had just climbed, forcing him crashing back onto his occipital bone.

The expected 'THUD' from the back of one's head hitting the earth never came. Instead, it was the 'PING' of Grandpa Ray's metal headboard spindles. Again Mark found himself wrapped in the confusion of a rude awakening. The events of this dream were much more jarring than the overwhelming green flies. Even though they were equally real to him, the drift into sleep this time was far more seamless; by all accounts, nonexistent.

Mark found himself bundled in Grandpa Ray's rust-stained white bed sheets wearing nothing underneath. Dripping from a clothesline hung up from the ceiling directly over the stove, were his drenched suit coat, pants, undershirt, underwear, and socks. Though he did not remember hanging them there, it was not inconceivable that he had done so. What was interesting was the left pant leg, which was covered in dried mud, indicating that perhaps aspects of the dream actually happened. Though Mark did not believe that the dead body of Mabel Andersen came to life and tried to hug him only a few meters from here, the disbelief did not calm the anxiety. *I have to get outta here. I'm startin' ta lose it.*

Mark clicked the radio dial back on to distract his paranoia while he re-donned his dry clothes. It was Van Beck reading from The County Crier:

'In response to the number of complaints the department has received regarding carnal knowledge, we would like to remind the citizens that public displays are against the law, even with married couples, no matter how long you've been married. Please keep your private lives private.'

Mark chuckled to himself as he pictured the sheriff responding to some of the old timers getting frisky out behind their tractors in Hayminster, trying to argue their innocence. *That must've been something to see.*

'Ash County is seeing an uptick in assaults being reported of late, up three hundred percent from the last month alone, whose numbers were already rising from the previous month. It is thought that the bug going around is likely responsible for the short tempers, but please folks, we ask that you please handle your differences peacefully. If you can't end your tussles agreeably, please call the Ash County Sheriff's Department and we can do our best to help you resolve the matter. Take it easy on each other. Be humble.'

Mark considered the disconnect between the neighborly request from the sheriff and the last second of Vince Winters's life as his spinal cord was severed.

'There are still no strong leads regarding the disappearance of Sara Siebert and Ed Deremer, last seen working at Hayminster Grocery last Wednesday. The Grocer is set to open its doors upon completion of the investigation by Friday morning. If you have any information regarding either party, please contact the Ash County Sheriff's department.'

The blood drained from Mark's face as he speculated as to what happened. On the back of his neck, the tiny hairs stood up as he examined the mud stain running up to the knee of his hanging dress pants. Again, Mark did not believe what he saw was real, and the mention of Ed now should not connect any dots. But Mark could not ignore the anxiety. It was a premonitory feeling of unrest and the urge to flee was suddenly all-consuming. Nonetheless, he sat through the feeling, pretending to be in control.

'Another nine cases of meningitis have been reported from Jotunborough General today. The quarantine triage is still being held at the Ash County Jail for the time being. Medical professionals are asking that if you feel any of the symptoms of meningitis, headache, nausea, or neck pain, to report to the jail. Doctors ask that you please stay away from the hospitals if you can, as authorities are trying to keep the contagion as confined as possible.'

Though Mark no longer felt the physical symptoms, he felt that the anxiety and the nightmares were the result of the infection. It had gone largely untreated and he believed the infection was not life-threatening, still he could not help feeling guilty. The anger that preyed on him from his interaction with Bill, his termination, the helplessness, the stress, the sickness, was the catalyst for this meningitis outbreak if Beecher was right about him being patient zero. Mark's ego overpowered his reasoning and now the town would suffer for it. *Ironic, the goal was to save the town; to change the world, but for the better.*

'In unrelated news, EnviroCore Axiom reports that plastic decomposition at Mount Trashmore is ahead of schedule by about twenty percent. "At this rate," CEO William Wildeboer stated, "by next winter, Ash County is going to have to do their skiing elsewhere." That is if this winter ever ends.'

279

The Sheriff enjoyed throwing in a few comments of his own if he was feeling clever.

'Tune in for the midnight reading and again in the morning. This has been Ash County Sheriff Tom Van Beck reading today's edition of The County Crier, on a very chilly April twenty-second.'

April twenty-second? Mark *was* losing large chunks of time. He vaguely remembered he and Reill planning the press conference for the vernal equinox, being symbolic of rebirth, as a kind of subliminal publicity strategy. Though it wouldn't have done much good, being there was still snow on the ground a month later. *There's no way I've lost that much time.* It seemed impossible, but it did explain the early presence of the crop duster. Convinced now that either his illness, or severe cabin fever was behind the memory loss, hallucinations, and paranoia, he knew he had to leave. If not to get out of isolation than to seek medical attention, whichever helped him first.

The rain was almost completely up the hill now at the edge of Ray's yard. The overcast night blocked any moonlight from illuminating the woods and Mark knew that if he did leave, he would be bringing the lantern. *It's time.* He clicked off the static of the radio, setting off in the rainstorm and darkness.

It wasn't long before Mark realized that the lantern was useless. Swearing and sloshing through giant puddles of mud, Mark decided he had no choice but to turn back before he got too far. The dreadful sounds of the mystery wildlife poisoned his feeling of security and he picked up the pace as he could. Behind him, the violent splashing of passing quadrupeds spurred him on even harder. But the fear had not struck him yet. It was not until, "Hey! This way!" echoed through the night, followed by the distinct sound of crying, that the fear ripped through him like the discharge of a captive bolt pistol. Mark fought through the fear and peered into the black, aiming his lantern in vain in the direction of the sound. The crying was horribly desperate, begging for relief from whatever was taking place, though using no words. The volume and intensity of the cries elevated and could now be described as screams. Mark's heart beat throughout his body, his arm quivering as he held up the lantern. The sound was unbearable, and he had to intervene.

"Who's there?!" Mark screamed. The surprising depth of his tone echoed for miles through Zululand. "Who's there?!" he boomed again, compensating for his fear by ignoring his better judgment. *Leave! Get the fuck out! You're going to die!* His analysts bombarded him with their logical assessment that he should save himself. *You can't see. You don't know how many. You have no knowledge. You need more knowledge!* But Mark stood fast, quaking where he stood.

There was silence now. No responses. No more screams. The light from Mark's lantern left light trails through the darkness as he traced the horizon. Two minutes or so passed before he decided that whatever was out there had gone and he turned back to wait out the night in Grandpa Ray's cabin. Then without warning, the familiar hoof prints of a horse pounded the ground in a rotund crescendo. Before Mark could even volunteer an explanation, the colossal beast behind the sound revealed itself in a sharp splatter of swamp water.

Slippy roared past him like a locomotive, spewing steam out his nostrils as he flashed by the dim light of the lantern. Close behind were the bipedal footprints of a human sprinting ever closer with just as much ferocity. But this beast did not brush past him. No, this beast blasted into Mark with all the force of a semi-truck, sending him airborne. The lantern flew from his grip and shined enough light to see the massive shadowy outline who struck him. Disoriented, Mark scrambled for the lantern, but was held back by the circus-like strength of the perpetrator's grip. Mark was no match for his attacker and soon found himself held down on his back. He struggled, but managed to maneuver his legs free enough to launch the man backwards. The burst of adrenaline animated the muscle fibers in Mark's legs and the race was on back to the cabin.

As fast as Mark could run in this state of panic, the monster's breaths were right behind him. Upon the sight of Grandpa Ray's lean-to, Mark prepared his dive through the back door for the hunting knife. However, the wet leaves at the threshold caused Mark to slip and instead of kicking the door in like a superhero, he fell through it ungracefully. His aggressor fell on top of his back and struggled at Mark's pants. Luckily, the slippery surface that caused the fall now worked in his favor. Mark's skin was slick enough to fend off the offender's grip and the handle of the knife soon found its way to his grasp. With an unanticipated burst of strength, Mark hurled the knife upward. The sudden unhanding confirmed that the blow was landed. Mark continued to thrash the Ka-Bar in the direction of his would-be rapist, slight pushback on his swipes the only indication his reckless slashes in the dark were making contact. Before long, it became apparent that Mark was connecting enough to get the upper hand and the animal tried to retreat. With this realization, Mark's slashes became more deliberate until the motion changed into staccato thrusts through layers of tissue. Sputtering and coughing now competed with the sound of the rain. Exhausted, and now convinced the half-dead being would not get up, Mark set out to retrieve the lantern, which he could see glowing several paces back. *That is a quality lantern.* Mark leaned over to pick it up, desperately trying to repay his oxygen debt.

Ambling back to the former predator, Mark curiously observed the injuries he inflicted. The man was a giant, perhaps a prison escapee who had spent the majority of his sentence on the bench press in the yard. As he set the lantern down to decide his next move, the glimmer of the flame bounced off the face of Grandpa Ray's splitting maul. "Oh," Mark huffed, "I forgot about this."

As calmly as if the target were a log, Mark threw the maul up over his head and then followed through with the momentum of the downswing. The impact separated flesh from skull but produced only the tiniest nick in the bone underneath. A second swing dug a slightly deeper crevice; the subsequent bounce rippling through every nerve in the periphery. Mark heaved a third swing into his victim's face, igniting a permanent convulsion. Pausing to rest a moment, he observed the spasmodic involuntary muscle contractions that inundated the body before him. "One more," Mark commented as he heaved the axe up high to deliver one final blow to the cranium. The wet thud sent chunks of brain and skull in multiple directions and put an end to the tremors.

Mark knew full well what he had just done but remained grossly indifferent. Adrenaline practically dripped from his pores, overcoming the seriousness of the act. The rain had died down considerably and the peculiar noises inhabiting the woods now caused Mark no fear whatsoever. As if accepting their challenge, but unable to articulate, Mark leaned into the night and projected a senseless, drawn out battle cry, "Faaahhck!"

The scream continued unto the third awakening. The radio was on, broadcasting Tom Van Beck, but the broadcast was not the relaxed sheriff reading the daily paper.

'The Ash County crimewave continues this sixth day of May at unprecedented rates. County officials are asking that citizens try to remain calm and resist the urge to commit acts of violence. In addition, a zero-tolerance order has been put into effect for gang affiliation and curfew violations. It is imperative that you travel in groups less than four and be indoors by sundown until further notice. Local deputies have been given the authority to use lethal force on anyone in berserker mode for their own protection and for the safety of the county. If you encounter a berserker, do not attempt to take the law into your own hands. Call police immediately. The Ash County Sheriff is still accepting new applications for volunteer deputies at this time. Interested parties should contact the Ash County Sheriff's Department via telephone.'

And that was it. *What was that at the end of the broadcast? Berserker mode? What the hell is going on? Is that another two weeks lost?* Not one word was mentioned about the intense flooding though Mark looked down to find the box of stick matches floating around the cabin floor. The peculiarity of the broadcast, the date of the announcement, the flood, the *nightmare* or *hallucination* or *whatever-the-fuck-it-was*, all combined with his numbing paranoia, convinced Mark that his mind was lost, or would be if he did not leave right now. The terrifying prospect of being stuck in a never-ending series of delusory purgatories was enough to send him out in the deluge, whether death would greet

285

him or not. *No matter what lies ahead.* Trudging out into the lean-to, Mark found no sign of the body from a few minutes ago; a few minutes ago in his mind anyway. With no choice but to blindly rely on an ethereal sense of direction, he set out into the eternal storm.

Even though Mark hadn't the slightest idea of where he was, he knew there were many steps between where he stood now and his return to civilization. *And then what? What of the town? What of the police?* As many steps that lie between, it was a far cry from the steps that lie between this moment in time and the *future* of civilization.

You are going to die out here. If you don't die of pneumonia or hypothermia, you will die of starvation, or else you will drown. You should have stayed in the cabin. Now if Ray returns you will not be there. You will be lost out here. The sloshing brown water swallowed him up to the ankles and he was sure that any minute he would befall another nightmare and awaken back in the cabin anyway. *So what's the difference?* By the end of the second hour, the physical signs of fatigue were amplifying the analysts. Chafing, wrinkled hands, and skin irritation blared just as loud. *You won't be able to do anything if you're in the hospital or face down in the mud.* But still he trudged.

By the third hour, the analysts became more and more convincing. *It should not be taking this long to get back to town. You are definitely lost. There's no end in sight. Cut your losses and turn around while you can.* The pain of his wet chafing socks added a limp to the inventory of misery, to include tingling fingers and a eustachian tube infection. But still he trudged.

At hour four, the rational analysts had begun speaking in the first person. *I need to rest. I am not going to make it. To hell*

*with the county, it never did anything but hold me back. I'm
starving.* Hunger pangs stung like a gut full of hornets. *I don't have
what it takes. I should have never left. Now I'm going to die out
here, alone, as if I never lived.* Each step was agony and his pace
had slowed considerably. He had forgotten why he ever left the
cabin; why he ever left the hospital. *Surely quarantine would have
been better than this.* But Mark had convinced himself that it was
too late to turn back. He convinced the analysts that he would not
hear them and no matter what they said or how loudly they said it,
he would march until he died if he had to. And then, they just
stopped.

No matter, for it appeared that God's plan was to stop him
after all. Before him, Mark beheld a giant river, wider than he had
ever seen in person. Living in the county all his life, he knew of no
river this size. At most, a stream that ran through and divided the
two worlds. If this was it, the downpour of the last month or so had
gone a long way to cut it deep into the earth. All he could do was
stand with his hands on his hips. With his analysts' abandon, a vain
and silent contemplation left him in a stalemate with Mother
Nature.

Mark stood at the water's edge. It must have been a mile
across and it wasn't exactly calm. Brown rapids rushed past him as
far as he could see from the right to the left, following the horizon
all the way. From where he stood on the bank, Mark saw two
choices and only one consequence. He could either choose to turn
around and walk another four hours in the frozen downpour and
rising waters, or he could jump into an impossible gushing torrent
and try to swim to the other side. The consequence of both was the
sensation of muddy water filling his nostrils and eventually his
lungs before he was washed away as a frozen, forgotten corpse.

Paradoxically, the choice of a much quicker death gave Mark confidence. It was not surrender. It was not a retreat. It was a decision. The better of two bad ones? Yes. But a decision nonetheless. It was action. It was resolve. It was courage.

Mark splashed both feet through the surface of the river and sunk in up to his waist. It was a good sign; as he did not expect to touch the bottom. Once in, the width didn't live up to its intimidation either. But as he waded through the water, he realized two things on which he had not counted. The bottom was slippery and uneven with rocks. Though he had stuck the landing, moving across it was a different story. Second and far less expected, was the matter of temperature. As cold as it was on land, the speed of the current was the only thing that kept this water from freezing solid. If it were much deeper, Mark may have drowned instantly, as shock would have forced a sharp inhale.

With each inch forward, the force of an avalanche tried to take him away. At halfway across, the fear that Mark had kept chained to the radiator was being pulled away from the pipes, and panic was steadily rising. In addition, the work it took to keep him upright began to take its toll. His legs started shaking as his muscles depleted all available adenosine triphosphate. "Fuck!" he screamed as he prepared to be washed away by the current. But the barb of fortitude and determination spurred him on. About three feet from the other side, Mark used the remainder of his strength for a last-ditch, do-or-die jump to safety. But he failed.

The shock took his breath as promised and the prophecy was now in the works. His nostrils filled with brown water as he was being washed away. Managing to cough the death back out of his lungs, he screamed again. "Fuck!" It was not so angry as before, but helpless and desperate now. Feebly, he kept trying to plant one foot on the riverbed before being taken further downstream, clumsily falling back down with a splash. Over and over, the attempts kept failing, each one taking a little more of his strength until he was simply trying to keep his head above water. Choking, he frantically searched for an answer. But he was getting tossed around so violently now that his senses were taking in mostly unusable information. Only seconds had passed since he had fallen, but the ordeal felt like aeons. He felt his head getting struck by sharp pegs. A series of tree roots had been exposed from the floodwater's erosion of the soil. Getting hit was enough to jut an arm upward in reflex. All four fingers wrapped downward to meet thumb, forearm muscles locked in rigor, clamping his hand on one of the roots. Legs floating freely on the passing waters, his fingers were the only thing keeping him alive. Mark breathed intensely, desperately trying to force his body to recover. Finally, as his forearm burned with exhaustion, Mark flung his other arm up to grasp another root. Abs now folding his body into a grip on the collection of roots, elbows stacked onto them and he began to climb as one would climb a ladder. With only one goal in mind, it was pure adrenaline that kept him going. He would not stop until he reached solid ground. Finally, in crippling fatigue, Mark collapsed on the stable safety of the earth. Shivering, gasping, the rain still battering him, he lay on the ground laughing with whatever breaths he could muster.

"A wave of violent crime has struck the Jotunborough Metropolitan area," the anchorwoman reported. "In the past week, a surge of violence has been recognized and police are finding it hard to keep up."

The talking head was then replaced by a police officer being interviewed in the field, "I've never seen anything like it," the officer admitted. "There's no rhyme or reason to it. It's not like it's one thing or one group of people causing all the trouble. It's kids, it's grandparents, it's teachers, it's normal god-fearing people assaulting, battering, and raping other god-fearing people."

The officer was replaced by the reporter in the field, "Officials say that the crime spike is a one-thousand percent increase from last year and that they are considering alternative holding methods for the incarcerated until this sudden outbreak of violence returns to normal. For Channel Four Jotunborough, I'm Diane Hoekwater."

"Thank you, Diane," the anchorwoman said. "In other news, Environmental Research and Development Company EnviroCore Axiom celebrates an early milestone at the infamous Mount Trashmore. President and CEO Bill Wildeboer spoke at a press conference late yesterday about the accomplishment."

"Today will go down in history," Bill started, "as the day we saved the world."

"The goal was to completely rid one acre of the phenol-based plastic in one week. That goal was surpassed by almost fifty percent, clearing one point four eight acres by last count," the anchorwoman remarked. "That is an estimated seventy-five pounds of plastic that has already been broken down and the company hopes to see that number double by the end of next week."

"At this rate," Bill continued, "all of the plastic in the

landfill will be gone at the year's end."

"Certainly the wave of the future eh, Chuck?" the anchorwoman bantered.

"Absolutely," her partner replied. "Garbage-eating bacteria. Who'd've thunk it?"

"That's it for now. Join us again at eleven. For now, stay tuned to Jotunborough Four's regularly scheduled lineup," the anchorwoman closed as the lights dimmed and the camera zoomed out.

The fadeout from the news was replaced with a flyover pan of an endless green pasture interspersed with sophisticated irrigation systems. Stock footage of wind turbines, solar panels, and futuristic-looking hydroelectric dams played under upbeat ukulele and xylophone music with a soothing narration about reducing carbon footprints, air purification, and climate change. A group of college-age kids in white lab coats, safety glasses, and wellies were all standing around some swampland hovered around a teacher-like figure staring upward at a vial of blue liquid in one shot. In the next, the camera moved past a lab bench full of scientists, all hard at work looking through microscope eyepieces or pipetting off samples. The final shot was a realistic globe being held by two hands. Upon zooming out and up, the audience discovers that the hands belong to President and CEO of EnviroCore, Bill Wildeboer, who pitches the new motto, "EnviroCore. Doing great things globally starts locally," followed by that unforgettable mouth full of teeth being borne to the public for all to see.

Everyone who was paying attention knew that there was some connection between EnviroCore and the strange behavior of the

county, but no one said anything. No one wanted to dig. It was
either that they were already affected and didn't seem to notice, or
the promise of prosperity the company offered blinded them.
Whichever it was, the widespread violent crime, public fornication,
and meningitis just fell out of the sky as far as Ash County was
concerned. Even the tabloid newspaper, which had made a name
for itself by criticizing or blatantly lying about the facility back
when it was Sciencia, didn't touch it. As far as the media reported,
EnviroCore meant the end of poverty and so, could do no wrong.

This ignorance was bliss to most, but least of all to Bill
Wildeboer. Superficially, Bill had it all. Everyone in the county, in
the company, in the media, held him responsible for ushering in
the new era. He was seen as a business genius; a fierce negotiator
that fought tooth and nail to make sure his beloved Ash County
would be the center of a new global powerhouse in an emerging
industry. 'Bill Wildeboer has secured the future of West Michigan
as the Silicon Valley of environmental science,' wrote Forbes. But
not very deep down, Bill knew that he was none of those things. If
it weren't for Philus pulling the strings, no one would ever have
known his name. He was a puppet, a figurehead, a lie. What's
worse, people were dying because of all his imagined success, but
chose not to hold him responsible for that part.

Bill turned away from the television and stared out into the
vast beauty of Valhalla National Park. A thin fog hung over the
ground like the ghosts of a thousand warriors. In concert with his
demons, they taunted him; mocked him. Bill stood from his seat
and stared harder now, holding the silver 1911 in his hand, barrel
facing downward. Bill squeezed his grip on the pistol and clenched
his teeth, as if he actually heard the voices.

Just down the hall sat a room full of executives from both

Axiom and EnviroCore, waiting on Bill to announce the completion of the merger and the shape of things to come. He wanted to tell them all about how they were getting rich off of killing people and how they were all fake. "Haven't you noticed the insanity going on?" he would say, then start squeezing off shots until the magazine was empty. He would go down in history as a madman and few would remember his name. But at least, his spirit would have dignity, no matter how history remembered him.

But no. This would not be the way it happened. Instead, he knew he would just go in and pander. He would go in and play the role, pumping up the crowd, congratulating them on jobs well done, saying things like, "We couldn't have done it without you." In this scenario, he would be in the history books next to the likes of Edison and Gates, as a fellow titan of industry. But his spirit would be damned. Bill Wildeboer would die as the lie he lived.

Though not a religious man, and slightly disgusted by his own ambivalence, perhaps he would let God decide. After all, he was the one who put him in this position. God had saved him once before. So he held the pistol to his temple again and put it in God's hands.

'Click' the pistol sounded as he pulled the trigger. Bill's eyes were open but for a flinch at the sound. 'Click Click Click' he pulled again. "Piece of shit," Bill said, believing now that the gun simply did not work. In an angry fit, he turned around and threw the gun on the desk.

"Bill?" Don Perry called, seeing the pistol land on the desk. Don entered the office cautiously, "Everyone is ready in the conference room. Are you alright?" Don knew first hand what Bill was capable of and decided it best not to pry. He simply repeated the statement in a different way, "They're all in there ready to make us rich. You coming?"

"I guess that's all that matters," Bill answered in a gravelly snarl. But he suddenly snapped out of the trance and perked up, "Let them know I'll be right in, will you?"

"Sure Bill," Don said, less than satisfied. "You sure everything's alright?"

Bill did not answer, but stated, "Get the fuck out," with his eyes.

Wildeboer sat readying himself mentally for the impromptu speech. Opening the drawer to put what he perceived to be a broken firearm away, his eye caught a glimpse of the Chivas. "Just one," he said aloud, filling his glass to the brim and chugging it. "One more," Bill said, refilling the glass. As he began making short work of the second scotch, he tinkered with the 1911, chortling sarcastically at the thought of divine intervention.

Bill sat manipulating the pistol, pressing the safety in and out, pulling the hammer back and dropping it, pulling the trigger over and over. He twirled it in his finger like a cowboy. He looked at his reflection in the window and acted like he was robbing himself. It was an embarrassing display, like a child who had found his father's gun while he was away at work, which was not very far off from this situation, other than the age of the child at play.

Bill had already ingested nearly a thousand dollars' worth of coke this day, but still had about half of the bag left. "Why not?" he asked himself, plopping a huge pile on the desk not even bothering with the rolled up twenty. As his nostril filled, his hands stroked the barrel. "That was the one," he said to himself, a little scared of the amount he had just taken in. It rocketed him and his pistol back in the chair as he came up from the dive. In a sort of cocaine-induced rigor mortis, his arms tightened up causing him to pull the stock set back past the pin which held the chamber open. Curiously, he noticed that the slide release had also popped up when he did it. He pressed on it, releasing the stock set back forward, thereby chambering a round. Unbeknownst to him, this was the missing piece of the puzzle that convinced him both of divine intervention several weeks ago, and that it was a defective weapon today. He examined the gun for a moment in both hands, more carefully now than before. Based on what he had seen in movies, he had some idea of what just happened, but could not resist the urge to test the hypothesis. So he pulled the trigger.

'BLAM' The pistol fired a round through the wall beside him. Bill dropped the pistol at the moment of discharge. His hands reflexively held his ringing ears. Acrid smoke wafted from the empty casing on the desk and filled the room. It would be a matter of time now until security swarmed the office. But Bill did not panic at all. As if admiring a curiosity, he stood up and picked the gun off of the desk and examined it again in both hands. His molars slightly held his tongue in his cheek as he mused, "Huh," as if to say, 'isn't that something?'

Bill calmly opened the drawer beside him and placed the gun and the cocaine back inside. He closed the drawer, locked it, removed his suit coat from the back of his chair and walked through the door into the hall. As he passed two frantic security guards, he said, "I'm fine boys," and continued to the waiting room full of executives. The gunshot only aggrandized his entrance. "Gentlemen," Bill heralded, "are we ready to become rich?" A hearty laugh and cheer ricocheted off of the wood paneling as the door closed behind them.

295

Mark had spent a considerable amount of time lying on his back staring up at the clouds that dropped the rain upon him. But since then, he had gained quite a bit of ground. The rain had stopped almost completely now, save for a drop every minute or so. It seemed the further he got from the river, the less it rained. But the day had been completely taken up by walking and it was now nearly dusk.

Though he had not eaten since the venison steak at Ray's, Mark did not feel hungry. On the contrary, the firmness of the ground beneath him, the relent of a relentless rain, and the awareness if his location enlivened him. At long last, he stared out at the emptying of the woodland onto a vast field at the threshold of a broken down fence. It was Lichten land. This was where Slippy could be seen from the deer blind. Sure enough, way off in the distance, Mark saw the tiniest speck where the Deremer men had spent many an hour. It looked quite a bit different from this vantage. Mark wondered if his father was in there now and if he could see him.

Suddenly, Mark recalled a memory of a much younger self looking through binoculars held by his grandfather. "Look, son" his grandfather said, "you can see all the way out to the end of time from here." Young Mark peered through the strange glasses in sheer amazement. His mouth hung open as his grandfather spoke.

"Where is the end of time?" young Mark asked.

"That's the entrance to Zululand right there where the grass ends," Grandpa explained with his index finger, "and Zululand is the entrance to Valhalla."

"What's Valhalla?" Mark asked.

"Valhalla is where all the soldiers go at the end of their time on Earth," Grandpa explained. "They spend the afterlife there.

It's the most beautiful place you've ever seen."

"What's a soldier?" Mark asked, still looking through the binoculars.

"A soldier is someone who makes a lot of sacrifices," Grandpa said, "and does brave things for his people."

"Do you think I'll be a soldier someday grandpa?" Mark asked.

"If you make a lot of sacrifices," he replied, "and do brave things for your people."

"Who are *my* people grandpa?" Mark asked.

"Your family and friends," Grandpa said, "anyone who is important to you. Your people can be anyone you choose."

Mark sat and soaked in the wisdom of his grandfather whilst scanning the horizon with the binoculars. "I can see the future with these things!" young Mark declared playfully. "I'll bet I could see the whole world from up here if I look hard enough!"

The words echoed in his head as he returned to the common timeline. It had been many years since he had thought of that day. It was quite remarkable how similar his father looked to his grandfather. They could have been twins if not for the twenty-year separation.

In the sixty-eight paces since he began his nostalgic drift, he had made it just beyond the broken spot in the fence and was now face to face with the mysterious grass that had taken over his father's life and sanity. The brilliant green shoots stood as tall as Mark, with a fuzzy seed at the cap. The swaying was even more dramatic up close. Even though the sky was overcast, there was no rain at all and the grass was not even damp. It gently draped across him as he made it through the blades. It was an eerie feeling. The grass was so thick that he had to rely completely on instincts and his sense of direction to make it through. Meanwhile, the gentle swaying of millions of blades of grass rubbing against one another sounded like people whispering. As he made it through, he could even make out a few of the words. *Helping sift it. See if it fits. Fist it said.* Then every once in a while, the whispering seemed to align itself into a chant. It was all he could hear. Whatever was being said, it was set against a completely silent background; the sonic equivalent to a black and white silhouette. It made no sense and of course it was his imagination. But that didn't stop him from hearing every word. *Stop... Stop... Stop... Stop.*

Suddenly, the common timeline dropped away from him again, and he found himself sitting around a dimly lit, smoke-filled room at a long shiny-lacquered wooden table filled with peanut skins and cigarette ashes. Mark's feet dangled from the chair, which had several breaks in the wicker mesh that pinched his tender skin. It was his usual boyhood Friday night hangout: the Jotunborough American Legion.

"Old Dean here doesn't understand the concepts of social order or morality," a gruff red-faced man grumbled. "You might even say that he's a fuckin' psycho!" The table erupted with laughter except for Mark, who just paid attention to his shoes bouncing off the legs of his chair.

"Dean doesn't know shit," one of the other drunkards spoke up, "otherwise you'd've moved out of this shit hole when you had the chance and left this fuckin' place to rot." They all spoke as if there weren't a small child sitting at the table with them.

"Fuck off Terry," Dean chuckled.

"At least he knew enough to keep his ass outta the grass," yet another pocky-faced, raspy-voiced gentleman piped up, "you can't be that psycho."

"No," the first man spoke again, "he has some stories that would make the lot of you shit yourselves." Dean smirked as he looked down at his beer glass.

"You didn't get there until '69, right Dean?" the second man said. "You guys just swept up after us." This statement caused Dean to laugh out loud.

"Tell them about the noses Dean," the first man said.

"What?" Dean asked, "You're fuckin' drunk Saul."

"What of it?" Saul chuckled with the rest of the table, "That bag you carry around with you."

"Oh," Dean glazed over, "that. It's fuckin' fingers not noses."

"Oh yeah that's right," Saul said, "he has a bag full of fuckin' fingers he carries around with him. That's how he kept track of all the baby-sans he fucked, whether they liked it or not. You sick bastard."

"Bullshit," the second man taunted, "you cut off their fingers?"

"Just the pinkies," Dean grinned.

"Bull-fuckin-shit," the second man kept on. "You never had your ass in the grass you fuckin' pussy. Are you sure you weren't keeping track of how many pinkies went up your ass?"

About three quarters of the table laughed. Dean's eyes shined wildly as memories overtook him. The grin drained from his face and he stood up slowly from the table. Everyone went quiet waiting for the reaction. But Dean just pushed his chair aside and left the bar.

"See," one of the men said as Dean walked out, "now you hurt his feelings." But without much silence, they returned to mocking and drinking as if he were never there. Less than two minutes later, the double action spring hinge door swung back inward presenting a fast-moving Dean. He proceeded to upturn a small, blue burlap sack which rained down tiny, grayish-green mummified fingers onto the shiny wooden table. If it weren't for the Dwight Yoakam on the jukebox, you could've heard a pin drop. He then bent down in front of the man who had doubted him and held up one of the smaller ones just an inch or so from the tip of his nose.

"This one couldn't have been more than twelve," Dean said calmly, staring deep into the man's terrorized soul. Mark was still far too young to understand what was going on, and continued to happily bounce the heels of his shoes off the silver legs of the chair, while the men at the table laughed nervously and tried to hold down their Pabst.

Why did I remember that? Fuck they're back. The analysts had returned.

Eventually, the endless wall of grass gave way to Deremer land. The grass had ended so abruptly that it startled him. After another half mile or so, Mark finally made it to the threshold of the three familiar deck stairs with the bland tan paint chipping away. As long as he lived in the house, he can never remember it having a fresh coat of paint. All these years, his father had sat up in that blind and never once had he painted the deck. The front door, which was never locked, looked just as shabby; paint peeling off in long strips of white. Between the dry rotted weather seal and the front door, there was an envelope addressed to Mark Deremer. The glue was unlicked and a single piece of paper, folded in thirds, waited for him inside. It was from Dr. Beecher. It read:

Dear Mark,

      If you are still alive, please meet me at my office. In case you don't remember, I have written the address below. Please come. No tricks. Life and death.

Mark was completely exhausted both physically and mentally. He couldn't imagine what Beecher would want, other than to put him in quarantine. Without a second thought, Mark crumpled up the paper and tossed it over his shoulder.

      The house lights were out; not unusual. Everyone was probably asleep already. The especially long winter made everyone more tired. Michiganders, one and all, are vitamin D deficient due to the lack of sunlight and a pitch black sky at 6 pm for half the year. According to the last WAC broadcast, it was May, but the air was still brisk and the sky was still black.

      The doorknob was just as unkempt as the door and has needed oil for the past twenty years or so. Turning it caused an awful squeak and it stuck in its turn whenever Mark let go of it. The door dropped open and Mark kicked off his shoes in the mudroom before entering the kitchen.

Mark flipped the kitchen light on from the mud room. He could not believe what his eyes beheld on the countertop. In the first few milliseconds of its viewing, Mark recognized the object to be dentures. Then that was scratched and determined to be some type of dental model, as it contained only the bottom half of the mouth. It was concluded that it must be some Halloween decoration. It became apparent once the rest of the kitchen was observed. A thin trail of blood led up to a human mandible, which seemed to be facing directly at the entry point, as if it were being displayed. It was apparent, as the rest of the scene came into focus, that the thin trail had spawned from a much larger puddle. From that puddle, dozens of other tiny trails had lined the walls and floor, spattered in every direction, all originating from the one giant puddle.

Mark's heart began to race. He had prepared as much as he could, but the flood came. It was a deluge. Panic erupted, bursting through vessels and nerves alike, crackling out of every hair follicle, every nerve, each and every square millimeter of flesh. He shook like delirium tremens and feared he might collapse. His emotions were a raging bull that Mark had agreed to ride bareback as soon as he flipped the lights on. He held on with every fiber of strength, desperately trying to stay conscious. Almost instinctually he walked toward the puddle, his heart increasing pressure and speed with each step. The living room adjacent to the kitchen was dark and details of the puddle could not be seen clearly. But a strange clicking sound crackled in the darkness, like tiny twigs being broken. *An animal maybe.* But Mark's attempts to downplay the situation were dashed upon flicking the light switch.

Illumination of the room revealed a thoroughly mutilated human body, soaked and lying in a small red lake. The skin of the body was stained pink, the clothing it wore, dark red. Whoever it was, was not dead. A slight jitter of the head was visible from where he stood. He took one step closer to see if he recognized it. The face, also stained red with blood, was bleeding from both eye sockets, which appeared as congealed blood pools, hardened and bursting out of swollen eyelids. The strange sound of tiny twigs breaking turned out to be the sound of the person's tongue, whirling around wildly and slapping against the roof of the mouth. Tiny air pockets wrapped in either blood or saliva were popping as the flailing tongue instinctually tried to find the lower line of teeth that it had neighbored its entire life. It wasn't until he looked with a little more focus that the sight of a sunflower pattern on the clothing found a match in Mark's memory. It was barely noticeable at first under a thick stain of red. He remembered criticizing the owner of the dress at one time that it was worn far too often, and the kids teased him about it. The disfigured semblance of a body twitching on the floor was that of Gladys Deremer.

The realization kicked the back of Mark's knees and he collapsed down on top of her. He looked one more time at the disfigured face that only had involuntary movements moving it in the dark pool underneath. It was her alright. The subtle distinguishing shape of the cheekbones had their place in Mark's memory. His head began to throb. Though he did not feel nauseous, a thick river of vomit erupted from his lips, right onto the body below him. He tried to catch his breath, but he could only heave desperate guttural squeaks past his epiglottis. He sat heaving over the convulsing body until he could inhale enough oxygen to start screaming. It was a cry he had not cried since he gashed a piece out of his head on a ditch drain when he was five. Seeing Gladys lying dead before him made him feel like a lost child, totally alone among a world of strangers. The only person in his entire life that had given him any feeling of security was gone, covered in gore, never to wake again.

The intense mourning was interrupted by another noise from his bedroom. He barely discerned it from his own crying, but when he did, he stopped. Mark listened intently, now full of fear that who-, or what-, ever murdered Gladys was still in the house. But the crying continued in the form of a baby wail. Mark got to his feet and followed the sound to its origin in his bedroom. *What in the fuck is going on?!* A flip of the switch illuminated his bedroom, but he barely recognized it as such. A baby in a crib sobbed with just as much emotion as Mark, wearing one thin splatter of blood from a different pool in the bedroom. On Mark's bed lie the corpse of his father, pieces of his shattered head stuck to the ceiling, the wall, and the side of the crib. The body was bent over with his hind end rearing up in the air and what was left of the head still trickling into the ocean already spilled from where the rest of it used to be. He wanted to scream and cry and vomit some more, but the reactions never came. He just stared blankly at the nightmare as if it were just that, a concoction of an overactive imagination. The child wailing was drowned out by his own heartbeat forcing blood through his vessels. Suddenly, from in the kitchen he heard the familiar voice of Sheriff Tom Van Beck. "Hello?" the voice called, followed by the emphasized syllables, "Jee. Zuss. Christ."

Two thousand volts blasted him back into consciousness. "Mark," the voice said, "are you OK?" The voice of Tom Van Beck had somehow transitioned seamlessly into that of Dr. Beecher. *Not a-fuckin-gain. How much time did I lose now? Where the fuck am I? What the fuck is this?*

Mark found himself in what appeared to be a home office, surrounded by deep burgundy-stained wood and antique medical instruments in glass cases. The night was so dark that the windows that weren't boarded up might as well have been painted black. The room was only slightly brighter, with the small flames of candles as the only light source. Dr. Beecher sat in a tufted wing back leather chair with a genuine look of concern on his face.

"What just happened?" he belted.

"The last thing you said was, 'That's when Van Beck showed up.'" Beecher answered softly.

"Where am I? How did I get here?" Mark asked in a panic.

Beecher stared at him trying to conceal his puzzlement. "You must have had a dissociative episode," he explained. "About fifteen minutes ago, you were outside banging on my door like you'd seen a ghost. This is my home. You are in Dwergenberg."

"Then what happened?" Mark asked, not getting any less agitated.

"I told you to come in and you sat down here, and you started telling me about a gruesome hallucination of your murdered parents," Beecher said.

"I guess I found your note then," Mark said, slightly calmer now. "Are you gonna call the cops?"

"Ah," Beecher said, as if he had realized something. "Where did you go that day you left the hospital? How long have you been gone?"

"Why?" Mark asked in paranoia.

"Well," Beecher said, "there are no more police. This whole county is now little more than a bunch of gorillas in human clothing."

"What do you mean? Like berserkers?" Mark harkened back to the term Van Beck had used for them in his radio broadcast, and the incident with the madman who attacked him.

"That's what they used to call them when they were only a few," Beecher explained, "now everybody is berserk."

"I heard the Sheriff mention 'berserker mode' on the radio yesterday," Mark noted.

"Van Beck was murdered several weeks ago," Beecher stated matter-of-factly, "one of the groups hung him up by the flagpole at the police station. Last time I looked he was still up there."

The hair on Mark's arm stood up before he spoke again, "I just heard it…"

"That broadcast has probably not been changed since it happened. It reruns automatically every six hours or something" the doctor interrupted.

"What the hell is going on?"

"Ever since we took that spinal tap," Beecher said, "the residents of Ash County have become increasingly aggressive. The incidence of violent crime was nothing like the county had ever seen. As I treated more and more cases, a pattern began emerging. The infected had several things in common. One, their place of employment. They either worked at, or had relatives that worked at, EnviroCore or the dump."

"Mount Trashmore?" Mark asked rhetorically, to which the doctor nodded solemnly.

"Two," Beecher continued, "aside from the behavioral and the physical symptoms that resembled meningitis, each one had thick green cerebrospinal fluid ooze out of the lumbar puncture needle. My team was working around the clock. But they just kept coming in, in greater and greater numbers. Before long my quarantine was full and so was the Ash County Jail. Van Beck called to send a bus load of offenders to me for treatment of their meningitis symptoms. Knowing what I knew, I thought it best to keep the contagion to a minimum. I brought the quarantine to him."

"You brought the quarantine to the jail?" Mark asked.

"I thought it would be better to keep it from spreading within the hospital. Surely, everyone in the jail already had it. So, yes, I moved the quarantine to the jail. It didn't matter though. The damage was already done."

"All because of me," Mark stated, remarkably absent of emotional guilt.

"I wouldn't bother with remorse," the doctor said. "Just because you were the first one I saw with it doesn't mean you were definitely patient zero. Besides, given the nature of the illness, I can't blame you for not wanting to be confined to quarantine."

"That bacteria spread from my lab," Mark admitted. "We named it partially for its green color."

"I know," Beecher said, "there was plenty of media coverage when we still had media coverage. You being the first one, the species name and color, your occupation; I put it all together. But I am just as at fault. I allowed Bill to talk me out of my better judgement. He told me that even if I did go through the motions to have you arrested, no one would do anything. Every cop in the state was at the press conference and they were all on his side. This was too big. And I was too small. Whether that was true, who knows. It's far too late for speculation. But I believed it."

The two sat momentarily in silence trying to ignore how readily they had allowed Bill to manipulate them. In Mark's case, there was not even a spoken threat. It was one that Mark had created all by himself, yet somehow he was able to blame Bill, as if the consequence of doing the right thing was overshadowed by Bill's reaction one way or the other. It was not fear, but more correctly, subliminal guidance. Whether or not it was real was up for debate.

"So what happened after the jail filled up?" Mark asked eagerly trying to catch himself from slipping down another rabbit hole.

"After the jail filled up, we set up tents and made a triage nearly five acres square. But that filled up faster than the jail. It was clear that the infection was exponential. So I called the CDC. Of course, government bureaucracy being what it is, they informed me I would have to go through the proper channels, i.e. my local health department. So I called the Ash County Health Department and they acted like I was some kind of kook. I told them who I was and everything I just told you. They said they started a report and would keep me updated, but acted like this outbreak of violence was not occurring. Strangest of all, they said they had not heard of the EnviroCore Axiom merger. You know this area as well as I do. Nothing this big has ever happened here. How could they not have heard about that?"

"It's possible she lives way out in Zululand or somewhere," Mark reasoned, "they have less contact with the world than anyone."

"Maybe," Beecher conceded, "but I called back a week later to find that the number was no longer in service. The health department! So I went down there in person to find the place locked up. Lights off. No cars in the lot. No explanation. I checked the website. Nothing. Still operational, but no explanation."

"OK," Mark agreed, "That is suspicious."

"Well, that is not the half of this phenomenon," the doctor ramped up, "a short time after that, the phones stopped working altogether. Then the internet stopped. Then electricity went out," the doctor made hand gestures referring to the lit candles surrounding them. "Then came the weirdest part of all," he paused dramatically as if he were telling a ghost story around a campfire, "things just started falling apart. Literally."

Mark was just as captivated with the story as Beecher was glad to tell it, "What?" Mark said in a hushed, drawn-out tone.

"We were working under candlelight at the hospital, because even the emergency generators would not work" Beecher continued. "It was a nightmare. People were dying every few minutes at first. It is basically impossible to run a health care facility without electricity. But try running it without plastic."

"Plastic?!" Mark nearly cried out in anticipation.

"Everything that was made out of plastic was disintegrating," Beecher regaled. "Everything. Name it. Tubes, bags, equipment, packaging, prosthetics, furniture, everything. I couldn't inject drugs or withdraw blood because the syringes were unstable. Patients were moved to the floor because their beds were melting within a few hours of lying in them. No more surgeries either because, of course everything was contaminated, but even if we tried, we couldn't create a sterile field. Even the personal protective equipment had holes being eaten in it. And, perhaps worst of all, if you had a medical device when you came in, you didn't anymore. If you needed plastic to live, you were dead."

All Mark could do was sit and listen in horror. "My god," he said, unsure of what other exclamation could capture his reaction.

"And it wasn't just the hospital," the doctor continued, "anywhere you went where plastic used to be, was a big melted hunk or a pile of grayish white powder. If the electricity didn't do it first, every single business collapsed within the month. No more grocers. No more diners. No more gas stations. But that didn't matter because vehicles didn't work either. The one good thing about all this is that Ash is so isolated that, as long as no one makes the journey out, we are self-contained."

Mark sat back and soaked it in with an eyebrow raise and a long exhale. *What about Vince Winters, the garbage man?* "What about Vince Winters?" Mark asked, acknowledging the timely return of his analysts, "the garbage man who was killed the day I left the hospital?"

"He was a garbage man?" Beecher replied.

"Yes," Mark said, now assured that the scene he witnessed in the hospital was not a hallucination, "was a spinal tap performed on him, by chance?"

"Probably not," Beecher sighed.

"Something wrong with that timeframe, eh?" Mark pondered. "How long after that were the crop dusters deployed?"

"I have no idea when," the doctor answered.

"But it was after that, yes?" Mark continued. "I remember seeing the plane fly over Zululand. Of that much I'm sure. That means it was at least later than that incident."

"You were hiding in Zululand?" Beecher prodded.

"I lost control of my vehicle back there," Mark explained. "Some old timer and his grandkids offered to tow it into town for me but they never returned. I figured they couldn't make it back through the flood."

"What flood?" the doctor asked.

"The flood that trapped me in Zululand for a month," Mark said sarcastically, "or however long I was gone."

"There was no flood," Beecher reinforced, "it has been rather dry actually."

Born of frustration and the renewed terror of all-enveloping dementia, a tear welled in Mark's eye. He held his breath, as if to suck the tear back into its duct. "I'm not crazy," he exhaled sharply, "I was trapped in that goddamn cabin. I thought I *would* lose my fucking mind. I was back there hallucinating. I swam through that fucking river! Just before I got home. Just before I came here!" Mark paused a minute to acknowledge what he and the doctor both realized, his clothes were completely dry. "Fuck," Mark lamented, leaning forward to bury his face in his hands, "I am crazy."

Beecher leaned forward to place his hand on Mark's back. At the hospital, he was not much for bedside manner. But this was his home. This was a crisis.

Just then, the tender moment was interrupted by the slamming shut
of a screen door. Mark forgot his sorrow in the chair, jumping to
his feet and replacing it with terror. He was too frightened to ask,
What the fuck is that? But the doctor answered as if he had spoken.

"That'll be Steve," Beecher said calmly, "hopefully."

"Steve?" Mark shouted, "Williams? Why is he here? He
should be worse off than anyone!"

"Well, he's not," the doctor replied. "Getting nowhere with
Axiom or Bill, I decided to do some digging. One issue of The
Crier featured a picture of Bill and Steve together in front of a
melted piece of plastic. On a whim, I went to the triage and
checked the roster, trying to match it to the name in the article. The
triage was split into violent and nonviolent cases. I checked the
jail, figuring his infection would have progressed markedly. But he
was moved to the less violent tent section. After a minute or so I
could tell that he wasn't as bad as the others. I told him who I was,
that I thought the meningitis outbreak was linked to his lab, and
asked if he could help. He agreed so long as I got him out of 'this
half-assed quarantine,' as he put it. So I used my status as
Quarantine Director to 'transfer' him. He's been here since then."

"Why is he staying here?" Mark asked.

"Well, it was obvious that I hit on something," Beecher
explained, "because Bill started calling here looking for him. He
was cordial at first. But after a few days he started threatening.
Then other Axiom goons were calling, lawyers, doctors, private
investigators…I told them I didn't know what happened to him and
to fuck off. Then people started coming over looking for him. Then
the radio was broadcasting it, promising a reward. Random
townspeople started coming over trying to break in. But that was
followed by a seamless transition to the berserker raids, so it was

better that neither of us were alone anyway."

"Raids?" Mark asked.

"Yeah, the difference was that the berserkers were looking for food. A new tribe comes by about once a night. Sometimes they just knock and ask nicely if there is any food we can spare. Other times, we have to chase them away." Beecher pointed to the hundred-year-old twelve gauge mounted above the fireplace.

"What are you going to do with that?" Mark asked, thinking about the plastic shell.

"Shit," Beecher said, jumping on Mark's train of thought. He walked over and popped the breach open to have powder and shot run out the front of the barrel onto the carpet. "Shit," he repeated.

"What is it?" Steve called from the back room.

"Would that thing have even fired?" Mark laughed, admiring the thick wrapping of twine which seemed to be holding the cracked stock together.

Just then, Steve emerged from the bedroom to see the last of the BBs hit the berber. "Shit," he joined in the disappointment. "Hey! Where the hell did you come from buddy?" he marched over to Mark with open arms, "are you sick too? We've been wondering about you." Steve looked different; larger, dirtier somehow.

"Yeah," Mark patted him on the back in the embrace, "I don't even know anymore."

"You sure don't act like it," Beecher noticed. "You don't appear to have the physical symptoms either."

"Which are?" Mark asked.

"When the bugs are at their peak," Steve piped in, "the affected's pupils become extremely glassy in appearance, differing from the rest of the eye. It appears silver compared to the retina. Aside from that, a deeper voice, enhanced muscle tone, more hair, everything you would expect an increase in testosterone to do. Shit, you should see what it did to the women, if you can still call them that. However, these unfortunate symptoms are more apparent if the individual has been infected for more than two weeks. The early symptoms are the same as meningitis, which is why it was misdiagnosed as such. Essentially, they are the same disease."

"Any theories about the symptoms?" Mark baited, ready to offer his, "I mean, why might these be the symptoms?"

"As you know," Steve could hardly contain himself, "Bisphenol A was first developed in the 1930s as an artificial estrogen. By the 1950s, it was discovered to be a highly stable polycarbonate resin, and became widely used in plastic manufacture. In the 90s, studies were coming out about large quantities of it feminizing animals in utero. Today there are about a million pounds of it produced annually. No turning back now. But that was just one more selling point *Vir* had to offer. It would clean up the plastic and 'rid the world of that nasty toxin.'" Steve spoke dramatically as if he were quoting some manufactured news story about EnviroCore. "By some counts," he continued, "ninety-five percent of the population is literally pissing BPA."

"So *Vir* was breaking down the BPA in our systems..." Mark extrapolated.

"Yes," Steve agreed, "and if the S curves were indicative of adaptations, as you hypothesized, then *Vir* adapted to break down the rings of the similarly structured estradiol in our systems as well."

"Ah," Mark interjected, "why then would there be excess

testosterone in the bloodstreams of the infected?"

"Ah," Steve reciprocated, "the doctor and I concluded that the body is responding to 'low-estrogen' signals and producing more precursor. Testosterone is a precursor for estradiol. In fact many androgens are precursors for estrogens."

"Why, that's goddamn elegant!" Mark shouted before Steve was finished with the last word.

"I know!" Steve shouted before Mark had finished his last word.

"That is definitely what's happening!"

"It has to be!"

"You guys really play off each other, huh?" Beecher chuckled. "It's like watching a ping pong match or something."

"And the timeframe," Steve continued in a more solemn tone, "I'm sure that the timeframe shift has something to do with me. When you told me to put my big boy pants on. I did. I contacted Ted Philus and told him we had something. Several years ago, when we worked for Sciencia, and got shut down by that Fuck-ass from procurement. What was his name? Greg Sauer. I went to Philus that day, but could never get anything to work. He told me to come back when I had something, but I never did. After a while I just gave up. I figured I would never get it, especially not without you, and did you really want to work with Philus? This was the opportunity. GLADIS worked. We had something. It wasn't pretty, but it was something."

The statement was a drop of thick purple dye into a clear glass of water. Its weight carried the dispersed particles down the concentration gradient and fathomed the deepest recesses of Mark's psyche. A shockwave rippled across his cognizance in effect. It wasn't the gravity of Steve's actions, it was that this information was somehow a crucial piece of the puzzle. The ramifications had not yet risen to the surface for cognitive review, but Mark knew it was huge, somehow.

"Philus?" it was all Mark could do to force his voice to speak the name.

Steve seemed to take great offense to the surprise in Mark's voice. His calm demeanor melted away to reveal the frenzied alter ego of the berserker, complete with pupils waxing silver. With a fiercely indignant tone set against a swelling and hostile posture, Steve launched into the cynical tirade defending his actions.

"I can't believe you thought that anything good could possibly come from this company. Don't you remember the Sciencia days? Didn't you find it the least bit odd that Ted Philus just up and disappeared without a trace? Just gave up his company? Just handed it over, packed up, and moved on to greener pastures? You're really sitting here surprised like they didn't chew you up and spit you out just the same as they did me? You've got some nerve bud. That little document that Bill had you sign, that means Axiom gets to keep all the money, all the credit, all the *glory*, for your invention, and if anything goes wrong, *you* get to take the blame."

Mark's jaw was locked tight. He hadn't heard a word Steve said following his admission to pitching GLADIS to Philus without him. "So you stole my billion dollar idea, the biggest advancement in environmental research in history, and just handed control of it to the cunning, baffling, and powerful Ted Philus, the most crooked man on the fuckin' planet?" Mark paused to gather his next words, "It was all you! You were the catalyst for all of this. You are the passed pawn in the endgame! You don't think he's been watching your every move from the fuckin' start? Planning based on what you do? And now you're here. With us. You ruthless little cunt!"

"It wasn't supposed to happen like this buddy," Steve barked back. "It started that I only needed him to back me and I would buy him out of his contract. GLADIS was dead in the water, so Ted was out of the picture. We parted ways and never spoke again. On the bright side, with all the plastic gone, there is no way they can be watching us."

"You," Mark paused and cocked his fist back, "Motherfucker!" With the expletive, Mark delivered a haymaker that ruptured Steve's eardrum. A loud slap was produced by Steve's cheek as gravity forced its contact with the linoleum floor. Steve quickly got to his feet to retaliate. A swift but wild swing narrowly missed the tip of Mark's nose, but a second hook was more accurate. The blow landed directly onto Mark's rubber bullet scar, breaking it open in a burst of dark blood once again. As the two grappled, Doctor Beecher tried to get in between them but was thrown clear. Several missed shots and a tradeoff of poorly executed wrestling holds ended the match in a collapse of exhausted respiration. The contest had restored both men to sanity. As they helped each other up, blood running down the side of both their faces, Beecher presented them with a giant glass jug of water, from which they both drank.

Once the two caught their breath, they retired to the couch in Beecher's living room, both pairs of pupils faded back to black. "Now seems like a good time to tell you that we discovered a way to quell the symptoms," Steve said, as if the last five minutes hadn't happened. "I'm sure you heard about the incident at Sideways? That biker bar on the north side? The reason I went to jail in the first place?"

"Brian mentioned something about it when I called from the hospital," Mark answered, "but he didn't elaborate."

"With the onset of the disease," Steve explained, "I started getting irritable, more aggressive, cockier than usual. It all makes perfect sense now. The testosterone flood. I don't know, man. I don't know what came over me. I just got this impulse to go in there. I had heard about it before and…well that's it. It was like a challenge, or something, that had come from thin air, daring me to go to this biker bar on the north side that I'd only heard about. Then I was in there and it wasn't enough. I felt like I could fight for some reason. I felt strong. I felt good. It felt like I could just rip the bar out of the floor and throw it. The more I sat there, having

319

accepted the challenge, the more I wanted challenges. So I found the hottest chick in the place and told her she was coming home with me, just like that. But she laughed at me. I let that go and tried to play my arrogance off like it was a joke and just kept talking to her. It felt like she was into me after a minute or so, but her girlfriends started leaving and she followed. Well, I just couldn't accept the defeat. So I followed them out to the parking lot where a bunch of assholes were getting in front of me and putting their hands on me. I just saw red. I don't know what came over me. I felt like I was barely conscious. I pushed one of them off me. Turned out I was as strong as I felt. The first guy fell backwards and smacked his head. Then two or three more intervened but I decided then and there that I was going to die or they were. I was as fast as I was strong and I kept pushing them off and they kept coming so I kept pushing them. Then I felt a huge blow in my side. I turned to see a Louisville Slugger coming at me for a second time. I grabbed the bat from the guy and clocked him a good one in the head. He did not get up. I swung it at the others but did not land any truer blow than that first one. I clipped a finger once, a back another time. They backed up while I was swinging at them. Well, it seemed like no time at all before the cops ran up to me with their pistols drawn, screaming for me to 'drop the bat and lay down.'"

"Jesus Christ!" Mark exclaimed.

"Yeah," Steve agreed with Mark's reaction, "but with that I had a theory. Once I was subdued and caught my breath, like what just happened, the symptoms, physical and mental, subsided."

"Meaning what?" Mark asked.

"Meaning," Beecher finally joined the conversation, "adrenaline is the cure."

"The cure?" Mark echoed.

320

"Well, not quite the cure I guess," the doctor hedged, "but with some experiments that Steve and I conducted, we concluded that it was a treatment anyway."

"One particularly frightening run-in with a berserker clan sealed the deal for both of us," Steve joined. "They started hacking at the house, they broke through the window," he pointed to the plywood nailed over the broken pane of glass, "we thought we were done-for. There must have been eight or ten of them all swinging axes and sledgehammers and crowbars into the house, trying to get in. The doc and I rounded up the most dangerous weapons we could find. We only came up with a claw hammer and a filet knife. But we managed to get one with the hammer. When that one fell, I picked up his sledge and just flailed it at the group, just like at Sideways. The doc got one of their axes and started swinging right along with me. My god it was terrible. We killed six of them and cut one down to the forearm. The rest retreated. The win, the excitement, you need it. It's what balances you out."

"It has to be more than just adrenaline," Mark dampened, "otherwise the raiders would have noticed the difference afterwards too."

"Yes," Steve defended, "but maybe they wouldn't have made the connection."

"Why not?" Mark struck again, "I think there is something else. Indulge me. There is an element missing from your hypothesis. Up to and including our little scuffle here a minute ago, there is a running theme. You were outmanned. You were afraid. But you fought anyway. You ignored your common sense and fought in spite of your fear. Bravery. *That* makes sense. The excess testosterone is just sitting around going unused. Bravery in the face of fear requires testosterone, of which there is an excess.

Do I dare suggest that you were afraid when you were fighting me?" Mark grinned slyly as he asked the question.

"I had a run in with a berserker out in Zululand," Mark said. "He was trying to assert his dominance. That's the theory I came up with anyway. I was scared out of my fucking mind. But I also managed to get the upper hand. I had no other choice but to put an axe into his head. I'll admit, as sick as it sounds, I felt a whole lot better afterwards. Clearer somehow, like I had finally scratched some ancient itch. In light of my 'bravery' hypothesis, it makes sense. I therefore suggest that all we have to do is scare the shit out of 'em. If we motivate them hard enough, they will disregard their fear."

"How do we do that?" Beecher wondered aloud.

"I know where there is a stock of food," Mark countered. "A whole freezer full of venison and salmon."

"Well why don't we go and get it for ourselves?" Steve reasoned.

"It's in Zululand," Mark said, "about ten miles past a treacherous, fast-moving river. I barely made it over. But…ya know…bravery. If we can get them to cross it, their symptoms will be gone. They will definitely make the connection, the ones who make it across anyway."

"That is the dumbest thing I have ever heard," Steve blurted.

"Come up with something better then, asshole!" Mark screamed back in short order. "We're running out of time here. We'll be dead one way or another if we don't do something."

"It's worth a shot," Beecher added.

"Jesus Christ," Steve blasphemed, "these bugs must be breakin' down your common sense! How are we going to talk to these people? We've had to *kill* some of them because they wouldn't listen. And, if we could get them to listen, why would they believe us?"

"The same reason we have to try this," Beecher retorted. "They have nothing to lose."

Steve sat silently pondering the plan. He wanted to stand his ground, but he had to admit that, at least it was something. Systematically, methodically, Steve searched for holes.

"We can't tell everyone," Steve conjured. "Plus, there are three of us and many of them. Any random group may have five or more. Plus, we are keeping the symptoms at bay. They are not. They are far more likely to catch us and kill us. Not just kill us, tear us apart. And not just tear us apart, but 'assert dominance' first."

"OK," Mark started, "think about how agitated you are getting right now. You are already forgetting the treatment. Have some balls!"

"Fuck," Steve acknowledged his lack of bearing, but remained stubborn, "well we might die!"

"We *might* die," Mark said. "But we *will* die if we do nothing."

Another pause followed Steve's weakening case. "How are we going to get the message to everyone in the county?" he said. "It's not like we can go knocking on doors or put an ad in the paper."

"We don't need to," Mark said. "You know how word travels around here. The only reason the goddamned newspaper even exists is because of hearsay. This whole county is one big sewing circle. As long as we reach a few, we have reached everyone."

"What if we just made flyers? Write: 'deer and salmon steaks, this location, this time.' We write it on stacks and stacks of paper. Then we just let them fly. What tribes aren't reached by the flyers will be reached by word of mouth."

"I'm not sure why we have to bother with any of this in the first place," Steve complained. "If we're going to venture out anyway, why don't we just run for the county line and send back the National Guard?"

"Because!" Mark shouted. "We are responsible for this...OK? Asshole? You! And me! And if we get to the county line, guess what, we just did it again, to another county!"

"We are all responsible," Beecher added. "Plus it's about twenty miles to the county line from here. Would we make that trip? If we did make it, do you think Axiom wouldn't cover it up somehow? They haven't accepted any responsibility so far."

Steve sat with his hands folded, fingers interlaced, knees bouncing nervously. He was out of reasonable arguments. It was like he was praying in vain for the bravery to come.

"What about GLADIS?" he said gravely.

"What about her?" Mark grumbled.

"Even though they won't take responsibility for the outbreak, they knew it was coming. I never did report the luciferase test of the lab either, even though the whole lab was fuckin' glowing. But somehow they knew, and when they realized the implications of a loose plastic eater, they fitted your office with ultraviolet germicidal irradiation bulbs, an all-metal generator, and restricted access to a very select few. I assume they wanted to protect GLADIS," Steve pointed to the puddle of black plastic that used to be Dr. Beecher's computer. "But they still couldn't understand the code enough to manipulate it, even with me there. They couldn't risk bringing in an outside programmer to try and figure it out. Also, as you know, for security purposes, they utilize a company intranet which can't be reached from the outside world. So they can't even remote in."

"How were they going to get her out of my office?" Mark wondered.

"Two ways I can think of," Steve said. "Just wait for this whole thing to blow over. Once it does, if it does, they can send in an outside programmer. Or else they can somehow get you to do it. Either way, right now she's just sitting there."

"So once this situation resolves, however it does," Beecher said, "they can just turn around and use it again and again, denying wrongdoing forever until they work out all the bugs."

"They don't have anyone guarding it?" Mark asked.

"Nobody knows what's in there," Steve replied. "The door is locked, the bulbs are on an automatic timer, and no one really works at EnviroCore anymore. Like every other place else around here, it's just an abandoned building."

"It's been months since this started right?" Mark reasoned, not particularly excited about what his new colleagues were hinting, "How do you know the generator still has gas in it? GLADIS could be a non-issue."

"Now who's forgetting his balls?" Steve needled. "I know it's a big generator, and I know the bulbs are on an automatic timer. How do I know?" Implying that he was one of the few with access, Steve produced his security badge and handed it to Mark as if it were a medal. "It would be an honor."

The house was steamy and congested from three men working in close proximity, but the air outside had to be thirty degrees cooler. The combination steamed the windows into a dripping condensation. Over and over again they wrote their message on the flyers:

Deer Steaks and Salmon Filets

Deremer/Lichten Fence

Follow the Arrows

The instructions, 'Follow the Arrows,' they all agreed, sounded much better than 'cross the rapids, then proceed ten miles.' The only problem was, there were no arrows. But the three agreed to leave in the morning to set them and to deliver the flyers. By 'deliver' was meant 'toss up in the air in strategic areas,' and by 'set the arrows' was meant 'nail them to trees near the river.' For now, it was too dark and they needed to be well-rested in the event they would need to outrun an angry horde of steroid freaks.

Over an oversized map of Ash County, the men discussed strategy; where the masses would likely congregate, where the flyers would disperse furthest, and safe hiding places nearby the route. The goal was to cover as much area as possible without venturing further out than was necessary. In addition, the men decided that since there were three, it would be wise to sleep in shifts.

"I'll take the first watch," Steve said. "It's too goddamn hot in here and you guys fuckin' stink." A smirk painted across his face before he turned and flung open the screen door, carrying a mesh firewood sack full of weapons. "I'll let you know if we're about to be murdered," Steve quipped as the door swung shut behind him.

The remaining members of the triad used up the last few

pieces of paper in the house by drawing large arrows on them. They figured roughly four per mile from the fence would suffice. Once the last arrow was drawn, they retired to the couch and passed the glass jug of warm water back and forth in a drowsy silence.

"I want to discuss your hallucination." Beecher reluctantly spewed forth.

"Which one?" Mark scoffed.

"Mark," Beecher paused, "it is clear that you don't remember meeting me before just recently."

"What do you mean?" Mark answered through a yawn.

"When you were very young," Beecher carried on, "your grandfather brought you and your brother to me for help."

The confusion was enough to recover Mark from his weary, "My brother?" His tone was doubtful, "I think you've got me confused with someone else. I hadn't met you until you came over to escort me to St. Catherine's. I would have remembered you, sir. You are not very forgettable, and I have a very good memory if I do say so myself."

"When, Mark, was the last time you saw your mother before the hallucination?"

"I saw Gladys…" Mark paused a moment to think, "I believe it was… I remember she was making a huge breakfast. It was the most food I've ever seen. She always makes the most food I've ever seen, she always has; seems like every morning she does."

"Every morning?"

"Yes. Pretty much."

"Why do you call your mother by her first name?"

"Well, that is her name."

"Isn't it disrespectful to call your parents by their first names? Why don't you call your father Dean?"

"I don't know," Mark said, getting frustrated, "I didn't consider her a mother I guess. It seemed like she was never there for me growing up."

"But you just said that you saw her every morning when she made you breakfast."

"Well, I mean, she was there, just, she was the one to…" he paused a minute to give himself a bit more time to rationalize and form a response. "She was there. She just… I dunno. She did have a way of making me feel more grown up. She never talked down to me or even treated me like a child. She trusted me to be rational; to find reason in chaos; to feel better. I loved her very much. I just felt I needed to distance myself."

"You just said you '*loved*' her. You still love her, don't you?"

"Well… yes of course. I don't know why I said that."

"You also said, 'distance yourself,'" Beecher prodded. "Distance yourself from what?"

"Hey what is this?" Mark was visibly angry now. It wasn't so much that he was annoyed with the doctor's questions, but that he was not able to answer the questions with the usual clarity.

"I do not mean any offense," Dr. Beecher said. "I am trying to help you remember."

"Remember what?" Mark asked in disgust.

"Remember what happened," Beecher said. "How long have you been living like this? Living in this fantasy world?"

"Doctor," Mark leveled, "I am trying to be patient here, but I must say you are not making it easy."

"The hallucination that you just described before you came

329

here," Dr. Beecher said, trying his hand at patience as well, "was not a hallucination. It was a memory." A wave washed over Mark. His ears became almost plugged as his head got very cold very fast. But he sat only in disbelief, making the face of a man who had just smelled a rotten peach. *There is no way.* "You have been living in that house alone since you were twelve. Your grandfather raised the both of you and gave you the house. He didn't want to sell it, he wanted to keep it in the family. Hell, it has been Deremer land since The Civil War. He knew that if he sold it, it would just be parceled up into subdivision. Your father was deeply disturbed and only ran the store with the help of your grandfather. Your grandfather lived upstairs at the store and put you to work so he could keep an eye on you for most of the day. As you grew up, you kept to yourself so much that no one ever knew you were under the impression that your parents were alive and still living with you at the farmhouse. You see Mark, that was not the hallucination. You have been living the hallucination. It has been your whole life."

Mark sat in silence, not believing a word. "Why are you telling me this doctor?" Mark asked.

"My god Mark," Beecher said. "You are old enough now to know the truth. You must have created this coping mechanism long ago and because you lived alone at such a young age, no one ever questioned your stability, and no one ever noticed that you'd been living among ghosts for the past twenty-five years. You saved a few really good memories of your mother to keep her living on in your conscious mind. I imagine you call her by her first name because it takes away the heavy emotional attachments connected with the word 'mother.' You don't call your father 'Dean' because there are no crippling vulnerabilities attached with that word 'father.' His loss did not affect you as did the loss of your mother,

Gladys."

Mark was still not convinced, not making the connection, still distanced from reality, "My father owns the store. I know that I am not hallucinating my father, OK? I've been noticing people acknowledging him since I was young. And why did you say he 'raised the both of you' back there? Who's 'the both of you'?"

"That man that owns the store is your grandfather," Beecher said. "He is the spitting image of Dean Deremer, but twenty years older. Plus, for all intents and purposes, he *was* your father. He was your legal guardian from the time of your parents' death until the age of twelve, when he let you live in the farmhouse." It was not an uncommon practice a hundred years ago to have the man of the house be a teenager. That Mark lived in the house at such a young age was not necessarily seen as being out of the ordinary. "When I said 'the both of you' I was referring to you and your brother, Ed."

"Ed?!" Mark laughed, "Ed is not my real brother. My grandfather adopted him. Ed's real last name is Sorbitt, son of Dean and Glad—" Mark stopped dead in his tracks. *How could I not have noticed?!* He suddenly recalled the story in The County Crier about the grisly murder-suicide in the Sorbitt household. It was exactly the same as the hallucination he had. Mark now recalled reading the paper about the 'Sorbitts.' This newly unearthed defense mechanism was doing such a good job of sheltering him that the last name was obscured in his memory as well, along with the first name of 'Dean Sorbitt's' wife. The reality of the situation began to dawn on Mark along with sheer terror left over from not processing the incident and leaving it buried for twenty some odd years. He suddenly found it very strange that his father spent nearly every waking moment out in the blind and that

Gladys was perpetually in the kitchen preparing meals. He simply picked typicalities of his parents from childhood and placed them in his working consciousness. The breakfast he ate every morning was from a real memory. It was the happiest his family had ever been, so his consciousness recycled that moment as often as possible, composing and adding in relevant conversation.

The multiple states of consciousness were constructed for this very reason, a defense mechanism. Whenever he started to put pieces of his parents' puzzle together, a built-in sensor would detect his imminent recollection of the incident and divert his attention like the click of a View-Master lever. His alternate consciousness would deal with the emotions behind closed doors and bury them behind Mark's back. Once and again, they could not be buried fast enough, or the emotions would rise too fast or with too much intensity and the black-outs would step in as a failsafe.

Mark had essentially created a parent for himself, protecting him from the harm of the real world. Though the parent was actually him, growing up behind the curtain, and now the parent figure recognized that if he were to be responsible for saving the town, he had to shake the coping mechanism and take ownership of his life. How else could he take ownership of the lives of so many others? All these realizations flashed at him in a second. Mark still sat dumbfounded at Dr. Beecher's pushing him over the line so brusquely. *Part of the lack of bedside manner I suppose.*

In the distance, a teapot began to boil. The whistle came up from a quiet low-pitched whine and sailed upwards to 20,000 Hertz. *I don't remember him putting tea on.* Suddenly whisking by the kitchen table on either side were packs of green four-legged creatures resembling dog-sized insects. Mark greeted them as if they were real. He jumped up and expressed genuine fear to the doctor sitting across from him. Dr. Beecher stood up with him, "What is it Mark? Stay with me," he said. Herds of them now kicking up dust all around them. It was his coping mechanism, arriving quite late to the game, perhaps by design of the parent figure. His multiple states of consciousness were no longer in play and a blackout could not be summoned at the moment. Plan C was, apparently, a real hallucination.

But with enough fear and enough panic, Mark's blood pressure raised enough to induce a fainting spell and he collapsed on the floor in front of the doctor. His body hit the wood-plank floor with a crack and a thud.

When Mark was a boy, he was most inquisitive, as children are. When he saw his parents' corpses, disfigured as they were, he naturally had thousands of questions. Of course the young boy did not understand death. He didn't understand motive or mental illness let alone that finding one's parents in this way at a very young age was horrific and possibly psychologically damaging in the long term. As a child, the world is new and the slate is blank. Most things are strange and confusing in this new world. A young boy does not know where to draw the line between what is strange and what is normal; and what is horrific for that matter. They haven't yet learned that some things are categorized as terrifying and psychologically damaging. So the questions he started asking his grandfather did not concern death, mental illness, or motive. Young Mark's questions had more to do with the details of the unusual scene, "Why was ma's tongue hanging out? What happened to her eyes? Where is she now? Is she still on the floor? What did she spill? Why did pa look like that? Where is pa now?"

The questions were more disturbing to Grandpa Deremer in that he *believed* that the boy was damaged from what he saw. In reality, Mark was truly only curious, and as the questions continued to be met with avoidance, his curiosity only grew stronger. Perhaps a straightforward discussion about what happened would have been better for Mark's development, but that was against societal norms.

In his best attempt at healing the boy, Grandpa spent as much time as he could with little Mark, taking him to the store with him every single day. The store became their second home. Mark would help unload trucks in the morning before school once he got a bit older. Then in the afternoon, he would walk back to the store and stock shelves or whatever odd job Grandpa had for him. It gave young Mark a purpose. The quick study that he was, he learned every detail about the process of running the store. In addition, he got a small amount of time to interact with the town. He developed his social skills in that little general store on the outskirts of Hayminster, which was possibly one contributing factor as to why they were so stunted.

It seemed like every day he asked a question about that gruesome scene. For years, he would come up with more and more questions with just as few answers as with in the past. Grandpa didn't know what to do and took him to see a much younger Dr. Beecher, who wasn't a psychiatrist, but did what he could for someone who needed his help. But Mark seemed to be fine by all other accounts, just a curious young boy who was trying to make sense of the world and his experiences within it. It was the nature of the questions he was asking that raised eyebrows. Mark began to make the connection as he grew a little older that the brutal scene of his butchered mother and headless father was not a normal thing to discuss. The other students began to isolate him, the teachers would chastise him for openly talking about it, and the whole of the town was whispering about him behind his back. Little Mark began to withdraw and eventually swept the entire experience under the rug to get everyone off of his back. He acted like he forgot the whole thing, which seemed to satisfy everyone. Dr. Beecher had a hunch that this was what was happening, but he couldn't be sure, and the last thing he wanted to do was try to remind a young child that he was orphaned by a notorious murder-suicide.

Of course he remembered it; unconsciously anyway. But the repressive burial worked wonders and each day that passed piled a bit more dirt onto the grave of that memory. As Mark's brain began to develop more fully, primal emotions would inexplicably rear their heads from far beneath the recesses. Mark felt the emotions of the incident, but did not try to unearth the past. By then, it was too deep to do it alone. Until now, he only kept piling defense mechanism on top of denial on top of rationalization on top of defense mechanism onto the memory's grave until he finally just began talking to and seeing his parents as if they had been alive and well the entire time. What he did not retrieve from memory, he filled in with extrapolations and character traits of other mentors. Since his grandfather was the one to raise him, and he felt more safety from isolation by calling him 'pa,' the name and association stuck. Not to mention the likeness of the two and the fact that Mark's last memory of his real father's face was a pile of red chunks. Grandpa never did anything to correct him either. He had no reason to believe that Mark would be lying about forgetting the scene. After all, he was only four or five years old at the time and, "What's the harm? For all intents and purposes, I am his father."

No one ever questioned any of his peculiarities after that. Anytime anyone remarked on any odd behavior, the response would always come back, "Can you blame him? Just think of what happened to him. How do you think you would behave if that happened to you?" Mark had carved out a safe little world for himself. He continued to work at the store, day after day, with Ed, his little brother.

Ed, on the other hand, was more seriously and more obviously affected by the incident. Not surprisingly, as he did not just come in and find the aftermath, but was present for the entire event. The poor child heard the savagery taking place in the next room from his crib and ultimately witnessed the final moments of his father's existence, even wearing some of it afterwards.

Compared to Ed, Mark was very well-adjusted. No one knew that he talked to himself or went to college on the advice of a hallucination. But in time, his brain began to heal itself, as brains tend to do, and the repressed root trying to grow from underneath the tombstone sprung itself up and the memory came crashing into reality with all the force of a head on collision between two speeding freight trains. One could argue that it was the stress, or the *Vir* infection. But the brain *was* healing and the proof was in reliving the incident. If Dr. Beecher had finished the much needed push, Mark's own mind had started it. Deep down he knew that, there is no way to know how strong you actually are until you have to be.

Mark awoke to a condensed beam of light shining directly into his pupil, just beneath the eyelid. The savory aroma of thickly cut bacon wafted into his nostrils. He rose from his covers similar to Ebenezer Scrooge after the visit from the ghost of Christmas future. Happiness filled his heart as the air filled with sounds of his mother laughing flirtatiously and his father speaking coyly to his mother. The words fell unheard, but the message bloomed like marigolds from the thaw.

Mark flung the door open from his bedroom, leading directly to the dining and kitchen area, to find the long farmhouse table vacant. The room was dark, with a cold stove top and overcast skies creeping into Mark's vision from behind the shabby red curtains. Despite his disappointment, he walked over to the table anyway and took a seat. When he did, he allowed a blink which opened to a table full of empty plates and silverware sitting neatly beside them. Seated in the places of his parents were their two corpses, just as they were when Mark found them that fateful night, his mother twitching uncontrollably, with dark red, hollowed-out eye sockets and a long, slithering, pink tongue desperately trying to find a foothold. Next to Gladys, sat Dean, wearing a blood-soaked black and white flannel shirt. On the neck of the body hung a few flaps of skin which covered shards of his skull. Mark studied the nightmare carefully. Every shining red inch of the scene was taken in, as it actually was occurring, projected onto his consciousness.

To his right, an increasing racket emerged from a desolate silence. A drum beat repetitiously. Finally, Mark summoned the strength to look away from his parents and discover some kind of ceremonial dance being performed in the living room. Two giant feathered men danced rhythmically to the drum and clapped along

338

with the long wooden beaks of their black, red, and yellow bird masks. A tall pole sat in the middle of a circle of tribesmen. From the pole hung taught cords attached to a warrior via buffalo bone piercings through his chest. The warrior leaned backward, tightening his face and pulling the flesh away from his ribcage. The warrior held his arms high in the air and hung backwards completely on his heels by his own body weight. The crowd and the drum beat went silent while the man hung in agony. In one action, both cords snapped and the warrior fell backwards out of view. Fellow tribesmen looking on stood up to cheer but were changed into howling wolves as they did.

To Mark's left, the distinct sound of a horse nicker drew his attention back to the table. Now sitting in his father's place was a live horse head. Its body sat, quite inexplicably, hidden underneath the table. In his mother's spot sat Grandpa Ray, who was caught in some kind of fast-forward loop that could not be understood. It was utter gibberish in between bouts of cackling and a tapping on his temple. Then, interrupting that nonsense, two shiny black objects flew quickly past his line of sight throwing him from a REM cycle into the common timeline with a gasp.

The next morning, Mark lit the burner on Dr. Beecher's stove and fetched a cast iron tea kettle and a bag of English breakfast from the cupboard above. One of the glass jugs of water nearby refracted the morning light into a vibrant spectrum on the gray slate countertop upon which it sat. But the sun's showpiece was distorted and subsequently shattered into oblivion as Mark stole a kettle's worth of water from it. The instant the first wisp of steam wandered up from the spout, Mark lifted the antique vessel from its fire and poured heated water onto a thin paper bag of the black crumbled tea leaves. Mark much preferred coffee to tea. However, somewhere amidst the Salvador Dali painting that was Beecher's kitchen, lay the disfigured remains of Mr. Coffee, model number R4-RB.

Surveying the wreckage of plastic that littered the room, Mark pondered how no one could have imagined that plastic would cause the downfall of the American Empire. He considered the symbol for lead on the periodic table, 'Pb.' It stood for plumbum, the Latin word for lead. A water resistant and highly malleable metal, lead was considered a perfect material for constructing Rome's network of pipes, delivering drinking water to its residents. Back then, no one could have guessed that it was toxic and responsible for the mass poisoning of Rome, spreading death and mental illness to anyone who touched enough of it. Some scholars would argue that it was the most potent contributor to the fall of the empire. Today, in Ash County, nobody could have guessed that a readily available, durable, and inexpensive material used in virtually all modern products would be related to the spread of a strange and contagious androgen-induced psychosis.

Breaking free of the train of thought, Mark began steeping his tea bag, deciding the English breakfast may be more enjoyable on the front porch. But when the door swung open, he found that he would not be drinking the tea alone. What he saw suddenly evoked the realization that he had never been awakened to take his shift as sentry. In the early morning sunrise, slumped against the staircase's wrought-iron spindles lie a deceased Steven Williams; his pale white face frozen in horror and missing the top of his skull. But that was not all. He found that whoever did this was not content just killing him. The perpetrators had removed the brain, leaving the dome almost completely hollow. Two optic nerves dangled from behind his eye sockets and remnants of the olfactory bulb lay tattered where the rest of the brain must have been unceremoniously ripped out. It had the semblance of a hollowed-out jack-o-lantern, with other bits of tissue serving as forgotten pumpkin innards. It was a disturbing sight, to say the least, seeing one of his only friends sitting upright on his porch, bearing the horrified sentiment of his last few seconds on Earth. But the way Mark handled it was perhaps more disturbing than the sight itself. He bent over slightly without a hint of surprise, fear, grief, or pain, and examined the corpse. He then pulled up the rocking chair beside him and sat, drinking his tea and staring out over the barren corn fields of Ash County as the sun continued its climb over the horizon.

With the last few drops of black liquid slurped clean from his mug, Mark retreated indoors to head Beecher off at the pass. Inside, he was already repeating Mark's tea ritual in the kitchen.

"Morning," the doctor said cheerfully.

"Morning," Mark called back with far less enthusiasm.

"Where's Steve?" Beecher asked, "He never woke me up last night."

"Steve's dead," Mark said flatly, "outside on the porch." It was not that Mark felt no emotion for Steve. But he lived in a different world now. The calming voice of his mother and the cocoon he had constructed to keep the world at arm's length, had been shed with one stout flay. *Oh well. No matter.*

"What?!" Dr. Beecher exclaimed, "What do you mean?"

"Well," Mark said, "I have a hunch, from the way they left him, that Axiom did not like him being here."

"How they left him?" Beecher repeated.

"They scooped out his brains," Mark said. "It's a message to us not to get any smart ideas."

Beecher stormed out, unable to break Mark's gaze before he got to the metal transition threshold separating outside from in.

"Jesus! Fuck! What the fuck?!" Beecher stuttered. He didn't stay outside for more than three seconds before marching back into the kitchen at a high rate of speed. "What the fuck?!" Beecher repeated, about three inches from Mark's face.

"I didn't do it if that's what your proximity is implying," Mark said calmly.

"How do you know it was Axiom?" Beecher sputtered.

"He didn't call for help," Mark explained, "which means it was either someone he knew, or ninjas. Plus, the body doesn't show any evidence of the brutal trauma or careless puncture wounds which are characteristic of a berserker attack. In fact, besides the missing brain and scalp, there were no wounds whatsoever. It was precise and calculated; professional."

"Why didn't they come in after us?" the doctor wondered.

"I do not know," Mark said. "Perhaps he did not let them know we were here. Perhaps we should not wait for them to come back."

Dr. Beecher nodded remorsefully and began packing for

the journey. Leaving your only friend's mutilated body on the porch as you carry on as planned should not sit well with anyone outside the limits of sociopathy. It was cold. It was callous. But both Mark and Beecher silently agreed that it was the best thing to do.

Mark and Dr. Beecher loaded up the huge stacks of flyers into two duffle bags and finished as much water as they could. Beecher did not have any portable containers that were not made of plastic, and carrying the large glass jug with them was not an option.

"Ready?" Mark asked, surveying the room one more time before they set out on the journey. Steve's access badge lay on the counter. Its picture of him brought a slight taste for vengeance to his palate. Mark walked back and scooped it up before they walked out and past the body, with the foreboding notion on both their minds that it could be them at any time now.

Not much was said during the hike. For one, they did not want to attract attention to themselves. Two, they were both too busy disregarding the fear of being sitting ducks for a random posse of dangerous lunatics to dismember. In some cosmic connection to the infinite dimensions, Mark felt empathy for his father walking in the jungles of Vietnam. Even though the doctor and the scientist knew exactly what they were doing and where they were going, even though they had rehearsed, discussed, and considered as many situations as they could think up before they left the house, each time they stopped to set a stack of flyers free, urinate, or otherwise make themselves vulnerable, writhing fear swooped down and pecked them without mercy.

They must have cast off thousands of leaflets, all on varying types of paper. There was printer paper, notebook paper, newspaper, magazine pages; pretty much anything they had that would fly. Mark and Beecher watched them scattering across the farms and vast fields of the county, flipping and flying, dispersing, diving hard in one direction and suddenly stopping dead or changing directions without warning. As unpredictable as the micro patterns of their flocks of messages moved as they were carried on the wind, the bigger picture displayed a consistent pattern. Mark began to trace the same fractal geometry that emerged in his visions of lightning bolts, tree limbs, ice breaks, and the waving grasses. *Unknowable, yet all-encompassing.*

An entire day of walking brought the men to the edge of Deremer land with empty duffle bags save for the papers with large arrows drawn on them. Curiously, in all that time, they didn't encounter one clan of berserkers. It was a good thing in the sense that they did not have to run for their lives or murder any more of their fellow citizens. On the other hand, it would be bad if they did not get the messages, or worse, if they had already fled the county in search of food, spreading *Vir* to the rest of the state. Nonetheless, they carried out the plan to a T with only one thing left to do.

They had made it to the broken entry point in the fence where the flyers instructed to meet. The sky had become overcast and a crater full of rainwater could not be avoided on the path to Zululand. Beecher in the lead, he made a feebly comical attempt to jump over it, seeming to land in the deepest possible region. "Goddamnit!" he groaned. They were the first spoken words of the entire trip. Mark decided to accept that he could not avoid it, but the expected cold of the small lake never reached his flesh. Looking down for an explanation, he noticed that he was wearing his father's jungle boots; the same ones that had sat unworn in the mudroom for decades. He had no recollection of putting them on before leaving Beecher's, or before that for that matter. *Fuck, please not now.* Certainly, he must have just grabbed them in his haste to leave the house after the vision of his parents. Even so, Mark felt this to be a sign that he was headed for a blackout, or in some capacity would be unable to maintain consciousness for much longer. If this were true, to acknowledge it as inconvenient would be quite an understatement.

Into the trunk of every few trees, another arrow was nailed until they reached the raging rapids, which had been whispering the promise to be every bit as intense as Mark's memory depicted, ever since they entered the woods.

Mark could not believe he had made it across the first time. "It's straight on through there," Mark spoke up over the galloping whitecaps. "Hopefully the promise of a few venison steaks will suffice to make them stupid enough to cross."

"Is there a quicker way back?" Beecher hollered, knowing full well that there wasn't.

"We should stay at my house tonight," Mark suggested. "There's no sense in making that same trip again for no reason. It'll be pitch black before we get halfway."

At ease that they would finally be able to sit down, they joyfully set off back to the farmhouse with a well-deserved sense of accomplishment. However, the warm blood that carried that joy soon would speed away, leaving dead-cold despair in its wake. Directly in their path stood what looked to be hundreds of large-statured berserkers; ragged and carrying a plethora of handheld farming implements or other makeshift weaponry. Whatever intellect Mark and Beecher had used to get them this far now gave way to raw instinct. The violent fury of the river behind them might as well have been the adrenaline in their veins, crashing into every post-synaptic receptor that would accept it. The object of their fear began excitedly hopping and screaming; crouching down into attack positions. The scene was reminiscent of a vast macaque troop preparing a raid on a marketplace in Jaipur. The three hundred meters between them gave little relief as the clan spread out and sprung down from the hills flanking their position at a horrifying and unnatural speed.

Mark's first instinct was to doubt his senses. As real as it was, he decided he must be living another nightmare. But that was irrelevant, as the fear gave him no choice but to behave as if it were real. Without even consulting one another for a possible plan of action, the two men plunged into the rapids. The temperature made them gasp in shock, and the current immediately carried them away.

Not more than five seconds later, the clan was rushing in after them. Neither the doctor nor the scientist were concerned, for at this moment, they feared the river would kill them first. Mark was slammed into a large rock protruding from the water, having crags suited just right for Mark's fingers, and he held tight. The rapids clung to him, making him heavy, pulling him from his meager safety with the force of a Clydesdale pair plowing him through the fields. With burning biceps and brown water washing over him, he scanned for Beecher, coming up empty. Enough time had passsed that flailing berserkers were now rushing toward him, grasping in vain at any possible foothold.

The speed with which they hurried into the water was nothing compared to that which carried them on the current. Frantic, terrified, the beasts held each other under trying to save themselves. In their struggles, many did not come back up, and just as many were washed away. The river made short work of thinning the herd and Mark began to fear that instead of saving them, he just killed them all in one fell swoop.

They were certainly afraid. The fear was not absent from the faces of those still on the bank either. But was the desire for food really driving them that hard? It did not seem that way. They looked like lemmings, just following the ones in front to their death. Some of the crazier ones were even laughing as they struggled through the current. Before long, a pattern emerged. Even as intense as the situation was, Mark noted the same fractal pattern in their rush. Though dozens upon dozens came charging into the river after them, attacking each other the whole way down, through the chaos, Mark saw order. As if they all had listened in to the conversation in Beecher's home office, they seemed to know, instinctually, what to do. Each and every one was scared to death, but continued on anyway, blindly disregarding the fear. It was a thing of beauty.

Through the commotion, Mark noted that some of them were making it up the bank on the Zululand side. Once over, the men started exhibiting peculiar behavior. While some sat to catch their breath, and some continued to run in the direction of the pointing arrows, others secured their stability with a firm grasp on some woodland projection in the bank and helped stragglers to shore. *They are cooperating?*

No sooner did Mark verbalize the thought than a particularly full pocket of water punched him free from the rock, tilting him upside down and barreling downstream. Pond water blasted up through his sinuses, making the task of righting himself that much more painful. Soon it became apparent that this trip through the river would be much less fortunate than his first cross over. His muscles were simply not as strong as he needed them to be. The freezing water added to the exhaustion and with several more gulps of the gamy river water, Mark could be sure he was going to drown. But before he could completely give up hope, something hooked the collar of his shirt, holding him still against the rushing current. Soon he felt other hooks and the sensation of rising as the grasps pulled him out of hell.

Once safely on the bank, one of the hands that grabbed the back of his shirt held out in front of him, awaiting Mark's. As he reciprocated, he was pulled to his feet by none other than little Ed. But Mark couldn't believe his eyes. It *was* Ed. But the blank stare of confusion that usually colored his face was absent. "You OK?" he screamed, to which Mark replied with a simple nod. With Mark's reassurance, Ed turned away from him to return to the fray and help others who were struggling to shore. Mark was beside himself. If he didn't know any better, he would say that the disability with which Ed had lived his whole life was suddenly gone.

Now more certain than ever that he was in a dream, he collapsed to his knees in exhaustion and watched the cluster unfold. Some of the men were still being washed away. But the ones who made it were forming long chains from the other side, helping to get as many as they could across. Some got to shore and shook hands, asking, 'are you alright?' and other mutterings about well-being that could not be deciphered. A few continued in the direction of the cabin, but without the bloodthirsty aggression that had personified them previously. They walked casually, as if nothing had ever been out of the ordinary.

This was a stark difference compared to the mob back on the Lichten bank. The berserkers were still aptly named on that side of the river as evident by the shining silver pupils on each one as they tore and swung at each other. Further up, it was a veritable orgy of violence, in which assertions of dominance, coma-inducing battery, and sickening acts of outright torture could be picked out of the anarchy. It reminded him of what some medieval battlefield might look like if all the combatants were violent psychopaths on a strict diet of bath salts and PCP. It was bedlam. There was no order and no cooperation. It was every beast for himself.

Even though Mark was witnessing what seemed to be a successful execution of the plan, he could not trust his senses, and so a feeling of safety did not register. All he could think about were the ones he saw heading toward Ray's cabin. He couldn't be sure that Ray had ever returned, or if he had even existed in the first place, if he wanted to be honest with himself. Nonetheless, he could not stand the thought of that poor old man being raped and beaten to death. So he gathered what strength he had left, reluctantly turned his back on the crowd, said a prayer that Beecher had died quickly, and started a sprint toward Ray.

Mark examined his situation. Less than seventy-two hours ago, he wanted nothing more than to get away from that cabin and out of these woods. A few months ago, however much time had actually passed, he was a simple study director; analyzing, concluding, testing, analyzing, concluding, reporting, repeating. With one step out of his comfort zone, he was addicted, trudging through a battlefield on a quest to rescue several hundred of his fellow citizens and a hermit he had only met once. As depleted as he was, both mentally and physically, he felt better now than he ever had. *What could possibly be the driving force to provoke such a paradoxical state of mind?* It was simple, he now had a purpose and what he did mattered.

As these thoughts churned, Mark sprinted through Zululand, noticing here and there a memorable landmark which assured him he was on the right path. The sound of wet leaves underfoot was all he could hear. Soon, a smell riddled with emotional associations drilled his olfaction. *Venison.* In the distance, sizzles and friendly chatter emanated from one focal point about eight-hundred meters ahead. Against the backdrop of a small, red cabin stood a crowd of people huddled around a campfire grill and a seated figure with a long white beard. As Mark's steps slowed to a halt, the bearded man stood and directed his stare towards him, inspiring his crowd to follow suit.

"Well, howdy stranger," the old man creaked. "Didn't expect to see you back so soon."

"What happened?" Mark asked.

"Well," Ray began, "the road was washed out. We couldn't make it back. I was surprised you weren't still here. How did you get out?"

"I tried making my way across the wash and was swept

away," Mark explained. "I nearly drowned."

"Holy Cats!" Ray exclaimed.

"But I was able to grab hold of some strong roots that were exposed by the erosion of the soil around it. I pulled myself up by the roots and out of the rapids. I finally made it out and back to higher ground," Mark was using a little dramatic license for Ray's sake, who really seemed to be enjoying it.

"That's amazing!" he shouted as he clapped his hands together.

"Sorry about the steak," Mark offered.

"Are you kiddin'?" Ray asked, "They were worth it just to hear that story!"

"And the wood too," Mark added. "I will replace everything I used."

"Son," Ray began again, "we knew there was a flood a comin'. We pretend like there is always sumthin' comin' and we get ready fer it. This time I had a feeling that it was gonna be extry rough and it was, so we moved ourselves out for a little while. But we've the provisions for just such occasions. They're fer emergencies and that's what you used 'em fer."

"Is the road still washed out?" Mark asked puzzled, "After all of that rain?"

"Nope," Ray answered succinctly, "it comes and it goes by and by. Car's all fixed too. Don't worry about that either. My friend owed me a favor."

"Who are these people?" Mark asked as if he didn't know.

"Oh them?" Ray turned around to include them, "These gals here said they found some flyers talkin' about venison steaks and salmon filets somewhere out this way."

Gals? They didn't much look like women, which he

remembered Steve saying was an effect of the *Vir* infection. "Hi
Mr. Deremer!" a deep yet feminine voice sounded. It was Large
Marge, the security guard who worked in the guard shack. Though
she had always had a large frame, and was probably stronger and
more masculine than most men, she was now nearly
unrecognizable. Her facial features and other secondary sex
characteristics were drastically warped from the testosterone
bombardment. Everyone in the circle apparently was suffering
from the same affliction, if they were indeed women. It was hard to
tell. But among them looked to be Shawna, the nurse that he had
aggressively propositioned at St. Catherine's, and also Sara
Siebert, Eddie's proclaimed girlfriend who was reported missing. It
was particularly satisfying to see her alive. *Why are all the women
here first?*

"Hi Marge!" Mark said as he walked toward Marge to give
her a hug, "glad to see you made it out of the hell."

"The what?" Marge questioned.

"This sickness," Mark hinted, "the crazy way that people
have been acting."

"Huh," Marge said, as if to say, 'well how about that,' "I
hadn't even noticed."

Mark took a moment to decide if she was serious or not.
Her expression said she truly did not realize that anything was
wrong. The others' facial expressions betrayed the same sentiment.

Marge, like the others in the circle, were an unfortunate
sight, for the bugs had affected them most of all, and they didn't
even realize it. Mark held out hope that, if his theory was correct,
their estradiol levels would stabilize and restore some of their
feminine qualities.

"Well," Mark dismissed, now addressing Ray, "you should

353

probably expect a few hundred more coming your way in the next half hour. Do you want to come with me and get out of here?"

"Well not if I'm expecting more company son!" Ray replied, "I'm sure I'll catch up with you again before too long."

"Where are the kids?" Mark asked.

"Oh they fly all over this wide world," he said, jokingly peeved. "My only worry is that one or both of them won't return."

"OK then," Mark held out his hand. "Guess I'll be on my way. If I don't see you again, thank you."

Ray took Mark's hand in his and pierced the gaze of his single eye deep into his soul before saying,

"All doorways, before going forward, should be looked to; for difficult it is to know where foes may sit within a dwelling.

Of his understanding no one should be proud, but rather in conduct cautious. When the prudent and taciturn come to a dwelling, harm seldom befalls the cautious; for a firmer friend no man ever gets than great sagacity.

A better burden no man bears on the way than much good sense; that is thought better than riches in a strange place; such is the recourse of the indigent.

He alone knows who wanders wide, and has much experienced, by what disposition each man is ruled, who common sense possesses.

But, a cowardly man thinks he will ever live, if warfare he avoids; but old age will give him no peace, though spears may spare him.

Thoughts, memories, and heart. I will see you again."

Ray's statement sent electricity through his hand to every nerve in his body. He then held up Mark's car keys, in much the same way that Steve had held up his security badge, as if it were a medal. As their handshake broke, Mark took the car keys and turned away from Ray's intense stare and climbed into the familiar heirloom station wagon. The car started without falter, even sounding stronger than he remembered, and he drove cautiously through the mud to his final destination.

Mark left the woods a new man. The barriers were broken, his eyes open. A vision of his multiple states of consciousness overtook his mind's eye. A semipermeable membrane in an endless grid broke all at once, leaving one singular, expanded consciousness.

At the bottom, the chain reaction from the surface burst through the thick membrane dividing conscious from subconscious, blasting Mark below. The dream world, the one of manufactured reality, suddenly made sense. It had not been disconnected from the common timeline at all. Looking down through the translucent surface from above, the information seemed warped and nonsensical, even frightening. But now, sinking in the cold, blue depths of the abyss, the water ran clear and pure as raindrops from the heavens.

Mark's blackouts and hallucinations were his own, that was not part of this disease state. They made perfect sense now, when posed against the background of subconscious. The dream of the green bugs, the female body in the woods, the River Gjoll, they were all communications from deep down. Not that Mark was a clairvoyant, but so many connecting nodes existed in this extensive network that constituted his intelligence, he was able to connect the dots based on the unseen information he already had. It was his way of understanding the world. Even his parents. Though they died when he was young, Mark held on to the good parts and pieced together what he thought good parents would be from his grandfather and from other experiences in his life. This oblivion he called subconscious had always been there, guiding him, just below the surface. It was a vast and tantalizing labyrinth that he refused to indulge all these years. Fear had held him back. He much preferred sitting at the desk of the rational analyst, making the most informed decision possible. But it was as if *Vir* had broken the spell and crazy old Ray spoke directly to it, spooked it, like a wild beast that had been long bridled. It gave him that essential missing ingredient which was thought of so fondly in days of old: heart. Mark now faced the fear and stopped the futility of trying to control it. He let go of the reins and let it run free and wild. He allowed the whims of this ocean to carry him away as a mere traveler, simply along for the ride. It was quite an awakening. He wasn't yet sure what to make of it, but he knew it was powerful.

Mark pulled the wagon up to exactly the last place he had seen it before he was sent to the hospital. Outside the lowered security arm beside the guard shack, Mark dismounted and approached the darkened building.

The sun had nearly set over Ash County. It had never been so quiet. Mark's was the only car that still worked leaving the night empty of a single engine noise for miles. The nonfunctional streetlights left the crisp spring air absent of the usual and constant buzzing sound. The EnviroCore building completed the town's image of an apocalyptic wasteland, complete with broken windows and defaced brick walls. Mark walked up to the entrance to find the plastic security badge reader but a grey spot mounted outside the door with frayed copper wires protruding from it.

Though he had walked these halls many times a day for the past ten years, he had never felt so afraid. Behind every corner, he expected a clan of berserkers ready to destroy him, or find some disfigured body rotting away. But he found neither. Just random piles of melted plastic and the occasional evidence of rabid violence.

Once he made it to his office as the former Vice President of Operations, he noticed a small red light which partially lit the metal badge scanner outside the door. It was probably the only lit bulb in the entire county. 'BEEP' the red light turned green as Mark swiped Steve's security badge in front of it, followed by the familiar sound of the automatic unlock. Inside was a much different scene than that of outside and the rest of the county. Nothing out of place, no melted plastic; it was like another world.

But Mark tried to remain focused on the task at hand. Upon booting the computer, he expected to spend a considerable amount of time trying to guess a security code or hack around it. But it appeared that *Vir* had provided all the security that was needed. There was no log-in screen whatsoever. If you were in the room, that was good enough.

Adrenaline pumped through Mark's system as he open the only folder on the desktop. Inside were two icons, one was the familiar cut-and-paste double-helix belonging to GLADIS, the other was a word document simply titled, 'new contracts.' Unable to contain his curiosity, Mark double-clicked on the word document. At the exact millisecond of the second click, the ultraviolet germicidal irradiation bulbs kicked on, nearly causing Mark's heart to crack his sternum.

As Mark began perusing the table of contents in the word document, it appeared at first to be exactly what he thought it was, legalese outlining the EnviroCore Axiom merger. However, upon closer inspection, it was much more than that. It became obvious, as he continued to expand bullet points, that this was a draft of a document that was only meant for the eyes of a small handful of people.

The first bullet point was titled, 'A Brief History of the Advanced Test System Research Project.' In the parlance of medical research, the term 'test system' was a euphemism for 'guinea pig.'

The page chronicled an experiment conducted in France in the early fifties involving an experimental medication in the town of Pont-Saint-Esprit. One day, about 250 of the town's citizens suddenly started screaming absurdities about giant fire monsters and jumping out of windows. Asylums, hospitals, and jails were packed full trying to restore order in the town and to save these poor souls from themselves. Conspiracy theories abounded as to what happened, most of them planted by the perpetrators in a red herring attempt. No one ever suspected that the well-known, well-trusted Axiom Pharmaceuticals would be the ones behind the 'poisoning.' In reality, it was an audacious new method of getting a drug to market. 'Advanced Test System Research' really meant 'Unsuspecting Human Subject.'

As many a frustrated clinical-trial physician will tell you, the metabolic effects of a drug do not necessarily transcend species. That is to say, just because a drug cures malaria in monkeys, doesn't mean it will cure it in humans. In the case of Pont-Saint-Esprit, it doesn't necessarily mean it won't send the humans running down the street after the hearts that have escaped from their chests either. After the situation was controlled and the smoke cleared, Axiom killed the Advanced Test System Project and buried all evidence that it ever existed. As Mark opened the next bullet point to read on, the timer on the irradiation bulbs clicked, engulfing the room in darkness again save for the glow of the computer screen.

Beneath the history was a small tome outlining new and existing government regulations from The Environmental Protection Agency, The United States Department of Agriculture, and The Food and Drug Administration. It read, "One exemption from MCAN reporting is the R&D Exemption. This is a complete exemption from TSCA § 5 reporting for certain R&D activities that are (1) conducted in contained structures, and (2) are subject to regulation by another Federal agency." Mark's eyes widened as he began connecting dots, "*Viridobacter circulofractus* is registered and complies with the Federal Insecticide, Fungicide, and Rodenticide Act, the Toxic Substances Control Act, and The National Environmental Policy Act in addition to its Research and Development Exemption. *Viridobacter circulofractus* is listed as a new microorganism on the TSCA Inventory of Chemical Substances and though it is exempt from the submission of a Microbial Commercial Activity Notice due to its additional governance under FDA and USDA, is FDA licensed and in compliance with the Public Health Service Act. In addition, EnviroCore has notified the Animal and Plant Health Inspection Service of *Viridobacter circulofractus* mass distribution and has obtained all proper permits. All relevant agencies are in possession of the *Viridobacter circulofractus* genome." All involved regulatory agencies were fully aware of the partnership between EnviroCore Axiom and Waste Management and had no complaints. All I's were dotted, all T's were crossed. In the end, the document concluded that the agencies and their counterparts, especially the EPA, were "excited to see the results." Mark's stomach acids boiled to the top of his neck. *It can't be. It just can't be.* In not so many words, *Vir* was exempt from regulation because it was 'experimental.' The question the experiment was asking: "Is this plastic-eating bacteria safe for Advanced Test Systems?" The Test System in this case was the population of Ash County, the answer to the question, was "No."

It had all the trappings of Ted Philus. Axiom was the company who had made their millions telling the world what to believe. Not many people questioned them and those who did ended up losing in one way or another. Just ask Steve. Before long, it didn't matter what Axiom said or did. They were so big and so well-established that they could do no wrong. Even in the face of blatant misdeeds, as long as they found a patsy or covered it up well enough, they came up smelling like roses; like it never happened.

In all fairness, the conglomerate had done a whole lot of

good in the world. They saved millions of lives and helped improve the quality of life for countless individuals. In the process of all that healing, they made a large fortune. After all, what is the harm in making money while helping out your fellow man?

When Steve came to Philus after quitting EnviroCore in a huff, Ted saw an opportunity and grabbed it with both hands. Imagine some German country bumpkin coming to Hitler with a map of allied strongholds and saying, "Thought you might find this interesting." Ted went to Axiom's door directly and pitched them 'one hell of an offer.' But Steve was in over his head. The problem was that he didn't understand GLADIS like Mark did. Two long years Steve tried to figure it out to no avail. Philus would have told Axiom that it was in beta, to which Axiom would have said, "Come back when it's ready."

So Steve just returned to EnviroCore; no hard feelings. But Philus didn't let go. He got to talking with Axiom and learned their story. Of course nobody liked the approval process. On the business end, the time and money wasted on declined applications would have been better utilized in a locomotive firebox. On the regulatory side, the approval process was antiquated and imperfect. From the perspective of the suffering public, people were dying, spending life savings on medication, or otherwise living shitty lives due to red tape. With viral vectors coming to the forefront as a contender to traditional medicine, the genetic modification prediction software named GLADIS was exactly what the world needed. If Axiom could show that the predictions were accurate, the approval process wait would be virtually zero. In fact, the approval process essentially would be GLADIS.

With the town of Vandeburgh and the rest of Ash County breathing down his neck anyway, Ted felt it was time to cash in.

Never really intending on leaving the company, he secured Bill as Axiom's first patsy, who put Mark in charge, who turned out to be the key to the golden city of El Dorado, handing over *Vir* on a silver platter. GLADIS made *Vir*, so GLADIS was ready. Mark could only speculate as to whether putting him in charge of operations was the plan all along.

But there were more pressing issues at the moment. No matter what happened, he would undo what was done, so that it never happened again. In case of emergency, programmers wishing to maintain copyright protection have come up with a simple virus; short, easy-to-write code affecting only the program itself. It gives the owner the ability to render the program inoperable in the event it is stolen. It simply deletes or duplicates random letters in the rest of the code. A shift of one letter may have the potential to bring the whole thing down. Mark added an algorithm which added about six million. He titled it 'frameshift,' after the type of genetic mutation which is the naturally occurring version of the computer virus code.

Mark opened the command prompt and began typing. Within seconds, 'frameshift' was ready to do its damage. When he closed the command prompt, a message appeared which read, 'run program with new code?' Mark hovered the cursor over the 'run' box ready to destroy his creation for the good of mankind, when the click of the timer lit the irradiation bulbs again. In the glare of the dark computer screen, the germicidal bulbs reflected Bill Wildeboer standing behind him pointing his father's 1911 at the back of his head. Without the slightest display of fear, Mark simply acknowledged the reflection with a deep sigh.

"Why didn't you just knock?" Bill asked, touching the barrel to the base of Mark's skull, "I would have let you in."

Unsure of what to do next, Mark looked around the room, noticing more than half of the 750 milliliters of Piercey's Scotch Whisky missing from its bottle. "You wanna drink?" With the gun in one hand, the other held a glass of the gold liquid of which Bill spoke. "I knew you were going to try something good," Bill pointed at him with the same hand wrapped around his glass. "You can move away from GLADIS now."

Mark wrangled the fear with the skill of a bronc rider, firing back, "How could you do this? To your own people? They trusted you!"

"First off," Bill stated, "there is no stopping Axiom. If you did, they would say it was their idea. Second, I do not have people. When are you going to realize that people are assholes? All these people you think you are helping could not care less if you live or die. Life is short Mark, worry about yourself. When you die and the people who know you die, it will be as if you never lived. You think there is something *more* to life? Let me clue you in on something…there isn't. We're all just tiny little bugs crawling after the next best thing. It's all about the here and now because we may all die tomorrow. Why can't you just be rich and be happy?"

Mark stood there a moment to contemplate the response. Bill was a man ruled by emotions. He couldn't possibly understand any better than Mark could understand *him*. *No matter*. He had to try.

"Bugs and human beings alike are the result of an infinitely large amount of chemical reactions. Every decision we make and even us talking right now, is a culmination of uncountable chemical reactions. Our emotions, the pleasure, the pain, the fear, the calm are all chemical reactions. The feelings of being brave, standing by your convictions, discipline, sticking up for yourself and what you believe in, helping others, personal sacrifice, all are driven by chemical reactions, millions upon millions of cascading chemical reactions. Many are instantaneous, but just as many may wait a lifetime for the right catalyst to come. When the catalysts don't come, the stagnation burns a hole and stinks to high heaven, like a mosquito ridden bog that does nothing but sit and grow scum, which dies and spawns more scum, in an endless cycle of waiting for something to happen."

While Mark was trying to change Bill's mind the only way he knew how, his fingers found their way back to the left mouse button. "There may be no stopping Axiom," Mark said, "but that doesn't mean we have to stop trying."

"OK that's enough," Bill said, pressing the barrel tightly against the side of Mark's head, scraping it against the rubber bullet wound that still festered underneath the patch of hair that grew over it. He could see the ornate lettering on the side of the 1911's pistol grip in the reflection on the computer screen, but he did not move from the mouse.

"Y'know the first time I used this fuckin' thing I was holding it to my own head," Bill admitted. "When I pulled the trigger, nothing happened. I was saved. I was sure it was divine intervention. I decided I had a purpose on this earth after all. Turns out I was just too stupid to realize how the gun worked. And I found that out because later on, I put a hole in my fuckin' wall playing around with it when I was drunk. It was an accident. Just as it was an accident that I didn't kill myself the first time. As I alluded to earlier, nothing really matters. There *is* no purpose. Everything is an accident. I'm with you on the 'chemical reactions' speech. If you do what you are about to do, if you finish downloading that virus, if you destroy GLADIS, you will be

pulling this trigger for me. You will die a senseless death and
Axiom will make the whole thing go away. You may not think so
but you and I are a lot alike. In fact, from where I stand, we are
essentially the same person. Yes, chase the chemicals. Chase the
dopamine and the adrenaline. But don't ever, ever, make the
mistake of attributing logic to the emotions that the chemicals
produce. Make the right choice here, Deremer." And Mark
obliged.

Mark's index finger slammed down onto the left mouse
key, which blasted a binary blip to the hard drive to finish the
'frameshift' code mutation. Just like Bill promised, the second
movement immediately followed the demise of GLADIS; Bill
pulled the trigger. The hammer pulled back and released upon an
empty chamber to produce the telltale 'click' sound of divine
intervention.

"Fuck!" Bill screamed, dropping his glass of whisky and
pulling back on the slide barrel assembly, desperately trying to
chamber a round. It was plenty of time for Mark to get up, turn
around, and tackle Bill to the ground. Mark was much stronger
than Bill remembered and he struggled to keep a grip on the pistol,
much less chamber a round. The two wrestled all over the office
floor. Neither was keen on giving up the gun, as doing so likely
meant death. Both were breathing heavily behind clenched teeth,
with grunts and screams as the two traded upper hands and
recoveries. "Goddamnit!" Bill grunted, renewing the anger that he
felt for the destruction of his hollow empire. Bill managed to get
his hand free from Mark's grip and Bill pulled the trigger, again
producing empty clicks. "FUCK!" Bill screamed with frustration,
realizing he had not been able to chamber a round throughout the
struggle. The two rose up with each other at the same time for long

enough to look at each other in the silver pupils and bloodshot eyeballs.

Mark gained leverage at some point and threw Bill onto his back. Mark held him down, as the two were exhausted, he again tried to reason with Bill, silently, through making him understand the realization that eventually one would lose, or they could both quit while they were both still alive. "Stop!" Mark said, "Stop! Stop! Stop! Goddamnit Stop!" Bill nodded his head as if he agreed to stop struggling and in fact Mark could feel the struggle in Bill decrease. Bill started to heave, and Mark let him turn to his side so that he would not choke to death on his vomit. The two men were sweating profusely, exhausted, and lying on the floor trying to catch their breath. Finally Mark got to his feet and outreached his hand to his fellow survivor to help him up. Bill looked up at Mark's outstretched hand and hung his head back down again, still not completely recovered from the struggle.

Finally, Bill got to one knee, cocked the slide barrel assembly back to chamber a round, and aimed the barrel upward at Mark, screaming the word "Stop!" before he pulled the trigger. With Bill's nod, Mark had assumed a mutual, nonverbal agreement. But in reality, he had only nodded his head. It meant nothing to him. Many would call the act dishonorable, but Bill was the one alive. Was it more important to be honorable or alive? *That all depends on who's asking.*

Mark saw the flash of the muzzle and nothing more. The .45 caliber round traveled at 800 feet per second from the cartridge out of the muzzle to reach the flesh of Mark's blinking eyelid. The ball exploded Mark's eyeball and continued drilling through his cribriform plate, leaving abraded skin in its wake. It continued its journey through the soft tissue of Mark's various brain structures before shattering an exit wound through the occipital lobe, enclosing occipital bone, skin, and hair follicles. The round continued to travel at a slightly slower speed through the glass window overlooking Valhalla National Park, sending glass shards scattering to the carpet of the office and onto the ground below.

Mark had not even noticed the blow, but felt his body inexplicably collapse, falling slightly backwards as an effect of his reaction to hearing the round click into the chamber. His lifeless body fell two stories to the lush, fertile soil of Valhalla National Park. He was dead before the round made the exit wound. But the remaining electrical signals spoke the body's last words, "No Matter."

Still on his knees, Bill examined the broken glass and the gaping hole the body had left in the window before it plunged out of it. He stood up, walked over to the hole, and looked down into Mark's remaining eye and then out into the blackness blanketing Ash County. Before he could look away, the irradiation bulbs flicked off again. But even from the blindness of the sudden light transition, even amidst the fog that crept over Valhalla, Bill picked out the tiny, flickering light of Grandpa Ray's campfire grill in the distance, feeding all of those saved souls who made it to the other side of the river.

Turning away from the window, Bill shuffled through a floor full of broken glass to Mark's desk. The computer screen showed a prompt telling the user that there was an 'Incorrect Logic Operation' and to 'Check for Errors.' Bill picked up the phone, pressed a single button on the phone's keypad, and held the phone up to his ear, "Ted?"

An ad hits the television screen filled with scenes of time lapse photography of forests growing, ocean tides, sun risings and settings, all flashing by at about one second per scene. The ad is set to a deep male voice narration, the ticks of a clock set to the changing scenes, and purely percussive instrumentation. "The world is changing fast. Gone are the days of 'standing by,' 'holding off,' and 'playing it safe.' The time to act is now. No more standing on the sidelines. No more 'research and development.' This is 'point blank,' 'all-or-nothing,' 'go time.' You can either jump now, or we'll wave to you from the other side. Either way, a new dawn... has come. Axiom. Brand new solutions to very old problems." The ad ends in silence but for the echo of the last percussive beat, with the image of planet earth being eclipsed from start to finish by the sun, by far the longest shot of the commercial, lasting four seconds, then fading the Axiom logo on top of the eclipsed earth.

Another ad now, much softer than the last. A flyover shot of the EnviroCore building amidst Valhalla National Park. Another flyover shot of a windmill farm on perfectly uniform green grass fields. A softer male voice narrates, "Imagine a perfect world." Flyover shots continue of a color-enhanced view of Lake Michigan, Sleeping Bear Dunes, Hartwick Pines, and the Porcupine Mountains. "A world where there *is* no carbon footprint," the voice continues over the shots of gorgeous Michigan scenery of all seasons, each getting more dramatic, "where biodegradability, sustainability, and renewability, didn't need mention." Wildlife, solar panels, fish jumping upstream, Tahquamenon Falls, "Where the only emissions were the gasps of awe, the breaths of fresh air, and the exhalations of relaxation." A shot of a young couple hiking through the woods, a bald eagle soaring upwards against the background of blue sky and fluffy white clouds, and a view from behind the bandana of an in-shape fifty-something, standing at the edge of a cliff overlooking a vast body of water. "Let us help bring you a simpler, cleaner world, where perfection is as far as the eye can see." The ad ends with a satellite view of Valhalla National Park, which zooms in on the EnviroCore building, which changes to a view of an airplane hangar-sized lab containing giant, pure white vats amidst all white lab equipment, which zooms down to a smiling EnviroCore employee wearing a white lab coat and white rubber boots and gloves, holding a vial of clear fluid. The camera zooms in on the vials of liquid, which transitions to a calm Lake Michigan flyover, which slowly zooms out to the planet earth. "EnviroCore Axiom," the voice concluded over a transparent EnviroCore logo that materialized over the Earth shot, "a perfect world, well within reach."

The ad fades to a breaking news flash on one of the major news corporation channels. "Good afternoon and welcome back," begins a well-established news anchor. "We are seconds away now from the live national press conference address of Bill Wildeboer, president and CEO of EnviroCore, who will address an historic joint funding venture between The US Department of Agriculture, The Department of Commerce, and EnviroCore's parent company Axiom Pharmaceuticals."

"Good afternoon," Bill Wildeboer greets from behind a lectern and two microphones. "It is with great pride that I announce this historic unification that takes place on the site where a towering landfill once stood. Great leaps and bounds have been made in recent months that will, in no uncertain terms, change the world. This is indeed a bright day for all involved in this union, the people of the world, and the history of mankind."

"Mr. Wildeboer," a reporter called from the audience, "how do you respond to allegations that a spurned employee sabotaged plant operations?"

"I can assure you that the setback was minimal and the plant is operating normally."

"Can you respond to reports of an outbreak of disease in the community?"

"Those rumors are unfounded but to be sure, as a precautionary measure, we did take blood samples from every man, woman, and child in the county. Those tests revealed no evidence of disease whatsoever."

"You were called in to rebuild EnviroCore from the ground up after the plant changed hands from its corrupt predecessor, is that correct?"

"That is correct, yes."

"How were you able to make such drastic changes in such a short time?"

"Well I had a lot of good people working to turn things around but I always say that going with your gut is the only way to make decisions."

"Bill, can you comment on the alleged saboteur being killed in an attack on you?"

"That person was, unfortunately, killed in the attack, yes."

"Can you elaborate at all?"

"Well, you can read the full police report but the perpetrator was a sick individual who engaged me in a physical altercation. I was forced to respond."

"Do you consider yourself a hero?"

"I did what needed to be done. I didn't think, I just acted. I like to believe that most people would do the same."

"Are you single?" a woman's voice trumpeted from the crowd arousing a low chuckle among the audience. Bill's only response was to laugh sheepishly along and grin a modest grin. The grin was shared just beneath the twisting mustache of Ted Philus, who relished every second of the coverage.

* * *

Made in the USA
Columbia, SC
23 October 2018